NIGHT SHIFTERS

CHERYL LEE

Order this book online at www.trafford.com
or email orders@trafford.com

Most Trafford titles are also available at major online book retailers.

Print information available on the last page.

ISBN: 978-1-4907-9431-0 (sc)
ISBN: 978-1-4907-9432-7 (e)

Trafford rev. 03/19/2019

www.trafford.com

North America & international
toll-free: 1 888 232 4444 (USA & Canada)
fax: 812 355 4082

Contents

Contents

Introduction

Ever stare into the dark and wonder if something was looking back at you? Ever think that you saw something so real but later, thought that maybe you did not and that your eyes were just playing tricks on you. On the other hand, perhaps you did see something so scary that you were too afraid to tell anyone in fear that people would call you crazy or would not believe you.

Ever feel like someone is standing behind you but, no one is there? Well get ready to take a journey into the life of Kyle Green, a young teenage boy whose nightmares becomes clues to the missing pieces of a puzzle about his life. As he learns more about the unknown, he will meet another young boy just like him who also holds the key to unanswered questions about him.

Which will help him learn to search for the truth about his past, present and future to save his family and possibly humanity.

He also falls in love with a girl who is strong spirited who captivates his heart and she too will help him on his journey. Follow a young man on a quest as he tries to end the nightmares and defeat the unknown. With help from his friends and a local schoolteacher, Ms. Creed who also learns that she will play a key role in this mystery.

Kyle will learn more truth about his parents. Keep your eyes open wide they are everywhere and you will never know when or where they might strike.

Chapter One

The Nightmares

My name is Kyle Green; I am sixteen years old.

I was very young when the nightmares started. I prayed every night that they would stop. It just felt so real; my breathing would increase, and I would break out in night sweats.

Something is chasing me and it is very fast. The woods are dark and cold and the night mist covers the trees like a silk blanket. I feel like an animal running away from its hunter. I can see their shadows moving in the moonlight. They used it to shield themselves. Despite the fact that I could not see them, I could smell them. The scent was very distinct but also hard to describe. Either way, I know they were there.

I kept running away from whatever was chasing me. I just knew it was something horrifying, even the sounds they made scared me. They were like a chainsaw in the night, ear piercing and gut wrenching.

I am still running as fast as possible; it felt more like slow motion. Regardless, they were getting closer. I can see movement all around me; I am trying to escape before they can get to me. My mouth opened to scream but, there are no words; no one could hear me.

There is a white mist moving fast in front of me. It changes paths constantly, ushering me in different directions. My instincts tell me to get to the clearing, a part of the open valley where the trees met at the top. All the while, they are getting closer and the smell is unbearable.

I do not know how I wake up but, when I do, my mom has to replace the sheets and pillows. Because of the nightmares, I would rip them to shreds.

My parents never understood why I would get these nightmares. They sent me to every shrink doctor they could find but, no one knew what was wrong.

They both took me to a festival one night and, even walking through crowds of people, I swore I could smell "them" as if they were close, watching me in the night. I could feel strange eyes watching me; I stayed close to my parents. They were busy talking with friends and neighbors and suggested I go and play. I guessed that they wanted me to be ordinary and make friends but somehow, I knew I was different. I did not have many friends and other children teased me because they thought I was weird.

I will never forget that night at the festival some of the bullies were teasing me and I ran off as I wandered around I watched people having fun, girls screaming, the sound of the music playing. As I walked, I felt the wind on my face and looked up at the sky filled with stars. The moon was full and bright that night.

Then, I stopped in my tracks. There was an odd smell in the air. I thought to myself for a moment, this only happened in my dreams, but; this was no dream, this was real.

I walked slowly and it got stronger I could feel something but, I could not see anything. It felt as if the night was watching me. I had to find my parents.

I walked as quickly as possible to get away. My breathing increased, my heart was pounding. I could feel them all around me; I could see the night air ripple like a silk sheet but I thought my imagination was playing tricks on me. I rubbed my eyes and just kept going.

There were so many people I could not see my parents. The wind started to blow harder. I felt driven to keep going, as if something was pulling me to safety somehow.

I saw a tent with bright lights up ahead and I ran inside only to turn back to see if I were still being followed. To my surprise, there was nothing. I had a sense of calmness immediately come over me. I looked around the tent that had interesting items inside, stuffed animals, and artifacts of all kinds. There was also a display of all sorts of candles, colorful charms, and books. It was a very strange place.

The charms glowed like sparkling diamonds. I deeply gazed upon it. I was surprised. I reached out my hand to touch it when someone spoke to me.

"May I help you young man?" I jumped.

"Sorry, I was just looking."

"Beautiful, aren't they?" the man who spoke said.

"Yes, they are." I replied.

"So, young man, what brings you to my place? Perhaps I could be of some service to you." I kept looking over my shoulder I felt them watching me.

"I'm sorry sir," I nervously started, "I didn't mean to-" I stopped in mid sentence. "Why didn't they follow me inside this place?" I had to ask myself.

"Son, are you frightened by something?" He asked me. "Well don't be afraid you are safe now."

For some reason I believed him.

"What is your name son?"

"My name is Kyle, Kyle Green."

"Well Kyle, my name is Benjamin. My native name is *"OTOAHHASTIS,"* he told me.

"What does that mean?" I asked.

"It means *"tall bull,"* he explained. I laughed a little.

"You don't look like an animal." I said.

"No son, when we are born we are given names by our tribal elders who say we carry the spirit and strength of animals."

He started to explain.

"We learn to be like them in many ways and learn to survive by watching them. My father was a tribal elder and he named me tall bull because I learned how to hunt and not to be afraid. He says the name represents masculine strength because I was so young and much taller than my older brothers were."

He winked at me and I laughed again. I looked around in such amazement everything inside was so wonderful.

"What are the charms for?" I asked.

"These are the charms of my people legend says they keep us safe from evil spirits and each one is very unique." He explained.

"What do you mean"? I asked.

"Well, it's a long story but, I will tell you."

And he began his story.

"Legend says there were a group of people selected from each of the tribes to come together to protect the people of the land. We call them "*QALETAQA*" which means "*guardian of the people*". Each of them received rare silver stones, which came from deep within the earth. There was a sacred ceremony with the chosen ones linking their souls to the stones."

"What happened to them?" I asked.

"Well some say that when they linked their souls to the stones as long as the light inside exists the darkness cannot harm us. We wear them to remind us that they are always watching over us."

Benjamin went on to say more but, by this time my parents found me and they were hysterical.

"Honey, we were looking all over for you!" my mother came toward me.

"Sir, I hope he was not a bother to you," dad said.

"No bother, I was just showing him some of my tribal memorabilia's," Benjamin said.

"Well, we must be going now, thanks," dad informed him.

"Bye Mr. Benjamin." I said my goodbyes.

My parents led me out of the tent as we walked they said hello and goodbye to friends. My mother says we have a busy day tomorrow and we need to get home so I could get some rest.

There were times when I thought my nightmares were becoming a reality. I was about twelve years old when my parents drove me out of town to a hospital. A doctor there claimed he could heal children of their nightmares through hypnosis. He had been successful in helping other children my age. He came highly recommended by other physicians.

The place looked more like an asylum for crazy people. However, it was also like a hospital. There were benches out front where people sat and it had a long driveway. However, I did notice the odd shape of the trees and how they met at the top. I just could not take my eyes off them.

Dad parked the car and we went inside.

"Hello my name is Dr. Frank D. Hill."

The doctor met with my parents to explain the session telling them that he videotaped so he could do further studies. He gave them a guarantee the nightmares would stop.

He placed me in a room with other children while he finished explaining to my parents about his success stories. I sat down, with them and watched them play. Another little boy sat alone none of the other children spoke to him.

I played with my football since it gave me comfort. It helped me focus on playing like my dad. He was the head coach of the local high school football team, the Arizona wildcats, and number one in the district. I want to play on the team one day when I get to high school.

I sat and played catch by myself for while tossing my football up in the air. I waited and I could hear the other children through the wall vents.

The rooms were like cells with monitors. I was still afraid and did not want to be here but, my parents wanted me to get better.

I could hear crying coming from one of the vents. I moved a little closer to listen, it sounded like they were praying. I sat down to the vent and spoke to him.

"Hello, are you all right?

"Yes…just a little scared," he answered back.

"My name is Kyle. What is your name?"

"Eric…My name is Eric Spearhorn."

"What are you here for?"

"I am here because I have bad dreams."

"Yeah, me to."

"What do you see in your dreams?"

"I don't know, it's hard to explain them,"

He informed me but he tried anyway.

"I see things moving about when others cannot. I know they are there. Sometimes it is as if I can feel them watching, waiting on me to fall asleep. My mom thinks it is because of my Grandfather tells me tribal ghost stories when he comes to visit.

She does not allow me to visit my Grandfather that much because of it; I can only see him if he promises not to tell me tribal stories. But it's who we are; she just doesn't understand that my dreams are real."

"The doctor says that sometimes we have to face our fears in the dark. I begged my mother not to take me inside, but she said it would help me get better. My father was not much help at all he just said be strong and brave and patted me on top of my head.

He is not my real dad; he died when I was younger. My real mom decided to move away, to get away from the memories."

"Why are you here?"

Eric asked as he finished.

"Nightmares, sounds like you and I have the same problem."

"Do you ever smell them?"

"Yes," I whispered.

I did not want the other children to hear me.

"I can't quite explain it. It is as if I know when they are near."

I never thought that I would meet someone who had the same dreams as I did. It gave me a sense of hope. With Eric's help, I convinced myself that I was in my right mind.

"The smell is it like nothing you had ever smelled before," he asked me.

"Yes. It is hard to explain. My senses let me know when they are near. It's even harder to escape."

"What do they look like?"

"I can't tell. They move like a black mist. I can hear them growl too."

"Shifters," Eric said.

"What!" I said almost aloud.

"We call them shifters; they blend in with the night and change into wolves. They have a distinct smell, and they are very mean. They don't like people who can expose them, they're like trackers almost."

"How do you know this?"

"My Grandfather is a tribal chief on our reservation and I have heard many of the Elders tell stories about them. He says only special people can expose them; that is why they can move at night and in dreams. If they get to you, they can kill you." He explained. "Suhnoyee Wah is what they call them."

"Suhnoyee Wah?" I struggled to say the name.

"It means 'night wolves'."

"What about in the daytime?

"Grandfather says they have ways to spot their victims. They sometimes use the animals,"

He began to explain.

"All I know is that they are dangerous and they love dark places. They can use the night to shift into many images."

"How do they survive?"

"They take the soul of the living by paralyzing them somehow. I think they hypnotize them; I am not sure, my Grandfather also told me there are also guardians that help guide the gifted ones and protect them in their sleep."

"How does your Grandfather know this?" I whispered.

"My Grandfather said there was a young boy in his tribe years ago who spoke of seeing a black shadow change into a half man half beast," he said, as he continued his story.

He told me that the boy drew in closer to the shifter and it picked up his scent. The boy tried to scream but he was traumatized by what he saw. Later, his mother noticed he was missing. His father and some of the other men in the tribe followed his trail into the woods. When they got to him, they saw the half man half beast standing over him. The boy was not moving.

The men stood motionless and in amazement at what they saw. They had encountered a shifter standing before them. They watched as the shifter transformed itself to blend with the night. The men did not know what to do. This was the first time they had ever encountered such a creature. The boy lay almost unconscious.

Eric told me that his Grandfather says, in his rage and thinking the shifter had killed his son, the father charged after it and the shifter immediately struck him down. He never saw it coming. The shifter took him by surprise. Grandfather held up his hand and began to say a tribal prayer over the remaining men and the shifter could not cross their circle. The boy lay not moving and his father wounded.

"What happened to the boy? I interrupted his story with curiosity.

"The boy tried to run but, he lost his balance. He knocked himself unconscious on a tree stump. The shifter was to ready to kill the boy but, Grandfather and the other men arrived before he could."

I could hear the suspense when he talked as he explained it to me.

"The shifter stood there looking at them, the men stopped in their tracks. The shifter pointed at them and spoke in a native language, as a sign to send them a message; but, it was more than just a message, it was a warning. The men hurried to get the boy back to the tribal doctor along with his father. The shifter had not wounded the boy however, the boy began to come out of unconsciousness and started calling for his father, but at the time, he did not know his father was badly injured. Grandfather says that the tribal Doctors noticed that the boy's father had an open wound on his chest from the shifter."

"What happened to him?"

He went on to tell me the rest of the story.

He said his grandfather was afraid to tell him more, but he said that he was brave enough to hear it. They called for the tribal Doctor and the Elders. His wounds were so severe that he had developed a fever and his eyes had turned pitch black. They selected a few of the men to stand guard outside of the teepee; no one was aloud to see in. The Elders kept watch over him all that night but he died of his wound.

They had a sacred burial; they placed his body in an underground tomb.

One day the boy and his mother went to pay respect to their dead and were surprised that their loved ones body was gone.

"How could that be possible?"

"The body was of another kind, a dark kind. He told me that one day I would understand the full meaning of the Suhnoyee Wah. It is why my grandfather needed to keep me protected. But, he couldn't until he was actually on the reservation."

"Does the reservation keep you safe?"

"Yes and no. The shifters cannot cross some boundaries. The boundaries are what keeps us separated," He explained. "Grandfather is working on me going to school on the reservation. He believes it's important so I could learn the ways of my people." He stopped for a moment. "My mother though…she not happy about it, she does not believe the stories he tells me."

Just by talking with him, I felt connected somehow; it was as if we understood each other very well. I just could not pull myself away from him; it is as if destiny wanted us to cross paths. He was just like me and though I could not see his face, I felt such closeness to him.

There were other children in different rooms and I could hear them screaming while their parents just paced the floors. Then the nurses came into my room to escort me out. I called for Eric but he did not answer.

I started to feel beads of sweat roll down my face. My father told me; I would be all right, that the doctor told him so. That he would make it all go away.

While my father calmly spoke to me, my mother just looked at me with tears in her eyes. I looked at them both frightened and full of fear. The doctor led me down a long hall with big lights. We came to a room at the end of a hall.

"All right young man, now you just lye down right here."

He placed these sticky probes on the side of my head and hooked them up to a machine. He placed another one right on my chest and just told me to relax. A nurse came into strap my hands down to the bed my mother looked worried.

"Is that necessary?" She asked.

"No, just a precaution," said Dr. Hill.

I wanted to scream but I could not. I couldn't move or speak; I had become paralyzed.

Another nurse came in and ushered my parents into another room where they could watch me through a big window. As I lay there, I could see them waving at me. Of course, I could not return the gesture because the nurse strapped my arms down to the side railings. I just gazed up at the ceiling and listened to the doctor. As he talked, I felt my pulse racing. The nurse dimmed the lights and told the doctor that they were ready to begin. He told me to breathe very slow and focus on the light.

"My voice will sound faint…just keep looking at the light," he told me.

My eyes were getting heavy and my body grew weightless. I could feel the nurse's hands on my head and, just before I felt my body drifting, I remembered the smell.

I could barely hear the beeps from the monitors and then it happened. What appeared to me was the room getting very dark, like a black cloak covering the room. My body started to shake and sweat rolled down the side of my head. I shook vigorously and tried to gain control.

It moved quickly around the room my eyes following its every move. The smell was unbearable.

"Where are you?" the doctor asked. I did not know what say, I was scared.

"Tell me what you see?"

"It's moving too fast," my breathing increased.

"What is moving fast?"

I started gasping for air. The room was so dark. The shifter moved hovering over me like a ghost, staring down at me. Its eyes were gaping wide and dark as a pit with no life inside. I could feel it pull at me as if it was trying to suck out my soul. My breath was leaving my body; I had no control. Could they possibly see it?

I didn't know what had happened. By the time, they turned on the lights everyone was standing over me asking me if I was all right. My mother was screaming at the doctor trying to figure out what had just happened. They went to another room so I could not hear their conversation. Doctor Hill explained to my parents that he had only just begun the procedure and that I was still conscious.

He told them that he could not explain what had just happened but only that I could have suffered a psychotic episode; that could have possibly triggered some neurotic brain cells similar to seizures. He also thought I could have been having delusions. The doctor wanted to continue further treatment but my mother could not take anymore.

By this time, my parents had me by my hand hurrying to get me out of the hospital.

"I'll get the car," dad said as we walked.

"Can I say goodbye to a friend?" I asked my mother.

"There's no time," she told me. However, I insisted.

The doctor interrupted and told my mother that she needed to sign some paper work since the procedure was unsuccessful. He wanted her to reconsider helping me since the nightmares were very intense. He needed another session for his research to determine what triggered them. My mom eventually agreed and left me in the waiting room.

I went to find Eric to say goodbye. As I went into the waiting room, I didn't see him; but, a girl told me that he was not there. She said that he went into the room but he never came out. I asked her how she knew and she said they always bring children back to this room but he never came back. By now, my mother came in, grabbed me by my hand, and we met dad outside. While my parents spoke harshly to one another, I tuned them out and tried to relax my mind. I tried to figure out what happened to Eric but decided that I would find out somehow later.

That night my mother gave me pill to help me go to sleep. She told me to try not to think about the events of the day, if she only knew how hard that was.

She sat looking at me long and hard. Then she jumped as if she saw something in my eyes. I could see that she started to say something but, instead, she kissed me on my forehead.

That night I must have slept like a baby. I do not believe that I had a nightmare; maybe somehow these shifters had decided to leave me alone for the night.

The next day as I was getting ready for school, it felt like only yesterday this all started. Many thoughts still ran through my mind. What do they want with me? Could I be the gifted one? So many doctors and my parents still say they do not know what could cause these nightmares. I thought about Eric a lot too. I really needed to find him. There was only one that I know who could tell me about him. I would have to be sneaky about it though.

I found it funny how time flew. The older you get the more responsibility you have. I had few friends around and Tony was my best friend. His parents moved to Patagonia last summer and we became friends right away. It was mostly because some of the local football jocks were picking on him because he carries around lots of books. Since the jocks could not keep their grades up they needed tutors, they had to apologize and be kind to him. Yep, you guessed it, Tony. He's really book smart.

We planned to meet up later at the library to study for midterms. One of our teachers, Ms. Creed, did volunteer work at the library; she is very good at helping students do extra credit work.

I went home to help my mother out with a few chores before going to the library. While I was helping though, I heard something that sent chills up my spine. The local news was on and they reported that a couple of hikers that were hiking near Wolf Creek made a gruesome discovery of a mutilated body. I just could not turn myself away from the television.

As I listened, the reporter explained that police had sealed the area and were not allowing anyone access to the campsite until their investigation was complete. No one was allowed near the site.

"At the moment, there are no witnesses and no one in the area has seen anything suspicious. Police say it looks as though it was an animal attack seeing that the victim's chest was ripped open." The reporter went on." The authorities have no further comments on the story.

"Honey,"

Mom called out to me.

"Do not keep your friend waiting. Kyle..."

She called to me but it was as if I could not hear her.

"Kyle honey, are you all right? Kyle, what is wrong?"

"Sorry I will be late for dinner. I rushed out of the house.

"Don't be long!

She said to me as I left.

"There is a storm approaching. I wouldn't want you to catch a cold."

I yelled back to her as I hurried out the door. Everything started to come back to me now, the story Eric told me about the boy and the shifter in the woods. I wondered what ever became of the injured man.

I arrived at the library before Tony. He had phoned and said he would be a little late so I decided to do some research on the Spearhorn reservation to see if I could locate Eric. There was a listing for several Spearhorns and decided that I would check them all out.

The actual reservation was about forty-five miles out of town and, since tomorrow was Saturday, I thought I would take a drive.

"Are you studying for finals, young man?" A voice asked; it was Ms. Creed. "Yes, I mean no…just looking up an old friend."

"Perhaps I can be of some help," she said.

Ms. Creed was a very nice person. She had helped a lot of people research their family history as well. She is a tall slim African American woman. She learned that, in the early 1800s, her ancestors lived on a reservation with Black Foot Indians. While escaping slavery, they sought refuge on the reservation. She also learned her great-great-great-grandfather fought in the civil war.

Ms. Creed is part Native American with a smile that could light up a room. She never married or had no children of her own; nevertheless, she considered her students as her children. We could always count on her to help us out. One of her many gifts was always lending a hand. She loved to get involved within the community.

"Why are you researching the Spearhorns?"

"It is a long story," I started.

"Well I'm all ears," she said laughing.

"My story's very complicated. I don't know if you'll believe me."

"Well why not?"

"It is a little complicated."

"Well, you can tell me; perhaps I can give you a bit of information. I am very familiar with the Spearhorns and I know all about their tribal background."

"What exactly do you know about them?"

"I know enough. They are very peaceful people. Over the years, the Spearhorns have expanded their reservation by building schools, libraries, and multicultural centers. This way, the children can learn more about their heritage. The Spearhorns' have a lot of influence in the community. They believe in taking care of their people, especially the elderly. Otherwise, they have donated books to this library and given charity to our hospital and senior centers. This is the way they express their kindness. We live in a new time now, some history whether true or false needs to remain history."

"Have there ever been some doubts about them?"

"Yes, truthfully, there has been some speculation from many yeas ago that Native Americans were very vicious people who robbed and killed for no reason. What people did not realize was that they were protecting their land to ensure the future of their tribe. They did their best to keep the government from telling them what they could and could not do on their own land. However, there were some treaties made and many negotiations. Therefore, everything we see on television about them being savages is not all the way true."

She continued.

"I am afraid Hollywood has its own depiction of how life should be. That is why for generations our ancestors told stories about the history of our people and kept records in books so that when you and I read them, we can understand our background. That is also, why we must remember our history; it is very important. It tells us who we are, why we are here, and how we can learn from the past. History has a way of repeating itself. As time changes, so do we but, there are some cultural trends that repeat themselves: music, fashion, dance moves."

"I never thought of it that way."

Ms. Creed had a way of explaining things so I could understand. She loved talking about her family history even about the early 1800s. When her ancestors escaped slavery, they sought refuge with a local tribe. The white man came to take them away; the tribal leaders refused to give them up though. In some cases, this sparked a war between the white men whom traveled onto the reservation to come to reclaim their so-called lost property. Some returned empty handed and others never returned.

Her great-great-great-grandmother was also a medicine woman who helped the injured braves who suffered from severe wounds during battle. During those times, there was a lot of intermarrying between cultures. Ms. Creed had many ties to Native Americans because she is one-fourth Black Foot.

We all had to learn not to be bias toward people. We must take our time to get to know them. Ms. Creed had a way of teaching people about their family history and locating distant relatives. However, I wonder if she could really help me with my problems. The doctors could not help me, but then again, who knows? I will just have to take that chance. She does know the Spearhorns and perhaps her information will be helpful. She also has connections to the reservation. I do not know if I really should tell her about my nightmares. There just had to be a reason for them though.

While at the library, I learned that the events of our day could have an effect on our dreams. The only thing was that my days are good except when the night comes. That was when my nightmares usually happened.

On the other hand, if I fell into a deep sleep, it felt so real. The sounds I heard, even the smells, were all too real. It was as if I had lived some of the events before.

I never thought I would meet someone with the same problems as me though. That was why I had to find him. He had to know more than I did. I wondered, perhaps he could answer many of my questions.

With all of this in mind, I decided that I would tell Ms. Creed; maybe not everything but, I would tell her enough. She was a smart woman and it was hard to play her as the fool. Some of the students thought that she could read minds. I just thought it was because she had been around a long time so, she could read peoples body language. She is always on guard but she did have some mysteriousness about her. You know when I ask her certain questions like why she does not have any children she quickly changes the subject. I believe in respecting people's privacy. If they want you to know, they will tell you.

She took a leave of absence for a while, something about her mother being sick. We didn't think she would ever come back to teach but, she did. She was absent for most of the school year and no one knew what had happened. Some said her mom was very ill and she left to take care of her. However, when she returned there was something very different about her. No one dared questioned it though.

Chapter Two

JOURNEY TO THE PAST

"Hey dude, I'm here." Tony had finally showed up.

"Well hello Tony," Ms. Creed said.

"Hello" he replied.

"So is this a private lesson." Tony whispered.

"Shut up, you dork! Ms. Creed has been giving me a history lesson on Native Americans, ok. So, why don't you just sit down and maybe you will learn something."

I told him.

"I thought we were going to study for midterms." Tony said.

"Something came up, is that ok with you?"

"Does this have something to do with your nightmares?"

"How do you know about that!" I yelled.

"Shhh," someone said.

"Some of the kids overheard your dad talking to one of the other coaches about how you used to scream in your sleep and talk about the 'unknown' chasing you. I never told you that I knew because you are my friend and I guessed it was none of my business."

"Well thanks." I felt a little relieved that I had a friend who really cares.

"What nightmares?" Asked Ms. Creed, "Kyle, what kind of nightmares?"

"Nothing." I scowled, "It is just nothing! I should have never come here! You have a big mouth Tony!"

"Kyle, I'm sorry, I didn't mean to."

"No it's okay," said Ms. Creed. I grabbed my belongings and turned to walk away when she said, "Suhnoyee Wah" I froze.

"What does that mean?" Tony asked.

"It means night wolf or wolves," Ms. Creed said. "Sit down Kyle and I will explain."

"What does this have to do with Kyle's dreams?" Tony asked Ms. Creed. "Sit down and I will explain."

I did not know whether to sit down or run. While in my thoughts, Ms. Creed placed her hand on my shoulder and smiled. A sudden sense of calmness came over me, almost like magic.

"I too have heard many stories about theses Shifters and your nightmares." Ms Creed said.

"What do you know about them?" I asked nervously.

"Your nightmares or the shifters?"

"Both."

"I too have heard people talking about your nightmares. I do understand what you are dealing with. On the other hand, the stories about the shifters were stories passed down from generation to generation in my family. I usually do not discuss it much because it is very hard to believe but, some things I do take to heart. It is the way that I remember the good and forget the bad.

"What if the bad does not want to be?"

"Then I must face destiny," she smiled. "Many years ago, the elders of ancient tribes told of horrific legends about the unknown beings, Shifters, as we call them. Nevertheless, some people believe that they are just superstitions told just to scare people. However, others believe these legends are true. I don't really know how they came to be; but, legend has it that a young warrior from the Shahwanee tribe was one of the fiercest in his colony. He was nicknamed Fearless One because he was never afraid of a challenge, anything, or anyone. Others tested their strength against him and failed.

The warrior brought many victories to his tribe and the Chief elders praised him for the honor but, there were others that thought he consider himself a God. This would cause many problems amongst the tribe."

As she spoke about this warrior, I had an eerie feeling come over me, as if some one or something was watching me. Then, my cell phone rang and I jumped.

"Oh, hi mom. Yes mom, I know I forgot, okay? I'm on my way." I quickly finished the conversation. "Sorry, I must be going." I explained.

"Oh my goodness, I didn't realize the time either," Ms. Creed seemed startled. "Listen boys, I will be teaching a class on ancient history here next week. We can talk more then. Can I drive you home?" she offered.

"No thanks, I rode my bike. I will be fine."

"Kyle, I must warn you to be very careful. There are many things that you don't know. Are you sure I can't drive you home? It looks really bad out there."

"No thanks. I don't live far from here; just a few blocks, I'll be home in no time." I told Tony I would call him tomorrow.

"Later dude." he said,

I hurried out of the library, jumped onto my bike, and headed home. The lightening started and then, the thunder.

"Please hold the rain," I mumbled to myself, "Just a few more blocks."

Just when I spoke, it started to rain. I begin to peddle my bike faster. That odd feeling was upon me again, as if something was following me, keeping pace with me. I just kept peddling faster and faster until I reached my street. As I did, I thought I saw something dash in front of me. It almost caused me to lose control of my bike. I tried to convince myself that it was just the rain in my eye.

I reached my street and finally I made it to my house. Dad was just getting home and I followed the car in the garage.

"Hi, son."

"Hi, dad," I greeted him as I kept looking back, staring at the darkness as if I was in some kind of trance.

"Son." My dad called to me. "Son is everything alright? Kyle!" He yelled. "Son what is wrong with you? Are just staring out in space; what is on your mind?"

"Nothing dad, just thought I saw something that is all."

"Well there is nothing there, son. Let's go inside, your mother is waiting for both us who, apparently, are late for dinner."

"Uh oh dad; I guess we'll be washing dishes tonight." I said laughing trying to put what had just happened out of my mind.

"There you both are. It's raining cats and dogs out there."

"Hi honey." Dad kissed mom on the cheek.

"Hi mom." I went to kiss her but she said not until I dried off first. I did it any way.

"Kyle, your soaking wet!"

"I know mom. I'll hurry for dinner."

I ran up stairs to take a quick shower to relax myself and let the steam take me away. I listened to the sound of the rain outside and the wind was howling unusually loud.

The more I listened the more I relaxed myself. It felt like I was drifting off to sleep. It was as if I was in a trance. A voice in the wind continued whispering to me. My eyes grew heavy and I could barely stand. I heard faint knocking and the sound of my name constantly. I could not break free.

The knocking increased and, like magic, I heard my name called again. I instantly snapped out of it.

"Kyle! Kyle!"

"Son, are you alright in there? What's that noise! Kyle, open this door right now young man!" My dad yelled. I gasped for air my breathing was heavy again."

"Okay dad. I'm all right."

"Son, you've been in there a long time. Your dinner is getting cold!"

"Okay dad. I will be down in a minute." I gathered myself together trying to figure out what just happened. I got dressed and went downstairs sorry mom, sorry dad. Mom placed on her hand on top of mine and asked was I feeling alright, and if I have had any nightmares lately, I told her no.

"Son," dad said. "Are you having in trouble with any of the kids at school?"

"No dad."

"Son, you are not doing drugs are you?"

"Honey, how can you say such a thing?" Mom yelled. "How could you?" Dad stopped mom in dead sentence.

"Son, I am just trying to figure out what's been happening to you lately."

"Dad, I am not doing drugs! I am not having problems at school! You know dad, I thought that you would be more understanding. Since I was little, I have been trying to convince myself that I am not crazy! I see images that aren't there! I hear sounds and I know that they are there. I have to tell myself that it is just my imagination and it is not happening to me! Why not commit me to an asylum and maybe you won't have to worry about me anymore!

"Kyle, honey we know you are not crazy, honey we love you." Mom said. "And we want what's best for you."

By now, I was standing up and pacing the floor.

"Son, please come sit down and we'll talk." Dad said.

"There's nothing to talk about. I'm going to bed."

In the back of my mind, I knew I shouldn't have spoken to my parents like that; but, the more I think about this, the more answers I needed.

I ran upstairs to my room and slammed the door. I could overhear my parents now arguing with one another. Dad suggested that mom call Dr. Hill; but, mom was not to keen on the idea. I *so* did not want this to be happening to me right now. My gut instincts were telling me to find out more; maybe seeing the doctor would not be a bad idea. After all, I could get my answers and maybe find out about Eric.

I decided to go back downstairs to talk to my parents and apologize. Before I could, however, the doorbell rang; it was Ms. Creed.

"Hello, I'm sorry to disturb you at this late hour but, your son left his book at the library. I thought I would bring it by."

"Please come in," mom insisted. Before my mom could call out to me, I stepped into the room.

"Hello Kyle. You left your book at the library and I thought that you might need it for your research."

"Ancient Almanacs of the Spirit World," my mother read the book's title. "Wow, what a huge book!"

"Yes, it's very interesting" Ms. Creed said. Mom handed me the book with a worried look on her face. "Well, I must be going." Ms. Creed started.

"Oh no, would you like to stay for some coffee?" Mom asked.

"Perhaps some other time, it is quite late and I must be getting home."

"Oh no, we insist," dad said. "Please, come in, the storm appears to be getting worse and the national weather service just issued a tornado warning for our area. Please come in."

"Ok maybe for a little while." The thunder and lightning increased. Mom ushered Ms. Creed over to the couch.

"Kyle, will you help me in the kitchen, please?" Mom asked smiling.

"Thanks again for bringing my son his book," dad said."

"You are quite welcome. Kyle is a very inquisitive student and it was no problem bringing it to him."

"So, Ms. Creed, what is it that you actually teach?" Mom asked.

"Jha'net, you can call me Jha'net." She stated. "I teach Ancient history and I do paranormal studies."

"That is very interesting." Dad said.

"Ms. Creed is a good teacher; all of the kids at school like her a lot." I also explained to my parents.

"Cream and sugar?" mom called.

"Both, please, thank you."

"Kyle tells us that you do a lot of research on ancestry," my father recalled.

"Yes I do, I love to read a lot and learn all that I can. Books are our friends; they help us learn our past so we can be prepared for the future."

"Very well spoken," dad said.

"I think its best that children should learn about their ancestors to give them a sense of where they come from. The more we learn about our past the more it opens a doorway to our future. In this day, age, and world though, technology makes this easier. To say that technology is advancing is an understatement. I do enjoy teaching my student, to make fun out of learning."

"No wonder they like you so much". Mom said. They all laughed.

"Well mom...dad, it's getting late and I should be getting to bed; long day tomorrow."

"Do you have plans, son?" Mom asked.

"Yes, Tony and I are going to take a drive up to the hills tomorrow."

"Just stay away from Wolf Creek, okay? There has been some strange things going on up there and I don't want you getting hurt."

"Yeah dad, I heard about the body they found."

"That is now missing..." dad interrupted.

"What do you mean missing?" Mom said.

"Well, apparently, they think that some one is playing a trick on the town morgue up there because the body they bought in is now missing."

"Missing?" Ms. Creed repeated. "This is very interesting..." She stared off into space for a moment. "When did this happen?"

"Well a friend of mine is a detective on the case. He said that, somehow, the body disappeared from the morgue. The strangest thing though was that the body was gone but the clothes remained untouched, like it dissipated right out of them. It has them all puzzled and no one can explain it. Some of the local tribes have been talking about some ancient myths but the police think that it is just some practical joke by some of the college kids. Stealing a body from the morgue is a serious offense though."

They all froze for a moment before my dad continued.

"The coroner states he was on duty when it happened; but, he cannot explain how someone can get into a room. According to the coroner, the door was locked and it requires a code key to open."

"Well he has a lot of explaining to do," my mother interrupted. "I heard on the news the body was severely mutilated. Why would someone do that?" Mom said.

"I heard that as well but it remains a mystery at the moment." Dad said.

I felt cold again and a little light headed I thought about the story about the tribal leader. Then, all of a sudden, the thunder struck so loud that it startled everyone. Soon after came the lightning and, crash, went Ms Creeds' cup onto mom's nicely polished hard wood floor. On impact, the lights flashed off and on. I nearly jumped out of my skin.

"Oh I'm so sorry. I'm afraid I got a little clumsy; please forgive me."

"Kyle paper towels, quickly." Mom said.

"I will check on the fuses" dad stated as he walked out of the room.

Mom and Ms. Creed were on the floor cleaning up the spilled coffee and the broken mug when mom noticed Ms. Creed's necklace. She just stared into it as if she was almost mesmerized.

"Your necklace has some sort of glow to it." Mom said.

"Oh this, it belonged to my mother. She passed it down to me from her mother and so on and so forth. It has been in my family for generations. Perhaps one day if I ever decide to have children of my own, I may pass it down to my daughter."

"You say that as if you don't want to have children." Mom said.

"Well I don't because of..." she paused in mid sentenced. "There all done." She turned her attention back to the floor.

"What kind of stone is that? Mom asked.

"It is a silver stone with a rare diamond inside." Ms. Creed explained.

"It's very pretty; I have never seen anything like it." Mom said.

"Like I said, it has been in my family for generations, handed down to the women in my family."

"Is there a reason why only the women receive them?" Mom asked.

"Perhaps I will have to share it with you some day." Ms. Creed said. "Well, I must be going now. It sounds like the storm is over. Thanks again for your hospitality and, again, I do apologize about the floor and your coffee mug."

"That is ok. Don't trouble your self over some spilled coffee."

"You sound like my mother." They both laughed.

"Good night Ms. Creed," I said.

"Good night Kyle. Don't forget to study; we have a test in ancient history on Monday. Remember, if you need help after school, you can find me at the library."

"I won't forget."

"Perhaps on page fifty-six in your book you will find some helpful tips that will prepare you for your test. Take a look at it, you might find it useful."

"Thanks Ms. Creed." I watched her get into her car and drive away.

"Wow, some night, huh?" dad said.

"Yeah she is a very interesting woman." Mom replied.

"She is very charming and she has a warm sense about her. I just can't explain it."

"Yeah I know. Mom, dad, about earlier, I am very sorry the way I acted; I did not mean to yell. It's just that I was angry and I sometimes I feel like I am alone."

"Son, you are not alone. We are both here to help you. We don't even understand what this all means but, we will figure it out together, okay?"

"Ok dad,...... "Well I am going to bed now, good night.

"And don't forget-"

"Yeah yeah, dad I know; stay away from Wolf Creek. We are just going to take a drive near the Spearhorn Reservation that is all."

"Good night honey," mom kissed me on my forehead.

I went upstairs to my room and set the book on the table. As I did, I noticed that there was a something sticking out from the book. I opened it to see what was on the inside and found a folded up news paper clipping with an article. It was on Eric Spearhorn, stating how a local teen was found after missing for several weeks in the woods.

The article reads:

Eric Spearhorn disappeared several weeks ago after he went missing on a hiking trip. Search and recue teams found him alive in the underground caves in the east canyons. He had fallen through a mineshaft that had given way underneath him. He survived by eating berries, herbs, and drinking water from an underground spring. He had suffered cuts, a fractured leg, and a bump on his head. He has since been undergoing treatment for slight memory loss.

He is currently living on the Spearhorn reservation. No one is aware of what happened to him but, due to his tribal teachings, he learned to survive on the land. Last reported, Eric has been doing well since his release from the hospital. The tribal chiefs are asking the local media to stay away from the reservation; they will hold a press conference giving them an update on the boy's condition.

No one can enter the reservation without an appointment or unless special permission is given. Due to recent events, the tribal chiefs are taking special precautions to be sure their students and others are safe. They are working with the local police department to help locate two other missing students who also went missing around the same time as Eric. Investigators have teams searching all over the hillsides.

With help from the police, the tribal elders are hoping to find the missing teens very soon.

I couldn't believe it; she found him. The only problem was figuring out how I could get in to see him.

I sat the paper down and fell back on my bed. Well, at least I knew where he was. I had to talk to him though. What if he didn't remember me? I really wished I knew what was happening to me. The odd feelings I get when I felt like something evil was near me was becoming nerve wrecking.

I thought back to when my parents took me to see Dr. Hill. There was something strange about that place...the trees. The trees meet at the top; I had seen it in my dreams. I would never be able to get that image out of my head, those soulless eyes staring down at me as if it was searching for something within me.

The images just kept playing repeatedly in my mind like a movie reel. I knew I wasn't crazy. I saw it hovering over me; it was real. I wondered what happened to Eric. He just disappeared from the hospital. I had to find out what happened to him. I had to get on that reservation somehow. Someone is going to give me the answers I need; perhaps it will explain the nightmares and sightings. Maybe I should just drive down there. No, that wouldn't work; they are not going to just let me on the reservation; it's heavily guarded. I need some serious clearance to get into that place.

On the other hand, maybe I could pretend to be a reporter for the local school newspaper; maybe they will let me on then. No way, come on Kyle focus they will check out your story. Think about what you are saying.

I felt a little frustrated, I took some deep breaths closed my eyes, and then I remembered what Ms. Creed said: page fifty-six of the book. I wondered what she meant by that. I reached over, grabbed the book from by table, and opened it up. I read the titled *Mythical Stories of Ancient Tribes*. There was piece of paper folded up inside the creased page of the book. I unfolded the piece of paper to discover it was from Ms. Creed. I began to read it.

Kyle,

I took the liberty of contacting Chief White Feather, one of the elders, and explained to him that a couple of my students were studying ancient myths on some of the local tribes for their term papers. I informed him that you would like to interview some of the local leaders to help them with their studies. He has agreed to let you on the reservation to attend one of his sessions. Please do not take any cameras or tape recorders with you, just a note pad and pencil.

Please respect them and follow their orders! Also, do not wander away unless you've been granted permission. Chief White Feather will have an escort meet you at the main gate; his name is John Morningstar, nick named Big John. He will take you where you will need to go. The tribal leaders will meet with you in their council building on the south end of the campus.

Once you are inside listen attentively and, once the session is over, you can ask your questions about your studies. Do not tell them about your dreams; stick to the subject on the ancient language. You will get the answers you need.

Good Luck!
Ms. Creed.

I couldn't believe it! How did she? Never mind. Why not tell them about my dreams or ask about Eric? This does not make sense. I had to find out all I could about Eric and the stories he told me. Maybe his grandfather will would tell me more. Why does he appear so secretive?

Oh, so many questions are in my head. I do not want to disappoint my parents but there has to be a reason why things are happening to me. Who am I, really? What is my background? Is there a connection? All my life I have known my parents to be honest with me, I think. Dad wants me to play on the football team.

My mother, I know she worries about me but I have always felt that she wanted to tell me something. She would always stop and stare at me and say in "due time." She would try to introduce me to some of the girls in our neighborhood but; I guess I'm too shy.

Shucks, I hadn't even kissed a girl yet. Maybe they think I'm too weird. Heck, I think I'm too weird. Not that the thought has *not* crossed my mind several times, I mean there is a girl at school and she is very cute...

"Aarrrgh!" I growled.

How can I even sleep with my brain on over load? I had better get to bed; I had a long drive tomorrow.

I glanced at the book and noticed an article on *The Secret Language of the Wolves.* I started to read some of it. The more I read the heavier my eyes got. I do not know when I drifted off to sleep but I had a dream.

I was running with a pack of wolves. It appeared as if I was one with them, we understood each other. Then, all of a sudden, we were surrounded by total darkness and there were eerie sounds coming from the woods. The wolves howled and surrounded me.

A tall dark figure emerged from the woods. The white wolf on my left stood next to me while the others appeared to be on guard. The figure did not move though. The white wolf growled even louder as more of them appeared. The wolves stood up on their hind legs like soldiers at war.

We passed through a clearing on the other side of the forest; it was like a barrier that the dark being could not cross. Once we got to the clearing, I was alone. The wolves were gone. I saw a young boy with his back to me. He did not move he just stood there. I went to reach out to touch him but, when he turned around, I gasped for air as my eyes widened. I could not believe what I was seeing.

The boy was a splitting image of me; he was my twin almost. He spoke in a language that I could not understand. The only word I recognized was "Suhnoyee Wah". He pointed behind me and I saw it again, the dark being. He was half man half wolf and shifting in the dark. It reached out to me and I felt fear grip me like a bear hug. I heard growling behind me. My heartbeat increased. I did not know what to do; I thought I was going to die.

The dark being moved slowly away from me. I turned my head slowly to see a white wolf towering behind me. The dark being stared deeply with his eyes fixed as if he was speaking a secret language. While he did, my legs weakened I fell to the ground. The two were now face-to-face. It looked as if they knew each other somehow. The dark being swiftly went away and the wolf leaned into me looking into my eyes looking deep within my soul. I stared back at it trying to get an answer.

The more I stared at it I could see my self in its eyes. Then it was gone I got up to chase after it.

"Wait!" I said, "What does it all mean?"

I was answered with a series of beeps, My alarm had been going off very loud.

"7 am…" I mumbled to myself, "Tony will be here soon."

Whoa…I thought to myself. What a dream…or was it a nightmare. There had to be some clue to my dreams, what did they mean? I hope I get my answers today; this is going to drive me crazy. I gathered my books and my note pads and filled my backpack with snacks and some bottle water. Honk! Honk! Well Tony is here.

"Come on dude it's time to hit the road!" He yelled.

Hold on okay!" I yelled out of the window. "I will be out in a minute."

I left my parents a note that I would call them when I got up to the hills. I ran down stairs, backpack in hand, and proceeded out of the door.

"Well it is about time." Tony said. "Dude you look rough, are you okay? Did you get any sleep?"

"Yeah, of course."

"Did you have another dream?"

"Well, kind a sort of. They are getting creepier with time."

"Well maybe you will get some answers today."

"Hey listen," I started getting Tony's attention. "No one on this reservation must not know about my dreams. Promise me you will not say anything! Tony! Promise me!"

"Okay, I promise. You should know that you can trust me by now right?"

"Yeah, sorry bud. Come on lets go."

We loaded up the car and took off to the freeway. It was nice that Tony offered to drive his car. I thought it was rather nice of Ms. Creed to arrange this. She really had connections.

"By the way, have you seen a girl at school taking pictures?" Tony asked.

"I haven't paid much attention." I answered as if I was going to be honest about it.

"Come on, everyone is talking about her."

"No, I haven't met her yet."

"Me either, but I hear she asked about you."

"Stop lying."

"I am not lying."

"What could she possibly want with me?"

"She is looking for new faces for her photo club."

"Whatever, how much further do we have to go?"

"We have about another thirty miles or so. Do you think you will find the kid you are looking for?"

"I don't know but, the stories that he told me have something to do with the dreams I have. There have been many weird happenings in up in those hills. Our town was so peaceful. Many people wonder what has been happening however; no one had any answers. Ms. Creed seems to be the only one though."

"Do you think that Ms. Creed has some type of connection somehow?"

"What do you mean?" I asked curiously.

"Well, she teaches a lot about ancient history and tribes and have you seen that necklace she wears? I swear it glows in the dark."

"Well silver does sparkle you know."

"Yeah, I guess you are right. I think my parents know more than they are telling me as well."

"Why do you say that?"

"Well, when I first started having these nightmares, they just argued a lot and my dad kept telling my mom that 'we need to tell him the truth.' When I would come in, they would stop talking about it."

"You know grownups."

"Well whatever it is, I know it's big. That is why I need to get answers. I have always felt that my parents have been keeping something from me."

My mom sometimes acted as if she wanted to tell me something. She would just stare at me though, as if she had more to say but could not. I thought she was afraid that she would lose me by telling me the truth.

"What do you think about the prank someone played on the morgue? Tony asked what I was thinking.

"I do not know. What you think about it?"

"I asked you first," Tony said.

"I have no idea really. It's impossible for a dead body to disappear from a locked room unless-"

I stopped in mid sentence and started to think about what Eric told me. It was the story about the boy's father being wounded and then his body disappearing with guards on duty. What happens to a person after a shifter has attacked it? Unless.

I drifted off in deep thought again.

"Unless…unless what?" Tony yelled at me. "Come on dude tell me!"

"It's nothing."

"Are you all right? You spaced out there for a minute."

"I was just thinking about something that someone once told me. I do not know but I feel like I am being pushed into my destiny and I have no idea what it is. It feels like a force guiding me towards the truth while evil is trying to scare me away."

"Well, do you believe in it?" Tony asked. "Kyle, what ever is taking place it's starting to have a serious affect on our town. I mean, I am no expert but I believe in the unknown. I might not experience things as you do but, I believe that there is always a war between good and evil."

I know that there is a connection somehow. As we approached the reservation, I hoped that I could get answers.

"Wow Tony, I am impressed to hear you talk like that. I never knew you felt that way."

"Well It is not everyday I get a weirdo for a best friend."

"Hey," I said, punching him in his arm.

"Hello...I am driving here."

"Well it is good to know that I have a friend that does not think I am crazy. I just feel that something is after me and I do not know why."

"Well if something is after you, I bet she is about five-foot-eight, nicely built, with long flowing black hair." We both laughed.

"Thanks, I needed a good laugh...She is cute."

"So you are interested in her?" Tony said sarcastically.

"Whatever man," I said.

"Maybe when I get back I can hook you two up!"

"No way would a girl like that ever be interested in a person like me."

All my life I felt that I was an outsider because of these stupid dreams and parents sending to doctor after doctor. I knew people talked and I often wondered why some of the kids at school stayed away from me. Maybe it was better that they do stay away; it is safer that way.

I ask myself why a lot. I know people have nightmares. What do you do when your nightmare becomes a reality though? Who knows, maybe I am supposed to be alone.

"You know that day at school when the football jocks were picking on me?"

Tony asked.

"I was feeling the same way until you came along. I did not think I could have friends either. Look Kyle, what ever this is I am going to help you get the answers you need. You're not alone; you have me, Ms. Creed, and your parents."

"Thanks Tony; I really appreciate it."

I told him as I looked out the window.

"Hey, check out the view of this place. It is so peaceful out here. The trees, the mountains, the fresh air, man I could live out here forever. What I would give to have a moment of peace, to be free from all this, I should be going to the movies, dates, doing teenage stuff. You know what I mean? What I would give just to have a night where I can dream peaceful dreams. My dreams are leading me to pieces of a puzzle that I do not even know how to solve. Everything seems to be a clue of some sort."

"Then maybe you should write down what you remember from your dreams."

Tony said.

"My notepad, you are right."

I reached in my backpack, grabbed my note pad, and started writing down things that I could remember from my dreams. Anything I could think of, I wrote it down. It was starting to look like a journal. The language I heard in my dreams and the images seemed so foreign. I began to draw them, black mists in the shape of a beast with long claws and teeth moving through night. It uses the night as a cloak to cover its true form. When it passes under the moonlight, it appears almost transparent.

I kept drawing and, the more I drew, I now know what my purpose was. Who was this warrior at one time? I asked myself how he became like this. Tony kept driving, I kept writing in my notepad, and more things came to my mind. The night I got home from the library, the sound of the wind blowing like whispers. This would help me to understand them more.

As we approached, I stared at the mountains and trees. The faces I saw in my dreams. I drew those as well, every distinct feature. The looks of fear in the eyes were like a warning sign.

The way they looked searching around the woods as if something was coming. Dark and light images moved around. I tried to capture every image of my dreams. I quivered as I looked upon them; I sometimes thought about what they are trying to tell me, or what do they want me to know.

The images in my head came to life on paper. I kept drawing, each page told a horrifying story, while others were like clues. I was glad Tony suggested I do this; then again, I really did not want to.

However, I had to find a solution to all of this.

"Hey Kyle, check it out, we are getting close."

"Yeah, I believe that is our welcoming party up ahead. Ms. Creed wants me to stick to the questions and, remember, we cannot wander around."

"Yeah, I got it."

"Tony, seriously, Ms. Creed must know a lot about this place so let's not disappoint her okay?"

"I just feel like there is more to the reservation. It may hold more secrets to everything. There is a lot of history here and I can learn more from the leaders here."

Tony replied.

"Well if you say so dude."

I really wanted him to know how I felt.

"I know so; it is just a gut feeling I have,"

"Well there is only one way to find out." Tony said.

Chapter Three

REVELATIONS

Tony and I arrived at the main gate of the reservation. He parked the car and, just as Ms. Creed said, Big John greeted us at the main entrance. His name says it all, Big John, also known as John Morningstar. He was about six feet tall and about 250 pounds of muscle. He appeared to be very intimidating but he seemed somewhat nice.

Speaking with a deep voice Big John approached us.

"Welcome to the reservation," Before you enter we must search your vehicle."

Tony and I looked at each with such surprise.

"Yes sir, whatever you say."

Big John explained the reason for the search.

"This is just a normal procedure that we do to be sure that illegal substances stay off the reservation. We like to keep things a little peaceful out here."

We got out of the vehicle as the security guards went through and under the car with metal detectors.

I leaned over to Tony.

"Ms. Creed did not mention this."

"Okay, all clear," one of the men said. Big John looked at us and spoke again.

"Please follow me up to the council building and I will take you to our tribal leaders. There, you will receive further instructions."

We followed him behind his big Dodge Ram pick-up truck, which by the way was nice.

The reservation was very big; they had schools, a library, and even a small family restaurant. The Native Americans sure had a lot of property to build on. We reached the council center and followed Big John in.

"After you," he said to us.

There were many kids our age that went to school on the reservation. We reached the council building at the south end of the campus. It was a beautiful building with a lot of Native American paintings and statues. As we went inside, we could not help but notice how nicely decorated the hallways were with memorabilia of ancient pottery, jewelry, weapons, and paintings.

As we walked along the long halls, I thought to myself how there was so much to see here. In some way, I feel connected with this place. I didn't know how but I just had a gut feeling, my stomach was in knots and my palms are sweaty.

Big John instructed us.

"Here we are. Go right in and take a seat. The tribal leaders are just finishing their lectures, they will meet with you once the session has finished."

"Thanks" we both responded.

We sat down and saw an elderly man standing at a podium decorated in multicolored garments speaking to a group of kids. I would assume this was Chief White Feather. I was not sure which one of the other men on the podium was Mr. Spearhead. I would just have to wait and see.

Chief White Feather was explaining the history of native tribes. He also explained that they had to fight to keep their land so future generations would be able to dwell on it. He spoke in such a way that his voice was very peaceful.

"For centuries, our people have fought to keep our lands safe," he calmly said. "We used the land that Mother Earth gave us to survive. Water, wind, fire, and earth are the most powerful key elements given to us; we must not take them for granted.

The earth holds many mysteries, untouched by man. There are many boundaries disturbed by man and burial grounds destroyed due to the loss of some of our land. Good and evil buried in the same ground should be entombed in peace forever, regardless of the life they once lived.

Many of us believe that when a loved one dies, part of us dies with them. Sacred burial prayers are spoken over the graves of the dead. The good spirits watch over us but the evil ones are bound never to cross the boundaries. There are many sacred burial grounds all throughout the earth. Some of them have been disturbed and it is our duty to see that they remain left alone for this reason.

My father once told me that to disturb the unknown was worse that raising the dead. Overtime, our people have learned to help each other keep the peace but there were some that chose another path.

Some believed they had the power to change the course of our history by breaking the laws of our people."

His speech was fascinating; every word he spoke was so profound. The way he talked, pronouncing every syllable, speaking clear so we could understand his distinct dialect. His words were mesmerizing almost like putting someone in a trance captivating their mind.

Tony and I were trying to take notes but, we were so tuned in to his speech we could not take our eyes off him. We tried to take as many notes as we could when Chief White Feather said,

"Now we would like to continue this session by hearing from you. Does anyone have any questions they would like to ask?"

"Yes, I have a question," one kid said. "How did our people survive when someone was seriously inured or sick? Surely they did not have modern medicine then as we do today."

The Chief responded.

"We used the land, my young one. Many of our people survived by using the resources provided to us by Mother Earth. Various plants and herbs were used back then to help with our people. As well, we would call up the gods of the earth to help us."

Many of the kids had questions and Chief White Feather answered them all; but no one else on the panel spoke. The men just listened and scanned the room with their eyes. I felt like one of them was staring at me. I begin to feel a little uncomfortable but maybe it was just my imagination.

Tony asked if African American slaves were ever owned by the Native American tribes and they told him

"Yes and no,"

Chief said.

"Depending if any of them were prisoners of war, some decided to join us for their freedom. African Americans who fled from slavery sought refuge on the land of the Chickasaws, Choctaws, Creeks, and Seminoles. Many of them were safe on the reservations where the white man could not come and claim them.

They considered them free people. Unlike us, our people were driven from our lands, taken to be slaves. Therefore, when they came to us we offered them safe haven and they dwelled on the land with us. We learned from each other and became people of peace."

Tony thanked him and sat down. Now that was interesting, I am sure Ms. Creed would like to hear more about that. I wanted to ask a question but I did not know what to say. They were asking if there were any more questions. No one raised their hands but, before they closed out, I stood up nervously waving my hand.

"Yes, brave one".

Chief White Feather said.

"Do you have a question?"

I knew Ms. Creed told me to stick to the studies but I just had to ask. My palms began to sweat again and I had a knot in my stomach.

The Chief saw I was hesitating so he asked again.

"Yes brave one? Is there something you want to say?"

I had a lump in my throat and everyone was watching me. I nervously responded.

"Yes sir. What can you tell me about the Suhnoyee Wah?"

There was silence throughout the room no one said anything. Now I really felt awkward and I really started to sweat and shake a little. All eyes were on me and I did not know what to do. Tony grabbed me by my arm.

"Come on, let's go. I don't think they liked your question."

Jerking away from him, I whispered.

"I cannot leave now."

There was murmuring in the room and everyone kept staring.

The tribal chiefs stared at each other until one of them stood up to approach the podium; he was old and seemed very feeble; the others had to help him to the podium. Once he raised his hand, they took their seats.

"My name is Chief Spearhorn, I am of the Cheyenne tribe; I never thought that I would ever hear that name again in my lifetime. Tell me young man, what is your name?"

I swallowed hard as I responded.

"Kyle,....." Kyle Green sir."

"Please, come closer," he said ushering me with his shaking hand.

As I approached him, Big John and others went to move near him, like to protect him. However, he just waved his hand as to usher them to stay put. I looked around as I walked. I could hear the whispers and feel the eyes on me.

I approached the podium and the Chief gave me a hard look. He told the others to dismiss the students and that he would meet with me alone. I looked back and they escorted Tony out with the others.

"Don't worry, your friend is in good hands. He will be fine."

He assured me.

"You have created quite a scare here young man."

The chief said.

"So tell me son where did you hear the name Suhnoyee Wah? Is this part of your studies?"

"Well, kind of. About five years ago, my mother brought me down here to see a doctor at a hospital and for..."

I stopped off in mid sentence, remembering what Ms. Creed said about not telling anyone about my dreams.

"Well anyway, I met someone who told me a lot about his tribe. We became very good friends. When I went to find him though, he was no longer there."

Chief Spearhorn rubbed his chin.

"So I see," the Chief said. "What was the name of the young boy?"

"Eric...Eric Spearhorn." I replied.

The Chief sat back in his chair and placed his hands on his cane. Which had the head of a silver eagle and diamonds for eyes; it was something to look at. He asked me what else Eric told me about them.

"Well, he told me that his mother never liked it when his grand father told him stories about their tribal history. She thought it was the cause of his dreams."

"What kind of dreams did he have?" He asked.

"He dreamed of things that he sometimes could or could not see but knew they were there."

"I see," the chief said. "So why were you there?"

I did not want to answer him, I was too afraid. By this time, Chief White Feather came in and whispered something in his ear. They both looked at me, then, again at each other. Soon after, Chief White Feather walked out again.

"Son, tell me about your parents."

"What do you want to know about them?" I asked.

"How much history do you have about them?" He asked.

"I'm not sure I understand what you are asking."

"Do you know anything about your background?" He said.

"No, just that both my parents married very young."

"I see," he said. "So why do you want to find Eric?" he asked.

"Well, because I feel that, I must speak with him."

"Son, I must warn you that searching for the past just might disturb your future. Are you sure you are ready to do that?"

"I am more positive than ever before. So, can you tell me if he here or not?"

I was starting to feel a little bit agitated so I just kept myself calm. I felt that the Chief was hiding something from me, something that he didn't want me to know.

"Tell me son, why this interest in Suhnoyee Wah?"

"I cannot tell you right now. I just want to know if Eric is here and then my friend and I will be leaving."

"Patience my son, patience, you will meet him due time."

"You told him the stories. Evidently, something is happening and everyone is sweeping it under the rug. The only person that seems to care is Ms. Creed..." I said in a soft voice.

By this time, my voice was escalating again and I did not want to be disrespectful. All I wanted to do was find out the truth.

"It is not time yet," he said. "All of the pieces of the puzzle that you seek will come together. However, they will come to you first before you go looking for them."

"Why do you think I am here?"

I was starting to get even angrier and I wanted to tell him about my dreams but, I remembered Ms. Creeds' words. Show no signs of disrespect, nor tell them about the dreams. I started to wonder why she would not want me to say anything about them yet.

"What I want you to do first is return home and speak with your parents. I think it's about time that they explain things to you about your past. Then I will arrange for you to meet Eric once he is well."

How could I forget? I am so selfish there, I go thinking of myself again.

"Chief, I do apologize. I heard about his ordeal and I am very sorry."

"That is all right young one. We must give him time to heal then, I will arrange a meeting," he assured me. "However, I will tell you this. Suhnoyee Wah is a very powerful being that my ancestors told me about. I was a young "OHITEKAH" meaning "brave" just like you that went searching for the unknown. It is what I found that had a great impact on my destiny. Therefore, young one you are near your destiny but be very careful."

He had a disturbed look upon his face.

"What was his name?" I asked.

"His name was Running Bear of the Shahwanee tribe. His father named him because, as a child, he showed great strength. As he grew older, he became the fastest in his village. He had the strength of a grizzly. Many thought he was a god, reborn. According to the legend, he was one that believed he was the strongest and the wisest; therefore, he had many followers.

Some say he connected with the animals after he defeated a pack of wolves in the wilderness. He helped win many of their battles and he thought he could persuade the Elders to give him power to start an army to prepare them for war. However, they felt that it was not the right thing to do. Running Bear thought he could force the hands of the Elders by making them believe Chief Iyotaka was weak and could not govern well.

He was distrustful and angry. Mostly because of a young woman, he was very fond of. Her name was Lei'liana her father sent her away to the Comanche tribe to learn the ways of the Comanche women. She was very beautiful and she wore a yellow feather in her hair that her father gave to her. She was very strong in spirit and she hunted along side with her brothers. She was very adventurous and smart. He wanted to make her his bride.

Since her father was the Chief, he felt it best to get his daughter away from him. The only way to keep her safe was to send her away to what some thought was the enemy's camp. However, that was not the case. He sent her away for her safety despite Running Bear being in love with her. The Elders knew his heart was corrupt so they watched him carefully. Running Bear would challenge the Elders many times to strike the enemy before they could strike them. This would not work because the Elders felt they were making peace with the Comanche's because of the boundaries. They warned him not to go against them for there would be a great price to pay.

They told him that he was not to cross the boundary because the blood contract between the leaders was sealed. Running Bear still would not listen. Chief Iyotaka told him wandering into another man's house would bring death and destruction to his own. This made Running Bear furious. He secretly went to the Comanche village to send a message to them."

"What did he do? I asked.

"Let's just say he was ready to start a war but, not just any war, a great war. The Comanche's were very smart people; they had many hidden caves high in the cliffs where they could keep an eye on anyone who cross the boundaries. Running Bear sent one of his followers to the edge of their territory to spy on them and report what he had seen. This would cause problems later.

He went to their camp, studied their movements, and watched them for days. He would report to camp and tell Running Bear that he saw Lei' liana with another warrior named "Queenashano" meaning "War Eagle". This made him furious. He was determined to get his revenge on the Elders and anyone who stood in his way. However, he did not know that the Elders had scouts watching him and one of them reported to the Council that Running Bears followers camped near the boundaries.

One day the tribal council called a meeting to banish Running Bear because they feared his actions would cause their village great destruction. The treaty between the two tribes would be broken.

At the meeting, Running Bear would not listen to reason, his rage, anger, and feelings of betrayal caused him to threaten the council members."

Chief Spearhorn took a deep breath and continued..

"See son it is not good for a man to be angry so much, it poisons the soul. "Running Bear was very impatient; he could not see past his arrogance and wanted control, but he was blinded by his own gifts."

Looking at me with great concern the Chief said.

"Never let what you do not understand cause you to take matters into your own hands."

"So what did Running Bear do?" I asked.

"Well, they told him to learn patience and that bloodshed among their people needed to stop. In addition, that he needed to embrace his inner peace. They told him that his anger had poisoned his soul and corrupted his mind so bad that he was dividing their people.

They gave him a choice to learn the way of peace or leave the village. Running Bear was very angry with them. He told them that they were all weak and they had put everyone in danger and there would be an invasion. He stormed out and sought refuge high in the hills on the east side of the valley. There he would have an army so great that he would become a great threat to all he knew."

He was about to tell me more but Tony came in all excited, apparently some of the girls gave him a tour of the reservation.

"Wow! This place is amazing. I think I am going to put in for a transfer!"

"I must be going and so should you. I understand that you have a long drive home and the hour has grown late. Your parents must be worried by now." He instructed me. "And remember, what you seek may also be seeking you."

The Elders came and took Chief Spearhorn away.

"What happened to Lei' liana?" I asked in such haste.

"Perhaps, another lesson some other time my son. I will see you soon."

They walked out of the room. Tony and I gathered our stuff and walked out to. Big John escorted us to our vehicle to see us off the reservation. We walked close behind them but not to close so they couldn't hear us talk.

"So did you find Eric? Tony asked.

"No, according to the chief, no one can see him just yet. He is still healing from his injuries."

Tony did seem a little concerned though.

"Well maybe it is for the best. So did you get the answers you were looking for?"

I just sighed and shook my head.

"No, just like grownups, everything has to be a secret. He told me it is about time that my parents tell me the truth about my past."

"Truth? What truth?"

"Well, remember I told you that I always felt that my parents have not been honest with me? My mother stares at me sometimes as if she wants to say something and dad says she should tell me the truth. Why do things have to be so difficult?"

Tony responded with surprising news.

"I do not know; but I did hear some of the kids talking about you."

I asked in haste.

"What did they say?" "That legend says only the chosen ones can see the Suhnoyee Wah." Tony was trying to whisper so that Big John couldn't hear him.

"Tell me in the car, not here." Tony nodded his head and we started walking toward the car.

Big John told us to follow him to the main entrance, wait until the gate opens then we can go through it. When we reached the gate, Big John looked at me. He had such an odd look on his face. I thanked him and told him that I would hope to see his smile again and he smirked a little.

"Take care, I will see you soon."

"Oh, are you coming up to Patagonia?"

"Well of course, I hear the fishing is great this time of year."

We drove off and headed home. I called my parents to let them know Tony and I were on our way but I got their voicemails. I hoped to be home in time for dinner.

"Tell me what all did you hear?" I asked in haste.

"Well the question you asked about the Suhnoyee Wah has some of the students a little scared."

"Yeah, yeah, go on."

Tony continued.....

"I found out how some students on campus are saying there have been meetings about the disappearances. The students are encouraged to stick together and not speak about it. I can surely tell you that something weird is going on here and, whatever it is, it has everyone scared. One of them told me that a week before Eric Spearhorn went missing; two students and a teacher went missing also, their bodies haven't been found."

I was in shock to hear that. Tony also said he wandered away by following the directory on the giant wall out front. He went to the library to see what else he could find out. He said it was like Fort Knox. There was one room in the back of the library, which they keep locked and you can only get in with a key card; therefore, he had to hurry because he was not supposed to be there. He did find an interesting article in a huge book with newspaper clippings that he thought I should know about. Tony looked at me with great concern and said.

"Kyle I do not know how to tell you this but..."

He paused for a moment.

"I found out why people are acting even more strange around here. The newspaper clippings I found was about a story that a reporter did on a local hospital here. It says the local authorities sited them for illegal adoptions on children sixteen years ago. The tribal council found out about this and was furious because the children belonged to the reservation. They have been trying to track the children down but some of them were difficult to find. In addition, their names were changed and the parents relocated.

The council filed a lawsuit against the adoption agency and petitioned the courts for the children's safe returned. According to the court of law, the department of child and family services brought the children back to the reservation where families could raise them."

"What does all of this have to do with me? I asked.

"I am getting there. The article also stated the tribal chiefs met with the department of child and family services to be sure that this would never happen again. All of the children that were illegally adopted were now accounted for. They found all but one.

"He paused again, I urged him to continue.

"Go on tell me! What is it?"

"Kyle, according to the reporter, the missing child is you. Eric had a twin brother."

Tony pulled another piece of paper from an article of a picture taken of the some students on campus. In the photo, it lists the names of the students. I felt sick; the picture of the boy I was searching for was my twin brother.

Tony also stated that is why when we reached the council building the students were staring they thought I was Eric.

I felt nauseous all of a sudden.

"Pull over man."

Tony pulled over; as I got out of the car, I fell abruptly to my knees. I did not know how to feel. Everything I knew or I thought I knew was confusing, my parents not my parents. It all made sense now. My head began to swim.

I looked at the article again and asked Tony to get my book. He retrieved my book from my bag and I pulled out the article that Ms. Creed gave me. It was the same article except the picture was missing. She knew…she knew all along!

"What did Ms. Creed know, Kyle?" Tony said.

"She knew that he..." I stopped in mid sentence.

"You know I hate it when you do that! Tell me!" Tony yelled.

"Ms. Creed, she knew the whole time. Look at the clippings they are the same. Ms. Creed put in this one in my book; it matches the one you took from the library."

"Kyle, think back to when you went to the hospital. Did you ever see Eric?"

"No, we just talked through the vents. I never saw his face but, somehow I felt close to him." I sat there for a few minutes trying to piece this all together.

"Did anything else happen at that place your parents took you that you can remember?"

"Something did happen, something terrible..."

"What do you remember?"

"I remember the nurses strapped me to a bed, put these probes on me, and told me to relax. I could see my parents through the window but then, they dimmed the lights."

By this time, my breathing started to increase. I took a deep breath and exhaled. I remembered the doctor telling me to concentrate on his voice until it faded. Then I felt weightless and I remembered the smell. My breathing increased again. I clutched my chest to catch my breath. Tony handed me my drink but then I started again.

"All I knew was that I was not alone in that room. It appeared somehow, hovering over me like a dark mist. It was pulling the life out of me. I couldn't breathe. I saw into its eyes as if it had no soul. No one else saw it but me. I know it was real though...I know it was."

"Hey man, I don't doubt you. Whatever is was you saw, I believe you."

The winds started to pick up. I could hear trees snapping in the distance.

"Come on Tony. We need to get going and we need to get going now."

We jumped into the car and Tony sped off fast. I kept looking back; Tony asked what was wrong but, I told him nothing; all I wanted him to do was to keep driving. I was quiet on the way home, I had so much on my mind. I had no idea what I was I going to say to my parents and how I was going to say it.

They always taught me to be respectful to others and to be honest but this time. I just needed to get some answers. I wondered how much did Ms. Creed know? Did she not want me to know?

On the other hand, she did say that she knew the Spearhorns very well. I was so frustrated that I slumped down in the seat and just sighed deeply. Tony turned up the radio and we listened to some of our favorite music artists.

Just as we did the DJ came on to broadcast the news.

"This is KBLZ radio, where you can listen to all of your favorite music hits from your favorite artist. And now the local news report:

'More bodies were found in Patagonia today near Junction Point according to the local police four bodies were discovered at a camp site. Local hikers discovered the mutilated bodies early this morning.

According to Police Chief Morgan, all campsites will remain closed until further notice. One reporter asked if a serial killer was responsible for the killings but no one knows as of yet. Police Chief Morgan did state that his department was working with the local and the state police to check all of parolees for the past few months.

"We are advising everyone to use precaution and contact the Patagonia police if they have seen anything suspicious.'"

Tony turned the radio off. This is getting worse. We both agreed. Tony said we should be home in about a half an hour but I asked him to stop at the store ahead.

We pulled over into a gas station and I went inside to use the facilities. Tony pumped the gas. We grabbed some snacks but, as we were leaving, one of the attendants spoke to us.

"Where are you going?"

Tony quickly responded.

"We're headed back to Patagonia."

"You boys be careful, there is a serial killer on the loose."

Tony and I glanced at each other for a moment.

"Yeah, there have been some strange things going on there."

"Well whatever, or whoever it is, folks out this way are scared. Some say they've seen packs of wolves near campsites so some of the hunters have set traps to trap them. Some claim that these are the biggest wolves they have ever seen."

I just had to ask.

"How can they tell?" I asked.

"Well, by the prints left behind on the ground."

I looked at the attendant somewhat strange the way as he emphasized his words. He acted as if he knew or had some kind of idea about what was going on.

He punched a few keys on the register and said.

"Your total comes to thirty-five even. You boys be safe driving home."

"Thanks we will," I said.

As Tony and I headed home, the winds were increasing.

"So what are you going to do?"

"Well, I need to talk to Ms. Creed. I think I will call her."

"You can try," Tony told me. I checked my cell phone but couldn't get any reception, only one bar.

"Well we are almost home. I will talk with her then."

"So did you find out anything else?" Tony asked.

"Yeah, the Chief gave me a little history on Running Bear."

"Who is Running Bear?"

"Ones whose name I should not mention."

"So what did you find out about him?"

"That he was a fierce warrior at one time and the people thought of him as some sort of god. They banished him because the Elders feared he would bring destruction to their village. First thing in the morning, I am going to do some research on him and see what I can find out. There has to be some connection."

I needed to know what happened to this warrior; there seemed to be a gap in this ancient mystery. Then it hit me, the book Ms. Creed gave me. I reached for the book and searched the index to see if I could find anything on ancient warriors. There was a section on *Ancient Warrior Tribes* and it listed their names. I scrambled through the book to find Running Bear. Then, under *Fierce Warriors,* I found him.

I began to read how some of his followers considered him a god because of his hunting skills and how he brought great victories to his people. Some said Running Bear had the spirit of a wolf, due to an almost fatal injury he suffered.

While he was out hunting deer, he encountered a pack of wolves deep in the woods. Legend says the wolves attacked him and he put up a great fight. When the other hunters found him, the wolves were dead and he was face to face with a monstrous beast. He survived the attack but was sick for many days. Running Bear healed from his wounds but some say he carried the spirit of a wolf: strong, fearless and he appeared to be changing. Some thought it was because he was near death. Others thought it was because his blood had mixed with the wolf because his bite wounds were so severe. He also had a previous run in with a bear when he was younger.

Running Bear would go on to earn the trust of his followers. When they went to battle, they would remain undefeated because of his presence.

I kept reading; I had to know more. Running Bear would invade villages killing off those he swore as his enemy. He would challenge the mightiest warriors and strike them down, killing them instantly. His name was spreading throughout the land and others began to fear him.

I came to an article on the Great War. I remember the Chief telling me about this. The more I read the more it played like a movie in my head.

The Elders took council to see what they could do with him. One of Running Bears followers betrayed the Elders by telling him the plot to bring them all down. Running Bears fury continued to increase his army of warriors. He decided to wage war with anyone who would defy him.

As well, he was very bitter towards Chief Iyotaka because the young woman he loved was still on Comanche's territory. Running Bear was determined seek his revenge against the council by kidnapping Lei' liana, no matter what. Chief Iyotaka sent a message for him to attend a council meeting with the other tribal leaders in the early morning.

That day, Running Bear and a few of his men showed up to meet them. The drums beating in the background alerted them that someone was approaching. When he arrived, some looked upon him in fear while others despised him. Chief Iyotaka spoke first.

"There have been many reports about you invading villages. You have broken the peace treaties we have settled upon. We have been making peace and you have been making war. Your father would be very disappointed in you. Your actions are going to cause a great war among our people if you do not stop."

Of course, Running Bear was furious at their accusations.

"You talk about peace; I am a man of war!" He shouted at them. "My father is dead because he turned his back on his enemy. He is dead because of you!"

"The council has decided to banish you from the village and the boundary. If you cross the boundary, you will meet your fate. You have allowed anger to overtake you and a man that is full of anger does not listen."

"You are weak and your enemy will destroy you. All this talk of peace has made you soft. If you see my face again it will not be my fate, but yours! Galutsá" He spoke the unfamiliar words before he stormed out.

One of the other elders spoke with concern.

"I fear for him, Chief Iyotaka."

"We must keep an eye on him," one of them added.

"This isn't over," another informed them.

"No," Chief Iyotaka said.

"I feel in my spirit that this is the beginning and we have not heard the last of him."

When Running Bear arrived back at his village one of his followers reported to him that some of the other women including Lei' liana visited Deep-Water Creek. They went every morning to gather fruits and berries. His followers also reported that there was a warrior with her at times. From what they saw, he appeared to be quite fond of her; the two of them hunted together.

Running Bear's heart grew even colder at the news. This was his chance to seek revenge upon those who betrayed him. He set off with some of his followers to capture Lei'liana. He ordered them to kill anyone that stood in their way.

Once they reached the creek, they laid low and waited for the time to strike. One of Running Bear's men aimed his bow and arrow struck one of the men in the chest. He fell into the water. Further downstream, Lei' liana was gathering water in pots when she noticed blood in the water. Soon after, the body surfaced. She screamed at the sight. One of the older men ordered his scout back to the village to alert the others but the attack had began. There was nothing that they could do; Running Bear's men outnumbered them.

The one who escaped made it back to his village to report the news. However, he was spotted and wounded in the back by an arrow. Thought to be dead, he made it back to the village; others saw him and ran to his aid. He could barely speak but, he told those around him what had happened. Running Bear and his tribe had attacked them and kidnapped the women. The young warrior died soon after from blood loss.

This angered War Eagle and his father Chief Wah'tayo. They gathered the horses and took off to Deep-Water Creek to investigate. When they arrived, they found the bodies of their fellow warriors decapitated and hanging from the trees by their legs. The warriors had cut out their hearts and drained the blood from their bodies. There was evidence left behind of Lei' liana. The yellow feather that her father had given her laid stained with blood on the ground.

"Cut the bodies down and take them back for burial." Chief Wah'tayo said.

"We should fight and fight now!" War Eagle said.

"No my son, we will have our revenge. Lei' liana is my responsibility; we must see Chief Iyotaka immediately. I will send scouts to locate Running Bear come we must go."

They took off immediately to see Chief Iyotaka. When they arrived, he was grieved of the news that his daughter was now a prisoner. Chief Wah'tayo told them what happened when they arrived at the creek and the council members shook their heads in great distress. He told them that he had scouts out searching the land to locate Running Bear's village.

"We must do something!" One of the men shouted.

"Then you are welcome to wait here until they return".

The next morning one of the guards beat the drums to alert them that someone was coming. Chiefs Iyotaka and Wah'tayo arose to their feet to see only one of their scouts return. His legs face, and arms were covered in blood and he could barely stand.

"What happened? Where are the others? Please tell us!" War Eagle said.

"Captured and killed." He stammered. "We arrived at the village at nightfall. They ambushed us; we didn't see them coming. Their skin painted black so they blended with the night. As we walked with our hands bound behind our backs, we saw the heads of our brothers. Their bodies mounted on steaks and placed near the entrance as a warning. We could hear the women screaming."

"Did you see Lei' liana? Did you see my daughter?" Chief Wah'tayo asked.

"Not at first but she is alive."

"How do you know?" he asked.

"I heard one of them say she was in the private chambers with him."

"I watched my brothers die before me. They strung them up in the trees upside down and cut off their heads. They made the women gather the blood in pots and take them away. His men brought me before him to find out why I was there. That is when I saw her. She sat next to him, her hands and feet bound. She must have put up a fight because Running Bear had marks upon his face. Lei' liana had bruising on hers."

The Chief groaned and ordered him to continue.

"He asked me why I was there and Lei' liana had this look in her eyes as if she spoke to me warning me not to tell." I told him I had traveled far to find food for my dying village and was captured. He laughed at me and said that I should have stayed in my land and that I was now his prisoner. He said he would let me live if I could make it past the clearing alive. The others started screaming and chanting. Running Bear had picked up one of the pots lifted it high in the air and started to chant."

"What did Running Bear say?" Chief Wah'tayo said.

"He said that he was one with the beast that walks in the night, his blood runs through his veins; He could hear his voice speaking and feel his power."

He continued.

"He told me to drink the blood of his enemies and devour their souls. And I would live forever."

As he talked more, he started to choke and they gave the young brave water to drink.

Chief Wah'tayo urges him to keep talking.

"Keep going, we must know what happened."

"I noticed that he was drinking out of the same pots the women collected the blood of our brothers in. He was drinking their blood. I called him a murderer.

He laughed and said.

"If you cut out the heart of your enemy and drink his blood you own their soul and their strength. Now you will suffer the same fate as everyone else."

Then he explained them how Running Bear arose to his feet and yelled out.

"Let the hunt begin!"

The young brave continued......

"They took me to the edge of the woods and I took off running. I ran as fast as I could. I stopped for a few seconds to cover my body in dirt and mud. I thought if I looked like them, they would not find me. However, they were smart. I managed to escape their bow and arrows."

Chief Iyotaka was very discouraged and angry.

"It is worse than I feared?" He has let the evil spirit overtake him and now he is worse that a savage beast."

He looks at the young warrior again.

"Can you take us to his village?"

"Yes, I can." The injured man said. "But it will not be easy; he has spies everywhere. Guards posted around the boundary lines and there are many traps to catch intruders. A path I found leads to the underground caves. If we take it, we can get in undetected."

"I will alert my people and tell them to prepare themselves for war," said Chief Wah'tayo.

"We will do the same." Chief Iyotaka replied.

The next day both tribes set out to find the location of Running Bear's village. It was on the east side of the valley high in the cliffs. They set up camp near the boundary and sounded the alarm to send a warning message.

One of Running Bears followers saw them and went give a report. War Eagle spotted him though. He followed him deep into the woods and attacked him. War Eagle brought him back to camp and he went before the council. They gave him a message to deliver to his leader. They demanded the safe return of his daughter or be ready to face war.

Once the scout was released, he reported the warning back to his leader. Running Bear went to the edge of the cliff and saw the tribes gathering. He called for his army to assemble.

By the morning, the war drums were sounding and the tribes reached the clearing. The smoke was a clear sign to Running Bear that the war was about to begin. Many of the other tribes were arriving to join in the fight as well.

His spy told him that there would be no negotiations and there would be a war. Running Bear ordered him to let the women go because it appeared they were out numbered. He turned to him and told him there was no room for weakness in his camp. The strength of a man's mind gives him great power but weakness will destroy his soul.

War is what Running Bear wanted. His heart was cold and he had no compassion. He told his people to get his horse ready; they would fight at dawn. The spy left to deliver the message to Chief Iyotaka's camp but, before he could get to the clearing, an arrow struck him down. Running Bear did send a message. A flaming arrow soared into the camp with a message saying,

"The way to a man's soul is through his heart."

However, Running Bear had a hidden agenda. He would enter the clearing dragging his prisoner behind him, to parade her in front of her father. He knew this would anger him and he wanted Chief Wah'tayo to suffer just as he did when his father died. At dawn, the tribes gathered.

As they approached the clearing, War Eagle saw Lei' liana with her hands bound walking behind the horse. Her clothes were torn and this made him even angrier. They waited until his army was in the clearing, and he said.

"You have defied your own kind and have brought death to your people. Release her now or die!" Running Bear laughed

"No,.. my brother. It is not I who is weak, for it is you! Let's see how strong you are."

Running Bear turned to one of his followers and said.

"Tsatsiyohisdi ageyutsa!"

One of the men freed Lei' lianas hands from the horse and released her. "Anagisdi" He said.

Ushering her to leave she walked slowly looking over her shoulder. When she saw her father, he started to run for her. She yelled for him telling him to stay back.

"No father!" She yelled again. "It's a trap!"

Running Bull took out his bow and arrow, shot it, and hit Chief Wah'tayo in the leg. He went down and Lei'liana ran to him but one of Running Bears men grabbed her. She fought him and he struck her down.

By now, War Eagle took charge and ran out to rescue Lei' liana. This was what Running bear wanted, the man who he thought wanted his woman. Running Bear raised his staff and yelled.

"Digatilásdi."

The warriors then charged each other the war was now on. Armies of warriors charged at one another. The Elders stood and watched but what Running Bear did not know that he had other enemies that would join in the fight. Other villages could see the smoke and followed it to the battleground.

Running Bears reputation of invading other villages was now back to haunt him. He would kill anyone who would not join him.

This would be the start of the greatest battle to take down a savage tribe.

I could not believe what I had just read. I had to find out more though. This all made sense to me now. We were just out side of town when the car started to slow down.

"Why are we slowing down?" I asked.

"I thought I saw something up a head, maybe it's a deer or coyote."

The road was dark and winding. Tony slowed down even more and I urged him to keep driving. I didn't want him to stop. A wave of fear gripped me and I looked behind the car only to see a dark figure move slowly across the road.

"Whatever you do, do not stop." I was very persistent. The car accelerated more and we kept going.

"What did you see back there?" Tony frantically asked but I only urged him to keep driving. I did not want to alarm him but I was afraid it was too late. I decided to tell him that I thought I saw something behind us. I kept looking in the rear view mirror, when the car came to a screeching halt. My shoulder hit the dashboard of the car.

I yelled.

"Ouch!"

Tony sat there frozen, he did not move.

I yelled at him again.

"Why did you stop?"

Tony's voice was very shaky.

"There is a herd of deer running across the road. Something must have startled them."

I turned to see a dark figure standing in the middle of the road behind us. Its black cloak moving in the wind, it stood there motionless just staring at us.

I slowly whispered to Tony

"Drive...drive."

"What is it?" Tony asked.

"Drive now!" I yelled.

Tony hit the accelerator and, the car took off fast. Tony started screaming as to why I had him driving so fast.

Looking behind us, I saw nothing. I softly whispered, closing my eyes.

"It disappeared.......It disappeared."

Tony was freaking out.

"Kyle, what is wrong with you man?"

Still driving fast. I had to calm him so he could slow the car down. But he was not convinced

"Please tell me what's wrong?"

"It's been following us," I said to myself.

"What? What do you mean following us?" He asked, still shaking.

"When we last stopped, I heard something. Why do you think I told you not to stop? I believe it has been tracking us."

I could not help but keep looking back behind us. I was checking to see if I saw anything odd but there was nothing. I pondered in my mind why it did not attack us. Why did it stand there looking us? There was no time to be afraid my emotions were too high.

Tony spoke out with great relief.

"Look! "We reached the county line we are almost home."

I felt relief come over me the fear had left.

At that moment, I remembered something. The boundaries, they can't cross them. I am almost certain the shifter was tracking us. I asked Tony if he was all right and he said he was fine, just a little shaken up. He did not know what to expect and wondered if he too was in danger. I told him I did not think so and that it could have been a warning for me.

His hands were still shaking as his white knuckles held the stirring wheel tight. I tried to calm him but he was too far-gone. Now I knew that I was in danger and possibly those around me. What just happened was very real.

A part of me did not want to go home. I wanted to go back to the reservation to get some more answers. I needed to get as much information as possible. I wanted to speak with Chief Spearhorn about the story that I had just read. Running Bear was evil and he blamed the Chief for everything. His drinking the blood of his enemies was more than I wanted to know. Then I thought of something I read. The story said that he had killed a pack of wolves except one. Could this be the cause of his change? I have seen the werewolves portrayed on television as they go man to beast, however this different.

To describe what I see is they are both half man half wolf. It uses the night to attack its victims as if it were a shield like a disguise almost. Nevertheless, in the light you can see both man and beast. That must be why, in my dreams, they move away from the white mist. It can expose them. Since he almost perished from his injuries, it seems almost like he became one with the wolf.

I wondered why the big wolf did not kill him. The book says Running Bear was face to face with this beast. He was very brave and did not show any signs of fear. Perhaps the damage was already done or the others arriving scared him off.

He was very angry with the Elders and felt that he had many enemies. The woman that he loved was sent away so she could not be near him. He had a lot of betrayal in his heart. He could not see past his anger and he was blinded by his gifts.

Then, I started to think about the gifts he had. Running Bear was described as having great strength, being a fast runner, killing a pack of wolves, and communicating with the animals. He had some powerful gifts. I also thought about the reservation. For some reason, I felt safe and secure there, as if I did not have to worry about anything. Perhaps, I could get another chance to go and talk with the tribal leaders again. I hoped I did not leave a bad impression with my persistence of getting answers. I just could not help myself though. I had to know if Eric was there and if he was safe.

I wonder if he even remembered me. If he was indeed my twin, and twins share thoughts and feelings, then he must also feel the connection. Twins...then that must mean chief Spearhorn is my grandfather. I have Native American blood in me. This is too much to take in.

The Shifters were after us because we are the chosen ones. I wonder if the same dreams I was having, he is having also. Moreover, if I can spot them, so could he. There have been some studies that paternal twins can sense each other and read each other's thoughts. I wonder if...I paused for a moment. No way, could that be possible? I had to push the thought out of my mind. After what just happened, anything was possible.

I sat there thinking of what I was going to say to my parents when I got home. If I am in danger, they were too. Do I leave, runaway? So many questions, I had no idea what to do. School would be getting out soon; perhaps, I could get permission to stay on the reservation for a while. I knew they would not turn me down. If I were away from my parents, they would be safe. I would have more time to do research later. Midterms were next week and I had to prepare myself.

As we approached my neighborhood, we noticed several cars in front of the house.

"Hey, that looks like Ms. Creeds' car and that truck looks familiar too."

"What are they doing here, holding a private meeting?"

"I wonder what is going on in there," Tony asked.

"I don't know but, whatever it is, it must be big and we are about to find out." Tony was very nervous.

Chapter Four

CONFRONTING TRUTHS

I didn't understand why they would be here; something was going on.

I gathered all of my belongings from the back seat of the car. Some of my papers got scattered when Tony made an abrupt stop.

"Have any idea what's going on?" Tony asked.

"You are doing it again?" I said.

"Sorry..."

"But no, not at all but, whatever it is, it must be serious."

"Do you think they found out I was in the library and took the article?" Tony asked.

"I do not know."

Tony and I went inside the house where everyone was waiting for us. My parents were both sitting on the couch along with Ms. Creed, Chief Spearhorn, and Big John. They all looked at us in such relief. My mother got off the couch and ran to us.

"Thank God, you two are all right. We thought you were…" She dropped off.

Dad stepped forward

"We tried to call you, when we did not hear from you, we got a little worried. Someone discovered two more bodies."

Dad was very hesitant to tell me, after seconds of silence he finally did.

"Two teenage boys fitting your description disappeared off highway 109 a couple of hours ago. The police said it was the same as the other victims."

By this time Big John came forward as well.

"They were last seen at the gas stations about an hour outside of town, driving the same car as you Tony. When we heard the news, we contacted Ms. Creed, who then called your parents to see if they had heard from you."

Dad was so scared he wanted to know if anything strange occurred.

"Did you see anything suspicious?"

Tony quickly answered my dad.

"No, we stopped at the gas station, filled the car, grabbed some snacks, and left. The gas station attendant did ask us if we were from here. We said yes and he explained about recent events happening out here. That's all."

Chief Spearhorn gave us both a hard look with his eyes.

"Is there anything else you would like to tell us, you look a little disturbed?"

Before Tony could respond to his question, I quickly answered this time. I did not want Tony to tell what we had just experienced.

"No, nothing happened just tired from our trip. So is that why you all are here?" I asked.

"Well, yes and no, son." dad said.

"Well, what is it?" I asked again.

"We are here to discuss something's with you that we feel you have the right to know."

Tony was not ready for this; he was probably thinking that he was in trouble for taking the article so he made up an excuse.

"I had better get home. My parents are probably just as worried about me too." See you on Monday."

I waved a friendly goodbye gesture to him.

"Yeah, see you later Tony."

Big John helps Chief Spearhorn to his feet.

"We may as well be going. Now that the boys are safe at home, we will be leaving now. "Yes, I must prepare for my speech at the library next week."

Ms. Creed followed.

"I'm afraid I must be going as well."

After everyone left, the atmosphere in the room changed. I was full of mixed emotions. My parents held hands tightly and looked over me. All I could do was pace the floor back and forth, rubbing my hands together.

"What is going?"

"Sit down, we'll explain."

How could I talk when I had so many questions to ask them? Therefore, I just blurted it out.

"Did you adopt me? Where did I come from and what about my birth parents?"

Dad went to speak but I stopped him.

"I found some information on the reservation...is that the reason they were all here?"

Dad started talking first.

"Son please let us explain."

"Kyle, you know we love you very much. Your mother and I want the best for you. I know this is a shock to you but, your mother and I didn't want to tell you until we thought the time was right."

By this time mom had a sorrowful look in her face.

"Kyle....."

She looked at me with tears in her eyes. She patted the couch softly and I sat down.

"Sit down and listen to me".

I sat down next to mom. I listened as they both began to tell me how, after they had got married, they tried to have children but could not.

After going to many doctors, they were informed that it was just not possible. My mother started to cry and dad consoled her.

Dad went on to say that, the doctors recommended adoption and put them in contact with a few agencies. There was a man that came to them and told them about a child that was ready for adoption because the mother had given him up. They immediately jumped at the chance and, after signing a few documents, the agency brought me to them.

"You were such a beautiful baby." Dad said, "And your mother was so happy."

Mom looked me in my eyes while holding my hand.

"We knew that you belonged with us."

Dad continued to explain that he knew the day would come to tell me.

I slumped back on the couch and did not say a word. I pulled out the folded piece of paper from my pocket that Tony gave me and handed it to them. It was an article about the illegal adoptions from the reservation.

My mother started to read the part about how the tribal elders tracked down the missing children, all except one.

"Son, this doesn't mean that you are one of those children?"

Taking the paper out of her hand, I slowly responded.

"I wish you were right."

I pulled the other newspaper clipping from my pocket and handed it to my parents with shaking hands; they unfolded the article to see the photo of the boy on the front page. They both stared in amazement. Dad looked in disbelief. There was silence in the room.

"You see mom, dad, I have a twin."

"Son," dad said. "We had no idea, do you know where he is?"

"Yes," I said calmly. "He is on the Tribal Union reservation."

"But you were just there, did you not see him?"

"Eric is still recovering from his wounds. Chief Spearhorn told me would get to see him when he is well. Can we talk about all of this later though? I'm really tired; it's been a long day…and night."

They both agreed we would finish in the morning. My mom kissed me on my forehead and dad patted me on my shoulder. She had tears in her eyes, looking at me as if she just lost a son. I gave them both hugs and told them everything would be all right and that I loved them.

I went upstairs to my room and fell on my bed. I had a lot to think about; all I could do was just lay there staring up at the ceiling. You would think a kid my age would spend his time playing video games, hanging out late, chasing girls, or something like that. I was chasing my past while horrific things are happening around me.

I took a deep breath to release energy from my body. I just kept staring while thoughts ran through my mind. I could hear parents talking through the walls; they were very worried about me. I feared for their safety. Maybe I should leave.

No, where would I go? I am just a kid.

Oh my goodness, I buried my head in the pillow. I really needed to get some sleep but I just could not. I grabbed my iPod and listened to some music. It always helped to calm my nerves. I wondered who the two students killed tonight were and where they were from. I just had to know. I turned on the television to catch the eleven-o-clock news.

"Patagonia is in shock once again as two bodies were discovered along highway 109 by a state trooper. The bodies are of two young men, said to be in their late teens or early twenties. The victims suffered wounds to their abdomen.

We are putting the public on high alert as we find out more details. It does appear that we have a serial killer, or killers, on the loose and residents are being urged take precaution."

The reporter stated that one of the bodies was discovered behind the car; the other was discovered just a few feet away. They apparently had a flat tire and pulled over to fix it. The Sheriff's department scheduled a press conference tomorrow morning. As local and state police continue their investigation, they are urging residents to take precaution.

I turned the television off. I grabbed my cell phone and called Tony to see if he was all right. He answered on the first ring.

"Hello."

"Hi Tony, it's me, Kyle. Just checking to see if you are okay."

"Yeah, still shaking. Luckily, my parents were not home to see me like this."

"Look Tony, I am sorry. Thanks for not saying anything in front of my parents."

"No problem but, why keep quiet. We could have been killed."

"I had a feeling that we should not have said anything. It just wasn't the right time."

"Who is keeping secrets now?"

"I know, I will tell them soon. I just wanted to be sure that you were safe."

"Swell, just swell. Look, I am going to bed. I will call you tomorrow, later."

I knew Tony was upset and scared, so was I. I just could not take any more surprises I just had to relax myself. I put my headphones on and listened to music until I could feel my body slip away into a deep sleep.

That night, I dreamed I was back in the woods, running away from the movements and sounds again. I am not alone. There were others with me. This white mist was leading us deeper into the woods. The further we went the more we grew in numbers.

Side by side, we ran through the first part of the clearing. I did not recognize any of them however.

We marched as if we were ready for battle. There we all stood lined up with our eyes widened, prepared and focused. The wind started to blow and then it howled. The trees snapped, as if someone was breaking them.

Then, I saw them. They moved slowly as silk composed of black mist. The Shifters transformed in the moon light. Their claws extended like huge sharp blades. They walked along side of one another like an army ready for war, growling louder and showing teeth. The others stayed near the clearing and did not break the line. The Shifters moved all around us, trying to intimidate movement of the line. We needed to get closer to the edge of the woods.

Then one of them shouted

"Diskualádodi!"

Everyone started running towards the woods. The Shifters were after us, using the land and trees against us. I could see them attacking the others. I kept running though.

One of the Shifters was getting close to me but I kept running as fast as I could. Its long claws reaching through the blackness caught my shirt. It ripped across my back. I kept running. I could see light up ahead and I kept going. The screams were louder and louder, the smell was getting stronger.

The growls sounded like chain saws, louder than ever. I thought I was going to die. As I ran, the bodies lay there with their chest ripped open. I witnessed bodies disappearing and transforming into the night.

Just a few more feet, I was almost to the clearing. The white mist was moving in my direction and some of the shifters were falling back. Then almost suddenly, I felt a hard hit. A Shifter knocked me down. I fell on my back and then; he appeared hovering over me, bearing his teeth. I clutch my chest, my heart was beating very fast and a lump was in my throat I cried out for help. I prayed for someone to help me. I just kept screaming. I yelled for it to get away from me.

The Shifter moved closer to me, revealing more of it self. With his claws pointing towards me, it was ready to strike. I moved backwards fast until I backed into someone. I turned to see Eric extend his hand with a silver stone speaking a native language. A light came from it and the shifter covered his already hidden face. Shifters could not stand to look at the light. The others he created also fled.

Then, it disappeared. I was still clutching my chest. Eric looked down at me and told me I was safe now. He turned away and walked through the woods. I called to him but he did not answer me. I asked him to come back he was no longer there.

I woke up the next morning with parents standing over me.

"Son, you had another nightmare." Dad said. "It must have been a bad one your shirt is torn to pieces."

"I am all right...it just felt real."

"Honey, let me call a doctor," my mother pleaded.

"No, no more doctors, please. I will figure this out on my own."

"Let us give him time dear," dad softy told mom..

"Thanks dad".

They left my room; I needed to talk to Chief Spearhorn right away. I did not know where he was staying.

I located him at one of the local hotels and called to speak to him. Patagonia was not that big of a town. The clerk said he was not in; therefore, I looked up Ms. Creed in the phonebook. I started to call her but I decided to go to her house instead. I figured face-to-face would be much better.

I ran downstairs and told my parents that I would be back later. I got in my car and drove off. I just had to get some answers from her. I arrived at her house and went to the door. I was nervous but I had to be persistent. I rang the doorbell and she answered.

"Kyle, what are you doing here?"

"Ms. Creed, I have to talk to you. May I come in?"

"Well, I am busy today. Can this wait?"

"No, this cannot wait. I must speak with you now." She hesitated for a minute.

"Sure, come in." She told me to go to the den area to have a seat. She would be with me shortly.

I walked in and, to my surprise; Ms. Creed had beautiful art in her home. I admired her taste for art. She had beautiful figurines and portraits of her family. I came across one portrait, it must have been a picture of her when she was little. The people behind her must be her parents. Ms. Creed walked into the den.

"What's the emergency?" she asked. I did not know where to begin so I started simple.

"Thanks for getting me onto the reservation." She replied with a welcome and asked me to sit down.

"Kyle, is there something wrong?" She asked.

"Yes," I said. "Everything is wrong. I had another nightmare last night, I was screaming so loud I woke up my parents."

"Go on."

"I was in the woods again and there were others with me. One of them spoke something and everyone started to run. There was black mist everywhere I saw the shifters slaughter them like cattle. They chased us through the woods. There were bodies everywhere with their chest ripped open."

By this time, my heart started to race and my palms sweating. Ms. Creed gave me some water, asking me to take my time. I proceeded to tell her how the bodies were transforming right before my eyes into the night.

"As we were running away, one of the shifters knocked me down. It stood over me staring into my eyes. I backed up into someone trying to get away from it. When I turned around Eric was there. He had a silver stone in his hand and it glowed very bright blinding the shifters. They immediately began to retreat. Eric looked at me, and told me I was safe and then I woke up. Ms. Creed these dreams are getting worse, my life, and those around me are in serious danger."

"Kyle, what else can you remember from the dream?"

"That is all, nothing else."

"You said Eric was in your dream…"

"Yes, he helped me get away from the shifter with a silver stone by blinding it."

Ms. Creed put her hand on her chest and clutched her necklace.

"Ms. Creed, this has to mean something, a warning of some kind. These creatures are following me."

She interrupted by saying.

"What do you mean by 'followed."

I explained to her when Tony and I were on our way back home we stopped at the gas station. Later we pulled over on the side of the road for a moment. That's when I heard the trees snap and the wind pick up. I told her how I urged Tony that we needed to get going and move fast.

As we drove further down the road, Tony slowed down he said there was a heard of deer running. Then I saw it in the middle of the road looking at us. I told Tony keep driving and not to stop. I do not know what it wanted but it made sure I saw it.

"I need to you to get me back on the reservation. I must talk to the Chief." I told her.

"Don't to worry, he's already here."

"What?" I turned around to see Chief Spearhorn come into the room.

"So your puzzle pieces have come together."

"How long have you been here?" I asked.

"I have been here long enough to hear what I needed to know." He said. "Ms. Creed would you mind leaving us alone for a moment, I need to speak with Kyle alone"

"Sure, I will be in my study." With that, Ms. Creed left the room.

The Chief sat down with his hands resting on his cane with the eagles head.

"Son, you are right. Danger is all around us. Please do not think you are in this by yourself. Everyone in this town is in danger until the killings stop. Therefore, we must be careful. Tell me...how much do you know?"

"I now know that my parents adopted me and I could possibly have a twin. Each dream I have, I come face to face with the danger. It stares at me as if it is searching for something. Sometimes in my dreams, I think I am going to die. This time Eric was there to save me. I saw it killing people as if it was creating an army of a completely new race. There must be a connection between my dreams and these murders.

I have seen enough. I believe the Suhnoyee Wahs are real. They are responsible for these deaths. The bodies of victim's chests ripped open and the disappearances from the morgue. Unless we have a crazy person on our hands desperate for corpses or these bodies are really disappearing."

I went on to tell the Chief more details I discovered while on the reservation. I asked him to forgive me for my behavior. Then I thought of something I never got around to asking Ms. Creed; why she did not want me to say anything about my dreams?

However, I felt that I was going to get more answers to my questions. He looked at me odd for a moment and said.

"Kyle...how long have you been having these dreams?"

"Since I was very little, my parents could hear me screaming at night and find my sheets and pillows torn."

I went on to tell him how in my dreams I can see them and smell them. Then how the white mist would lead me to the clearing and the shifters could not cross the boundaries. Then he looked at me and said.

"Nasgiya yinulistaná suyedá sakuu"

"What does that mean?" I asked.

"I believe you already know," He said. "I am afraid there is much, much, more you have to learn. Come to the library tomorrow after school to my meeting. You will find it interesting."

"How is Eric?" I asked.

"Eric is well; he is getting stronger...as you saw in your dream." How odd for him to say that but it kind of made sense. "Don't worry you will see him soon."

His voice was very shaky and he had a look of concern on his face. He told me not to worry, the spirits will keep him protected. Ms. Creed did not know what to say but I had to ask her why she never wanted me to mention my dreams to the Chief. She looked at me as though she was afraid. However, I had the feeling she was afraid, not for me be but for herself.

Due to the murders, the school district decided to shorten classes so students could get home before dark. Everyone was to walk in groups and report anything suspicious. The whole town was on alert.

Ms. Creed told me to go home and she would see me at the library tomorrow.

I headed home with so many thoughts running through my mind. I expected more from the Chief, all this waiting was wearing down my patience. They know more than what they are saying. I knew they were afraid as well. I wondered how these creatures could die. There must be a way to kill them.

I was on my street when a car passed me driving slowly. The windows were dark so I couldn't see who was driving. The car was an older model sedan with a dent on the right side. I had never seen the car in the neighborhood before. Maybe they are looking for someone. Who knows but I will keep a look out for it.

Chapter Five

Ancient Legends

I arrived home to find my mother standing in the kitchen looking out of the window. She looked disturbed. I called to her but she did not answer me. I called to her once more. She was staring out of the window, as if she was in a trance. I gently touched her on the shoulder and she jumped.

"Sorry… what's wrong?"

I explained that I called out to her and she did not answer me. She apologized and stated she was just daydreaming. I did not believe her though; she had something on her mind.

"Sit down and I'll fix you lunch," she offered.

"No thanks, I will just go to my room," I said as I looked back at her again. "Are you all right?"

"I'm fine."

"Hey, I saw a strange car in the neighborhood, an old black sedan. Have you seen it?"

"No, perhaps they're looking for someone," She suggested.

I asked her again if she was sure about felling okay.

"Just fine son my mind is full of thoughts and worries for you right now."

My mom was definitely a worrier, I told her as a family we would get through all of this. As I turned to go up stairs, she reminded me about something.

"Oh, and don't leave the house, your dad is coming home with a surprise for us."

"I'm just going to my room to do some research."

I went to my room, sat on my bed, and just stared up at the ceiling again. I had to find out more about the war and find out what happened.

I got on my laptop to research and there was a lot of information on Native American wars. Therefore, I had to narrow my search a little. I added names of some of the warriors and there were so many. Until I came across an article titled *The Blood War*. I clicked on the link; it was on the war that I was reading earlier.

In the 1870's through the 1890's, there were many wars but there were none like this one. Legends say the tribe of Running Bear became one of the fiercest tribes in all the land. Many feared his army was multiplying and would become unstoppable. Since the Chief elders had banished him, he would seek his revenge. Running Bear searched distance lands gathering an army of warriors to help him defeat those who betrayed him. The Elders wanted peace in the land but Running Bear wanted war. He thought that turning your back on your enemy made you weak and that only the strongest would survive. He was not afraid to look death in the face, according to legend he had seen death. I tried to gather as much information on him as I could.

There was another link on the Forbidden Lands. I would research that later. Therefore, when I met with Chief Spearhorn again, I could ask him more questions.

Dad came home and asked me to help him out for a while. He wanted to talk to me. Mostly, to let me know that he spoke with Chief Morgan, he said that there had not been any murders lately but they still wanted everyone to be careful. Dad said after school was out he wanted to know if I would like to help him with football camp. Just so, I could get my mind off my troubles. I told dad I would think about it. He said that was fine.

He also talked about how he wanted to take us on a getaway for while. I told him that would be good. He said that we owned a cabin up near mountain peaks and there is fishing creek up there where we could do some fishing. I told him that we should get away and relax a bit. Dad said he was glad to hear me say that. He suggested we leave on Sunday. He asked if I had any special plans and I told him no.

With a smile on his face, he said he was taking us away for a few days. Since it has been scary around town it was about time we did something as a family.

Dad went to go talk with mom. I went back to my room to find that my cell phone was buzzing. It was Tony leaving me a message to come hang out at his place. I decided to call him later. I needed to relax.

There is a long day planned tomorrow after school. Chief Spearhorn would be speaking and, since I had a personal invitation, I was going to get a front row seat. I decided to call Tony back and reached his voice mail. I left him a message saying

"Tag, you are it."

Then I hung up. I started to think more about Eric. I could not believe I had a twin brother. Maybe I should not get my hopes up yet. That still needs proving. How much did he know about me I wonder?

I pulled out the article Tony found and stared at his picture. There was a lot of resemblance between us. Eyes, nose, and ears. His hair was longer and darker. I wondered what I would say to him when I met him. I also wonder who our real parents are or if they were even alive.

Since the adoption was illegal, did they try to find us? There are just too many loopholes. Do I pursue it or leave it alone? I do not want to hurt my parents. After all, they did raise me and didn't ask for any of this. They both just wanted a child to love and take care of. I wonder what my mother was thinking about earlier; she was in a seriously deep thought. When mom does that, she knows something and I wondered if she is afraid to tell me. I have a feeling in time she will.

After school let out the next day, I hurried over to the library to hear Chief Spearhorns speech. There was a lot of media coverage and people everywhere. Even other Native Americans from distant reservations were there. Some dressed in their native attire and colors. I went in and there was no room to sit.

Then one of the officials tapped me on the shoulder and told me to follow him. I had a seat in the reserved section. I was surprised to see Tony there also.

"I didn't expect to see you here," I lightly punched him on his shoulder.

"Wouldn't miss it for the world." He looked at me smiling and said, "Guess who is here?"

"Who is here?" I asked surprisingly.

"Your photogenic girlfriend and she's looking as good as ever."

We both looked up at her. She was very pretty snapping photos of everyone. She had on a black leather jacket, white shirt, and dark jeans. She wore her baseball cap backwards and silver hoop earrings. I just could not take my eyes off her. I watched her take pictures of all of the officials, and the crowd. I was in such amazement by her.

She could never be interested in a person like me. Besides, it would be too dangerous. Maybe she had a boyfriend or she could be a lesbian I shook my head.

"Kyle, would you like a bib for all that drool on your shirt?" Tony said jokingly.

"Whatever dude, come on sit down it's about to start."

We sat down in our seats. Then, Ms. Creed stepped to the podium to welcome everyone. She began her introduction.

"It's a privilege and an honor to introduce such a man who represented his country and his people very well, Chief Spearhorn."

She spoke about how he was an influence in his community and ours by the contributions he made. There were others on the panel. Some I had never seen before. I did recognized Big John and a few other men from the reservation. They must be the security.

After Ms. Creed introduced Chief Spearhorn, the crowd applauded. He thanked the crowd with his humbled voice and said.

"Thank you, town of Patagonia, for your hospitality. You have treated me with kindness." He started by acknowledging others on the panel as well. There were Native Americans from all sorts of tribes here.

Many of them had traveled to hear him speak. Then the Chief began to talk about the wars.

"There are many of you gathered here to learn about our native history. I am here to talk about an ancient one that we talk about seldom; however, he is a part of our ancestry. Regardless of our history, whether it is good or bad. We can take from them. Learn and teach our children the correct path to take. Educating our children is very important.

My father once told me, '*A man that travels down a dark road without receiving instruction first will find himself blind until he opens his eyes.*' We must continue to keep our eyes open. Do not let hatred and anger blind you, as you will learn today about a warrior blinded by his very own gifts. Even though he wanted to prove that he was the best, he spent his life convincing others what he already knew deep within."

Chief went on to talk about the many wars between tribes some tribes were territorial. It would mean death to cross into their land without and escort from a representative from the tribe. Others did not care. Some of them took it upon themselves to kill the innocent for the good of the land. If they did not protect it, their race of people would die.

"Many of our people back then were people of peace. They worked hard to keep the land plenteous for their families. The fathers taught their sons how to hunt to bring food back to the villages. Some of our young men grew up to be strong like their fathers. As other wars went on, many of our people suffered many fates. Their spirit lives on in us. We remember them in song by the beating of the drum.

Some of the other tribal leaders from many different tribes wanted to make peace with them by calling a truce. Some of them wanted this treaty and others did not. They felt that the land was better off left alone. We encountered many pioneers and helped them to cross rough terrain just to get to the lower valley on the other side. Many travelers suffered death crossing over into lands that was unknown to them and some they even kept prisoner.

Many, many moons ago there was a tribe called the Shahwanee's who had a warrior that was very strong. He was not afraid of anyone. When he was a young brave, he along with other young braves would have to prove their strength. They would show the elders how they could defend the land and provide for their families. He knew he was a strong warrior and often proved himself to his father that he could be among the greatest.

His name was 'Liwanu', which meant 'growl of a bear.' One day his father and the other hunters took the young braves deep into the forest to show them how to hunt dear. Liwanu was sharper than his fellow brothers were and always watched carefully. He would prove to everyone that he was the best by wandering away into bear territory.

Liwanu came across a carcass of a deer and noticed a huge bear. The bear towered over him like a giant. The others heard the noise and took of running in his direction. Liwanu was face to face with the beast and it chased him. He knew he could not defeat the animal alone. The bear chased him deeper into the woods and the others feared that he would die. They kept running towards him. Liwanu ran and saw a huge rock; he jumped on it and turned to face the bear with his spear. Ready for battle, the bear lunged at him and knocked him off the rock.

By the time the others arrived, they thought he was dead. They heard a groaning sound and Liwanu was underneath the bear alive. His father ran to move the beast from him and with only few scratches, he was proud to see that his son was alive. Liwanu told his father that he felt strange somehow.

As the beast lay on him dying, he looked deep into its eyes and saw the life leave the bear. He said he was in a trance and could not move. The bear made a strange sound as life left him. He said it was as if the spirit of the bear went into his soul and he felt a connection with the forest but he could not explain it. On that day, his father decided to change his name to Running Bear because his son showed great strength of a bear and destroyed it.

His father told him that he now possesses the spirit of the bear and that it was a gift from the gods. He also told him to use his gift wisely never let evil overtake him or it would mean death to us all. The young brave had proven himself to his father and would go back to his village and celebrate.

However, this young brave would go on to have a life changing experience that would have a great impact on his village for a long time. My ancestors talked about him, his life would become legendary. It is on record in our archives about Running Bear and other warriors of his time. Our people keep them as a reminder of our ancient past.

Though our people survived war, plagues, and droughts, we survived by drawing strength from one another. We learned the way of the land and sky to show other how to survive as well. Mother Earth provided the way for us and we repay her by keeping the land pure from waste and other debris. We should take care of the earth she is our homeland to destroy it we would be destroying ourselves.

When we need help, we call upon the spirit of the earth to help us. We used the plants to heal our sick the animals provided our clothing. As the earth provides us with the materials, we need to survive. We can only repay her by taking care of her.

I have asked the wind dancers to give a demonstration of how we thank mother earth for being kind to us. We dance and give thanks for what we have."

The Chief took his seat and the dancers came forward. Each one of them represented an element: water, fire, earth, and air. The dancers were dressed in beautiful colors from head toe. The drummers were beating the drums it was very exciting to watch. In the background, others wore masks. It was very exciting to see this, and then others joined in the dance. After the dance was over Chief came back.

"The moon festival is approaching; however, due to the events happening here, I want everyone to be careful and use caution," he instructed everyone. "The council will have a meeting next week to determine if it will go as planned." Once again, the chief thanked everyone and took his seat.

"Thank you everyone for coming." Ms. Creed came forward. "There are refreshments being served on the pavilion in the back of the building." As she spoke, Big John approached Tony and me.

"Would you like to get your picture taken with the Chief?" he asked. We gladly accepted the offer.

We went onto the stage and stood next to Chief Spearhorn all of the photographers rushed like paparazzi and starting taking pictures. As they did, my eyes scaled the room and, right in front, there she was taking photos. I did not want to look directly at her so I focused on the other photographers. Then, it was over. I watched her pick up her camera bag and leave.

"When can I come back for a visit to the reservation?" I turned to the chief.

"Anytime,... when school is out."

"I would love for you and Tony to come back," Big John joined in, "but, you have to finish the school year. On the reservation, we give the students a grand bonfire. I will let you know and send the invitation." We both gladly accepted.

Chapter Six

A New Friend

The next day at school, it was the last week of finals before school ended. I was feeling good that the nightmares were calming. Some nights I did not even dream. I felt the more I pieced things together, the stronger I became. The local police stated that the town crime dropped and no one had filed any missing person's reports in weeks. However, they still had an ongoing investigation.

I was gathering more information as I did research on Running Bear and would write down anything or faces that would appear in my dreams. I thought about Chief's speech, when he said as the bear was dying, its spirit entered Running Bear. It made perfect sense.

As I walked the hallway to my class, I saw the signup sheet for football camp. Dad was getting very busy with volunteers. My locker was close by so I needed to grab more books, as if I did not have enough already. I needed to hurry. I did not want to keep Mr. Wong waiting.

He was my science teacher and he was very strict.

As soon as I opened my locker, more books and papers fell out.

"Oh, crap what the...I thought I cleaned this thing out." I guess not.

I bent down to pick up my junk pile and shoved everything back in. Then, I took off running down the hallway when I collided with someone. Books and papers went flying everywhere.

"Hey, what's your hurry?" Oh, no it was the photo queen. I had knocked her down.

"I am so sorry, I do apologize. I did not mean to."

Gathering her books and papers, she responded.

"That's all right,"

"Here, let me help you up." I extended my hand out to help her.

However, she resisted and spoke a little harsh.

"I can manage on my own thank you very much. So where is the fire?"

She knelt down and started picking up her books.

"Here, let me help you with those."

"Oh, no thanks I can manage." My hands started shaking again. "You're Kyle, right?" She asked.

"Yes, yes, my name is Kyle." We both stood up at the same time.

She calmly introduced herself.

"My name is Elsha, Elsha Morgan."

Smiling at me was better than her fist in my face.

"Hello Elsha, you wouldn't happen to be kin to Police Chief Morgan would you?"

I nervously asked.

"He's my uncle. My dad is Dr. John H. Morgan he works at the hospital and part time at the morgue for forensic studies."

"Oh," I said in relief. "I saw you at the library yesterday."

"Yeah, I took some cool pictures of you and your friends; I will have to show you sometime, once I develop them."

"Cool."

"Well I have to be going now."

She handed me my books and of course, I was all thumbs, they fell again.

"Sorry, I would help you again but I am already late for class."

Wonderful, I was also late. As she walked away, she waved at me and said.

"See you later."

With books and papers in my arm, I bolted in the door to Mr. Wong's class. He was very strict on people who were late and he usually kept them after class. I snuck in quietly as he was writing the class assignment on the board. I sat down easy in my seat. Tony was laughing at me. I frowned at him.

"It was very nice of you to join everyone for class. Would you like to explain why you are late for class?"

I swore this guy had eyes in the back of his head. Mr. Wong did not tolerate tardiness at all; I bet he would be on time for his own funeral.

"Locker trouble sir I do apologize for being late."

I hated being the center of attention; I wish some of the kids would stop staring at me.

"Since this is the last week of the school term, I will let you slide this one time."

I thanked him and took out my notebook to write down the class notes. Only this was not my notebook. Oh no…she must have it. This was not good. Maybe she wouldn't even look at it. We did collide very hard. Maybe I put it in my locker by mistake. I would check after class. I borrowed paper from Tony and started working.

Mr. Wong was talking about how forensic science has helped solve many cases through DNA. The technology we have today is more advanced now from when we first started. With new information, we can go back more then eighty years to solve cases.

Mr. Wong told us that he has always been fascinated with science. He explained more to us by saying DNA tells us secrets that we never knew and has put us on a journey of new scientific breakthroughs.

As Mr. Wong talked, I thought about Elsha I could not believe we ran into each other literally. She appeared to be very nice. I also thought about my notebook. I hoped that it was in my locker. I prayed it was in my locker. No one needed to see that. I must have grabbed it by mistake this morning. That meant my science notes are at home sitting on my desk. Way to go Kyle.

Mr. Wong teaches tenth and eleventh grade science and he believes in notes. He acts like a college professor sometimes. Perhaps he will go easy on us students today. Yeah right, Kyle when does Mr. Wong ever go easy on any of his students.

After Mr. Wong was through giving his science, lecture class was over. I went to my locker and Tony followed me. He wanted to know why I was in such a hurry. I told him no rush. I just need a few items from my locker. Then he wanted to know why I was late for class since I am always punctual. I told him that I ran into someone. Tony was persistent when it came to asking questions. I told him he should become a reporter. He just had to know everything.

After searching through my locker I slammed the door shut.

"Darn! It is not here."

"What are you looking for in there?"

"My notebook I must have dropped it when I ran into Elsha."

I did not want that to slip out of my mouth. Well, too late now Tony was all ears. He just had to know where and when.

"I didn't see her coming around the corner. We ran into each other and our books fell. She must have picked up my notebook by mistake. I have to get it back."

"Well then just get a new one," Tony suggested.

I turned to him and giving him a mean look.

"That notebook had important information in it."

I made sure he heard me. Then I walked away.

"I will see if I can find her after school, I have to go I do not want to be late for another class."

The rest of the day, I tried to stay focused. I should be worried about my book but she came to mind more often. People say love at first sight is true. Well in this case, it is true. She was very pretty, my mind drifted a little bit. What was I thinking? She had my notebook. She will probably think I am some kind of freak. Anyone who reads that will know that I have terrible nightmares. Maybe she was laughing at me behind my back or perhaps showing her friends. I could not help but think that.

"No way, she would not do that," I tried to convince myself.

I had better pull my brain back to focus on class; thank goodness, it is the last class of the day.

As soon as class was over, I ran to my locker to check it one last time and nothing. I emptied out everything and placed all of my books into my bag. Now I was worried. I met Tony in the hall and he asked if I could give him a ride home because his car was in the shop. I told him no problem but I had to find Elsha first. He agreed and we stopped at just about every class and asked some of the students. Tony suggest I just forget and he would loan me his. He also thought that perhaps Elsha would bring it to me.

Tony wanted to know why the book was so important. I had to tell him details of my dreams were in that book. He did not say a word. This was a first...Tony was speechless. I hoped Elsha would return my book soon. My parents and I were leaving Sunday to go out of town for a few days. I drove Tony home and decided to stop by the library to check out some books and return the one that Ms. Creed gave me.

The librarian said she would not be in today and that this book on the Ancients was her own personal one that she had purchased from the library. Therefore, I would just hold onto it and take it to her home later. The librarian asked if she could help me find something for me and I told her that I would just look around. She also reminded me that the library would be closing early today to prepare for inventory. I called my parents and told them I would be at the library for a while and would be home soon. I wanted to hang out at the library and do more research on Running Bear.

I doubt that I would find anything but Chief did say they had archives. Maybe I should visit their library. Since Eric and I could possibly be twins, that makes Chief Spearhorn my grandfather. Surely, they would have to let me on the reservation. Big John said they would be having an end of the year celebration for all of the students, maybe I will use that time to research.

I found a corner way in the back of the library near the audio booths. It was very quiet and secluded. With the exception of a few staff members, no one was in the library, thank goodness.

I sat and read for a while. I thought about how nice it had been that my dreams were becoming mild. I wondered how much more I could take if they got intense again. I relaxed on the lounge and read my book I found on The Forbidden Lands. It was very interesting. It talked about when people who were evil had died. The witch doctors, or spiritual priests, would say a sacred prayer over the body so that spirit could not cross back over. It was important to the Native Americans. They believed that once the spirit crossed over, a prayer had to be spoken so it could never enter our world again. That was why burial grounds are sacred and should go undisturbed.

There was a cave mentioned called catacombs in different parts of the world. There were other names like underground cities of the dead. In western mountain areas, tribes often deposited their dead in caves or fissures in the rocks. Their tombs were sealed and a high priest or priestess would say the prayer so the spirit could rest for all eternity.

Many believe that the dead walk among us. There are sprits trapped between two worlds and cannot crossover. They wander around aimlessly until they can get to the other side. Some say, we have the gift to help lead them into the light. However, others believe that some dark forces seek prey on the living because there are ties that still connect them to someone in the natural world. Some of these are just myths but the Native Americans have special prayers and dream casters that catch evil spirits. It only works if the sacred prayer is used.

As I read, my eyes became heavy. I did not know when I drifted off to sleep in the library but, I did. I had another dream.

I could see a group gathering, preparing for something. I did not know what they were doing. As I moved in closer, I saw a huge flat rock shaped like a platform. The sky was clear and the moon was full and bright. A chief tribal leader stepped forward dressed in his native attire. Upon his head was a big headdress filled with large colorful feathers. He had war paint on his face and a long staff with the head of an eagle with diamond like eyes. He held it tightly in his hands and the eyes began to sparkle.

He spoke in a language that was ancient. He pointed his staff toward the trees and said,

"Nihi tlayeli galutsá dadahnawasdá."

The dark beings did not move and the young warriors held their places. The chief tribal leader stared into the darkness and began what sounded like a prayer. White mist began to surface from the ground the chief prayed louder.

Then, there was a great silence; no one moved. I could feel a wave of fear come over me. A smell gripped the air like thick smoke; I could not escape. The sounds of growling intensified in the woods and then he appeared from the trees. I was unable to move. The creature had to be about seven or eight feet tall.

The tribal chief did not move the staff in his hand but the eagle eyes glowed even brighter this time. The Shifter moved and transformed because of the light was like the others in their human form.

There they were, face to face. This was not a war but a gathering of two leaders.

"Why was I here again what does this all mean?" I thought aloud. I had to get closer to see.

The Shifter transformed into a man standing very tall. He had a stocky build and a scar on his face.

"It couldn't be so..." I said to myself. The Chief spoke to the shifter in ancient language. Somehow, I could understand them.

"Why have you summoned me here?" The Shifter asked.

"Your evil upon this world must stop." The chief replied. "You may have crossed over into this world, but you will never cross the boundary lines. We will protect our people."

"True." The shifter started. "But I will have my revenge upon your people. I may not be able to touch you, wise one, but I will kill those who come around you. You and your generation will parish for what you did to me. I will not rest until I have my revenge. You cannot protect them from me much longer"

The Chief did not appear intimidated by the creature at all.

"Your spirit is restless mighty warrior. As my ancestors defeated you in your mortal life, we will defeat you again even in death."

The Shifter laughed.

"I am the shielded by the night; I am the darkness that people fear. I will not stop until all of the first born of the bloodline are mine."

Then the Chief raised his staff and spoke.

"Your curse will not rein forever."

Then, the Shifter pointed his finger over everyone who stood around.

"As long as their blood flows, I will remain. I will seek you and hunt you down like cattle. Your children will cry out in the night. I will have my revenge."

Then the Shifter stepped away from the Chief and transformed from man to wolf, blending with the night. The chief continued his prayer. He extended his hands toward the crowd and called for the other spirit leaders from different tribes to join him on the big rock.

Four men stood back to back and each of them extended their staffs towards the four corners of the earth north, south, east, and west. The three others stood side by side also facing opposite directions representing heaven, earth and the spirit of the souls. They prayed the prayer of "galákuodi galikuo-gi." Which are the seven sacred prayers. A white mist moved throughout the land in each direction the men faced. Covering the land as far as the eye could see.

After the prayer, the seven men joined their staffs together and it created an illuminating light that extended into the heavens. The ground shook and seven sacred stones appeared. One stone per tribe and each of them placed the stones in a sacred pouch. This was to protect them from the Suhnoyee Wah for all eternity. When evil was present, the stones would glow or sparkle keeping them safe. The Chief Elder gave each man instructions on how to take the stones and break them down into pieces. Each piece of the stone was to be given to the firstborns of every tribe after that person died the stones were to be passed down to other firstborns of the same generation. The stones were to be worn for protection.

I heard a noise behind me. Then a hand on my shoulder, I turned to see it was Eric and had blood all over him. He pointed to the woods and said,

"Galutsá nasgi iyuwakodi." Meaning *Come, it's time.*

I could hear a woman screaming out in pain; I followed the sounds to a village. I went inside a hut to see a woman lying on a bed full of bear furs. She was very beautiful to look at. Men that looked like spiritual leaders and doctors stood around her. The midwives were comforting her and she screamed even louder. The men had long staffs decorated with yellow and black feathers and attached to them were dream catchers. They were saying prayers for the woman because she was giving birth. She pushed harder and harder and delivered a boy.

The women immediately gave the child to the spirit leaders and they carefully examined him. They nodded their heads in agreement and placed the child on another bed of furs. The woman screamed again. She gave birth to a second child, another boy. They also examined this child and placed him next to his brother. The woman had give birth to twin boys. The chief elder came in to the hut and looked at them. He ordered the midwives to leave.

By this time, a great storm approached and the winds blew hard. Darkness fell and the people scattered. The chief elder turned to the spiritual leaders and said.

"Nihi tsitsanáta gado hnadága." They nodded their heads in agreement and took the children out. The mother screamed at them saying

"á-tla, á-tla," repeatedly, I knew she was screaming no. Then a warrior entered, he appeared angry.

"Where are they?" The chief elder told him it was for the best, they would be safer this way.

The chief elder continued.

"I feel danger is approaching and we must get them to safety."

The spiritual leaders were praying people were screaming outside in the village. I looked to see wolves moving fast like black mists attacking the people dragging them into the darkness. The chief and the others prayed louder and the hut shook. One of them set the staff at the entrance and blew white smoke from a sacred chanunpa pipe to fill the room. The Shifter tried to get in but it could not cross. It growled louder and louder and then it was quiet.

I walked towards the entrance to see if it was gone. My breathing increased, I had to know if it was safe. I looked out of the hut only to see dead bodies laying everywhere. There were men, woman, and their children as well as destroyed huts everywhere. I heard a noise directly behind me I quickly turned around to see an elderly man with a long staff that made noise when he shook it.

He drew a circle around me speaking in an ancient language. He waved the staff all around me and then he put paint on my face. His skin was dark and his eyes were of a crystal blue color. He placed his thumb on my forehead. From his sacred chanunpa pipe, he blew a strange smoke in my face as he spoke in his native language. I felt lightheaded and fell to the ground. My eyes were opening and closing. I felt as if I was spiraling through time I heard someone call my name.

"Kyle...Kyle, wake up. I don't think you would like to spend your weekend here."

I jumped to see the Liberian standing next to me.

"I am very sorry."

"No problem." She said smiling at me.

I gathered my things to leave. I looked at my watch to see the hour had grown late. How long was I out? I had better get home. I quickly hurried out the door when books went flying and all I heard was,

"Ouch!" She fell backwards at hit the ground.

"Darn it, not again..."

"What is your problem, Kyle? Why don't you watch where you are going!"

"Sorry, I am so sorry my mistake. Here let m-"

"No!"

She ushered me away with her hand.

"You have done enough already!"

She picked up her books and hurried into the library before it closed. I did not mean to however this was the second time I had accidently knocked her down.

I just had to apologize to her so I waited next to my car for her to come out. I just had to make this right. She must think I am a real jerk or something. My dad always said real men apologize even if the woman thinks he is a jerk. Therefore, I figured I had better fix this or at least try. I waited for her to come out of the library.

"What are you stalking me now so you can knock me down again?"

I really didn't want her to think that I was stalking her.

"No, I am not. I wanted to be sure you are okay."

"Well for what it is worth my rear end hurts and I almost had to pay a late fee because of you. And I just missed by bus ride home!"

Now I really felt bad, I must make things right with her.

"Can I make this up to you somehow?"

"Yeah, how about paying close attention to where you are going next time."

"Then at least let me take you home."

"Never mind I will walk, I am not going to fall for your little scheme."

"Scheme, what scheme? You think I planned this?"

By this time, I was getting a little irritated with her.

"Look, I am sorry. Please let me take you home, it is the least I can do."

She stood back and looked at me for a second.

"Only, if you promise to be careful next time okay."

"Scouts honor." I awkwardly opened her door; I was so nervous.

"So, do you always hang out at the library?" she asked.

"Sometimes, I go study with some of the other students from school. I hardly ever see you there though."

She explained her reason.

"I just had some photography books that I needed to return. Since I had to drive all the way home, she left school a little bit early. My dad gave me a ride back into town. We were going to meet up later but plans changed, I told my dad I would catch the bus but, no thanks to you, I missed it."

I murmured under my breath.

"No wonder I couldn't find you."

"Excuse me?"

"I mean, I was looking for you. I needed to ask you a question."

"Okay, well what is it?"

"When we bumped into each other today-"

"You mean when you knocked me down?"

"Okay, when I accidentally knocked you down. I believe we accidently mixed up our books. I think you have one of my notebooks and I need it back. Oh and here, I have yours."

Reaching behind my seat to retrieve her book, the car started to swerve a little.

"Here, allow me." She said holding the steering wheel. I reached her book and handed it to her.

"Thanks I was looking for this."

"Well I just stuffed my books into my bag. I must have yours at my house then. I will look for it."

I did not have much to say after that. It was hard not to stare at her she was beautiful.

"Pretty isn't it."

Her comment caught me off guard.

"What?"

"The countryside."

"Oh yeah, it is very pretty." Whew, close one.

"I love the country. My dad and I do a lot of horseback riding out here."

"You ride horses."

"Yeah, all the time, I live on a ranch in Hunter Valley. It is just a few more miles up ahead on the left past the huge rock. Have you ever been on a horse?"

"Me, no, I have never tried it."

"You should it is very relaxing and fun. I am taking my horse out in the morning for a run, would you like to join me?"

Oh, boy it's payback time. Surely, she is going to set me up or something.

"Sure, except that I do not do well with horses."

"Have you ever tried?"

"No…"

"It is very easy, just like riding a bike."

I shook my head as I drove.

"That is easy for you to say."

Elsha then inquired about my summer.

"So do you have any plans this summer?"

"No, not much planned here. How about you?"

"No, just plan on staying around here, helping my dad."

"You would think people would leave this place and get away for a while."

"Well I have a way of finding a place quiet and serene, no one to bother you at all. Just peace and quiet."

She looked down and discovered my book.

"Forbidden Lands…very interesting book. You're into Ancient Mythology?"

"Something like that." I said. "I have been studying ancient legends for a few months now."

"So you do have a hobby."

"I would not call it a hobby, just learning more I guess. I see you like photography."

"Yes, I do and it has always been a hobby of mine. I enjoy capturing moments that will leave fond memories."

We approached her neighborhood and she told me to turn by the big rock. We pulled up to this huge house with tall trees on each side that went along a stretch of driveway. The house was like a beautiful mansion, like the kind on that television show, *Dallas*.

I could see the horses running around inside a six-foot white picket fence. There were also two German shepherd dogs approaching the car.

"Beautiful aren't they?"

"Yeah, they are huge creatures."

"There are my dogs. The dark brown one is Tango and the light brown one is Boomer. Well, thanks for bringing me home, I really appreciate it"

"It was the least I could do since it was my fault."

"Here," She reached for my hand and placed a piece of paper in it with her address on it.

"This is just in case you get lost."

I really could not believe that she invited me over.

"See you tomorrow morning at eight o clock. I will look for your book."

"Great, thanks. See you tomorrow."

As I headed home, she was all I could think about. She was nice but, then again, this could be a trap of some kind. I thought to myself for a while, no way Kyle just stay cool.

When I arrived home dad was in the yard fumbling around with fishing string.

"Hi son. Care to give me a hand since you are a little late?"

"Sure dad. Sorry for being, late I gave a friend a ride home from school."

He must have been at this for hours. He tangled up in wires and string.

"There I think I got it, son." It had been along time since dad had used his fishing gear.

"I'm excited about our trip."

"I am too. Remember to finish the camper, okay."

"I will get it done right after I finish helping you."

"You can wait until morning"

"I have a few things to do first…"

I tried not to think about my dreams but for some reason though; they did not bother me as much. All I could think about was Elsha. I had to admit, I've had a crush on her since the beginning of the school year.

Tony called me, I told him I ran into Elsha at the library and he said he already knew. Someone had seen us talking. People do talk in small towns.

"So did you ask her out?"

"No, she asked me to go on a horse ride with her, but it is not a date. Besides, I think she may have my book."

"Way to go, Kyle."

"Look, I have to get going. I have to finish getting things ready for our family trip."

He begged me to tell him all about it once I got back home. I told him I would.

After I talked with Tony for a while, parts of my dream plagued my mind again. I thought about the bloodline. I for a moment thought I got it now. More pieces of the puzzle were coming to me. I ran to my room quick to write down everything I could remember.

Both leaders, one good one evil, were standing face-to-face, communicating with one another. They had the stones and said a sacred prayer.

As I drew, the images became life like. I must have been at it for a while; mom knocked on my door. The mail had arrived, she handed me a letter. It was from Big John.

"It must be important." She said.

I opened it up and it was an invitation to a summer bash on the reservation. I could bring two of my friends and there would be an all-night bon fire and a closing ceremony.

"Wow, it sounds like the Olympics.""

"Well son, you should go. I think it would be very good for you to start getting out more and making new friends."

"Thanks, I really appreciated it." She gave me a hug

"Dinner will be ready soon."

Now would be my chance to find out what I could. I connected pieces together of my dreams, gathered clues and took new notes. I had to find some way to fill this gap.

Chief Spearhorn said that they keep records in their archives, I wonder. When Tony and I were on the reservation, he said he snuck into the library. Surely, they do not have things lying around like that. Then again, Tony is very clever. I remembered him saying there was a door that has a key pad on it. That must be where they keep the records.

I decided to get on the internet and research more. Where to begin, *Illegal adoptions of Native American children,* there were many articles perhaps I should narrow it down by they year.

A Local Reporter Investigates Illegal Adoption Ring

Bingo the article was just as I remembered when Tony discovered it.

Local reporter investigated illegal adoptions of children from the tribal union reservation. There were about twenty children illegally adopted when the mothers gave birth at the Fairway hospital. Because the women did not live on the reservation at the time, their relatives did and their files are on record.

According to the law, Native American children could not be placed foster care or adopted into non-Native American families. It was very important that the children learn about their heritage this way. Moreover, the reservation would take care of their school and medical needs.

The Department of Child and Family Services worked closely with the council members on the reservation to be sure that the children would be returned. However, one child was never found. Some feared the child might have been kidnapped or sold on the black market; officials struggle to find him.

Once the other children returned, the council members continued their lawsuit and since then the case had been sealed. The public could view no other documents. The reservation now keeps record of all documents concerning this case.

Great, now I was going to have to go to the reservation and find out. I wonder if they would even let me in. The Chief is my grandfather, so then he also could tell me who my parents are and if they are still alive. All I had to do is ask right. If they had known this all along, then why not tell me? Why not take me to the reservation? Something was not right here. Another gap in my life that is all I needed.

Oh well, I had a busy day tomorrow. Riding horses with Elsha and packing for my trip. My parents must have more information about the adoption. I wonder where they kept them. I have to get the answers somehow. Perhaps I could contact the reporter to see what he or she found out. The reporter worked for the Patagonia Times. Reporters work late so I would call and find out.

I called the newspaper and asked is someone could tell me who the reporter was. The person on the other end said it was along time ago so; they placed me on hold for what felt like an eternity. Finally, someone remembered I was on hold. They did inform me that the reporter was a woman by the name of Veronica Banks however; she no longer worked for the paper. She quit after that story hit the news.

I asked if they new where she was and was told she lived on the outskirts of town near temple cove. However, they were not sure if she still lived there or not. I would have to check the white pages and get her number.

I started yawning time hit the sack. I had a busy day tomorrow. Research is on hold until I got back.

Chapter Seven

UNCOVERED SECRETS

I had no idea what I was getting myself into. Imagine,... me riding horses? Hah, I must have been crazy to accept. I mean, I love motorcycles but I was not too sure about wild kingdom.

She looked at me and just smiled. Elsha assured me that I would be fine. She said the ride would help keep me relaxed. She has been riding all of her life. This was my first time ever. How was riding a horse going to keep me relaxed?

We walked out to the pasture and stood by the fence.

"Horses sometimes choose their riders so I want you to stand inside the gate and wait. Just relax and do deep breathing. The horses can sense fear in people. They are very misunderstood creatures; we should not take them for granted."

I went inside the gate and it shut behind me. She told kept telling me to go out further.

"Which horse is yours?"

"The black on one the end, his name is A Knight's Dream."

"Where did you come up with that?"

"Have you ever read a fairytale book?"

"No, I don't read fairytales that much."

"Well, she is like a princess awaiting her knight in shining in armor. If you can picture it that way..."

"Oh, that is a good one."

Elsha encouraged me to keep going forward. I could see the horses approaching. She told me to watch out for the white one. He was new and no one could get close enough to ride him.

Her dad had about ten horses and they were very beautiful creatures. I stood there and waited.

"How will I know which one?" I asked.

"Think of something unique that only the horse would do that only you would know."

Then she told said.

"Close your eyes and concentrate."

The horses spotted me and started in my direction. I closed my eyes and stood still. I could hear them getting closer.

"Okay...I can do this," I said to myself. The first horse that bumps my right shoulder and rubbed my face would be the one.

As I stood there, I could hear them around me. The horses were moving around and making noises. Then I felt a nudge on my shoulder and then one of the horses blowing air through its nostrils gently rubbed my face. I opened my eyes to see this beautiful snow-white creature staring at me.

"His name is Wind Star." Elsha said. "Beautiful, isn't he?"

"Yes," I said.

"I am very impressed. This horse never lets anyone near him."

She showed me how to get on him. I placed my foot in the stirrup and pulled myself up. I couldn't believe this animal chose me to ride him.

"Be still, become one with the horse." Elsha instructed me. "Stroke his main and caress his side. This way he is gets comfortable with his rider."

She spent about an hour showing me how to ride. Falling off was easy but staying on was the hard part. She reminded me to become one with the horse and reassure him.

"Become one with the horse…" I kept repeating it to myself.

Wind Star was a fast horse but I needed him to slow down. I gently pulled on his reigns and the horse obeyed. I did everything she said. I kept myself calm and focused. I could feel the horse release air from its stomach and yawn. It sounded like Wind Star was getting comfortable with me as his rider. We spent the day riding through the trails. We had to be careful for wild animals; horses could sense danger and they scare easily.

"This is why I bring the dogs; they are good at keeping watch." Elsha told me.

She took me to a hidden valley just beyond the trees; it was breath taking. A valley plain so beautiful…like on a postcard. My eyes could not believe what I was seeing. Tall trees, fresh green grass, beautiful flowers everywhere.

We stopped and listened to the wind blowing through the trees and we could hear water from a nearby creek. Elsha brought along some snacks for us incase we got a little hungry. She was very well prepared. We stopped for a while to rest. Once we rested, she said we would head back up to the trail.

We untied the horses and she let them roam free.

"Do you always let the horses roam?"

"The horses know their way back home," she assured me. "Besides, I use the dogs to help round them up.

"Do you come here often?" I asked. It sounded like a cheesy pickup line.

"Every chance I get. Sometimes I come here to study, take pictures, or when I've had a bad day. I come here to get away from it all. I love the outdoors, how about you?" She asked.

"Well, yes I do. I never knew this was here though. How did you find it?"

"It is just beyond our property line besides, I like it. It is quiet, secluded, and no one is around to disturb you. I think this place is sacred somehow."

"What do you mean?"

"Just beyond the tall trees is a small entrance to a cave. I think the Native Americans dwelled here centuries ago. I didn't touch anything inside but, I did find some clay pots, a spearhead, and some drawings on the cave walls. I took pictures of what I found."

"Did you tell anyone about it? I would like to have a quick look."

"No," she quickly replied. "I believe that nature intended for us to leave well enough alone and not disturb it. To disturb the cave would be disrespectful."

I figured I had better leave this one alone. She also told me how she took pictures of the cave by extending her arm into the cave with her camera lens and took pictures. She said she never went in the cave, she was too afraid she would disturb or mess up something.

She mentioned how she wanted to tell Chief Spearhorn when he was here but could not get near him. It appeared only special people like me could get near him.

She nudged me in my shoulder and started laughing.

"Tell me. How do you know the Chief?"

"I met him through Ms. Creed."

"Ms. Mystery Woman with a Secret…" She said softly. I looked at her frowning.

"What do you mean by mystery woman?"

"You mean you don't know that Ms. Creed has a secret?"

"Secret, what secret could Ms. Creed possibly have? What are you talking about Elsha?"

She turned to look at me.

"One day, I stayed after school because I asked if I could use the lab to develop my pictures. Well Ms. Creed was in the other room, I heard her talking on the phone with someone and she was upset. I thought it was about all the mysterious disappearances of the bodies from the morgue. However, this was something different."

"Go on," I said.

"Well, whoever she was talking to, she said something about them not bringing someone here, that it was too dangerous. Also, that no one must ever know about 'her' and did they get the stone necklace she sent. Then, I guessed the person on the other end was saying something, like when she was coming for a visit. She said she couldn't come to Rocky Point. Something had come up here and that she could not leave yet. It would have to wait until the end of the school year. I knew it was something serious because Ms. Creed's voice changed, as if she was crying or something. Then she said 'She knows, she made a promise and she will be there she just needed more time.' I said it before and I will say it again, the mystery woman with a secret."

"That conversation could have been about a relative wanting to visit or something."

"You have the relative part right."

"Elsha, what are you talking about?"

"Ms. Creed has a daughter and she does not want her to come to Patagonia."

"You can't be serious. Ms. Creed doesn't have any children."

"Then why would she ask the person on the other phone if they received the check and what about this stone necklace? There is something about her and she is hiding it."

I paused for a moment trying to collect my thoughts. Ms. Creed never mentioned children, and the necklace she's talking about that much is true.

"Wait a minute, what makes you think that all of this true and besides you were in another room."

"Well, Mr. Smarty pants; while I was listening I dropped a bottle of rapid fixer on the floor. She heard it. Then she came into the room and found me on the floor. She said she did not know anyone was here. I told her I did not know either because she startled me. Then she asked me how much did I hear. I figured she wanted to know how much of her secret I had heard."

"It is called privacy, doll." I said sarcastically.

"Let me finish, motor mouth. I had my iPod with me so I turned it on so she could hear the music coming from my earphones. She told me that she would call the janitor to help me with the spill. Just before she went back to the adjourning room, she asked what I was doing there after school. I told her I got permission from Mrs. Johnson to develop the pictures from Chief Spearhorns speech at the library. She told me she would love to see them and to stop by her class once I had developed them. Then she looked at me again and said, 'Are you sure you did not hear anything'. I said not with these on, holding up my earphones."

Do you believe me now?'

She spoke with such an attitude. I apologized to her and explained I did not mean to make her upset.

Then she responded.

'I am not upset.' I know you like Ms. Creed who doesn't. However, I know what I heard. I would not make any of this up. Oh, and one more thing do not ever call me doll again, okay. Remember, my name is Elsha."

"My apologies Elsha and my name is Kyle, not motor mouth."

We both looked at each other and laughed.

"Did you tell anyone about Ms. Creed?"

"No, you're the first. So, don't you say anything to anyone. I want to respect her. Besides, I hear a lot of things but I keep it to myself."

"What other things have you heard?"

"Am I on trial now?"

"No, I'm just curious."

"Are you asking me have I heard things about you? Well, if you just want to know, I have. It does not change anything though. Look Kyle, I could care less about what people say, I draw my own conclusions about people. You are unique in your own way, even when you are sleeping. Oh yeah, I forgot, that day in the library, I did not mean to disturb you. I thought you were reading."

"I was, I must have dozed off. I like the library it is a very peaceful place and it is never crowded on Fridays. I do not have many friends. Tony is my best friend. How about you, do you have friends?"

"I don't spend my time worrying about who likes me and who doesn't. I am my own person and I can handle myself. What does it matter anyway?"

"Hey, calm down I just asked."

"Sorry, I did not mean to be defensive. It is a habit I have."

We kept talking for a while. She told me about her hobbies and asked if I had any. I would have told her what I did in my spare time: Instead of me chasing dreams my dreams are chasing me.

"You are a nice person Kyle and I enjoy being around you."

I was speechless well at least I know she enjoys my company.

"So have you developed any more pictures?" I said trying to keep up in conversation.

"They should be ready in a few more days."

"Elsha, you have helped me in so many ways. I cannot tell you how but, one day, I will. Just me being out here like this, around you, I have no fear at all. I mean there are situations I do not talk about, however, when I am with you, nothing. There is just a strong and positive atmosphere. I really do not know how to explain it all to you."

By his time, my heartbeat picked up and then my palms were sweating.

"Elsha, what I am trying to say is....never mind." I stopped and just looked at her.

"I know what you are trying to say, Kyle." Oh, no she has a boyfriend. "I am just not ready to date yet, I hope you understand."

"Yes, I do. I would never pressure you. I mean. I am not very good at this." I said trying to laugh. "I respect your decision. What I meant to say was I enjoy your company and would like to continue that as a friend of course."

"I would like that very much," she smiled at me. "Come on I have to get the horses back."

We gathered the horses and started back. It was a quiet ride to the ranch. I could not help but stare at her; she was so beautiful. Her black hair was just flowing in the wind like silk. I loved the way she smiled at me.

The ride felt like hours but we finally reached the ranch. We came down the hill and Elsha's father was waiting for us. She waved to him as we approached.

I was very nervous about meeting her dad.

"Hello, my princess. Who might you be young man?"

"Daddy, this is Kyle Green. We go to school together."

"Oh, yes, your father is the football coach."

"Yes sir," I said nervously.

"How was the ride?"

"Bumpy, sir," I said rubbing my hind end. "Very bumpy."

"Well, you will get used to it. My princess here is the best teacher anyone could have."

"Daddy, why are you home early?"

"Well honey I have to go out of town for a few days."

"Why?"

"The police down at Rocky Point asked me to come there to help them with an investigation. Some remains were found near the border and, according to the coroner, they are similar to the ones we have here. I will need for you to stay at your uncle's place while I am gone."

"Sure daddy."

"Kyle?" he called.

"Yes, sir."

"You keep an eye on my princess; do not let anything happen to her."

"Daddy, you know I can take care of myself."

"I know that dear but I will feel safer knowing that someone is watching you." He looked at me and winked.

"Yes sir, I will sir."

"I am going to have to take the dogs and some of the horses with me so, the ranch hands will be here soon. Oh, by the way sweetheart, a package came for you. I believe those photos you were waiting on have arrived. I put the box on the kitchen counter."

"Thanks Dad…wow that was fast."

"So Kyle, what do you think about Wind Star?"

"He is a very nice horse sir, very fast too."

"Yes, I have to agree. I don't really know where he came from. One day I found him wandering in the wild with no tag. No one has claimed him yet so I named him Wind Star, because he's fast like the wind and, if you look a the mark on his chest, it is shaped like a star. I tried to capture him on many occasions but he was just to fast. I figured if I gave him time, he would come around again and when he did, I was ready for him."

"How did you capture him?" I asked.

"Well I really did not have to. We were rounding up horses one day and, as the gate was open, he ran right in. I figured this is where he wanted to be. I learned that a horse that runs free will make his home where he wants. When he is ready to leave then, he will but so far, he likes it. Therefore, I keep him around. As I think about, it if memory serves me correct, you are his first rider. None of my other ranch-hands could get near him. I think he likes you."

"I think so too, sir." Rubbing Wind Star he responded by neighing and moving his leg back and forth.

"Wow, I have never seen this horse respond to anyone like that before. Son, you must have a special gift." Wind Star agreed neighing behind me.

"Come on Kyle, let's go put the horses away."

We walked over to the fence and released the horses. We watched them run with the other horses. Wind Star was dominant over the other horses. They responded to him as if he were their leader.

"Well, I have to be going now. I promised my dad I would help pack for our weekend trip."

"Cool, where are you going?"

"We have a cabin up in the hills near Mountain Peak. My dad wants to take us away for a few days and spend some family time there."

"That sounds like fun. My dad used to take my mom and me up there to camp out and ride horses."

"Where is your mother?" I asked.

"My parents divorced when I was much younger. They both received joint custody of me until one day my mother decided that I was interfering with her career plans...more like boyfriend career plans. Therefore, she decided to run off with some rich person and sail around the world. I guess she figured cruising around the world would be better than having a child glued to her hip."

"Do you ever hear from her?"

"It depends what part of the world she is in. I will get a post card from Monaco, Rio de Janeiro, or some other part of the world letting me know that she loves me. In addition, how she and her boyfriend would like me to visit them for the summer cruising around the world. She sends me gifts on my birthday and at Christmas. She knows I love photography so she is always sending me the latest camera gear and pictures for my scrapbook."

I could see talking about it was making her a little upset so I told her she did not have to explain anything else to me. She said it was ok and that she was used to it. She said her mom has been begging her to sail with her and Francisco. That is his name. She is waiting on me to spend a summer with them.

"Are you going to?"

"No, I would rather stay here instead. Besides, I do not think I want to be stuck on a boat with my mom and her boyfriend telling me about their adventures on the sea. I would rather throw myself overboard." We both laughed.

"Thanks her for teaching me how to ride. Can I see you again?"

"Yeah, at school," she laughed.

"Oh, you got jokes."

"Well you said you wanted to see me again right?" With a smirk on her face, she laughed again.

"All right, all right, I will see you at school then."

"Have fun this weekend." She said.

"I will."

I got in my car and drove off. My cell phone was buzzing in the seat. Oh, I forgot about my phone. Six missed calls. I picked up my phone and listened. Dad reminded me to finish the camper when I got home. Then my mother called to remind me to help dad. The last call was from Tony wanting details and for me to call my parents.

What a day this had been, I would definitely have to write this one down in my book.

The book! Oh, I forgot to ask her about my book. It was too late to turn around now, my parents would kill me. Oh well, it was not as if I didn't have paper around and I have not had any dreams lately either.

I arrived home just in time to help dad get all of the fishing gear ready for our trip.

"How did things go?"

"Very well."

"You look different and you almost have a glow," dad pointed out as he looked over me. "Who is she son?"

"What?" I said pretending like as if I did not know what he was talking about.

"You heard me, the last time I saw a look like that was when I first met your mother".

"Ok dad, her name is Elsha."

"Oh, Chief Morgan's niece that takes all of the pictures?"

"Yeah, that is Elsha."

"She is a very pretty girl."

"Thanks."

"So what did you two do today?"

"Horseback riding, her dad has about ten horses, and one of them happened to have chosen me as a rider."

"That is interesting."

I happily replied as I reminisced my day.

"Yes, it is."

"Son, I am glad that you are spending more time doing things as a young kid should. In spite of everything that has happened around here. I am glad to see that someone other than your mother is keeping a smile on your face. Were finished here for now, you better wash up before dinner you don't want to get horse hair all over the table."

"Okay dad."

We walked in the house and mom was setting the table. I could not be happier. My parents were smiling again, my nightmares were now pleasant dreams; this was too good to be true. Our family had survived many obstacles and now we were able to sit down and talk about them like a real family.

However even though the nightmares subsided, I still had that feeling occasionally that something else was going to surface. It was like the calm before the storm. At least, for the moment, I was going to enjoy this moment with my parents. I needed this and so did they.

I told them all about Elsha at dinner, mom was very anxious to know more about her.

"I want to meet her."

"I will invite her over next week sometime."

Mom gave me this calming smile as she responded.

"That's fine dear."

We would leave early in the morning and dad wanted me to get my rest. I told mom I would do the dishes and dad said not to be up too late.

I wonder what *she* was doing. Was she thinking about me at all? Many things played in my mind repeatedly. Could Ms. Creed have a daughter? What will Elsha's dad find at Rocky Point? Ms. Creed's daughter is there. What about the cave Elsha found? Either way, all I could see was her smile. I could not help but to think about her she was beautiful and I think that I was in love with her...like wet feet...wet feet!

"Oh no!"

Water was everywhere. I was so caught up in my daydreams, I let the sink overrun. I grabbed the mop to soak up the water quick just in case my parents came downstairs. My cell phone rang and it was Tony.

"Hey dude, I have been trying to reach you all day."

"I have been busy getting ready for my family trip tomorrow."

"So tell me how today was?"

"It was nice we did some horseback riding, I met her dad, it was cool."

"Did she have your book?"

"I forgot to ask her."

"If I were in your shoes I would forget the time of day that girl is hot!"

"You are such a dork. Look, I have to go we leave for Mountain Peak in the morning and I cannot stay up too late. I will see you tomorrow."

"Later lover boy" Tony said. He was so crazy.

I finished the kitchen and went to my room. She was all I could think about; I tried to get her out of my mind. She plagued my mind worse than my dreams. I could only imagine what she thinks of me. Our first meeting was not a good one, nor the second but I was glad we got the chance to spend time together. She had a tough side to her though and she was outspoken.

***

"What a day, Kyle is a very nice person." Elsha thought to herself.

He is a little awkward but nice. He looked somewhat disturbed. Despite of what I heard about him, everyone has some kind of problem. All it takes is just getting to know a person. I really enjoyed Kyle's company today. I am glad we got a chance to talk, he is unique, Wind Star would agree to that. Today I believe he overcame a fear that he did not know he had.

When he was in the fence, the horses were like a magnet to him. Wind Star did not let anyone near him or even try to ride him, only Kyle. He was not so bad after all. Look at me, my dad is a doctor and a forensics specialist. My mother, well, that is another story. She just chose to live a life childfree. Still she tries to be a mother to me while away.

I grew up hating her for not being there. I remember some of the arguments my parents used to have. Mother would get mad at dad for not being home because he was going to school and working late nights. He was taking care of his family. She said there was never enough money; she could not see it was due to her spending habit. Therefore, I guess they decided to part ways. I wanted to stay with my dad. He spent time with me as much as possible. Well, she expected the television to take care of me while she talked on the phone or was just too busy to watch her little girl.

My parents met in high school and, of course, my mother got pregnant with me. They both went on to college after that. Money and a new baby did not work so well but they got married anyway. They both tried to make it work but things were just too different. Dad worked hard, went to school while my mother stayed home to take care of me. I guess at one point she grew tired so the arguments came and went I knew she wanted to leave. Dad would make sure he spent as much time with me but mom kept complaining.

Therefore, she started seeing other people; it hurt my dad… bad. He said he saw it coming and he tried to tell her that once he finished school, times would be different. If she had waited for him, she would see he did very well for himself. He had this house built and he wanted me to be in a safe place and to be sure that I would always be happy. She on the other had met her boyfriend at some social club and now she is sailing the world.

I guess they both got what they wanted. She got her rich man and her freedom and daddy got his princess. Speaking of my dad, he is one of the most eligible bachelors in town and he is very good looking. I got my hair from him and I have my mothers hazel eyes.

Dad was preparing to leave for Rocky Point in the morning. He wanted me to stay with my uncle for a few days until he returned. No problem, I liked my uncle. He is the Chief of Police and he is very nosy, comes with the territory I guess.

My uncle likes to ask me if any of the boys are interested in me. He wants me to let him know and he will run a check on them. I thought he was joking but he was serious. My uncle was very protective. I felt sorry for my little twin cousins when they get older.

I went to the kitchen to get my package and the rest of my books. Dad did not like clutter so I had to be sure the countertops stayed clear of my books and things.

"Yep this is it, Photo Specialist, the film developers." I looked over the package. I also noticed I received an envelope from my mom; it must have been more pictures of the lavish life style.

I took my package to my room, set them on my computer desk, and put my books on the floor next to my bed. I liked to read before going to bed; I would rather just reach down and pick them up. If dad saw this, he would have a cow. I opened the box to see that the developing company had sorted my pictures per my request.

"What do we have here: School Academics, Recreational, and Exploration and Public Relations."

These photos were in different folders and labeled according to their events. I looked at the pictures and put them in order for my scrapbook collection by category. Of course, I couldn't help but be organized. I got it from my dad; he is a neat freak and has to have everything in order.

"Now on to the next one."

By the time I got to Exploration, I was a little tired so I decided to get them sorted for each of my books.

"Public relations."

I picked up the picture of Kyle and the Chief. I assumed the other kid was Tony. He was a handsome young man, talking about Kyle of course. I stared at his picture for a moment. He does have mysterious eyes though. I decided to keep this one up on my mirror just until I was ready to put it in book. I wonder if he would like a copy of it. I will just keep it out to give to him so I will not forget.

Now onto the next set of pictures. I took these pictures when I went out in the forest a while ago, such a wonderful place, quiet, secluded, and pretty. I was somewhat surprised that they arrived so fast. I was not expecting them for another couple of days. Oh well I was glad I had them now.

As I looked, I could see the clay pots and some sort of drawings on the wall. 'Hmmmm....Interesting. I sat down to my computer and scanned the pictures in one by one to see a large image. I have made an unbelievable discovery here; surely national geographic would love to see something like this.

However, I do not want the news media and strangers poking around here and then my secret place will become a tourist attraction. Perhaps, I will keep this to myself just for a while and maybe contact the reservation and let them know about my discovery. The images on the wall were like some kind of ritual. It appears to be men on a rock holding up staffs, a full moon.

In addition, there is some sort of half-human half wolf thing.

Other photos showed eyes peering through the darkness. This was creepy. The more I looked at the images; I could feel a chill come over me. There was some ancient writing but I could not quite make it out. I enlarged the images but it was no good, this must have been when I ran out of flash.

One last picture shows a body with black mist rising out of its chest what kind of ritual was this. I must go back to the cave and take more pictures. I do not want to disturb the sacred grounds though. This time I will be careful and take my flash, my extended lens, and my video camera so I can also record.

Great, I will make plans for my next expedition. It was really getting late and I had to get to bed. Dad was leaving in the morning and I wanted to see him off.

"So tired..." I stumbled over my books. I forgot those were there. I picked them up to place them on my bookshelf. "Wait a minute...this was not my book. Hmmm... property of Kyle Green. What kind of book is this," I wondered.

He was quite the artist. I laid down on my bed and looked at the pictures. The images were so life like and very detailed. The notes talked about the events that took place in each dream. I was in shock at what I was looking at.

Therefore, the rumors were true he did have nightmares. Kyle was not crazy; his nightmares were very real and they were definitely haunting him.

"I should not be looking at this. Surely, this was an invasion of privacy," I thought aloud but I just could not put it down.

Since he was little, Kyle has seen the dark images of half man half wolf. He talked about the smells, sounds, ways he knows when they are there. He can feel them watching him, eyes peering through the night.

Repeatedly, I whispered the words he wrote in his book:

"Eyes peering through the night...dark beings...the photo." It dawned on me.

I looked through each of them and I could not believe it. The images are the same as on the cave walls. Kyle, poor Kyle, he must have been going crazy out of his mind. I could only imagine what he was going through. The doctors, the night sweats, this all has to mean something.

I kept looking through the book until I found more and more chilling details of Kyle's dreams. Only special people can expose the creatures if they survived. Kyle's details were very clear. I was going to help him find the missing pieces to this puzzle. I know this is dangerous but I had to help him out as much as possible.

Chapter Eight

THE EXPEDITION

Rainstorm...

I am definitely not going anywhere in this weather. The thunder and lightening was terrible. I called the ranch-hands to check on the horses and they were fine.

When lightening storms are severe, the horses could get spooked. Therefore, we put them in the stables so they would feel safe.

I called my dad to see how things were going. He said it was a little tricky, the terrain was very rough up in the mountains but the horses did okay.

He was meeting with another forensic doctor to discuss some new information that had just recently surfaced. He would be leaving first thing in the morning but they asked him to stay another day to assist them on another case. I asked him if I could go home in the morning but he suggested I spend one more day at my uncle's place. He said he would make it up to me when he got back. I agreed. I told him that I loved him and would see him soon.

My uncle was cool. He did not get to see me as much because he was so busy. Because of his title and position, he was very busy trying to solve murder cases.

Since I was staying one more day, my uncle asked me if I could watch the twins while he took his wife out to dinner. Since he had been busy working so much, he finally got a break to spend time with his family.

My uncle rented some movies for the kids and I sat down to enjoy the movies with them. I could not help but to think of Kyle I just hoped he was able to relax with his family and have fun.

As the children watched the movie, I looked through his book some more. I must return it to him when he gets back. I would have to go and search the caves to get more clues. I would have to go by the cave tomorrow and be home before dad gets back. Good thing the trail is up the hill behind our house.

After a while, the twins fell asleep and I put them to bed. My uncle called to check on us. I told him we were fine the children were asleep and I was catching up on some reading. He said they would be home in a few hours they were going to catch a late movie. I told him to be careful the storm appeared to be getting worse.

I hung up the phone and took out my laptop. I had stored my pictures on it for my research. I looked up the area where dad had our house built. I researched our town in Arizona back several hundred years, looking up maps and pin pointing geographical areas.

Back in the early 1920s, archeological scientist discovered cave dwellings along the hillsides of Arizona with Indian scouts. They were granted access to the reservations for research only. However, they were not allowed to remove any artifacts they found; they were only allowed to take pictures and notes of what their discoveries.

I did find other articles on archeological ruins for Patagonia I did find there were caves and burial grounds here. I would have to see if our land was on the map.

According to the map that I found, Hunter Valley used to be a dwelling place for Native Americans years ago. Somehow, the colony of people vanished. No one knew what happened to the natives. Some say the people left to escape famine or they died due to plague. Other archeologists speculated the people sought refuge deep within the caves to escape war.

The geographical map showed caves deep within the mountains. The caves were unreachable due to landslides. However, another scientist, by the name of Jeremiah Flynn, said there was a story told by the natives of a hidden sacred place where different tribes used to dwell. In his book, he stated there is an old Indian tale that talks about a sacred burial ground of ancient warriors. They called this place The Forbidden Land. Only certain people could go and walk the grounds; kind of like keepers of the grave, making sure they went undisturbed.

From generation to generation, the elders selected one person from each tribe during the high moon. They would dedicate themselves and their lives as guardians of the dead. It was rumored that a sacred prayer sealed the entrance to the cave centuries ago to keep people from ever entering or disturbing the tombs.

Others thought the stories were fabricated just to keep people away; seeing that the cave was also a diamond mine possessing the richest jewels.

Kyle was reading a book on The Forbidden Lands. The more research I did the more interested I became. I looked at Kyle's drawings and discovered another clue.

Kyle stated in his dreams he would be in a clearing describing it as a place beyond tall trees in an open valley. There he would see the dark images. The drawings of bodies laying with the dark beings hovering over them were very chilling. I started comparing them with the photos I took of the cave. Some of the images were too dark but I could barely make out the writing on the wall.

It was getting late so, I turned off my laptop, grabbed my journal, and started making a list of the materials I would need for my expedition. I would definitely need my camera with the extended lens, tripod, video camera, oh-yeah, extra batteries, flash light, my camera rods, bottled water, and a few snacks.

I placed the list and the photos in Kyle's book and placed them in my backpack so I would not forget. I wanted to see how far in I can go without setting foot inside.

After making my list, I checked on the kids, you would think they would be scared to sleep with the thunder and lightening as loud as it was. Despite it, they both were sound asleep.

I went back to the living room and curled up on the couch to watch some late night television. However, I decided to read instead. I drifted off to sleep for a while. My uncle came home. Even though I was sleeping, I could hear him talking.

The storm had knocked the power out so they had to get a rain check on their movie. My book must have fallen on the floor my uncle picked it up and placed it on the table for me.

"She's just like her uncle." My aunt, Faith, said.

"Really, how?" My uncle replied.

"You always fall asleep with a book in your arms." She covered me with a warm blanket. I snuggled deeper into the couch and fell into a deep sleep.

The next morning I woke up to the sound of birds chirping and the sun beaming through the window. I could smell bacon an eggs cooking in the kitchen. My aunt was preparing breakfast and my uncle was sitting at the table drinking his coffee.

"Good morning, sunshine."

Trying not to yawn I replied.

"Morning,"

"Sleep well last night?"

"Yes, I did thanks."

"Your dad called while you were sleep; he should be here sometime this afternoon it appears the storm is headed his direction and he wants to get on the road."

"Thanks unc."

"So what are your plans for the day? You are welcome to stay as long as you like."

"That is okay. I want to finish putting my scrapbooks together so I will be headed back home soon."

Then my aunt Faith walks in holding a tray full of delicious food.

"Breakfast is served."

After breakfast, I packed my things and my uncle tried to convince me to stay. He received a call and had to report to work. Faith thanked me for watching my cousins. She gave me a big hug saying,

"Here, go buy yourself something nice."

Slipping me a fifty-dollar bill, she kissed me on my forehead.

I considered her as a mother more than I did my biological mother. She was there when I needed someone to talk to about boys, periods, and other things. My aunt was very cool, I could not imagine having twins but they did run in the family. My uncle says the twins are just like me, always inquisitive and wanting to know more.

Before I could leave my aunt asked me to hang out with her.

"Do you want to do some shopping in town?"

"No thanks, I'm gonna go home to check on the horses. Can you give me a rain check?"

I wanted to stop by the bookstore on my way home to see if it was open too. Since my aunt paid me for babysitting, I would use the money to purchase a new book. Smith's bookstore just happened to be open but closed early on Sundays. Thankfully, I had perfect timing.

I searched the directory to see if they had any books on Jeremiah Flynn, only one left in stock.

Bingo! The Forbidden Lands.

I paid for my book and headed home. I could see the storm clouds rolling over the mountains. I hoped dad would make it out of town before the storm hit Rocky Point.

When I reached home, I could see the ranch-hands putting the horses back out in the fields to run. Horses do not like to be in small places for a long time; they need much bigger space. That is why when dad built the barn; he made sure the horses felt like they were not in a box. Therefore, if they were to get spooked they will have room to run and not hurt themselves.

I waved to Rodrigo and the others; he was dad's longtime friend he took good care of the horses. Our families have been close for years. I met Rodrigo at the main gate.

"Can you mount A Knight's Dream for me?"

I went inside to gather my things. I took out my list and double-checked everything I would need. I placed the book on my desk and changed clothes. I almost forgot my hat and gloves. I put on a long sleeve shirt, black jacket and some dark jeans. Grabbed some snacks and headed out. Rodrigo met me at the gate with my horse.

"Where are you going, senorita?"

"Just out for a ride to take more pictures for my scrapbook collection. I won't be long."

"Okay senorita, you be careful out there and keep your eyes open. Some of the men spotted some wild animals yesterday, are you sure we cannot assist you?"

"No thanks, I am not going far and plus I have my cell phone with me."

The animals must be following the herds we usually get a lot of deer and elk out here. They must have spotted the coyotes.

I headed up the trail on the horse; it was about a ten minute to fifteen-minute ride to the cave. I knew Rodrigo looked out for me; he had a concerned look on his face when I left. We usually never take the horses without the dogs because they act like security.

There were a few clouds in the sky; I assumed we had another storm approaching so I had better hurry. I reached the valley just beyond the tall trees. I tied A Knights Dream to a tree placed the feeding sack on her for a while then proceeded to unpack my backpack. I had to be careful because the ground was still wet. Good thing I had my riding boots on. I had Kyle's book and my photo with me. I placed my bag on my shoulder and headed to the cave. I loved it out here, so peaceful and quiet. The view was breathtaking. The horses loved it, plenty of fresh grass to eat. The springtime was the best the butterflies migrated flying around in a rainbow of colors.

I proceeded to the cave and set up my equipment. I started taking pictures and notes recording my information.

I must have been at it for hours. The sky started to grow dark a little.

Whispering my thoughts out loud.

"Just a few more minutes,"

I noticed before in the photo there was a little light coming from the back of the cave. Perhaps there was an opening somewhere; maybe it would be big enough for me to lower my camera down into it.

I climbed on top of the rocks to set up. It was slippery due to the rain. Not an easy thing to do when you have about twenty-five pounds of camera equipment on your back.

Finally, I made it and caught my breath. I put my camera around my neck and walked slowly so I could find an opening; and I did. I walked along top of it; it stretched far back. I do not know where the light could have come from but then, I found it.

Slowly, the rocks under me feet begin to crumble. Suddenly, the cave gave way and I fell in. I fell hard against the rocks not once but twice and landed on my back. I do not know how long I was out. I cut my head and I was bleeding. I lay there in the dark just seeing the light outside. There must have been another passage when I fell and knocked it loose. I do not know how far down I was though.

I tried to reach my phone but I could not move. I picked up my camera and luckily, I had the light attached to it. I shined it all around the cave and I could see the drawings. The images were just as I saw in my photos. This is what Kyle saw in his dreams. His nightmares painted on these walls. Each detail told a story of war and symbols of sacrifice.

I started snapping pictures with my camera. I could only hold my arms up for so long though.

I was alone in the dark. I talked myself, tried to calm and slowed my breathing. I could hear A Knights Dream neighing on the outside. She must have sensed danger.

"Stay calm, Elsha, just stay calm."

I could not help but think about dad; he will be so worried about me. I closed my eyes and tried to focus. The clouds covered the sun and the wind was blowing; the temperature was dropping fast. No one knows where I am and I do not know what is lurking in this cave. Oh, I did not want to think about that either.

Dad is going to ground me for the rest of my life. Surely, he was on his way back home now, he will come find me. I was starting to feel cold and I was fading in and out. I tried to hold on and told myself to fight but I just could not. I felt myself slipping away again.

***

"Hello."

"Hi Faith, it is, me John."

"Well hello, how are you?"

"Doing well, listen is Elsha still there with you and Frank?"

"No, she is not. She left early this afternoon? Is there any thing wrong?"

"Just a little worried. I have been calling the house and her cell phone and she is not answering either of them."

"Maybe she is out with friends."

"Perhaps, I will keep trying to reach her."

Faith was now worried too; she called her husband to see if he had seen Elsha. He stated he had not seen her since breakfast this morning. She explained to him that John called and was very worried. Frank said he would ask some of the officers if they spot her car to call it in.

Because he was the Chief of Police, he had a trace placed on her cell phone. John reached the house and there was about a few hours of daylight left. Elsha had been missing for about six hours now and no one had heard from her.

Word started to spread through town that Elsha was missing. John finally reached home; Elsha had parked her car in the garage. John went through the house calling for her but she did not answer. He went up to her room and she was not there. His brother, the Police Chief, had arrived.

"Did she leave a note?" Frank asked his brother; but, there was none, no phone messages either.

"Have you contacted her friends?"

"No, she doesn't have many friends…except there was a boy she just met. I think he said his name was Kyle. She had taken him horseback riding the other day."

"Kyle Green? I know who he is; his dad is the football coach at the high school. Try not to worry I will have one of my men call it in."

The hours started to grow late and daylight was just about over.

By this time, more officers had arrived to form a search party. John and Frank were talking when one of the officers approached him and stated that Kyle and his parents were vacationing at Mountain Peak; it was about twenty-five miles east of Hunter Valley. Chief Morgan told the officers to see if he could reach one of the officers by radio.

They were also informed that another storm was approaching and it could be a bad one. With only a little daylight left, the search may have to start in the morning. With other park rangers checking all of the cabins they hoped to get in touch with them to see if, Kyle knew anything about Elsha's whereabouts.

Kyle and his parents were having a great time together. It was very nice up in the mountains. Kyle referred to it as the place where Elsha took him: quiet and serene.

Kyle and his dad finished fishing and headed back to the cabin when a park ranger told them that they were evacuating the campgrounds. There was a serious storm approaching and he encouraged them to get down the mountain or we would end up stranded. It was a drive to get up to the cabin so it did make sense.

***

Mom was on the porch waiting, she had already started packing our things. She turned on the radio to get an update on the weather but all we were able to get was static. We were just about to lock up the cabin when there was a knock at the cabin door. Dad opened the door and it was the same park ranger.

"Are you Mr. Green?"

"Yes, I am."

"Can I see your identification, just to be sure?"

"What is this all about?" Dad asked.

"Well sir, we have a call from a Police Chief Morgan and he would like to speak with your son."

"What for?" Mom said.

All I could think about is what Chief Morgan could want with me.

"Sir if will follow me down the mountain, I can patch a call to you. I am afraid we will not get good reception here due to the lightening striking one of our towers. Do you have a CB radio in your vehicle?"

Dad was getting irritated and worried.

"Yes I do."

"Good, as soon as we get down the mountain past the mile marker post twenty-one, turn your radio to number two. We have another tower there and we should be able to get good reception."

Dad agreed and we loaded up the rest of our things and started down the mountain. We talked amongst ourselves trying to figure out what was happening.

I had no idea Chief Morgan and my dad were very good friends. Whatever is going on it must be very important. I wondered if they have found more bodies.

On the other hand, was someone we knew hurt or missing? I checked my cell phone and no bars. I hoped it was not Tony…no way not Tony. Then again, I wonder whom. Dad knew many people so it could be anyone.

We were almost down the mountain dad started to turn on the radio we past the mile marker and we were on frequency two. We could barely hear the people talking. The winds were starting to pick up. Dad could not go fast because of our trailer we pulled behind us. It was blowing strong and we could feel the truck shaking.

Chapter Nine

SEARCH AND RESCUE

We reached the bottom of the hill and started onto the main road. Then the park ranger-notified dad that Police Chief Morgan was ready to speak with him.

The ranger gave dad the cue to go ahead.

"Go ahead Chief."

"Tom, this is Chief Morgan, I am sorry to have to bother you at this time but, we need to speak with your son. It is an urgent matter."

"What is this all about? Frank what's going on?"

"We just want to know if he had heard from Elsha."

I nodded my head no; I had no idea where she was.

"No, not since the other day when they went horseback riding Frank,"

"Thanks for the information." Chief Morgan said.

Dad tried to ask him more questions but the radio was out. The storm was picking up and lightening was interfering in everything. Why were they looking for Elsha? What was going on? Dad and mom were wondering the same thing. Hunter Valley was not far, so dad said he was going to stop by and see. He knew Chief Morgan very well and he would not ask questions if something was not wrong.

As we approached the big rock, I showed dad where to turn in. The place was swarming with Police cars with their lights flashing. They looked like they were getting ready to start a search. We all got out to be greeted by an officer who was about to tell us we should not be there but Chief Morgan stopped him.

"What was going on?"

"Elsha has been missing since this afternoon and no one knows where she is."

"I can help you look."

I stepped forward and offered to help as well.

"So can I. I'm in.

Elsha was my friend. I checked my phone and I could see that Tony had been trying to reach me. I listened to his messages and he was in a panic. He said that the Police have been all over town asking if anyone had seen Elsha. I called him to let him know that I had just found out. He told me that he was close by and knew they were going to start a search; he was on his way to help.

I waited for him to arrive; it is good to have a friend by your side when the girl you like is missing.

People started to gather and the sun would be going down soon. Elsha's dad came running out of the house with a paper in his hand.

"Do you know anything about this?"

"No," I told him.

Then he turned to his brother John.

"It looks more like an expedition. Do you know where Elsha could have gone?"

John was starting to panic; you could see fear all over his face.

"I'm not sure; she does a lot of riding all over this place."

Then in interjected to tell them what I knew.

"I may know where she could be. Elsha took me on a ride the other day to one of her favorite places."

By this time, Rodrigo heard the news and came to offer his assistance. He explained that he was the last to see her and pointed in the direction she went. Then we heard a noise and saw Elsha's horse, A Knights Dream. She had been wandering around and, just like Elsha said, had found her way home.

Her rope was tangled in the brushes and some of Elsha's belongings were still on her. We ran over to get the horse and she appeared to be okay, with the exception of some claw marks on her side. Now we all started to worry.

Police Chief Morgan immediately started the search and John went to gather the horses. Elsha dogs, Tango and Boomer, could sense something was wrong. Even Wind Star was running a round; something was in the air and I could feel it all over me.

With the news media showing up and police cars everywhere, this place started to look like ground zero. Divided up into groups of ten, the search and rescue teams set off in different directions.

Everyone received instruction to radio if they found anything and to keep checking their frequencies. Meanwhile, I just could not sit around. Chief Morgan questioned me.

"Are you sure that's where you Elsha took you?"

"Yes."

Elsha's dad looked at Rodrigo with an anxious look.

"We needed the horses!"

Tony had now arrived and he offered to help. I told him that I really appreciated it and thanked him.

John walks toward Tony and me with a few horses.

"Since Wind Star will only let you ride him, I thought it best if you did."

Tony was not much of a rider but he got a real quick lesson. We started off, I lead the way and the others followed. I could sense danger was lurking, Wind Star knew it too.

We had reached the clearing in about ten minutes the sun was just going down over the mountainside. We had to move fast so we picked up the pace on the horses and Tony had to hold on. Wind Start moved like a lightening bolt.

"Become one with the horse..." I kept repeating to myself.

Elsha's dad had hoped her phone was on so he checked his GPS and picked up a signal.

"We're on the right track," he yelled up ahead.

I started to remember now. We got to the clearing of the valley plain and I saw the tree where we had first tied the horses. The paramedics also were behind us on ATVs and with their medical kits.

We got off the horses and Chief told everyone to get their flashlights and stay together. We called out to her but we did not get a response.

John had lost a signal again so we had to start the search. Tony, dad and I stayed together and Chief gave instructions that if we came across anything to use the signal flares. We were also given walkie-talkie radios to stay in touch. We set off to search for her.

***

Elsha lay inside the cave going in and out of consciousness; she would flash her camera to scare off anything that might be in the cave. With every flash, she thought she saw something.

There were noises in the cave; her battery life on her camera was going out. She heard noises but thought it was the wind. She was very brave but also very scared at the same time.

***

We searched everywhere and no sign of her. Her father did not want to give up.

As we were searching, I remembered Elsha said something about a cave. I had mentioned it to my dad and he asked me did I know where it was.

"Elsha never showed me because she thought it was sacred. She did say she took pictures of it."

Dad encouraged me to focus my thoughts about the cave.

"Think and think hard, son. We have got to find her."

It would be hard to find in the dark so I focused for a moment. I closed my eyes and tried to remember where she pointed.

Wind Star was getting restless and stomped his hoofs to the ground. I told dad to radio John and Chief Morgan and I told Tony follow me. Wind Star acted very strange and was on alert.

Elsha's blanket must have fallen off her horse because I had found it. Tony ran to give it to the Chief and I moved on. I had come to a little pathway and saw the brushes.

"Elsha…" I whispered her name.

I moved closer to the cave. I could see the flashlights coming toward me. I took a deep breath, it was very dark inside, there were rocks piled in one area, and I shined my light up. Silly girl she had climbed on top and fell through.

I called her name and no answer. Her camera rod was lying on the ground and I went in slowly. Nothing could have prepared me for what I saw next. The drawings on the wall, each detailed picture brought my nightmares to life. Now I know I am not crazy.

The dark images on the cave walls reached out to me. A part of me wanted to run, fast. My heart raced and my breathing increased. Elsha was in here and I had to get her out. I told myself to be brave I called to her and no answer. I secured my backpack on me, took out a flare, and shot it into the air to let the others know I had found the cave. Dad radioed me but it was just static.

I walked slowly shining my light all around on the inside. The drawings were coming to life almost, each chilling detail made me shiver. Dad and the others had arrived and ordered me out of the cave. I walked backwards and told dad I had to find her.

Dad was very serious, and did not want me hurt.

"We don't know if it's safe or not."

Elsha was my friend and I cared a lot for her, my impulse told me to keep going.

"I have to do this."

I could hear Wind Star neighing even louder as to give a warning. Chief Morgan ordered me out of the cave to let the experts handle it but I refused.

I was shocked. As I faced them to discover writings, and more drawings then I stepped back and fell. My flashlight fell inside an opening inside the floor of the cave. I yelled for dad and they all ran in. The cave was unstable. I was hanging on tight but there was nothing but sand and rock. The more I moved the more the cave gave way beneath me. Dad told me to hold on he yelled for someone to grab some rope. He was holding me while my body dangled beneath me. Slowly, I slipped through his fingers and down I went. I could hear dad screaming my name.

"Kyle,.....Kyle,....!"

I made a loud sound when I hit the ground. I must have landed on some ancient pottery. I saw my flashlight and went to reach when I heard someone groan in pain. I shined it all around I must have been in some type of a secret chamber.

"Elsha..." I called out to her again.

I didn't know how far down I was but, I saw another opening. Down below, on the floor beneath me and there she was; it was Elsha. She was lying there not moving. She must have hit her head she was bleeding badly.

"Are you alright down there?" I could hear dad calling.

"I'm okay."

"More help is on the way."

"I had found Elsha and she's hurt," I yelled back.

The wind was picking up outside; the storm was near. I could see bits of lightening flashing. I took off my backpack and took out some of my camping gear. I tried to figure out how I could get to her. No one knew about this cave but Elsha. There was no way of knowing if this was the only way in.

I looked at the drawings on the walls and knew I was in a dangerous place. My instincts told me that we had to get out of there and fast. I could hear dad calling to me but the wind was very loud. I heard Elsha moan again, she was only few yards beneath me so I tried to reach out to her. I could barely touch her when I heard something else, something worse.

"Elsha…Elsha!" I kept calling her name. "Please wake up please." She moved her head a little. "Open your eyes Elsha. It's me, Kyle."

"Kyle." She said.

"Yes, Elsha I am here. Your dad is here, they are going to rescue us."

I needed her to keep talking to me so, I would say non-humorous things. I did not want her to use any muscles in her body at all. Therefore, I told her that I rode Wind Star with no problem.

The cave was very unstable; I could hear rocks falling from above and faint voices. Dad and the others must be working recklessly to get us out. I tried the radio again but I could barely hear. I thought if I moved around inside the cave, I would get a frequency. Elsha started coughing she was trying to get up.

"Don't move." She refused my request. "You're stubborn…"

"You sound like my father."

"Are you okay?"

"My head is hurting…"

"Try not to move; I don't know how bad you're hurt. We needed to stay here until they got us out."

The cave was very dark; the flashlights helped a lot. I looked around to examine the cave and it was evident enough each drawing on the wall told a chilling story of everything I had been searching for.

According to the drawings, priests were holding up staffs and they were glowing. One of the drawings showed a picture of a man standing in front of the cave with his hands raised. His staff was glowing. Pictures of a full moon and stars show that this took place at night.

More rocks were starting to fall in on us. I needed to find a safer place to move Elsha. I had to get her out of the place she was. I called out to her again.

"Elsha..."

She slowly responded.

"You need to get me out of here..."

"Can you reach my hand?"

I realized that her backpack was still on her; she could move just a little bit.

More rocks were falling; they must have been trying to drill or something. I knew I had to hurry and make a decision. I stretched myself out on the floor of the cave. She was trying to move.

I reached further and caught her wrist; I pulled slowly and she moaned in pain. I had to pull her up.

"Can you take off your backpack?"

Elsha was able to slip out of her backpack. I encouraged her to hold tight.

"Hold onto to me."

As she held onto me I slid backwards slowly on my stomach. With short breaths, I inched backwards. When she was halfway out I reached around her, put my hand on her waist, and pulled her out. I held her for a few minutes then I fumbled through my backpack and found my camping lights. She had a huge bump on her head; she thanked me for getting her out. She whispered to me to get her backpack and I told her that she did not need it. She begged me to get it for her.

With more rocks falling, I had to move Elsha out of the chamber soon. I quickly moved to the opening and reached down as far as I could and grabbed her backpack. With the lights, I searched for a safer place to move her. My light caught a drawing on the wall that showed our exact location. I followed the pattern and it pointed in another direction of the cave. I went in first to make sure it was safe, it looked liked a place where the natives must have slept.

It appeared safe I pushed against the walls to check the density of the cave. It felt like solid granite.

I picked up Elsha, moved her to the chamber, and went back for our backpacks and lights.

More rocks started to fall in as I grabbed the last of our items. I could hear a little sound coming from the walkie-talkie. I played with it a little bit and tried to reach my dad. The cave was dark and cold so I placed my jacket under her head.

I had now been in the cave for hours. I know our parents must be going crazy by now. I had to do something to reach my dad.

I checked on Elsha to see if she was all right, she was sleeping. I took the radio and walked through the cave to see if I could get a signal. I switched the channels back and forth to see if I could hear anything. Then finally, I heard someone talking. I was only a few yards away from Elsha. I called to the person and could not make out whom it was.

I moved further into the cave until the sounds came clearer. Then, nothing, the sound was gone. I went back, sat down next to her, and placed her head on my lap, gently rubbing my hand over her bruised head. I grabbed my bag and luckily, my first aid kit was there. I cleaned her wound and she talked in her sleep. She said things about her dad and then she said something like dark images, flashing lights.

She spoke my name a couple of times stating repeatedly that she must help me. Then she was out again. I could only imagine what was going on up there. Surely, they were trying to figure out a way to get us out of this place. I scrambled around in the dark to see if I could find some wood to make a fire. I just had to keep Elsha warm.

Without knowing the extent of her injuries, I knew I had to do something. I placed the lights around in a circle so I could search a wider area. There was wood in the cave, I gathered what I could and started making piles. It is a good thing dad taught me some survival techniques. You never know where you will end up or what you will end up in so, always be prepared.

My dad taught me a lot. He is the outdoors type. I never thought I would be; nevertheless, I am glad I took an interest.

Once I got the fire started, I knew it would not last long. I needed to find more wood. I could see more images on the walls around us. I grabbed Elsha's camera and took some pictures. Thinking if we ever made it out, I would show these to Chief Spearhorn. No one would ever believe what we had found but we had the proof.

I tried the radio again and there was still a lot of static. Elsha was still unconscious. I checked her breathing again, her pulse was steady. I did not want to leave her but I had to find more wood. I took her flashlight and walked to where we both fell in. They must have been trying to get through and caused more rocks to fall so my way was blocked. I started searching other parts of the cave and found some old pots and a few tree roots. I started back towards Elsha to add more wood.

When I heard the radio making noise, I picked it up and yelled for dad, there was a lot of interference in the cave. I tried moving to different areas but nothing worked. I went to check on Elsha and she was sleeping. I added more firewood and left her to search for more. I must have been at it for hours. Lurking through the cave searching for what I could.

I thought about my parents again, and what they must be going through by now. I know they are in a panic and I am sure that Chief Police Morgan had everything going on as planned.

Once the fire was going and it appeared like it should last for a few hours. I decided to go back and move some of the rocks. I needed to make a pathway just in case I needed to move Elsha again. I blamed myself for dropping my book. If I had been paying attention, she would have never got her hands on it. Nevertheless, how was I supposed to know this would happen to us? I mean she had no idea what was in this cave until she started taking pictures. Elsha sure has a mind of her own; she is smart, strong, and well capable of taking care of herself… until now.

I had to keep moving, so I thought about things to keep myself going. I thought about Eric and what he must have went through when he was missing. He fell into a cave also. He survived by remembering his tribal skills and he found food. I doubt if I would find any food in this place. I am sure that Elsha packed some snacks; she was always prepared.

You would think a person would be scared trapped in a place like this. However, I did not have time to be; I was in survival mode and knew I had to take care of Elsha. Her father told me to take care of her while he was gone. So much for that how was anyone to know what she was up to she does have a mind of her own though and she is tough. I guess you would have to be.

Her mom left her, her dad is busy, and her uncle is the Chief of Police, can't get any better than that. I felt tired so I pushed myself even harder.

I do not know how many rocks I had moved. I kept my momentum up and the more rocks I moved the more wood I found. It was as if mother earth was graciously supplying me with what I needed. I tried not to focus on the cave drawings. I put it out of my mind as much as I could. I did not want to think of anything that would set my mind into a panic. Every so often, I would stop and take a break.

The dust from the cave made me cough so I tied my shirt around my face to shield it from the dust. From time to time, I would go back and check on Elsha. Her breathing was still steady and I would tickle the palm of her hands to see if she would move. I also did the same thing with the bottom of her feet. Good, she had use of her arms and legs.

I moved more rocks and found more wood. The more I felt my body tiring I pushed even harder. I shined the light above me and more rocks blocked it, I did not want to risk tampering with it and having them fall on top of me so I worked carefully under it. I could here more rocks falling above us so I know they are working aimlessly to get us out. I could not give up I had to keep going.

After a while, I could do no more I was exhausted and needed to rest.

Chapter Ten

THE ENCOUNTER

I went back to where Elsha was, sat down to relax myself, and closed my eyes. I must have been asleep for about an hour or two when the sounds from the radio awakened me. I looked at my watch; it was almost midnight Elsha was mumbling again.

I spoke with her and she responded by calling out to me in a soft whisper.

"Kyle…Kyle…."

"I'm right here."

"How long had we been in here?"

"Almost ten hours now. Our parents are working hard to get us out of here."

She tried to sit up I encouraged her to stay still.

"Don't move, Elsha I don't know how bad you are hurt."

Of course, she didn't listen to me. She sat up holding her head in her hands.

"Are you okay?"

"I have a headache and I'm a little dizzy...this is what I get for exploring."

"Elsha what were you thinking, this place is dangerous for anyone to be in?"

Still holding her head, she got enough strength to tell me.

"After you had left, I opened my package to look at the pictures and I noticed some of the drawings inside the cave. Then, while I was putting my books away, I found yours. I noticed that your drawings were the exact same as what was on the cave walls. I decided to explore the cave only to get pictures, not to go inside; I found a little opening on the top and was going to extend my camera down inside. That's when I fell, not once but twice."

I explained to her that there was no need to explore, then I explained to her how we found out she was missing I scolded her a little.

"We had to cut our trip short due to the storm; your father asked me if I knew your whereabouts. I told him I did not know. Your uncle started a search party and had an all points bulletin out on you."

She laughed softly.

"That is just how my uncle is. I have something important to show you."

She reached for her book. By the way, she moved I knew she was still in pain. So I offered to help.

"Here let me to get it for you."

I sat next to her and she began to show me what she had discovered.

"Each picture I took is identical to the cave drawings and then I derived a conclusion. Whatever is happening in our town and other places has something to do with these drawings. Comparing the stories about each body, that was found mutilated. Each piece fits a puzzle some how and this cave holds the answers."

I really didn't want to focus on this right now, but it was much needed information. So I encouraged her how we needed to get out of the cave. We did not know how deep the cave went but we had to find another way out.

"We need to focus on getting out of this cave first. I moved some of the fallen rocks that blocked the way we fell in. We have to try to get out."

I was not sure how long our lights would last. Being down inside a dark cave was not very appealing. I examined the chamber we were in to see if I could find something. Perhaps the natives left tools behind.

Elsha tried to tell me more, but I would not let her talk, she needed to rest. I was afraid her head injury might be more serious than I thought. She said she was fine and wanted to help me. I told her to stay close to the fire.

She could not help but stare at the drawings on the wall.

"They look life-like don't they?"

I replied.

"Yes they do. I followed the drawings on the walls and found this place."

Then she had a good idea that would help us both, I was starting to feel a little bit claustrophobic being in here so long.

"Maybe if we followed the patterns, we will find a way out."

It was a good idea and it was worth a try. I would stop at nothing to get her out of this cave.

"Can you stand up?"

"Yeah, I think I can."

I helped her to her feet and we checked the walls to find a clue.

There were drawings of all kinds; we could not make out some of them because the images were faded.

There were pictures of men and women holding torches following strange symbols. Each symbol depicted life-like drawings of warriors, priests, and village people. We searched for any opening we could find, some which led us into different areas of the cave.

We stopped when Elsha got dizzy and fell to the ground. I wanted to stop but she insisted that we keep moving. I had a gut feeling that I did not need to argue with her we had to keep going.

The cave walls described how there once was a village here. The images showed a dark skinned man who while pointing to the cave, visited the people. With his hands, extending out in front of him was as a sign that the people should stay away from the cave.

Other pictures showed women and children gathering baskets and placing them at the edge of the cave. They bowed down as if to worship something. We both studied the drawings and took pictures.

We moved all throughout the cave until we came across a huge wall like stone. It must be a secret chamber of some kind. The writing on the walls showed a priest standing on the opposite side of it. A white cloud circled the stone. There were seven glowing stones around the rock. We did not have time to study it.

I encourage Elsha that we should keep moving. Elsha took more pictures of the drawings. The symbols must mean something. She took out her book and searched for anything she could find.

I wondered why she had purchased the book, The Forbidden Lands. She had marked the pages where the maps showed our geographical area.

"The cave is on the map, there was a group of people that dwelled here long ago."

It had been about thirteen hours now we needed to keep moving. Elsha stated......

"If we search for the torches on the wall, it might lead to another way out."

We needed to get higher. As we searched, we did find more drawings and it showed men going into the cave with torches but by a stream. This must be the way.

We followed it along a long corridor, which brought us to a small opening in the ceiling of the cave. It was just big enough for Elsha to fit through.

"Stand on my shoulders and climb up."

She proceeded to climb up and did as I instructed.

"I can see a little bit of light."

She told me. I handed her the rod and told her to poke through it carefully. Little by little, the earth gave way.

As she dug, tree vines and rocks fell in on us. She yelled it was a way out but it would require more digging. We were at it for hours and our bodies were so tired. We rested on each other for a while and then started again. The cave ceiling was becoming unstable around us. We were no longer safe there. Before trying again, I looked at her and reassured her.

"I'm going to get you out here."

We kept going until we finally broke through the ground; this must have been a secret entrance to the cave long ago.

Then, I had a bad feeling come over me. Elsha was tired and I had to move quickly. I stood her weak body up on her feet.

"I'm going to lift you up again but you have to climb up the vines to get out,"

My body shivered as a cold chill came over me.

"Kyle….what's wrong? You're shaking."

"Don't worry about me; you need to get to safety."

I put her on my shoulders but the more she pulled, the vines kept breaking. Elsha was so scared.

"I can't get out!"

"You have to try. Keep pulling!"

The more I encouraged her the harder she pulled, she was able to get a hold of a vine and pull herself out. Panic was setting in on me as I started to hear strange noises.

"There's a radio up there. You need to hurry though; there isn't much time."

In sheer panic, she yelled back to me.

"How is there no time? Come on Kyle hurry!"

The sound was coming from inside the cave and I needed to keep moving away from her so I gave her strict orders.

"I will follow the cave to the north end. Contact Chief Spearhorn at the tribal union reservation and hurry," I yelled.

"I won't leave you here; I got out now so can you come on!"

The cave was becoming unstable fast.

"Elsha…, go, hurry!"

As the entrance started to collapse in on top of me, I could hear her screaming my name. With the rocks falling, I quickly moved through the cave finding my way to different parts to keep safe. I could only pray that Elsha made it out the rest of the way.

I pushed myself to keep moving, I was so exhausted. I could hear more of the cave collapsing behind me. I moved my hands along the cave walls; it was very damp; I could hear water above me.

As I came to another small opening, I shined my light and saw a chamber on the other side. I moved through it as fast as I could. I came to a huge rock I could feel the air from the outside. I tried to move the rock but it was too heavy. There was a tiny opening at the bottom. I tried clearing some of the earth from around it. The ceiling above worried me because it looked unstable. However, there was just enough room for me to move.

I got down on my hands and knees and dug under the rock. It was working, the more rock and sand I cleared away, the opening got bigger.

The wind was howling, I started to tremble in fear again, I felt so strange. I just had to get out. My senses told me that the Shifters were getting closer.

I ran the light against the wall to search for another way out, there wasn't one. This was the end of the line. The drawings on the cave revealed more horrifying details of dark images hovering over bodies. The people bowed down to the beastly image.

Men taken into the cave bound together laid on a flat piece of rock. Images drawn of half men half beasts appear from the shadows and consume them all. Transforming their victims, other drawings showed the men's faces in other parts of the cave. Their souls bound to the earth, never to escape.

I thought to myself for a moment. That is why the priests prayed over the cave so they could not cross the boundaries or leave. Something happened here but, what, I asked myself.

I searched the walls for more clues. These were the stories told from generation to generation. My eyes followed along the walls of the cave there was an imaged engraved into it. It was of a horrifying being, its eyes peering through the night as if it were watching me.

I shivered hard and tried to keep my focus. I was so exhausted and tired. I had to keep digging though. I thought if I could remove some rocks from on top of the huge one, I could possibly climb out. This only made matters worse. I was so desperate to get out, I caused a rockslide from within the cave and more fell on top of me.

As the rocks fell, one hit me in the head and I fell down. I was in and out of consciousness and bleeding quite a bit.

I encouraged myself to keep moving.

"Come on Kyle get up."

My eyes were deceiving me; I kept seeing images of a man standing on a ledge waving a staff and praying almost. The sky was black and the moon was full. The white mist was moving all about him circling him like a cloud. I knew I needed to move but my legs felt as if they were paralyzed. The voices were getting louder and louder. I must have been dreaming, somehow.

"Get up Kyle, get up."

I could see light from the outside. Then I heard it again, a noise that set my chill factor on high. I forced myself to get up and dig more and more.

With the sound getting closer and the smell of burnt flesh hitting my nose, I knew I was going to die. My head ached so badly, I must have been delusional. I swore I saw a horse running in my direction, neighing very loudly. I kept digging.

Finally, I was able to see the outside. The horse was even closer than I thought it was, kicking against the side of the cave. I started to crawl out and pushed my bag before me. I tried to move as fast as I could. I was half way out of the cave when I felt nostrils in my face. It could not be but it was. Wind Star had found me. I could not move another inch, but the horse was nudging my face. I pulled up on his rope and stood on my feet.

Dazed and disoriented I managed to pull myself onto the horse. The wind blew and made an unusual sound as if someone called my name. My senses were off the charts but I was not alone. Because standing on the rock behind me, was the biggest wolf I had ever seen. It growled at me and its eyes fixed on me watching my every move. Then it turned its head up toward the sky and let out a loud howl, as if it was sending a message.

The wind picked up and the night rippled like water. The wolf lunged at us and Wind Star moved fast as lightning running through the woods. I could hear more of them around us I held on to him as tight as I could. Wind Star was kicking his hind legs up in the air but he kept his stride.

My breathing was so severe I felt myself losing consciousness again. How could this horse have found me before the others could? Elsha said the horses knew their way back home. I could not tell which direction the horse was running my head was down and all I knew was I was in serious danger. The Shifters were persuing us.

The night moved around us like dark cloaks, shape-shifting wolves were all around us. With me on his back, Wind Star increased his speed and charged even harder. I fought to stay on him but I wobbled from left to right.

Suddenly Wind Star came to the creek and jumped high into the air. One of the Shifters must have countered his jump and striking me on my back. My shirt tore open; I could feel something wet run down my back.

The horse had managed to make it to the site where everyone was waiting. My eyes were opening and closing, my back burned with fire, and saliva dripping from the side of my mouth. I felt myself going numb. My hands lost their grip and slid down the side of the horse.

With my head leaning on the horse's mane, Wind Star had made it and the sun was coming up. I could hear people shouting as the horse walked toward the crowd with me on its back. I was so exhausted that I fell off Wind Star, I could not hold on any longer. The sound of drums in the background was very odd. I felt myself slipping away into a dark realm spiraling downward pulled by a force so strong. I could see faces of people that I cared about fading in front of me.

You will never know where destiny will take you, some people are prepared and some are not. Others embrace it and take what it offers. I was born with a gift to spot evil, with gifts come consequences and great sacrifice. Without darkness, there can be no light, and without light, there can be no darkness. Each given a chance to rule, one leaves another takes over. I was changing inside my blood was turning black as night.

The sound of drums was all around me. Images of light and darkness clashing into each other like a battering ram. Two warriors opposite each other stood in the middle of a field as if to do battle. Wolves uncovering themselves from the darkness stepped out from under their dark cloaks undressing themselves from the night. Indian Chiefs with huge feathered headdresses waved staffs in the air with glowing eyes of eagle's heads attached to them. They were saying prayers and some blew smoke from their sacred pipes. The sky filled with white and black smoke.

The fight between good and evil had started. The cry of the wolf was loud like a war cry. Screams came out of the night as a woman travailing in childbirth. I was in a tug of war between life and death. What will I become, will I ever see my loved ones again. The dark man in my dreams stood on a high cliff, his eyes rolling back in his head, his face, and chest painted with war symbols. Just like the ones, I saw in the caves.

Others warriors started to surface. The battleground took place near the cave just outside of the clearing. This was in deed a war. My body was struggling to survive. I was lying in the balance caught between two worlds. Darkness filled my eyes; I could see the gifts it was offering me.

Gifts to have unimaginable strength, power, and control the ability to transform with the night and shield myself from the world. The drums were getting louder and louder and I could hear people singing a war cry like song.

Fire rose up like an inferno in the mist of the warriors in the field. The dark skinned man stepped forward his painted tattoos glistening in the night called on the "Ekua adanádo" Which meant Great Spirit. He and others stepped forward. Four of them faced the four corners of the earth, and three representing heaven, earth, and the spirit of the souls.

They each stood in position and aimed their staffs high into the air night was turning to day. The darkness was fighting to stay in my body; it was spreading like poison.

I tried to fight it but I could not. There were many strong forces in this place between heaven and earth. Evil will always present itself in many shapes and forms. There are those that can determine between the two.

It is a choice we are given as humans, whether to do good or evil. I do not know why I had to be one of the chosen.

Evil can offer you many gifts. I feel as though I am held between two worlds, my soul spilt in two. Good and evil are fighting all around me. Some have come to protect me, while others have come to claim me.

I have been haunted and hunted all of my life; great warriors are here to standing in the balance lined up like soldiers watching this spiritual war. Eagles are flying high with their eyes glowing, fighting with dark transparent images.

Voices are calling out to me; another force pulls me into their direction. I notice a woman standing with two little boys at the edge of the woods, she points to an opening where the seven men with the staffs glowing are standing. The sky is rippling like a bubble getting ready to burst.

A gateway has opened one of the Chiefs looks into my eyes, which are black as pitch he blew a ring of white smoke around me while my body fell against the ground.

My mouth opened and a cloud of black mist exited my body. I was changing again I felt like I was floating. I could see silhouettes of people standing around me. Bright lights illuminated everywhere. The Chief looked at me and said in his native language **"Nihi naánige ayásdi nakuu"** which means *you can enter now.*

He ushered me to go through the gateway.

As I walked, I looked back at him and he said,

"This battle is just the beginning of your journey."

I could hear sounds of faint voices in the distance, my body floating in time and space. My mind flashed faces of blood stained warriors fighting in great battles.

I watched as the shifters transformed themselves to blend in with the night, hiding as though they were waiting for time. This war was over for now, but will there be another one. There are always spiritual battles taking place between good and evil. Men will one day have to choose one or the other.

I thought about my family; how I could protect them, keep them safe. The fate of humanity is at hand. Evil has presented itself in many forms the call of the chosen ones have been sounded; it is time to take a stand.

It is hard to fight the unknown with the natural eye, sometimes you have to travel into their world to learn about them. However, when they enter into your world you have to prepare yourself.

Some of us, chosen ones, are destined to fight without any warning; we learn our fate when it is too late. I now know that I am apart of something that will change my life forever.

I wonder if I will be normal or what will become of me. What will happen to me now? What will I become? Life can be so precious.

Never take it for granted. I am the chosen one it is something I will have to live with for the rest of my life. Did I change? One can only wonder.

Printed in the United States
By Bookmasters

More Light on the Expanding Universe

Les Hardison

MORE LIGHT ON THE EXPANDING UNIVERSE

iUniverse books may be ordered through booksellers or by contacting:

iUniverse
1663 Liberty Drive
Bloomington, IN 47403
www.iuniverse.com
1-800-Authors (1-800-288-4677)

ISBN: 978-1-4917-7860-9 (sc)
ISBN: 978-1-4917-7859-3 (e)

Library of Congress Control Number: 2015918351

Print information available on the last page.

iUniverse rev. date: 02/29/2016

CONTENTS

CHAPTER 1

INTRODUCTION

My first book, *A New Light on the Expanding Universe*, was an attempt to explain a different concept of how the universe we live in is put together and functions. It was based on the assumption that light really does not travel at 300,000 kilometers per second but instead goes from one place to another in no time at all; that is, the emission of radiant energy from one atom and the reception of that energy by another atom are simultaneous events. They happen at the same time, judging from the standpoint of the local time at the observer's location. This is equally true for two observers moving with respect to each other in our three-dimensional world.

To make this happen requires five dimensions: the three we observe when we look around us; a fourth, which is the direction the entire universe is moving as it expands at the *apparent speed of light*;[1] and a fifth dimension around which our entire four-dimensional super universe is wound like a vast number of strings representing our lines of sight.

I tried in the first book to keep the subject matter somewhat limited, which is pretty difficult if you are trying to describe the entire universe, from electrons to galaxies, using a single, relatively simple set of rules. So I left out a lot of things. Some because they were not important to the overall scheme of things, some because they would have made the book too long if they were included, and some—I have to admit—because I hadn't thought of them yet.

[1] The *apparent speed of light* is italicized here, as it is a phrase used in a special sense. In this case it denotes the velocity, approximately 300,000 km/sec, which is usually defined as the speed of light in a vacuum, but is, in my view, the speed at which the universe is expanding into the fourth dimension.

BRIEF REVIEW

For those of you who may not have read the previous book, *A New Light on the Expanding Universe*, or fail to remember all the confusing points raised in the book, a brief review is in order. Without it, I would have to introduce each of the subjects in this book by reviewing the background throughout the book.

This review is intended to provide enough introduction to the material that you can pick up where I left off without having read the previous book. And you can, of course, skip over the review if you remember it all or if you know what I was saying in the first book and disagree with it.

My whole concept of the physical sciences is based on the belief that light and other forms of electromagnetic radiation are transferred from one point to another instantaneously without having to pass through the empty space between the emitting atom and the receiving atom, and without any change in time taking place, at least from the standpoint of the observer witnessing the transfer. Nothing else, neither physical bodies nor other kinds of waves, can do this.

The mechanism for the transfer depends on a fourth dimension, similar in properties to the three dimensions we experience but stretching out in a direction from the here and now in a fourth direction we do not perceive that is perpendicular to the three we do. This is the direction of expansion of the universe, and it is also the direction in which time changes.

In addition, there must be a fifth dimension that is not similar to the three we live in. It seems to have no properties that are important to us, except that the four-dimensional universe I described is wound around a tiny spherical kernel so that points in our four-dimensional space-time continuum actually come into physical contact, although they are separated by significant distances in three-dimensional space and time. This is like two points on a piece of string being wound around a large ball of twine and lying essentially in the same place, although they are a significant distance apart along the length of the string. They can be spaced at any distance along the length of the string, as long as they are an even number of multiples of the circumference of the ball apart.

The observations of radiant energy transfer show that light moves through a vacuum at a speed that seems to be the same to any two observers, whether they are moving relative to one another or not. This leads to the conclusion, reached first by Einstein in his special theory of relativity, that time is measured differently by observers moving relative to one another. This seems to me to be true and necessary to account for the observations.

On the other hand, the measurements of the apparent speed of light seem to me to be misinterpretations of the data. I think the physicists actually measured the speed of expansion of the universe long before Hubble introduced the concept that it is expanding. However, their experiments were set up to measure the speed of light, and they believed that is what they measured. If one grants that the universe is expanding at the apparent speed of light, then it is necessary that radiant energy moves instantaneously from place to place, or at essentially infinite speed.

The question is, how could it look like it was taking a finite amount of time for the light to move from one place to another when it is actually moving instantaneously? The answer is that the observers did not actually see the light moving from point A to point B in a finite amount of time. You can only see a light coming from a distant source toward you, and when you see it, it appears that it was emitted at the moment you see it. Yet if you shine a light away from you (which you cannot see) and then it is reflected back to your eyes, it appears that the reflected light was emitted at the moment you saw it. If you had a superprecise stopwatch, the watch would show an elapsed time.

This led me to conclude that there are two ways of looking at time. Galactic time is time that is exactly the same everywhere throughout the physical universe as it exists right now. All points in the universe are at the same exact galactic time. However, no one can see anything that exists at the same moment in galactic time he is experiencing.

Each individual—or one might suppose, each atom in the universe—experiences his own local time. His local time encompasses all the universe that he can see, in all directions at the moment. Everything he can see is in the galactic past, according to galactic time, and all the galactic present, except his location, is in the local future.

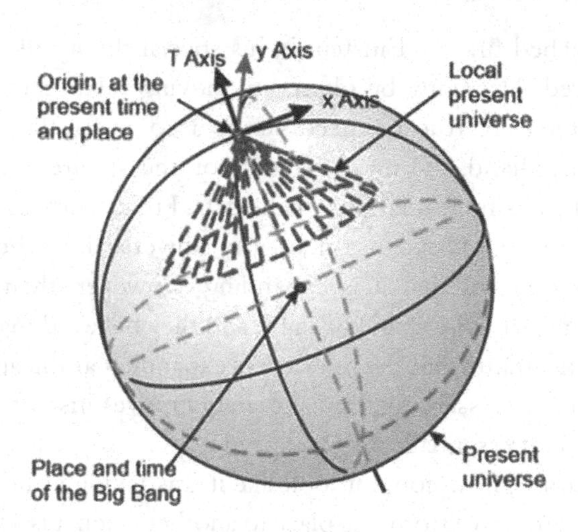

FIGURE 1
THE LOCAL UNIVERSE WITHIN THE GALACTIC UNIVERSE

The sphere pictured in figure 1 represents the universe as a two-dimensional x–y world with no z direction—the surface of a sphere. The observer at the origin cannot see any of that sphere; he sees instead the two-dimensional surface of a cone stretching out in in the x and y directions around him and into the galactic past. The x–y sections of the cone are circles growing in diameter with increasing distance.

They also represent distances stretching farther back into the galactic past. In the real world, distances from the origin would be spheres of growing diameter with increasing distance and would look like the real world as we see it. It is not the surface of the sphere that we see, although at close range it is hard to tell them apart.

This picture of how we see the world around us is a little strange, but it helps account for the properties of light and leads to a theory of gravity and electromagnetism that is consistent with the observations of physicists. It also provides answers to all sorts of questions that have bothered physicists since Einstein, Planck, Bohr, Schrödinger, Heisenberg, and many others established the foundation for the Standard Model of the Universe, which is accepted by most physicists as being the best available description of the world we live in. This leads to the question of what time it is at locations other than our own. Are distant objects really in our past, or are they in our present as they appear to be?

In addition to the different picture of the way time is viewed, I listed a number of other conclusions I have drawn about the way the laws of physics should be interpreted that are different from the commonly accepted interpretations. I also have listed them here because they may be helpful in understanding some of the further ideas put forward in the following chapters.

GENERAL CONCLUSION

1) The velocity of light is essentially infinite. It doesn't take any "time" to get from one place to another. It is not really a velocity, like the rate of change of position of a fish swimming through water, as it does not traverse the distance between the source and the receptor.
2) The universe is the three-dimensional "surface" of a four-dimensional hypersphere. It is expanding in the fourth-dimensional direction at a rate equal to the *apparent speed of light*, c.
3) The expansion rate is essentially unchanged from the time of the big bang, at which time the universe occupied a small volume. Hubble's constant is a measure of the rate of expansion of the universe. It is numerically equal to the reciprocal of the age of the universe, and the "constant" is decreasing linearly with the passage of time.
4) The three-dimensional universe is many times larger than the part that is observable because there is a "horizon" between the present moment and the time of the big bang that prevents us from seeing or learning about parts of the universe beyond the horizon.
5) All matter in the universe has a substantially constant, uniform velocity, c, equal to the *apparent speed of light*, or about 300,000 km/sec in the direction of the fourth dimension. This is basically what makes $E = mc^2$.
6) The fourth dimension is a real, physical dimension. It is not time. In this four-dimensional space, the passage of time has a direction and may be thought of as a vector.
7) Gravity is the result of slight differences in the distance matter has traveled from the time and place of the big bang to the present; the more massive an object, the shorter the distance. The differences between the lightest and most massive objects is very small compared with the diameter of the universe, but they are large enough to account for the phenomenon of gravity. Bodies with mass tend

to accelerate toward each other due to the tipping of the three-dimensional space toward them in the fourth-dimensional direction. This distortion of space may actually be what constitutes mass.

8) The relative accelerations of the massive bodies in three-dimensional space obey Newton's laws when referenced to the *local universe* in which they are measured. Most of the deductions made by Albert Einstein in his special theory of relativity apply only to the theoretical calculations of position and velocity, were they measurable in the spherical *galactic universe.*

9) Electrostatic and electromagnetic attraction are similar but more complex deformations of the three-dimensional universe in the direction of the fourth dimension. However, they probably involve a twisting of the space around the direction of the time vectors in the four-dimensional universe.

10) Light, along with electromagnetic radiation in general, is comprised neither of waves nor particles (photons) but is actually the effect of direct transfer of kinetic energy over spatial distance and time differences by physical contact of the source and receptor atoms.

11) The science of quantum mechanics was developed to account for the discrete levels of energy transmitted by presumed electromagnetic waves. The unit of energy was called the *photon.*

    I do not believe radiation consists of either waves or particles, nor do I believe that photons exist. This leads me to be suspicious of many of the particles named and studied by physicists. These include gluons (transfer particles that are supposed to hold nuclei together), gravitons (which are supposed to be the particles that conduct gravity, much as photons are supposed to conduct light), and ultimately the Higgs boson, which is theorized to be the transfer particle responsible for the mass of the elementary particles.

12) Nils Bohr's concept of the atom does not paint an adequate picture of the hydrogen atom and does not seem to apply to heavier atoms. I proposed a different picture in which electrons can orbit nuclei below the synchronous velocity without "falling into the nucleus." This model is applicable to all atoms, not just to hydrogen and helium.

13) Planck's constant is a measure of the radius of a five-dimensional, hyperspherical "kernel" around which the four-dimensional universe is wrapped. It does not adequately represent the energy transmitted as radiant energy, although it seems to be consistent with the perception

of light by the eye and with optical properties of light in general. All these processes depend on the frequency of rotation of the electrons in the source atoms, rather than the amount of energy transferred in each radiation event.

14) Schrödinger's wave equation is simply a statistical probability function that applies to the likelihood that an atom will be in the proper time and place to exchange energy with another atom. It does not have to do with waves at all.

I have not, in the book you are about to read, said anything significantly different from the ideas put forward in the previous one, but have instead expanded upon them and in some cases tried to answer questions posed by readers of the earlier book.

CHAPTER 2

THE LIGHTLESS UNIVERSE

This section deals with some of the properties of light that arise by implication if the velocity of light is taken as infinite and the perceived velocity of light is assigned to the velocity at which the three-dimensional universe is moving through a four-dimensional space.

In particular, it covers the properties of light associated with transmission, refraction, reflection, and visual perception. The importance of these is that they all make sense when viewed in the framework of the expanding universe in which light is an instantaneous transfer of energy and involves neither waves nor particles. All the properties of light help support the overall picture I have proposed for the way space and time are related.

THE "FREQUENCY" OF LIGHT

The phenomena of transmission, refraction, and reflection were described in detail by Sir Isaac Newton in his book on optics published in 1704.[2] He had no knowledge of atomic structure, but he was well aware of the "rules" that seemed to govern the transmission of light from a source to a receptor. Like everyone else, he presumed that light traveled through space like sound waves, or golf balls, or anything else perceived to move from one place at a given time to another place at a later time. The evidence all seemed to support this assumption.

The perception of light by the human eye is a truly marvelous process, but much of it depends on the same optical properties of the lens of the eye as telescopes, microscopes, and cameras.

[2] Isaac Newton, *Opticks: Or, A treatise of the Reflections, Refractions, Inflexions and Colours of Light. Also Two treatises of the Species and Magnitude of Curvilinear Figures* (London: 1704).

It will be demonstrated that the optical properties of light, although wholly defined by the amount of energy transferred in a single emission/absorption episode, are related not to the energy content of the transmission, but rather to a "frequency" that is related to the energy by Planck's constant, according to

$$E = hf\,, \qquad \text{Equation 1}$$

where

E = "Energy" associated with the transfer event
h = Planck's constant
f = Perceived frequency of light.

If there are really no light waves moving between the emission source and the receptor—nothing at all passing through the intervening space if there is no material present in the space—the concept of the frequency of light does not seem to fit into the picture at all.

However, many of the properties of light, like the colors we observe in the spectrum by a prism, are proportional to the frequency of rotation of the electrons rather than to the energy involved in the emission. This is because perceived light is ordinarily the result of thousands or millions of such transmissions of energy, so the energy of a single transmission is not sensed. The total energy received by the receptors is perceived as the brightness of the light, while the energy of each individual transmission is perceived as the color. This is quite analogous to the perception of the total energy of sound as loudness, while the frequency of the sound waves is perceived as tone or pitch.

Both sight and hearing are responses to the square root of the energy of the source, and this is proportional to frequency. So, in most of the following work, "frequency" is used when talking about the optical properties of light. It is simply a measure of the change in orbital frequency of the inner electrons of the emitting atom and receiving atom, rather than the frequency of light "waves" traversing the space between them.

Light can be emitted from atoms that have either one or two electrons orbiting the nucleus, in the case of hydrogen and helium atoms, and in the innermost orbit for all heavier atoms. These electrons have all the properties required to account for the observed properties of radiant energy transfer in the visible light range.

Larger and more complex atoms also have a pair of electrons in the inner orbit that are likely to rotate at the same orbital radius as for either hydrogen or helium but which are capable of much higher orbital velocities because of the greater electrical charges on their nuclei. Therefore, the heavier atoms are likely to be able to emit radiant energy at higher energy levels than hydrogen and helium. The higher energy levels would be described as having higher frequencies.

Because visible light has energy levels that are characterized by frequencies in the visible range, it is much simpler to talk about "light" and to presume that it is emitted by hydrogen and helium atoms in the sun and stars than to continually reference electromagnetic radiation from whatever source. However, all the discussion should apply to radiant energy transmission ranging from gamma rays on the very high-energy end of the spectrum to long radio waves on the low end. All radiant energy transfers should be governed by the same rules. Low-frequency radio transmissions may also involve the transfer of free electrons in addition to the inner-orbital electrons.

SPEED OF LIGHT IN TRANSPARENT MEDIA

Light is emitted and absorbed in simultaneous events when viewed from a local time reference. This yields an infinite velocity for light in a vacuum. The imposition of a transparent material, such as glass, water, or air, between the emission source and the ultimate receptor involves some time delay. While the transmission of radiant energy from atom to atom does not involve the passage of time, the conditions for the transfer to take place are not present continuously, so each absorption and reemission does take time. The transmission of light through transparent materials is thus necessarily slower than instantaneous transmission through a vacuum.

The emitting atom and the absorbing atom must be very precisely arranged in space and must be separated by a time difference that is a precise number of multiples of the minimum orbital path length of the electrons. So when an atom of a transparent material absorbs energy from an external source, it does not instantaneously pass it on to the next atom toward the interior of the material, but rather waits until a suitable receptor atom is in just the right time, place, and orientation for the transfer to take place. This results in a little time delay before the next step can take place.

The energy is first absorbed by a receptor atom in the surface of the transparent material closest to the emitter. In order for this transfer to take place, the absorber atom must have an orbiting electron or electron pair aligned properly with the emitter and spaced at one of the many acceptable distances from the emitter in both time and space.

The result of this first transfer of energy is that an atom in the transparent material becomes energized,[3] having exchanged energy levels with the primary emitter. Now, in order to serve as an emitter in turn, a second atom somewhere in the transparent material must be lined up properly with the surface atom so that a second transfer can take place.

The probability of this alignment occurring in a given very short time period is high, but it is likely that the situation required for the second energy transfer to take place will occur only after a finite time has passed. When the second transfer takes place, the energy level of the original excited atom at

[3] Throughout this book, energized means that the orbiting electrons in a particular atom have a significantly higher orbital velocity than that assumed by the bulk of the atoms in the material at the same temperature.

the surface will be exchanged with the second atom within the transparent material.

The process is repeated for each atom along the path the light takes moving through the material. Each of these transfers involves energizing an atom within the structure of the transparent material to exactly the same level as the original emitting atom had prior to the beginning of the process.

It is likely that the property that distinguishes transparent materials from opaque ones is that the transparent materials have many potential receptor-donator atoms lined up and held in random positions so that at any time there are many that will be lined up with the orbital plane of the inner electrons perpendicular to the initial path of the light.

To illustrate this process more simply, imagine an experiment set up on a table in a laboratory, as shown below, with some phenomenally accurate instruments to measure the energy transmitted and the time of events. The table has in one corner a very tiny light source that becomes energized from time to time by reflecting light received from a source, such as the sun. When energized, it very quickly retransmits the energy across the table to an incredibly sensitive detector, which receives the energy. In the center of the table, in the direct line between the emitter and the absorber of the radiant energy, is a place to set up lenses, mirrors, etc.

For an initial experiment, light will be transmitted from the source at A to the receptor at B, with nothing (neglecting the small influence of air in between, as Michelson and Morley did). Two phenomenally precise clocks are located at A and B, and they record the emission and reception events for each single transmission of energy. The clocks are synchronized when placed side by side.

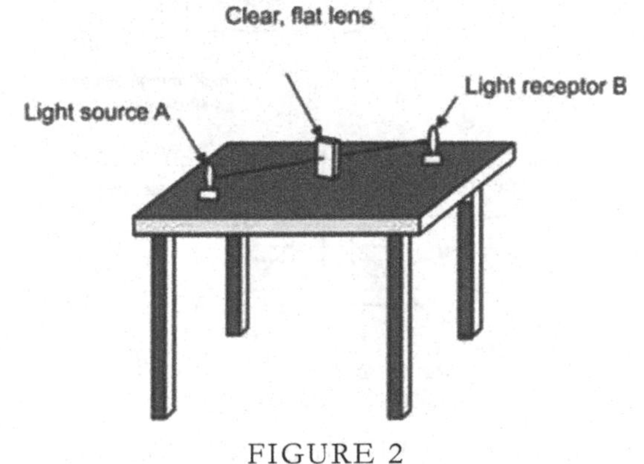

FIGURE 2
LAB TABLE WITH SOURCE AND RECEPTOR

The experiment begins with light source A transmitting a single burst of energy to receptor B and timing transit of the light from A to B. After the event has been recorded, the time difference between the two clocks, Δt, can be determined. It is found to be equal to d/c, the distance between A and B, divided by c, the *apparent speed of light.*

Both clocks were synchronized and read what I have called galactic time. But an observer located at light source A would, at the time of the event, observe that the clock at location B did not read the same as his clock at A. Rather, it showed an earlier time, and the difference between the two clocks was d/c. So he corrects the reading of the location B clock to match his by subtracting d/c from all the readings and concludes that the time of transit of the light from A to B was zero.

In short, the speed of light would be c if measured in terms of the galactic time but infinite if measured in terms of the local time at location A. The same would hold true using location B or any other point from which observations could be made.

This is a little easier to understand by showing the picture on a three-dimensional scale including the fourth-dimensional T direction through which the universe is moving at the *apparent speed of light*, c. In this view, our three-dimensional directions are limited to x and y, the plane just above the table top, and presume that z is zero throughout

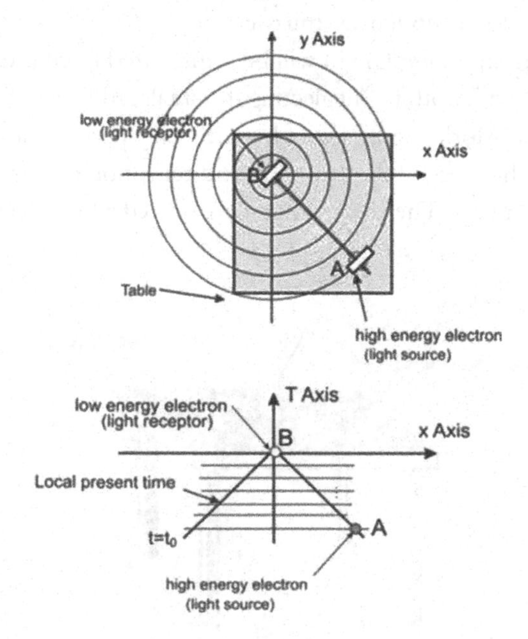

FIGURE 3
LIGHT TRANSMISSION WITH AN UNOBSTRUCTED "PATHWAY"

The upper view in figure 3 is a plan view of the experiment showing the arrangement of the source and receptor on the diagonals of the table. In this picture, there is nothing between the source and receptor but air.

The light emitted by the source at A from time to time is recorded on our super precise time clock, as is the time of receipt of the energy at receptor B. The two times are shown to be exactly the same according to the local time as observed from either end. That is, there is no time lapse at all by local standards.

For a second experiment, imagine a flat lens of clear glass has been placed on the table somewhere along the line of sight between points A and B, just as shown in figure 2. The transmission of light from A to B is no longer through empty space but now involves the transmission through the flat glass lens, as shown in figure 4.

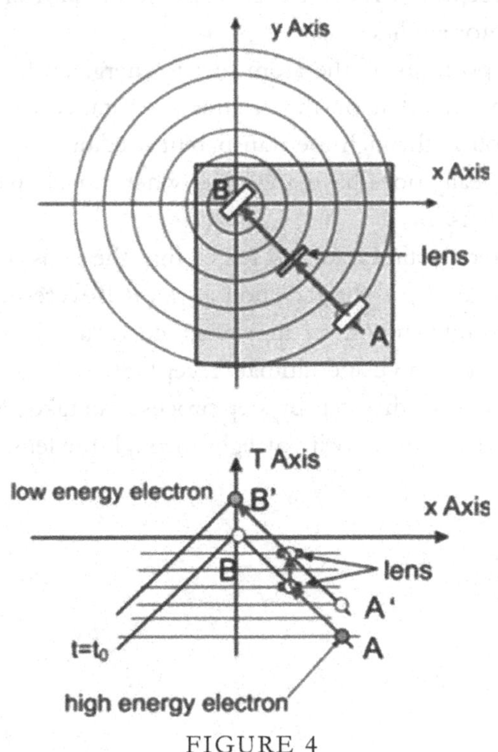

FIGURE 4

LIGHT PATH WITH A CLEAR PERPENDICULAR LENS

Now, the closest atoms to the emission source along the line of sight are those in the nearest surface of the lens. When an atom in this surface is suitably lined up with the emitting atom, an instantaneous transfer of energy between the two will take place. The arrival of the energy at the glass surface and the emission from the source at point A are simultaneous.

The absorbing atom on the surface of the glass can absorb the energy and retain it as kinetic energy of the atom, or it can emit it as reflected light to a third receptor outside the lens, or it can pass it on to another atom within the body of the lens. A piece of high-quality optical glass will, for the most part, find a second receptor atom within the structure of the lens sooner than it will find one outside and will complete the exchange of energies immediately when such a match is found.

This relaying of the energy from an energized atom to one with a lower energy level, which then becomes the emitter, goes on until the transfer to an atom on the opposite side of the glass occurs. At this point, another transfer to the ultimate receptor at B occurs. This last step requires no time after the emitter and receptor are lined up.

Because the position of the atom that is energized to the higher level does not line up with that of the emitter instantaneously, light does not move instantaneously through the transparent medium as it would through a vacuum. Light really does have a velocity when traveling through matter, such as the glass lens.

Our supereffective timers would tell us that the emission of light from point A and the receipt of the radiation at point B were not simultaneous, but rather took a finite amount of time when corrected for the difference in clock readings at the source and ultimate receptor.

Figure 5 shows how this step-by-step process can take place, introducing a time interval and a finite velocity of light through the lens.

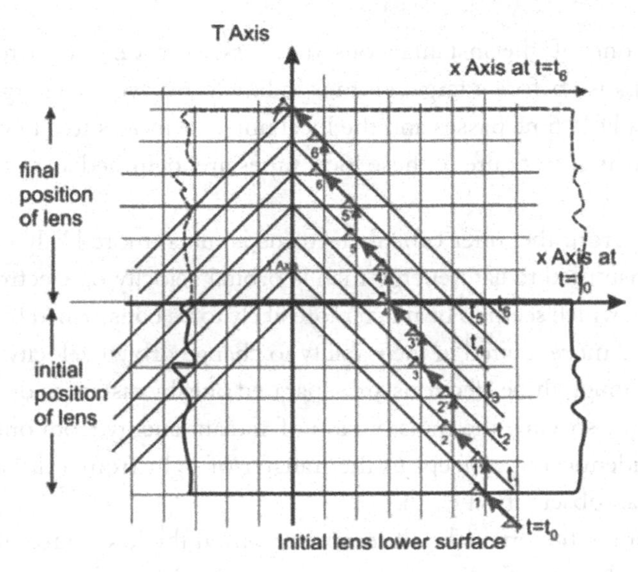

FIGURE 5
RADIANT ENERGY TRANSFER WITH
AN ORTHOGONAL LENS

The importance of showing this process in the diagram with the cones representing the local time in the two-dimensional analog universe is that the local time cone is moving in the T direction, just as the lens is moving.

Figure 5 illustrates the internal working of the transparent lens, which is shown as having seven atoms aligned so as to transmit light incident at ninety degrees to the surface. The reason glasses and other transparent materials transmit light without altering its direction is that they haves atoms arranged at random throughout its structure that can absorb visible light at just about any angle of the incident light. These all have a fixed orientation so that at whatever direction the light source hits the surface, there will be some atoms properly aligned at the surface and within the body of the material.

The light is "transmitted" along a line perpendicular to the orbital plane of the electrons in the atoms involved for both the emitting atom and the absorbing atom. These orbits are represented by the bases of the lightly shaded triangles in figure 5. The proton is at the apex of the triangle, and the base represents the orbit of the electrons. All are shown with the same orientation of the proton and the inner electron orbit because the condition for transfer of energy from one electron orbit to another is that they be oriented parallel to each other.

Every one of the instantaneous transfers from one atom to another involves a pause before a target atom is in line to receive the energy. During this pause a little time passes and the local universe moves to a new location along the T axis. In figure 5, these local times are identified as t_0, t_1, t_2, t_3, t_4, t_5, and t_6.

Energy from the inner orbital electrons is much more likely to account for the transmitted radiant energy than is orbital velocity of electrons in the outer orbits, which seem to be much more likely to be constrained by chemical bonding and more limited in their ability to change orbital velocity.

Even though these electrons are separated only by distances on the order of the atomic spacing, the transmission of radiant energy from one atom to another is identical in concept to the transfer of light from a distant star to the eye of an observer on earth.

In figure 5, the original first receptor atom in the lower face of the lens at time t_0 is shown with the electron in gray, at the lower right corner of the tiny triangle representing the atom. The associated proton, or atomic nucleus, is shown in black and plays no role in the transfer of radiant energy.

In this example, the original emitting atom is presumed to have a higher energy state of the orbiting electrons, perhaps consistent with the temperature of the filament in an electric lightbulb rather than with the temperature of the ambient air or the lens. All the other electrons in the lens are at lower energy levels commensurate with the temperature of the laboratory. As the excessive energy state is passed from atom to atom, the receiving atom acquires exactly the energy level of the original excited atom. The lower energy state (orbital velocity) electrons are shown as unshaded circles.

The process of transmission of radiant energy during a "transmission event" results in the final receptor on the far side of the lens from the source ending up with precisely the same level of excitation as the atom in the source from which it originated.

EFFECT OF FREQUENCY ON THE SPEED OF LIGHT

It is well known that the frequency of radiation and the properties of the medium of transmission (other than a vacuum) determine the speed of light through the medium. The frequency of radiation is essentially the orbital frequency of the emission source. When light passes through a transparent substance, it does not simply move through it, but rather becomes a part of the transmission process. That is, the surface atoms in the transparent material receive the energy from the emission source at the same local time as it is emitted. They then become excited atoms, and serve as the energy source for and retransmit the energy to a second atom within the transparent material. This then becomes the energy source for a third transmission. The orbital velocity of the high-energy atom is transferred to the lower-energy atom as the two atoms exchange energy levels (and possibly exchange the orbiting electrons themselves).

According to this theory of light transmission, the frequency is necessarily an integer fraction of the *apparent speed of light*, so it might be represented as

$$f = \frac{v}{2\pi r_0} = \frac{c}{N2\pi r_0}, \qquad \text{EQUATION 2}$$

where

f = frequency of orbital rotation
v = orbital velocity
c = *apparent speed of light*
r_0 = orbital radius.

In the equation, r_0 is also equal to the circumference of the spherical kernel on which all the lines of sight in the universe are wound. All the values are referenced to the galactic system of time keeping, in which c appears to be the velocity of light.

The value of N, the divisor of the ultimate orbital velocity an electron could have, is an integer, such that, if N=1

$$f_c = \frac{c}{2\pi r_0}, \qquad \text{EQUATION 3}$$

then

$$\frac{f}{f_c} = \frac{1}{N}. \qquad \text{EQUATION 4}$$

This insures that the all the electrons shown in figure 5 will eventually have the orbit of the electrons of the atom in position 1 lined up with those of that in position 0 only when they are both in the line of sight shown by the arrows. Only when they are so aligned, can the initial transfer take place. As soon as the two electrons are lined up (which can only happen when they are both on the line of sight along the right edge of the cone in figure 5), the initial transfer will take place.

When there are two orbiting electrons in an atom, if one of them is lined up on a line of sight with an orbiting electron in a second atom, the second electron in each atom will automatically be aligned. The second electron in the receptor has its own separate local time cone, which will include the second electron of the emitter.

This actual transfer is instantaneous once the conditions are right. The delay has been in waiting for the two electrons to line up properly so the energy can be transferred either by direct contact of the two electrons, or because the electrons actually exchange places in their respective atoms.

The second step repeats the process of the previous one, but during the time required for the two electron orbits to line up properly, the electron at position 1 has moved in the T direction to position 1', and the exchange of energy with atom 2 takes place instantaneously.

Exactly the same waiting interval may be required before the second atom can transfer its energy excess to the third. So, at time $t = t_0 + 2\Delta t$, the third electron receives the high energy level, and the second returns to its original state.

This process is repeated four times more to result in the electron at the surface becoming the possessor of the excess energy at time $t_0 + 6\Delta t$, or t_7.

The final step in the transfer involves the last electron within the lens waiting for the ultimate receptor electron to line up properly, which takes on average another time interval Δt, so at $t = t_0 + 7\Delta t$, the energy finally reaches the ultimate destination outside the lens.

The conditions necessary for the exchange of radiant energy from one atom to another seem relatively straightforward, but they require some explanation in order to calculate the effect of the frequency of light on the refraction process. This explanation is consistent with the theory advanced previously that the velocity of light is essentially instantaneous in a vacuum and that the mechanism of radiant energy transfer involves distant atoms being brought into contact by the wrapping up of our space time on a fifth-dimensional kernel. This brings atoms far apart in space and time into close contact if the geometry of their relative positions is correct.

If one looks at the exchange as a simple mechanical process whereby one electron moving at a relatively high velocity catches up with and impacts a slower-moving electron. A perfectly elastic collision (whether the two electrons actually come into contact or simply come closer together than normal but separated by the distortion of space around each of them due to its electrical charge) will be the result. If they are both orbiting protons at the same orbital radius, the necessary conditions for this simple energy exchange to occur are:

1) The orbital planes must be parallel. This requires that axes about which the electrons are rotating must be parallel.
2) The orbital planes must be separated in space and time by an integral number of distance units, each of which is equal to the orbital circumference of the hydrogen atom in both the three-dimensional world and in the T direction, where time can be measured as $t = T/c$.
3) When conditions 1) and 2) are satisfied, the electrons associated with both atoms will, for all practical purposes, be traversing the same orbit. This condition must exist long enough for the faster of the two electrons to "catch up with" the slower-moving electron.

Conditions 1) and 2) are satisfied by atoms that fall on the conical elements comprising lines of sight in the two-dimensional analog model and have spacings that put them in parallel planes separated by an integral number of basic radii, r_0.

The third condition imposes a time limitation. Many atoms may be positioned properly with regard to their planes of rotation and space/time separation but simply be out of phase with the emitting electron at any given time and so not be involved with energy exchange. The probability of being suitable has to do with how close the two are to being in phase at the moment in question.

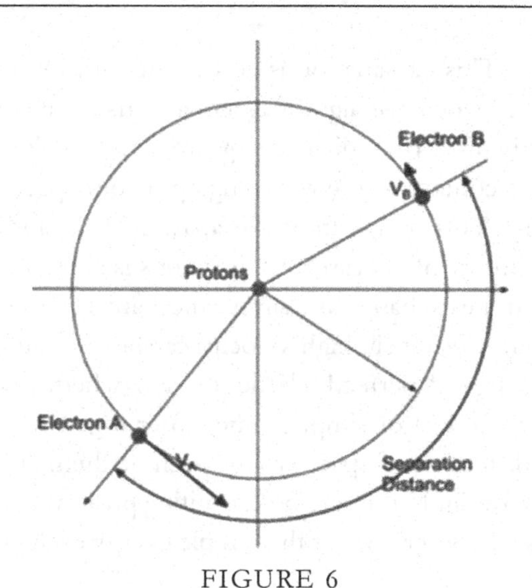

FIGURE 6
CONDITIONS FOR RADIANT ENERGY TRANSFER

Figure 6 is a schematic of two atoms lined up properly in space and time for energy exchange. All that is required to complete the energy exchange is for the fast-moving electron, designated Electron A in the figure, to catch up with the slower-moving electron, Electron B. The geometric conditions have to be in place long enough for this to occur.

One can guess how long on the average this should take for various combinations of energy levels. In figure 6, if the velocities of the two electrons are known, the relative velocity is simply

$$v_R = v_A - v_B \text{.} \qquad \text{EQUATION 5}$$

In this example, a single orbiting electron has been used for simplicity of illustration. In the real world, two electrons are likely to be in orbit in each atom. As pointed out previously, if the two orbital planes are parallel and the spacing in space and time is correct, the second electron from each atom will be doing exactly what the first one does at any given time but is held in position on the opposite side of the orbit.

The time required for A to catch up to B is dependent on the distance between them when the chase starts, and there is no way of knowing this. However, it is likely that many such transfers will take place before a significant amount of energy has been transferred, and using the average time seems warranted.

The maximum time required will involve the initial placement of the fast electron just ahead of the slow-moving one, so that the distance between them in the direction they are going is $2\pi r_0$ for the case where only one electron is orbiting per atom. The shortest distance is if the fast-moving electron is dropped right behind the slow one and the distance is essentially zero. Thus the average distance for many such transactions is likely to be half the maximum, or πr_0.

The time required for Electron A to impact Electron B is therefore about

$$\Delta t = \frac{d}{v_r} = \frac{\pi r_0}{v_A - v_B}. \qquad \text{EQUATION 6}$$

The frequencies of rotation of the two electrons can be taken as f_A and f_B, so

$$\Delta t = \frac{\pi r_0}{2\pi r_0 f_A - 2\pi r_0 f_B} = \frac{1}{2(f_A - f_B)}. \qquad \text{EQUATION 7}$$

This appears to give an absolute measure of the time required for the transfer of the energy to take place, provided we know the frequency of rotation of the electrons involved in both the sending and receiving ends of the transaction and there is only one electron involved from each atom.

Because this situation exists only for hydrogen free radicals, which are rarely present in solids under ordinary temperature conditions, figure 6 could be redrawn with two electrons per atom, or four in the same orbit when the conditions are right for the transfer of energy from one atom to the other. Under these conditions, the maximum and average distances for the electrons to travel before a collision would occur is half that given above.

$$\Delta t = \frac{\frac{\pi r_0}{2}}{2\pi r_0 f_A - 2\pi r_0 f_B} = \frac{1}{4(f_A - f_B)}. \qquad \text{EQUATION 8}$$

Note that this equation suggests that the speed of light in a medium is dependent on both the frequency of orbital rotation of the electrons in the emitting atom and in the atoms in the lens. However, we observe that the separation of light into various colors by a prism seems to depend only on the frequency of the orbital electrons in the emission source and not on the frequency of the unexcited electrons in the prism. This is easily explained.

In order to emit light in the visible spectrum, it is necessary for the emitting bodies to be very hot. This is true for the "initial emitters," or original light sources, like the sun, an incandescent lightbulb filament, or the electronically excited phosphor in a fluorescent lamp. But light can be reflected or transmitted by bodies at low temperatures where individual atoms are energized without the bulk material attaining a high temperature.

The natural radiation from materials in the ambient temperature range is at a far lower energy level than that of the hydrogen and helium atoms in the sun, which provides our natural sunlight, or the glowing filament in an incandescent lightbulb. The frequencies associated with prisms, mirrors, and eyeballs in their natural, unexcited state are far, far lower than the excited atoms which emit light. So it is not unreasonable to neglect the orbital frequency of the atom in the receptor and write:

$$\Delta t \cong \frac{1}{4f_A}. \qquad \text{EQUATION 9}$$

Now, assuming that this value is a critical property of the light being transmitted, we can rewrite the equation for the velocity of light in the transparent material of the lens used in the example as follows:

$$v = \left(\frac{\Delta x}{n\Delta t}\right) \cong \left(\frac{\Delta x}{n}\right) 4f_A, \qquad \text{EQUATION 10}$$

where

n = total number of retransmitters in the line of sight through the lens
Δx = thickness of the lens.

Thus the velocity of light in the transparent medium is inversely proportional to the transmitters per unit length of the lens times the frequency of the emission source, provided the emission source is much hotter than the receptor. This is certainly true of visible light emitted from the sun, and it is probably a close approximation for very energetic radiation in the form of gamma rays, X-rays, etc. The approximation may not be valid for lower-frequency radio waves, in which case the temperature of the lens or the transmitting medium might be significant with respect to the source and

$$v = \left(\frac{\Delta x}{n}\right) 4(f_A - f_B).$$ EQUATION 11

This says simply that the ratio of the velocity of light in the transparent medium is proportional to some property of the transparent medium times the frequency of the source. If the transparent lens is absent or has the same properties as a vacuum, the value of n is 1 and the velocity of light is infinite in terms of the local system of measurement, or c using the galactic or universal system. For actual transparent materials, there are finite values for both Δx and n, and finite transmission speeds result.

The ratio of the number of transmitters per unit thickness is proportional to the refractive index of the transparent material, or

$$v \propto \frac{f}{n},$$ EQUATION 12

where

n = refractive index of material.

Thus the speed of light in a transparent material is inversely proportional to the refractive index and proportional to the frequency of the original source, for most radiation, and proportional to the difference in frequencies of the source and receptor for lower-frequency radiation. This accounts for the complete lack of color distortion of light transmitted from distant galaxies, where there is no difference whatever in the velocities of the different colors. Were this not so, we would see the reds, blues, and greens coming from a star at different locations because of the rotation of the earth.

One other point is worth touching upon before leaving the subject of the transfer of energy between atoms. The preceding discussion has presumed that the planes of rotation of the atoms line up perfectly at the time the transfer of momentum from one atom to another takes place. This is not necessarily so.

Misalignment of the planes is not an impediment to transfer taking place for hydrogen free radicals, where only a single electron in the inner orbit is involved. Figure 7 illustrates this point. Here two orbital planes in three-dimensional space are shown with a 20-degree tilt of one relative to the other. However, at the point where the planes intersect, the velocity of the high-energy electron is just exactly the same in both direction and velocity, as it would be if the two planes were parallel. It is apparent that if the two planes remained stationary with respect to each other, the energetic electron would not overtake the slow moving one but would instead pass above it.

However, the point is made that while radiant energy transfer is most likely to take place between atoms whose orbital planes are parallel to each other, it is possible for transfer to take place between nonaligned planes.

However, this is likely to be the case only when hydrogen free radicals are involved. These have only one orbiting electron, as shown in figure 7.

With molecular hydrogen, or helium, or any heavier atom, there will be two orbiting electrons in the inner orbit. One of these cannot lose its energy independent of the other. Both are going to have to orbit along the same path and at the same velocity. For all these atoms, the energy exchange necessarily requires that the orbital planes are parallel, so the two high-energy electrons are both traveling in the same orbit as the electrons in the atom absorbing the energy. It is a requirement that both the emitting atom and the absorbing atom line up perfectly, or nearly so, with respect to the normal three spatial dimensions when more than one electron is required to exchange energy in a particular radiation event.

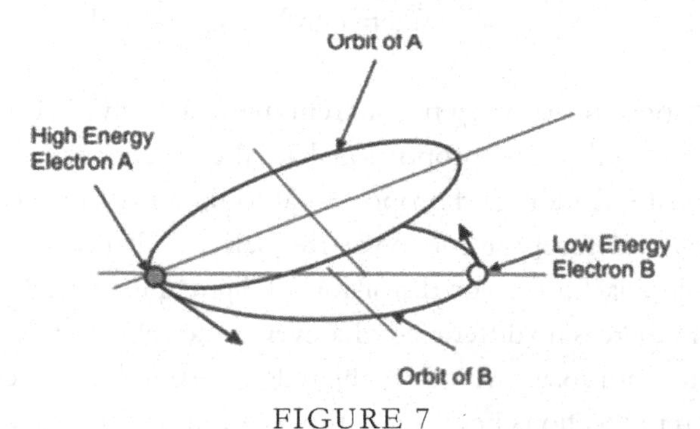

FIGURE 7
ENERGY TRANSFER WITH MISALIGNED ORBITS

Nonaligned transfers are limited to hydrogen in the free radical form. This condition is unlikely to exist under earthlike conditions, where hydrogen is much more likely to exist in either molecular form (two atoms sharing two electrons) or ionic form (one atom with no electrons), and precluding energy transfer. Figure 8 illustrates this point.

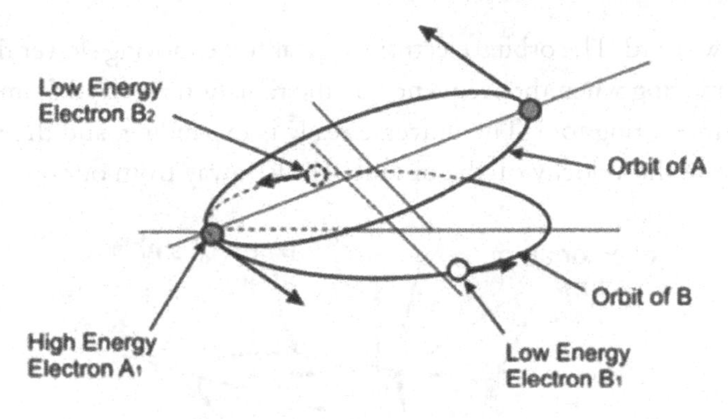

FIGURE 8
ORBITS AT AN ANGLE FOR HYDROGEN
AND HEAVIER ATOMS

Radiant energy can be transferred from one atom to another if the orbital planes of the two atoms are very exactly aligned and remain so for the tiny interval of time required for the fast electrons to catch up with the slow electrons.

However, this condition only exists if the atoms have no velocity relative to one another in three-dimensional space.

If they do have any relative velocity, the alignment in the three spatial dimensions could be exact, but the emitting atom's path in the T direction would be tipped in relation to that of the absorbing atom. While these appear to line up properly, the orbital planes would be tipped relative to the T direction.

Energy transfer can still take place with essentially all the momentum (and therefore all the energy) of both electrons. It is apparent that the energy transfer will not involve the total energy of the emitting atoms if the orbits are out of parallel in the transverse direction also. Likewise, the emitting atom will acquire not the total original energy of the receptor atom but only the component of the energy of the receptor that is in the orbital plane of the emitting atom.

The red shift observed for light emitted by galaxies very far from our own has been attributed to the velocity of the galaxies away from us as a result of the expansion of the universe. It is because of the different direction of time, or the T axis, which always points outward from the present position of the universe in four-dimensional space, that we see the frequency of the light shifted downward. The orbital electrons appear to be moving slower than they really are moving when the frequency of the radiation received from them is used as a measuring tool. The universe really is expanding, and the red shift does indicate the velocity of the distant galaxies away from our own.

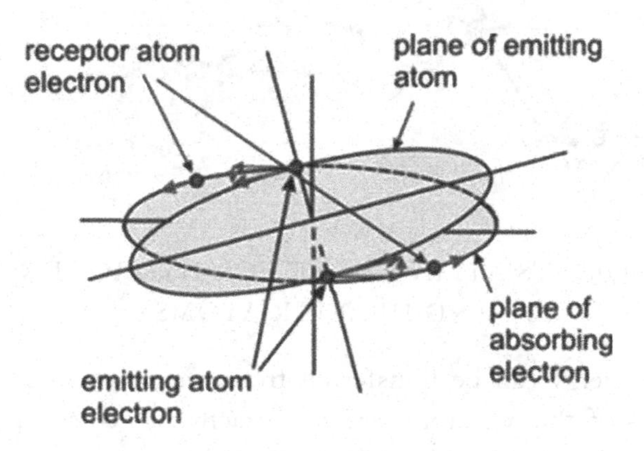

FIGURE 9
RADIANT ENERGY TRANSFER BETWEEN
NONPARALLEL PLANES

It is also apparent that, in the experiment described, the atoms are all essentially at rest with respect to each other so that all the energy transfers in this experiment will be done at the full value of the emissions of radiant energy received from the source.

REFRACTION OF LIGHT

Refraction of light is a common property assigned to light waves, and it is the basis for the design of all sorts of optical equipment, from eyeglasses to microscopes to spectrographs. The well-known phenomena observed in rainbows or when a triangular glass prism is used to separate the colors of light in sunlight are examples of light being refracted.

The laws of refraction are well-known and can be summed up by saying light that passes from a vacuum, or near-vacuum, into a transparent substance appears to bend as it enters the transparent material such that the angle it makes with a line perpendicular to the surface is decreased. The velocity of light in the medium is generally accepted to be lower than in a vacuum, and the bending is more pronounced the slower the velocity in the transparent medium is. That is, there would be no bending at all if the light moved at the same velocity as in a vacuum; the slower the velocity, the more the bending. The degree of bending in passing from one medium to another defines the index of refraction of the two media, according to Snell's law:

$$\frac{\sin\theta_1}{\sin\theta_2} = \frac{n_2}{n_1} = \frac{v_1}{v_2}, \qquad \text{Equation 13}$$

where

θ_1 = angle of incidence
θ_2 = angle of refraction
n_1 = index of refraction of the first material
n_2 = index of refraction of the second material
v_2 = velocity in medium
v_1 = velocity in vacuum.

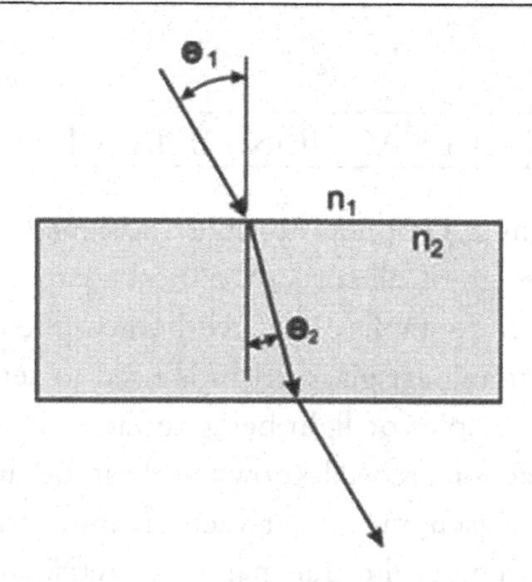

FIGURE 10
ILLUSTRATION OF SNELL'S LAW

The index of refraction of transparent materials is always greater than 1. It varies with the wavelength of the light such that longer wavelengths, toward the red end of the visible spectrum, have lower indices of refraction and are bent more than the higher wavelengths. The frequency of light in empty space is, in these cases, calculated by dividing the *apparent speed of light*, c, by the *apparent frequency*, f.

The presumption that light and other forms of electromagnetic radiation are transmitted instantaneously requires a different viewpoint when dealing with refraction, but this idea offers not only a clearer picture of the results of refraction but also the reason it occurs.

In figure 5, the lens inserted between the source and receptor in the example had flat, parallel surfaces and was inserted at right angles to the path light would have otherwise traveled between an emitting atom and a receptor atom. The light was slowed, but its path was still straight through the lens in the direction it was traveling originally. There was no refraction, just a slowing down of the light.

However, Snell's law would still apply, although it would look like this:

$$\frac{\sin\theta_1}{\sin\theta_2} = \frac{n_2}{1_1} = \frac{c}{v_2}.$$ EQUATION 14

All these relationships are based on the wavelength of light, which is simply the presumed velocity, c, in vacuum and v_2 in the transparent medium.

The whole equation is based on the *apparent speed of light*, c. If, instead, the velocity of light in a vacuum is taken as infinite, as observed by a local observer, the velocities must be corrected, using the relationship

$$\frac{v_L}{c} = \frac{\frac{v}{c}}{1-\frac{v}{c}}, \qquad \text{EQUATION 15}$$

where c is the velocity of the universe in the fourth dimension.

The use of the refractive index in the conventional Snell's equations produced a result for the velocity of light v through the transparent medium referenced to the universal coordinate system, and now this must be converted to the local coordinate system. So, where v_2 in equation 15 was the velocity of light in the transparent medium,

$$\frac{v}{c} = \frac{1}{n_2}, \qquad \text{EQUATION 16}$$

and

$$\frac{v_L}{c} = \frac{\frac{v}{c}}{1-\frac{v}{c}} = \frac{\frac{1}{n_2}}{1-\frac{1}{n_2}} = \frac{1}{n_2-1}. \qquad \text{EQUATION 17}$$

Thus, if the refractive index of the material were 1.5, the velocity of a particular beam of light passing through the transparent medium would be 2c, as compared with infinite velocity in a vacuum. The velocity of light through atmospheric air, with a refractive index of about 1.0003, would be c/0.0003=3333c.

Now, sufficient groundwork has been laid that the experiment with the orthogonal glass prism described in figure 2 can be repeated with the clear, flat lens turned at an angle to the "path" of the light radiating from the source to the receptor. With the flat glass lens turned at an angle to the light path, the lens will now act as a prism and will produce a separation in space between the points where different colors of light are received by the detector.

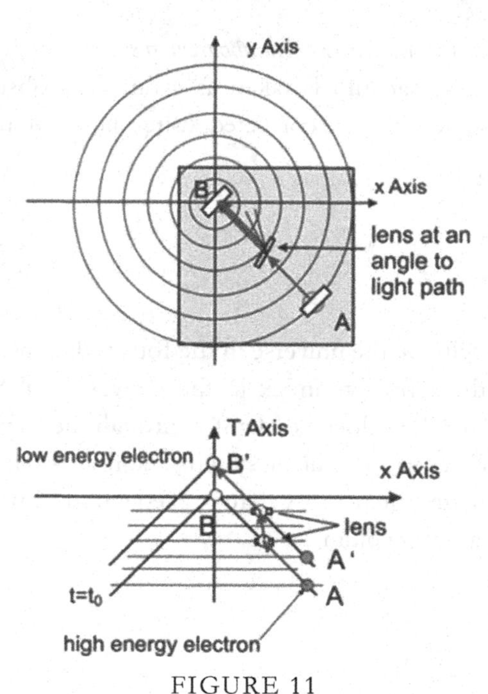

FIGURE 11
TRANSMISSION OF LIGHT THROUGH AN OBLIQUE LENS

The flat pane of glass is not as good a separator as is the familiar triangular prism, but it will produce the desired separation. The speed at which light passes through a transparent medium is determined by the physical properties of the medium and the frequency of the electrons orbiting the atoms within the source of the light.

Figure 11 is a repeat of figure 4, but instead of interposing the flat lens into the line of sight at right angles to the light path, it is inserted at an angle to the line of sight. There will of course be refraction of the light, as demonstrated by experiment.

When the light travels through the lens at different speeds, which are established by the properties of the lens and by the frequency associated primarily with the orbital velocity of the electrons in the emission source, the light of higher frequencies passes through the lens faster because each transfer takes less time than for lower frequencies. Because the light is traveling faster, it must traverse a longer distance in a given length of time. Thus the path length for the higher frequency is longer than for than for the lower frequency.

The longest path length would be if the light went directly through the glass at the same angle as it impinged on the glass, as would be the case if there were no lens there at all and the time of travel through the space would be zero. Speeds slower than infinite require a longer path length such that the lengths are equal to the thickness divided by the cosines of the angle of incidence, θ, as indicated in figure 12.

The symbol θ_S represents the angle of the shorter route taken by the lower-frequency light, and θ_L is the angle of the longer path. One can write an equation for the separations by "wavelength" based on the time of travel through the lens for each of the colors in the white light.

The speed of light through the transparent material can be calculated from:

$$v = \left(\frac{\Delta x}{n}\right)\left(\frac{1}{\Delta t}\right). \qquad \text{EQUATION 18}$$

The mechanics described lead to a slightly different interpretation of the rules of optics than contemporary physics produces, but the results of the experiments and the rules derived from them are correct. By way of defining these slightly different interpretations, it is necessary to look at the nature of the perception of light and the influence of frequency on the time delays involved in aligning the emitting and receiving atoms.

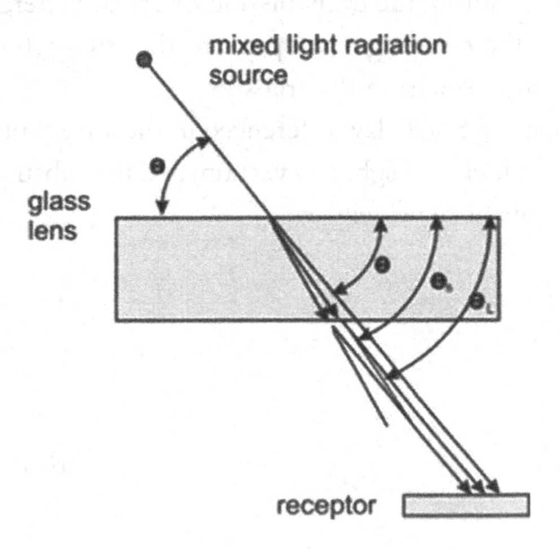

FIGURE 12
SEPARATION OF COLOR BY AN OBLIQUE LENS

The conventional expression of Snell's law

$$\frac{\sin\theta_1}{\sin\theta_2} = \frac{n_2}{n_1} = \frac{v_1}{v_2}, \qquad \text{EQUATION 19}$$

where

θ_1 = angle of incidence
θ_2 = angle of refraction
n_1 = index of refraction of the first material
n_2 = index of refraction of the second material
v_2 = velocity in medium
v_1 = apparent speed of light = c,

which references velocities to universal time. However, the measurements are made by observers using local time, so the proper interpretation of the velocities can be recast in terms of the observed velocities in the local time system, where the velocity of light is infinite.

The frequency of light can continue to be thought of as the rotational frequency of the electrons in the energized emitting electron or electron pair, and the "wavelength" as the *apparent velocity of light*, c, divided by this frequency. Physically, the wavelength is the distance the light appears to advance in the time-like T direction during the transmission of radiant energy per revolution of the electrons in the emitting atom prior to the energy transfer and in the receptor electron subsequent to the transfer.

The restatement of Snell's law referenced to the local time of the observer requires an infinite velocity of light in a vacuum and the substitution of the local velocity, v' for the universal velocity, v.

$$n = \frac{c}{v_2}, \qquad \text{EQUATION 20}$$

or

$$v = \frac{c}{n}. \qquad \text{EQUATION 21}$$

Substituting

$$v' = \frac{v}{1 - \frac{v}{c}}. \qquad \text{Equation 22}$$

$$v' = \frac{c}{n-1}. \qquad \text{Equation 23}$$

Here v' is the local velocity, and c is the velocity of the universe in the time-like T direction.

Vacuum, with a refractive index of 1.0 yields an infinite speed for light, whereas a lens with a refractive index of 1.5 yields 2c. The velocity of light in air, with a refractive index of 1.0003 gives a speed of light in air of 3333c. In each, the values of n and v refer to a specific frequency of rotation of the atoms in the inner orbit around the nucleus of the mitting atom.

The frequency of rotation of the electrons in the receptor atom prior to the transfer of radiant energy to it does not appear to have much effect on the transfer, other than to set a lower limit on the amount of energy that can be transferred. It does, however, suggest that increasing temperature of the transparent medium lengthens the time required to transfer radiant energy from an excited atom to one in a lower excitation state. Warming the transparent material should cause a slowing of the process of transferring energy from the excited atoms to those at the normal state for the ambient temperature, which will result in a decrease in the velocity of the light travel through the medium, and result in a higher refractive index at the higher temperature. This is illustrated in figure 13, which is a plot of the refractive index of water at various frequency for four temperatures.

It may be the case that this small effect is as I described it for solid media, where the molecules and atoms are bound fairly securely in place. In a liquid, the atoms and molecules are in a constant state of motion, and it might be possible that this provides more opportunities for emitter and receptor atoms to line up properly for the energy exchange in a very short time interval.

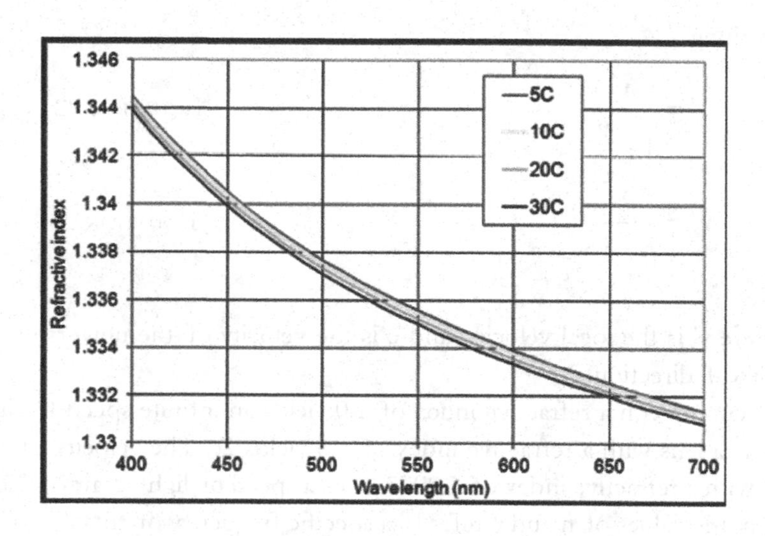

FIGURE 13
VARIATION OF IAPWS REFRACTIVE INDEX
OF WATER WITH TEMPERATURE

http://www.philiplaven.com/p20.html

ABSORPTION

The transmission of light through transparent substances is not ordinarily perfect. Some of the light incident on a surface may be reflected and some absorbed in the transparent medium. For nontransparent materials, the majority of the light incident upon its surface is reflected or absorbed. Both absorption and reflection appear to be more complex processes than transmission or refraction.

Absorption occurs when light transmitted from an original emitter finds a receptor on the surface of the absorbing material that is capable of interacting to produce a radiant energy transfer event, but where there are no immediately available internal receptors that are capable of accepting the energy absorbed by the surface atom and retransmitting it, as is the case with transparent materials.

Thus the energy transferred to the surface of the opaque material must either be retransferred to receptor atoms outside the body in question or transferred to other internal atoms that transmit it in random directions until it is eventually converted to random motion of the atoms, or heat.

Classical blackbodies are theoretically constructed solids that reflect no radiation whatever and absorb radiation of any frequency, converting all of it to heat, which results in the increase in thermodynamic internal energy of the body, measured as an increase in temperature. This is a two-way street—blackbodies also radiate light at a rate dependent upon the surface temperature.

The theoretical rate of emission from blackbodies is given by the Stefan-Boltzmann equation of radiant energy

$$P = \sigma A T^4, \qquad \text{EQUATION 24}$$

where

P = rate of energy emission, Joules/second
A = area of radiating surface, square meters
T = absolute temperature, °Kelvin.

The value of σ, the Stefan-Boltzmann constant, is given by:

$$\sigma = \frac{2\pi^5 k^4}{15c^2 h^3} - 5.670400x10^{-8}\, Joules / \sec meters^2 \,°K^{-4},$$

EQUATION 25

where

k = Boltzmann constant
c = apparent speed of light
h = Planck's constant.

True blackbodies absorb radiant energy irrespective of frequency. They do not exist in nature. Most real solids are considered to be gray bodies, which absorb only a limited amount of the incident radiation and reflect or transmit the remainder. They emit radiation at a rate which is a function of the absolute temperature of the body, according to the Stefan-Boltzmann law,

$$P = A\varepsilon\sigma T^4,$$ EQUATION 26

where

P = power, Joules/sec
A= surface area, square meters
ε = emissivity.

The emissivity of a surface is simply the fraction of the radiant energy transferred to the surface (from the inside or the outside) that is emitted to external receptor atoms. The transmittance is the fraction of the radiation that is passed through the medium, and the absorbance is the fraction that is kept within the body and converted to heat. Thus, the three factors should account for all the energy being transferred to the surface of the solid by radiation.

$$\varepsilon + \rho + A = 1.$$ EQUATION 27

All three of these quantities are functions of the frequency of the light impinging on the surface of the object, which accounts for the appearance of color in the everyday world. A true blackbody would have an emissivity of 1.0 and an absorbance and reflectivity of 0.

A very perfect mirror would have a reflectance of 1.0 and emissivity and absorbance of 0.

A perfect pane of glass would have a transmittance of 1.0 and emissivity and absorbance of 0.

All objects may be considered to have all three properties to some extent. A pane of glass may show a reflection of our faces on the surface if the lighting conditions are right yet transmit most of the light from brightly lit objects on the other side to our eyes while absorbing a small fraction of sunlight to make the pane warm to the touch.

This is also true of less apparent cases, such as the passage of X-rays through a petroleum pipeline to look for internal flaws in the welding. Visible light is the only form of radiation we are adept at sensing and interpreting, but all forms or radiant energy follow the same patterns.

Light, as we experience it, originates mainly from the sun and to a much smaller degree from the tungsten filaments in lightbulbs, the fluorescent coatings in fluorescent lamps, and the chemiluminescent tails of fireflies—but mostly from the sun.

The sun's rays consist of a broad spectrum of radiation, only a fraction of which is in the visible light range. The light we can see is associated with emissions largely from hydrogen atoms and helium atoms at very high temperatures. However, hydrogen and helium atoms are not the only possible sources of visible light. Heavier atoms, such as tungsten in lightbulb filaments, are also capable of producing visible light when heated to temperatures in the range of 2000°C. In general, the radiation emissions from all bodies increases as the temperature of the emitting surface increases.[4]

[4] Black body curves of Planck for various temperatures and comparison with classical theory of Rayleigh-Jeans, from Darth Kule, as published online in Wikipedia, June 2010. http://en.wikipedia.org/wiki/File:Black_body.svg (2010-06-05).

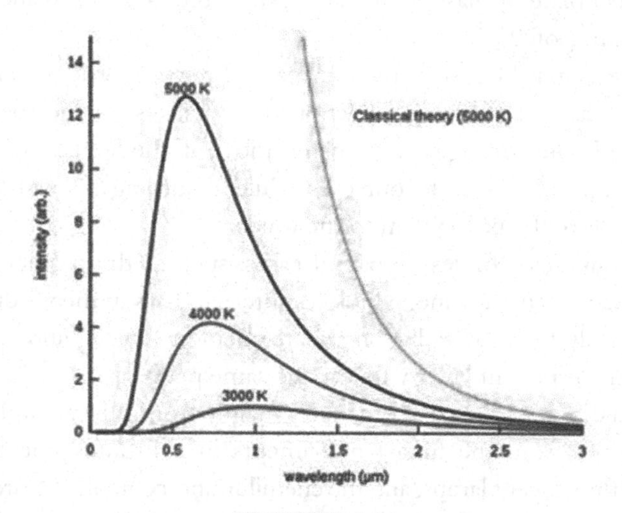

FIGURE 14
RADIATION ENERGY VS TEMPERATURE FOR BLACK BODIES

The frequencies of radiation from blackbodies (or gray bodies, which do not emit all frequencies) are plotted in figure 14. Here and in the following paragraphs, frequency and wavelength are classically defined, and the evidence indicating that there are no "light waves" is ignored.

Planck's law relates the frequency of the radiation to the temperature and is the basis for the above curve.

$$(f,T)df = \frac{2hf^3}{c^2}\left(\frac{1}{e^{\frac{hf}{kT}}-1}\right)df, \qquad \text{Equation 28}$$

where

E = energy per unit time in the frequency interval dv
h = Planck's constant
c = *apparent speed of light* in a vacuum
k = Boltzmann constant
f = frequency of radiation
T = temperature in °Kelvin.

The frequency at which the power per unit frequency is maximized is given by Wein's law,

$$\lambda = \frac{.002897}{T}, \qquad \text{EQUATION 29}$$

where λ = "wavelength."

As

$$f = \frac{c}{\lambda}, \qquad \text{EQUATION 30}$$

the maximum frequency of emission at any given temperature is approximately

$$f = \frac{cT}{257.19}. \qquad \text{EQUATION 31}$$

This is the frequency of the orbiting electrons in the surface atoms of the blackbody giving rise to the radiation.

To be consistent with the theory of the nature of electromagnetic radiation presented here, the light from both the sun and the lightbulb filament arise from the rotational energy of the electrons in the innermost atomic shell.

While the velocity of the electron may be a substantial fraction of the energy level necessary to cause the electron to escape from its orbital path (the ionizing energy level), this is not at all true for, say, a cold tungsten element in a lightbulb that is turned off. The greater positive charge on the nucleus of the tungsten atom allows much higher velocities of the electrons in the inner orbit.

This does not preclude the tungsten atom from reradiating to another potential receptor directly in the line of sight to the original source, but it is much more likely that it will radiate to another tungsten atom within the same crystalline structure that will not direct the radiation toward a timely exit. In short, the movement of the radiant energy within the tungsten crystal structure is likely to preclude transparency to visible light. Most of the radiant energy impinging of the surface of a tungsten crystal will be either reflected or absorbed, and the tungsten will become slightly warmer as a result. Thus we would say that tungsten has a relatively high absorbance for visible light, moderate reflectivity, and essentially no transmissivity.

Most materials, including tungsten, have a very distinctive pattern of absorption of visible light and tend to reflect frequencies that we interpret as the color of the material. Green paint, for example, tends to absorb most of the light in the visible spectrum that falls on its surface but to reflect the frequency range that we see as green. Green paint comes in a wide variety of hues but also in several groups with respect to the degree of dispersion of the reflected light. High-gloss enamels tend to appear almost mirrorlike, reflecting the green and other frequencies in a very regular pattern, while flat finishes appear dull and do not have the shiny, mirrorlike quality.

The "easy" paints to manufacture are those that reflect substantially all the visible light spectrum—the white paints—and those that reflect none—the black ones. They use pigments to produce the desired reflectivity, which are quite simple chemically, like titanium dioxide, TiO_2, for white paints and carbon black, C, for black ones.

Colors in between require a wide variety of often complex dye materials to bring about the reflectivity we expect. However, the important aspect of the discussion of color is that the light we perceive when we look at a green-painted shutter did not originate in the shutter, but rather in the sun or in some device that mimics the sun's ability to generate visible light over the entire frequency spectrum we are capable of seeing.

REFLECTION

The reflection of light appears to be a more complex process than either transmission or refraction. Both of the phenomena considered so far have to do with the properties of the transparent medium through which light is transmitted from a source to a receptor. Reflection seems to be independent of the properties of the bulk material and is involved mainly with the surface rather than the properties of the bulk material. Thus a highly polished piece of steel and the surface of a perfectly quiescent pond may both appear to be excellent mirrors, although they have markedly different levels of absorptivity and transmissivity.

To be highly reflective, the surface must be very smooth. That is, it must have essentially no microscopic hills or valleys. Also, it must be composed of material which has the ability to receive radiation from across the whole visible light spectrum and to reemit it without any change in the orientation of the atoms having taken place during the extremely short time required for the absorption and retransmission to take place.

The frequency of orbiting electrons in the emission source atom is exchanged essentially without change to intermediate atoms and finally to the receptors in our eyes or in photoelectric detectors or cameras. It is the energy level of the emitting electrons that establishes the "frequency" of the light being transmitted. This frequency affects the index of absorption and of refraction of the light. However, it seems to have no influence in the case of reflection.

Still water surfaces, highly polished metal surfaces, and silvered mirrors all produce very crisp, well-defined, reflected pictures of ourselves and the world around us. The picture does not seem to depend on the properties of the mirroring substance, other than that it be very smooth and completely reflective.

The simplest case is that of orthogonal reflection. This is what one sees in the mirror every morning. The mirror is at right angles to our line of sight, so the light appears to leave our faces, strike the mirror, and return directly back to where it came from. This is also, incidentally, the essence of Michelson's classic experiment to measure the speed of light.

This arrangement is shown in figure 2, the lab table with a simple optical experiment set up on it. Instead of a transparent glass lens, picture a high-quality mirror mounted at the center of the table, and the light source being moved over next to the receptor—a supersensitive photocell.

Here the cone representing the local universe at the present moment in the two-dimensional analog of the real 3-D universe is shown with an atom (the receptor) in the "unexcited" state and ready to serve as a receptor for radiant energy from any suitably excited atom at the right place in space and time at the cone's apex. You might imagine that the atom is yourself looking in the mirror expecting to see your own image.

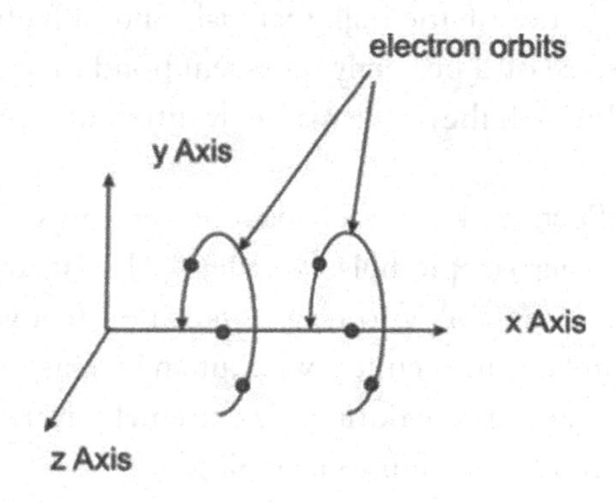

FIGURE 15
CONDITION FOR RADIANT ENERGY TRANSFER

An earlier version of yourself stood before the mirror just a picosecond before, and light that originated in the sun reflected off an atom in your face (along with many other atoms; but for now, just one is considered). In order to see your face in the mirror, there must be atoms in the mirror that are precisely aligned with some of the receptors in your eye (ignoring the intervening lens in your eye for the moment).

The mirror is presumed to be directly in front of you, so your line of vision is perpendicular to the mirror in three-dimensional space. As only the x direction is shown in the diagram, in addition to the T direction, one must imagine that the atoms are so aligned that the electron orbits in the three-dimensional world are parallel and at right angles to the x axis, as shown in figure 15.

In three-dimensional space, the two orbital planes are perfectly aligned, both lying in the y–z plane, although at different values along the T axis.

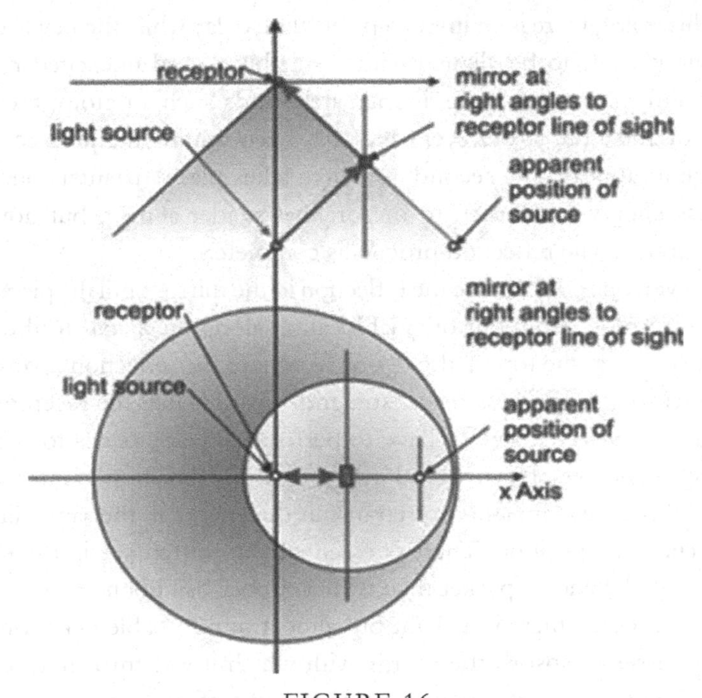

FIGURE 16
REFLECTION IN A MIRROR AT 90 DEGREES

The electrons are not synchronized or lined up in the y–z plane, nor are they necessarily moving at the same velocity. However, it should be clear that if there were a third dimension, z shown in the picture, the z dimension (perhaps the height above the lab table) would have to be equal for both the receptor and the mirror.

Now, to receive light from the earlier version of yourself, the earlier version must also be aligned perfectly with the orbital path of the electrons in the atom in the mirror. Again, the electrons are not expected to be in synchronism with the mirror's electrons, but they must be in planes exactly parallel in space and placed such that they may be made to overlap by superposition on the surface of the universal kernel. This requires that they lie on a line forming an element of the mirror's local present time—a line of sight—and that the spacing in the T direction (essentially, the time difference between them) meet exacting criteria.

When these conditions are all satisfied, then and only then can the transfer of energy take place from the source atom to the mirror. And it does.

At this point, there is an imperceptible time delay while the newly excited mirror atom waits to be aligned with a suitably placed unexcited receptor atom. It almost, but not quite, immediately finds such an atom, the future position of the atom in our eye, which has been waiting the picosecond for the image to appear. The second exchange takes place instantaneously, and the excess energy is returned to the original sender almost, but not quite, instantaneously. The reflection process is complete.

However, one does not see the reflection in the mirror until the picosecond it takes us to move from our original location along the T axis to the future location, shown at the top of the figure 16, where the reflection is observed.

The reason this process seems straightforward is that the receptor atom in the mirror surface does not have to perform any acrobatics to complete the reflection process. It is oriented with the proper direction to interact with the original source atom and can retransmit the energy in the same direction without changing position. There is essentially no difference in the reversal of course of the energy packet than with a rubber ball bouncing off a brick wall. In both cases, there is a slight but almost unnoticeable delay while the ball compresses to absorb the energy with which it was thrown against the wall and the time when it expands, releasing most of the energy.

The image one sees, or that which is seen by the receptor on the lab bench, appears to be on the far side of the mirror at a distance just equal to the distance between the real source and the mirror. What has happened is that the line of sight, along which the light source would have been seen from the receptor if it were turned so as to see the light directly from the source, has been replaced, at least for distances beyond the mirror, by the lines of sight that comprise the local universe of the mirror. Because you cannot see through the mirror, the light received by way of reflection from the mirror takes the place of any light that would have come from the direction of the mirror were it not in the way.

The mirror presents a picture that has been rotated by 180 degrees, so that instead of seeing the light source adjacent to the receptor, it now appears to be well behind it, at an azimuth angle of 180 degrees rather than 0 degrees.

As was the case with refraction, the case of a mirror turned at an angle to the incident light source is more complicated. The mirror cannot be turned at an angle to the T dimension, so it is necessary to look at the top view in the schematic shown in figure 17 to illustrate oblique reflection.

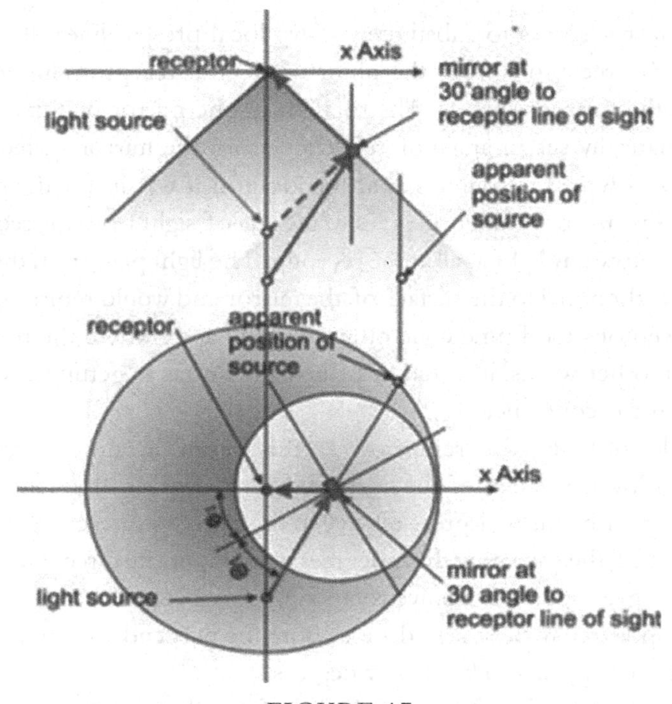

FIGURE 17
REFLECTION IN AN OBLIQUE MIRROR

In figure 17, the mirror is turned at an angle of thirty degrees with respect to the receptor at the origin. It cannot show the viewer events in the future before one arrives there, so it is necessary for the viewer to see something that is in his local present. The mirror must be in his local present for him to see it.

Although the images that appear in the mirror may not be in the viewer's present, they must be in the local present time for the mirror and in the viewer's local past.

In figure 17, the mirror is turned thirty degrees counterclockwise to its position in figure 16. This is, by the simple geometry of the situation, the angle of reflectance that will be measured by the receptor at the origin, or the apex of the cone representing the *local present universe.*

This cone is represented by the larger circle in the lower schematic and by the forty-five-degree lines in the upper one. The smaller circles in figure 17 represent the cone that comprises the mirror's *local present time.* The source must be in the mirror's *local present time* to transfer radiant energy to it, meaning it must be on the surface of the smaller cone.

The mirror serves to substitute its own local present lines of sight for those of the receptors from the point where the receptors line of sight intersects the mirror's surface. The rotation of the mirror by thirty degrees has automatically set an angle of reflection from the mirror surface to the receptor, and were the source still at the location it was in for the previous case, with the mirror at ninety degrees to the line of sight from the receptor, it would not show any light at all at the receptor. The light path from the source would be orthogonal to the surface of the mirror and would return to a point on the receptor's local time cone other than the apex where the receptor is located. In other words, it would miss the boat, so far as getting a reflection in the mirror is concerned.

We do not see the reflection at this point in time because the counterclockwise rotation of the mirror by thirty degrees offset the location of the receptor by thirty degrees relative to the mirror's surface. It also offset the location of the source by thirty degrees in the opposite direction, resulting in a sixty-degree apparent relative rotation of the image. Whereas the image originally appeared to be at zero degrees from the perpendicular to the mirror surface, it now appears to be at sixty degrees.

Thus the angle of incidence of the light from the source to the receptor appears to be thirty degrees, just equal to the angle of incidence, and both are equal to the angle of rotation of the mirror from the direct line of sight.

Obviously, reflection works and produces images in which left and right are interchanged but up and down are not reversed. Mirrors can be made of all sorts of materials, from water, which serves moderately well if it is still and clear, to silvered glass, to polished chromium, as well as many metals that are crystalline and many kinds of glass that are noncrystalline. What the mirrors all have in common is that they must have extremely smooth surfaces so that the surface is flat and clearly defined and does not contain much in the way of microscopic irregularities. In order for the mirror to know which way to direct the light it receives, it has to have a surface whose direction is very clearly defined and the same orientation at every point.

The question is how does the absorber/reemitter atom line up properly with both the source and the ultimate receptor when they do not lie in a straight line perpendicular to the mirror surface? In short, why should the angle of reflectance equal the angle of incidence?

In order for an atom in the mirror's surface to transmit radiant energy toward the receptor at the origin, it must be aligned exactly with the orbital plane of the receptor.

The mirror functions as a mirror because of the property of having many atoms aligned so they will be able to match both the source and ultimate receptor atomic alignments. It is likely that this condition requires that the positions of surface atoms, which are relatively fixed in solids, be such that the orbits are parallel with the surface of the mirror and therefore with other atoms in the surface of the mirror. Thus the orbital planes of the mirror's surface atoms are locked in place, and many of them are parallel to the surface. The receptor atom orbits are not so likely to be similarly locked in place or are more randomly distributed. A receptor can be presumed to align with the mirror's orientation in order to complete a radiant energy transfer event.

In order for the mirror to receive the radiation from the emission source, the emission source must also be exactly aligned with the mirror atom in all three of the normal spatial dimensions and must be in the local present of the mirror. The local present of the mirror will have only one element of the local present in common with the local present of the ultimate receptor and one element in common with the source. All things in the direction from the receptor to the mirror but beyond the mirror will be obscured by the mirror. All the other elements of the local present of the mirror will lie within the local past of the receptor.

In order for the orbital planes of the receptor, the mirror, and the source to all lie parallel in all three dimensions, the orbits of the atoms in the source must be aligned with the surface of the mirror and so must the orbits of the ultimate receptor, as shown in figure 16. Here it will be seen that the angle of reflection—the angle of the arrow from the mirror to the receptor—exactly matches the angle the mirror is turned with respect to the direct line of sight. The angle between the line of sight from the receptor to the mirror and from the mirror to the source appears to be exactly ninety degrees. This is not accidental, and will always be the case with reflected light or other forms of radiation. The point of great interest here is that as the rotation of the mirror is changed from zero degrees (exactly facing the receptor), the location of the source needed to have the radiation relayed via the mirror to the receptor must move away from the receptor. The distance was zero in the initial case with the mirror at right angles, and it becomes infinitely distant as the mirror rotation approaches ninety degrees.

It will appear to the observer at the origin that the original source, which he sees as a reflection, will not be directly at the center of the mirror in his line of sight but rather at a position along the x axis at the appropriate distance behind the mirror. What he will see as the angle of incidence is exactly his own angle of reflection.

This also has some significance in explaining how the surface of water acts as a mirror to some extent and appears more reflective as the angle of reflection (the angle the line of sight of the viewer makes with the surface of the water) increases.

Finally, it casts some light (no pun intended here) on the reason why colors are perceived. The atoms that constitute strong reflectors of color of one or another light frequency have atoms within them that are aligned with the surface and have only a limited capability of absorbing and retransmitting light. This implies a pair of electrons orbiting a nucleus of an atom in which the orbital velocity range is very limited. In short, hydrogen atoms cannot be the principle constituent of the dye, because they are in most circumstances capable of handling many of the frequencies of visible light.

CONCLUSIONS

All the commonly recognized properties of light, including the optical laws of absorption, emission, transmission through transparent substances, refraction, and reflection are compatible with the proposition that light is transferred instantaneously from one atom to another, even when the two atoms in question are separated by considerable distances in both space and time.

In fact, the proposed nature of light makes some of the properties, such as the finite velocities of light in transparent materials and the refraction of light, easier to understand. It does not require light to have a wavelength or frequency, nor does it hint at any wave/particle duality.

Some of the necessary properties of mirrors are explained, at least superficially, by the requirement that they have many surface atoms with electron orbital planes that can be exactly parallel with the bulk surface. This property is the one that gives a reflective material its reflective properties.

Dyes and other materials perceived to have strong colors are composed of material that can serve as reflectors (but not mirrors) for only a selected few frequencies. They are likely to be of considerably more complex molecular structure than hydrogen.

CHAPTER 3

MAKING PEACE WITH PLANCK

The essence of this story is that Planck's constant, defined by

$$E = hf\,, \qquad \text{EQUATION 32}$$

where

E = energy of a photon
h = Planck's constant
f = frequency of light wave,

appears to relate to the perceived frequency of light waves but does not adequately represent the energy levels of the orbiting electrons that emit the energy we perceive as light.

In the previous book, it was suggested that Planck's constant is completely inappropriate when dealing with the energy of the orbiting electrons in the inner orbit of hydrogen and other atoms and that the energy involved is proportional to the square of the frequency. This is true of essentially all processes involving energy associated with rotation, oscillation, or wave actions. So I recommended using a different version of Planck's constant,

$$E = Hf^2\,, \qquad \text{EQUATION 33}$$

which fits the energy transfer description involved in my alternative theory of light transmission.

However, when the emission spectrum of hydrogen at high temperature is broken down in frequency by a prism or spectrograph, the distinctive emission bands have "frequencies" that are proportional to the energy transfer, as suggested by the Planck's constant in equation 30.

When energy is transferred from one atom to another, the energy of the emitting and the receiving atoms are respectively decreased and increased by an amount of energy that is in proportion to the difference in the square of the frequencies. This is the amount of energy that is transferred and is characterized by

$$\Delta E = H(f_2^2 - f_1^2)\,. \qquad \text{EQUATION 34}$$

When the eye perceives the transmission of this sort of packet of energy, it does not respond in proportion to the energy content but rather to a perceived frequency. The perceived frequency of the transmitted light is established much in the same way the frequencies are separated by a prism.

That is, the frequency of the electron orbit changes, rather than the energy involved, is what determines the speed of light in the transparent optical material and therefore the degree of refraction or separation of the various frequencies in a prism. Thus it appears that, while Planck's relationship does not describe the energy levels involved in the transmission of radiation, it does accurately describe the frequency of light perceived by the eye or by the degree of separation of the emission bands on a spectrograph.

The apparent conflict between the two expressions can only be resolved by differentiating between the frequency of the orbiting electrons in an atom and the perceived frequency based on the bending of light in by a prism or the lens of the human eye. So,

$$E = H(F_2^2 - F_1^2) = hf \qquad \text{EQUATION 35}$$

where

F = orbital frequency, sec^{-1}
f = perceived frequency of light, sec^{-1}.

This does not in any way impact the presentation of the model of the hydrogen atom and atoms of heavier elements presented in the previous book.

The use of Planck's constant by Bohr in the development of his model of the hydrogen atom was inappropriate, as the electron orbits do not have wavelike properties in themselves. However, the use of Planck's constant seems to be justified when dealing with the perceived frequency of light or other radiation, either by the human eye, by lens or glass prism, or by other optical device.

CHAPTER 4

ROTATION OF ELECTRONS AND PROTONS

It has been argued in this book that light is transmitted energy that moves from the orbiting electrons in one atom to those in another by direct contact. This contact occurs through space and time by virtue of the entire universe being wrapped around a tiny five-dimensional hypersphere on which the emitter and receptor atoms touch each other.

The analysis of electrostatic and electromagnetic "forces" suggested that the warping of the 3-D universe that occurs in the vicinity of charges represents a swirling or rotating effect on time in the space surrounding the charges. The swirl around the electrons goes one way and that around the protons goes the other. This accounts for the electrostatic attraction and repulsion, and also for the magnetic forces.

However, it does not explain why the warping of space does not affect uncharged particles unless there is a secondary effect on space that amounts to an offsetting effect in the opposite direction of the depression caused by the swirl. This is very much like an antigravity effect, in that it causes the time vectors in the space around the charged particles to bulge outward, forming a hill that offsets the depression in the vicinity of isolated charged particles so that they have no effect on the space around them other than the slight gravitational effect of their masses.

A New Light on the Expanding Universe presented this, but there was no hint as to how the swirling effect came about or what relationship between electrons and protons causes one to go one way and the other the opposite direction.

Some additional thought on the subject led me to an interesting speculation. There is no physical basis for this, and it must be regarded as simply a possible explanation for some otherwise inexplicable things.

REVISING THE KERNEL

The protons in the nucleus of an atom and the electrons surrounding them occupied essentially the same location on the surface of the five-dimensional hypersphere, around which were wound all space, matter, and the fourth spatial dimension, T, through which the universe is expanding at the velocity c. The picture was as shown in figure 18.

The circumference of the kernel was presumed to be equal to the radius of the orbit of the hydrogen atom, or r_0, and was presumed to be the same for all atoms.

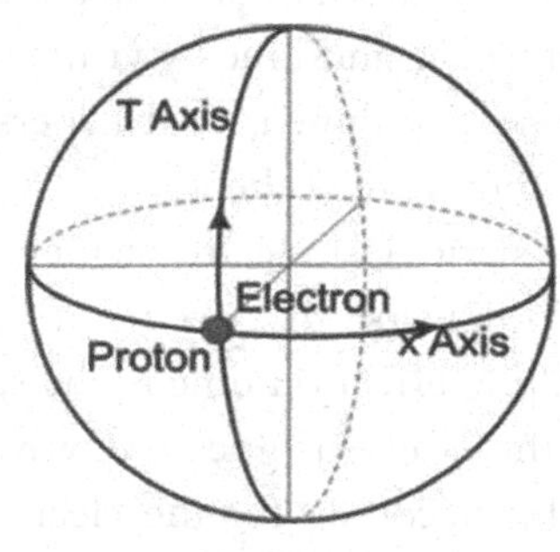

FIGURE 18
THE X-T PLANE WRAPPED AROUND THE X-T-U KERNEL

However, the question of why the protons and electrons have opposite spin directions raises questions about this picture and the possibly that the kernel is twice as large as previously assumed. If so, the circumference would be $2r_0$, and the radius would be

$$r = \frac{r_0}{\pi}. \qquad \text{Equation 36}$$

The picture would now look like figure 19, with the electron on one side of the kernel and the proton on the other. Because light is totally dependent on the exchange of energy between the electrons, with the protons merely acting as anchors for them, there would be no loss of generality in the ability of the atoms to exchange orbital velocity, just as postulated in the first book.

It is apparent that rotation around the axis of the kernel, which has an electron at one end and a proton at the other end, would produce rotation of both the particles and the space around them, as required to account for electrodynamic properties of electrons and protons. Because they are on opposite sides of the hypersphere, the electron and proton will spin in opposite directions. The spin is complex because there are protons and electrons scattered all around the equator of the hypersphere, each with its own "private" T axis. This requires the hypersphere to be spinning in all directions at the same time.

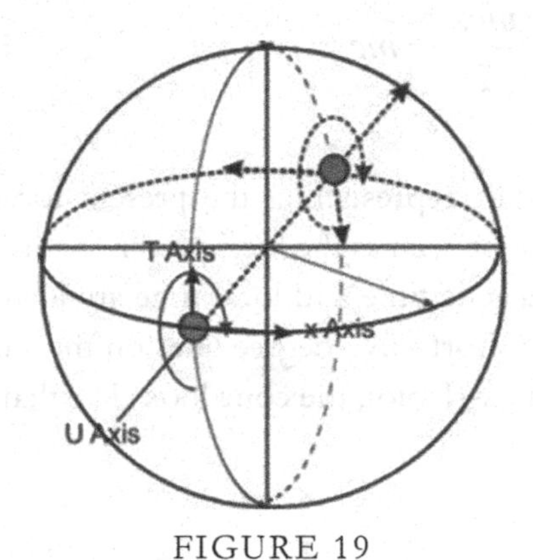

FIGURE 19
ROTATION OF THE KERNEL AROUND THE T AXIS

This would be difficult for a three-dimensional sphere but apparently easy for one with five dimensions.

Also, the electrons and protons located at right angles to the ones shown will have their own spin around their T axes and in addition will be rotating at the radius r around the T axis for the proton and electron shown.

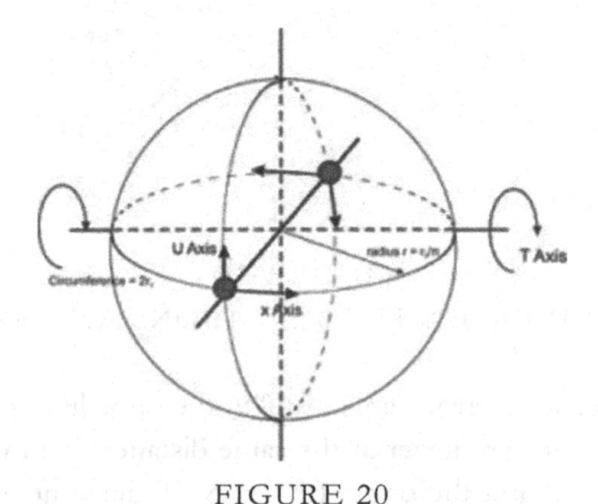

FIGURE 20
KERNEL WITH U AND X AXES, ROTATION AROUND T AXIS

The rotation with the electron and proton located at the quarter points between two T axes around which rotation is taking place shows the velocity of these points in the U direction is c, at right angles to the three spatial dimensions and the T dimension, adding another energy term to that based on the movement at the apparent velocity of light in the T direction:

$$E = \frac{mc_T^2}{2} + \frac{mc_U^2}{2} = mc^2. \qquad \text{EQUATION 37}$$

How does the cone, representing the present local time, fit onto the kernel, and what would be seen as the local present by an observer at the apex of the cone, where galactic time and local time are identical? Here, the rays of the cone show up as forty-five-degree lines on the surface of the x–T, or y–T or z–T plots. In an x–T plot, the cone looks like that shown in figure 21.

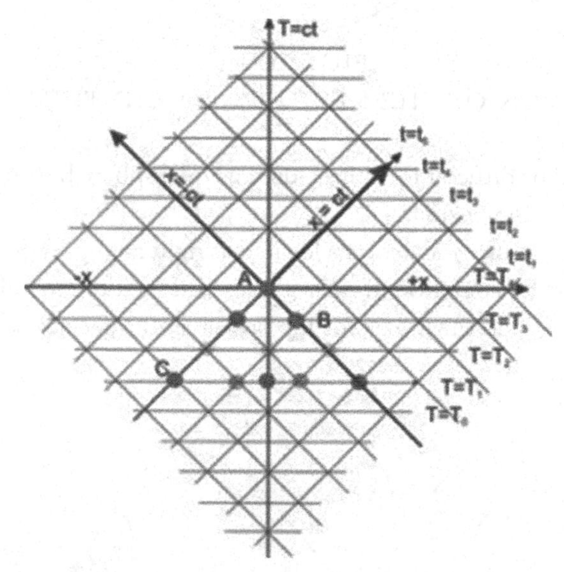

FIGURE 21
LOCAL UNIVERSE WITH ELECTRONS AND PROTONS

The protons and electrons are all still in the same lines of sight, but the difference is that they are never at the same distance from the origin. That is, if there is a proton at the origin (the apex of the cone representing the local present), then the electrons will be at the next level down, where there will be no protons. The protons, if there are any forming compounds with the proton at the origin, have to be in the second level down, or the fourth, or sixth—only even-numbered steps. The electrons in the outer shells, or in other atoms forming a compound, have to be on the odd-numbered layers: one, three, five …

In this picture, the electrons spin one direction and the protons the other, as they are on opposite ends of the same rotating axis. Both have the energy mc^2, half of which comes from translation in the T direction, and half from translation in the U direction, which is related to rotation around the T axis.

The only thing I am having trouble with at the moment is the neutral particles, which could very well be formed by the combination of an electron and a proton.

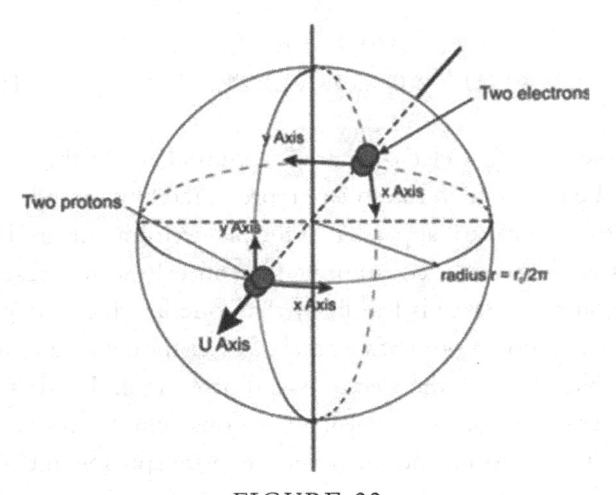

FIGURE 22
THE HYDROGEN MOLECULE WRAPPED AROUND THE UNIVERSAL KERNEL

The combination must be made in such a way that the spin of the electron and proton are retained, because there is nowhere for the energy to go when a neutron is formed by combination of an electron and proton. If one assumes that the neutrons and protons cluster together at the nucleus of heavier atoms than helium, the inner orbit still contains the two relatively mobile electrons, while a second orbital level is available at twice the orbital radius.

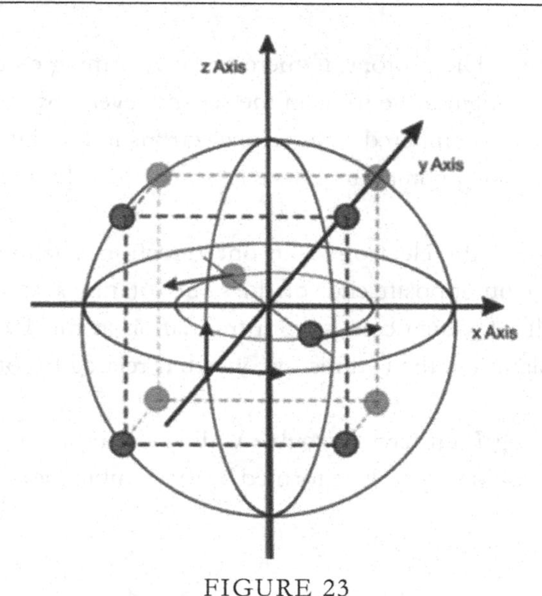

FIGURE 23
ELEMENT WITH TWO COMPLETE ELECTRON SHELLS

In this picture, eight electrons are accommodated at the corners of an imaginary cube inscribed in the sphere represented by the circle in figure 23.

By way of summary, it appears that the picture of a universal kernel with the protons and electrons constituting an entire local universe occupying a single site on the surface is less likely than one in which the protons and electrons are on opposite sides of a kernel of twice the diameter. This accounts for the opposite spins of the electrons and protons, and adds some weight to the argument that both electrons and protons spin in two directions: one the time-like T dimension, and the other the more ephemeral U direction.

CHAPTER 5

HOW FAR BACK CAN WE SEE IN TIME?

When looking into outer space from any present position in space and time, one sees the universe stretching out in all directions. We can see into space so far away that we cannot distinguish stars or even galaxies. However, telescopes gather more light than can be seen with unaided eyes, and objects that are farther away can be distinguished.

Presumably, increased size and perfection of telescopic lenses would allow us to see things at much greater distances. Is there a limit as to how far back in *galactic time* we can see? Would vastly more powerful telescopes be able to see stars and galaxies all the way back to the time of the big bang? The purpose of this chapter is to explore the limitations that may prevent anyone from ultimately witnessing the beginning of the universe, even with the use of the ultimate telescope. It will also suggest that the properties of light itself prevent us from seeing anything more distant than about two-thirds the diameter of the present universe—and only a small fraction of that.

The search for the outer limits requires a more sophisticated analysis of the way light travels over great distances and explains the shortcomings of the approximate methods for measuring distances to nearby stars and galaxies. These are very good approximations, as long as the distances and time periods are small compared to the overall size and age of the universe.

In addition, the look backward provides some indication that the velocity of recession of the galaxies does not appear to follow Hubble's constant for those farthest away. This gives some weight to the argument for a universe built along the lines advocated here rather than on conventional cosmology.

THE SHAPE OF THE LOCAL UNIVERSE

The previous book, *A New Light on the Expanding Universe*, described the present three-dimensional universe as a three-dimensional surface of a four-dimensional hypersphere that is quite uniform in size and expanding at the velocity c, the *apparent speed of light*, in the fourth-dimensional direction.

However, a human observer cannot actually see any of this hypersphere at its present location (at the present *galactic time*), save the tiny space he occupies at the moment. All the rest of it lies in the observer's *local future*. What one can actually see at any given instant is a view of the universe as it was, by galactic time standards—just a nanosecond ago for objects that are close at hand and up to millions of years in the past when the most distant stars are viewed through telescopes. What he can see is described here as his *local universe* at the *local present*.

The local universe is what one sees when looking out the window or looking into the night sky. Everything seen is in the *galactic past* but comprises our *local present*. The difference in these two systems is negligible for objects close at hand and for velocities that are relatively low compared to the *apparent speed of light*. For measurements that stretch out to a substantial fraction of the size of the entire universe, the differences are enormous. The galactic universe used by physicists is no longer approximated adequately by making measurements in the local universe and using them without correction.

The assumption that nearby space is linear rather than curved and that light moves in straight lines between two points, creates errors. It is necessary to look critically at this approximations and to correct for the errors in order to get the larger picture, which is very different when it includes distances that are significant as compared with the size of the entire universe.

For locating nearby objects in space, the shape of the three-dimensional galactic universe can be represented to be like the surface of a two-dimensional balloon expanding in the fourth-dimensional direction. This is not quite the shape of the *local universe* at any given instant.

Because the three-dimensional universe is vast and the dimensions so large that the portions of it close by do not have any apparent curvature, this linear model appears quite precise.

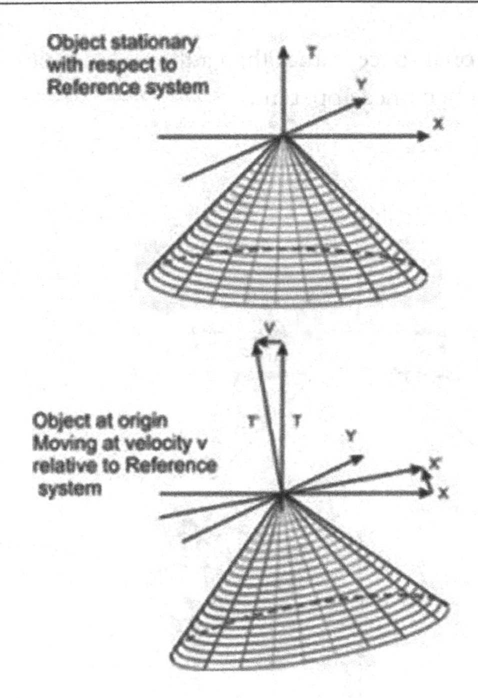

FIGURE 24
THE LOCAL SHAPE OF THE LOCAL UNIVERSE

The *local universe*, when limited to the relatively nearby volume of space (say a few light-years in any direction from the observer's location), can be presumed to be a cone with its apex just touching the surface of the hypersphere representing the *galactic universe*. All the things one can see at any given instant are located within the surface of a cone, as shown in figure 24.

Close to the observer, the cone appears to have straight sides and a ninety-degree apex angle if the T dimension is depicted with units of the same scale as the space dimensions. The "viewer's lines of sight" are straight lines extending outward at forty-five degrees to the horizontal plane representing the *galactic present.*

SHORTCOMINGS OF THE LINEAR MODEL

This model is based on an approximation to the true picture. If the area under observation is expanded somewhat, the curvature of space (or the surface of a balloon representing the present universe as a two-dimensional thing in a three-dimensional space, rather than a three-dimensional thing in a four-dimensional space) becomes apparent.

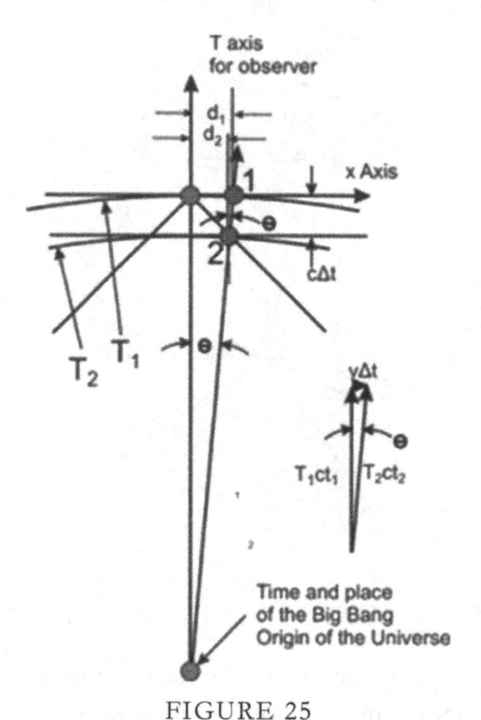

FIGURE 25
ILLUSTRATION OF THE ERROR IN THE LINEAR MODEL

The measurement of points along the surface can be approximated by the straight-line distances along the x axis, but in reality they are the distances along the curved surface. The distance to an object, such as a galaxy, seen through a telescope to be at point 1 is not exactly the distance measured along the x axis. It is instead the distance along the curved path from the observer to point 2 in the curved path at time T_2 in figure 25. This distance is exactly

$$s = T_2\theta = ct_2\theta \qquad \text{Equation 38}$$

where

$$T_2 = ct_2 \qquad \text{Equation 39}$$

$$\theta = \frac{s}{T_2}. \qquad \text{Equation 40}$$

The velocity of the object in question, due to the expansion of the universe, is the distance traveled in three-dimensional space divided by the time since it started moving away from the big bang,

$$v = \frac{s}{t}. \qquad \text{EQUATION 41}$$

Because

$$T = ct, \qquad \text{EQUATION 42}$$

$$\frac{v}{c} = \theta. \qquad \text{EQUATION 43}$$

The linear model would have equated the velocity to be only the component of velocity parallel to the x axis, or

$$\frac{v'}{c} = \sin\theta, \qquad \text{EQUATION 44}$$

where the primes represent values referenced to the galactic system of coordinates and unprimed values to the local system of measurement.

In order to correct the linear model for the curvature of space, it is necessary to multiply the accurate distance value observed by

$$\frac{v}{v'} = \frac{\theta}{\sin\theta} \qquad \text{EQUATION 45}$$

to obtain the linear approximation. Unfortunately, there is no simple method for computing this ratio other than using the sine of θ, but it can be approximated by using the series approximation for the sine of an angle:

$$\sin\theta = \theta - \frac{\theta^3}{3!} + \frac{\theta^5}{5!} - \frac{\theta^7}{7!} + \ldots \qquad \text{EQUATION 46}$$

Because our observations of events in the past are limited to about the last half of the life of the universe, the angle θ is between $-\pi/4$ and

$+\pi/4$, so θ is always less than 1 in in the area of interest. The sine can be approximated by

$$\sin\theta \approx \theta - \frac{\theta^3}{3!}\,, \qquad \text{EQUATION 47}$$

and the ratio of velocities for distances along the arc to velocity measured along the chord by

$$\frac{v}{v'} \cong \frac{\theta}{\theta - \frac{\theta^3}{3!}} = \frac{1}{1 - \frac{\theta^2}{6}}\,. \qquad \text{EQUATION 48}$$

This correction factor is used when correcting for the error in measurement when the distance along the chord is taken as the distance around the arc, whether dealing with the present universe or the hypersphere representing an earlier expansion stage. The approximation in equation 48 produces an error of less than 1 percent when dealing with local velocities between zero and the highest velocity we can measure. For practical purposes, there is no reason to correct for the curvature of space in the fourth-dimensional direction, as it is negligible in most cases. It is simpler to think of the model using radial coordinates and simply avoid using the linear approximation.

THE FIRST APPROXIMATION

A much larger picture of the universe must also take into account that the lines of sight, heretofore assumed to be straight lines at all points, are probably curved also.

In the local universe, they appear to be at forty-five degrees relative to the surface, or rather from a plane tangent to the surface, of the sphere representing the galactic universe. This seems to be true when the coordinates for distance and time are chosen as consistent units. That is, if distance is chosen in light-years or light-seconds and time in years or seconds. It also appears to be true for fairly large distances, but extension of this notion to time and distance extending beyond any means of observation is speculative.

With this caveat, it is reasonable to assume that light is always emitted from and received by atoms located on lines that lie at a forty-five-degree angle to the surface of the sphere representing the universe as an expanding two-dimensional balloon.

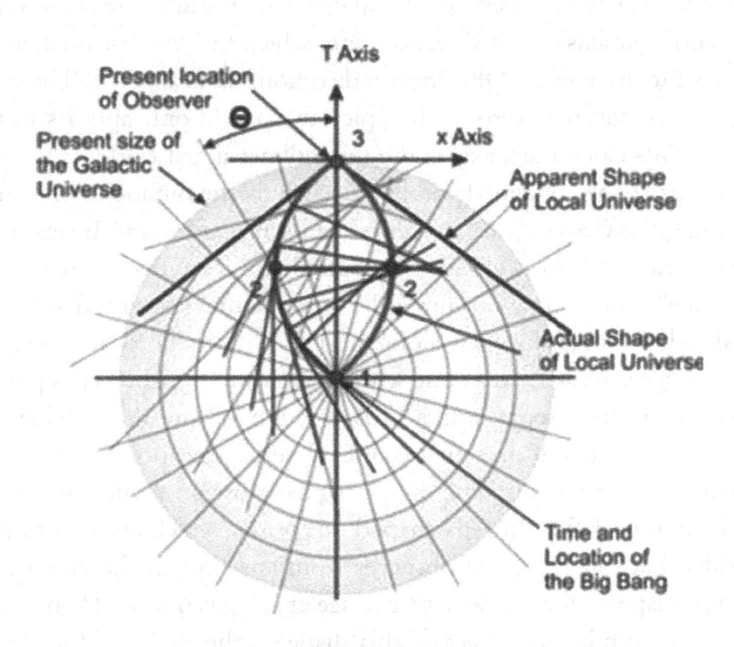

FIGURE 26
THE ENTIRE UNIVERSE,
AN APPROXIMATE LIGHT PATH FROM A PAST EVENT

A first approximation to the positions in time and space from which light may be emitted and detected by an observer in the present time is illustrated in figure 26. This also represents the line along which past radiation events appears to move from a source to the receptor at the origin of the coordinate system, although nothing actually traverses the space and time between the emission and the reception of the radiant energy.

This assumption leads to the conclusion that the path light takes in reaching a present observer from an emission source in the remote past follows an arc and changes slope as the universe expands. The curved path which fits the forty-five-degree requirement and provides a continuous path from an emission source, no matter how remote, to the present that follows a nearly circular arc connecting the distant source and the present receptor. It is, in the vicinity of the observer, approximately the conical shape used in the linear model to deduce the relationships between local times, distances, velocities, and so forth throughout this book and in the previous book.[5]

Figure 26 depicts a cross section of the entire four-dimensional universe as a circle with the x coordinate representing distance from the observer and the T axis indicating the direction of expansion of the universe at the velocity c. The fourth-dimensional T direction (into which the universe is expanding) is taken as the ordinate and the linear x direction as the abscissa. The y and z dimensions are taken as zero for this picture, so light only appears to move between points along the x axis in the three-dimensional world.

The lens shape contained within the circle is the outline of the surface representing the viewer's local universe at a particular instant. It was derived from the idea that light is always transmitted at a forty-five-degree angle to the "surface" representing our three-dimensional universe and that it can be received and reemitted anywhere along this line. Near to the local observer, the forty-five-degree lines form a cone with its vertex at the observer's position.

The outer circle represents a cross section of the three-dimensional galactic universe at the present instant of time. The point at the center represents the location and time of the big bang origin of the universe. The task at hand is to define the lens-shaped *local present*, which consists of all the light paths that can reach the observer from any time in the galactic past; that is, the shape of the universe he can see at any given time. Then it will be possible to determine the effect of this shape on the ability of the observer at the origin to look back in time and space toward the big bang.

Starting with the point that represents the origin (the point of the lens-shaped volume or the top of the local time cone), one can rather easily establish the slope of the lines that define the top of the cone geometrically.

A square inside the circle represents the cross section of the two-dimensional analog of the universe, with the corners at the points shown in table 1, where R is the present radius of the universe.

[5] Les Hardison, *A New Light on the Expanding Universe*, 2010, self-published. Available from Amazon.com or Kindle.

TABLE 1
CORNERS OF THE SQUARE

Corner name	x coordinate	y coordinate	Slope
Top center	0	R	+1
Left	-R	0	
Right	+R	0	-1
Bottom center	0	-R	

Looking at the right-hand branch of the cone, which slopes downward to the right from the observer's location, it can be seen that the slope of this line is given by table 2.

The way this slope changes as one moves backward in time to intermediate points between the present time and the time of the big bang, it is reasonable to generalize this slope to other, smaller circles representing earlier sizes of the universe. Smaller circles, each representing an earlier state of the universe, have radius r, determined from

$$r = \sqrt{T^2 + x^2}\,. \qquad \text{Equation 49}$$

The corners are now as shown in tTable 2, and the slope is

$$\frac{\Delta T}{\Delta r} = \frac{T - x}{T + x}. \qquad \text{Equation 50}$$

The outline of the lens-shaped region can be established graphically by simply rotating the inscribed squares for each circle of decreasing radius until the corner is centered on a radial line that intersects the circle of radius r at an angle and makes a smooth, continuous curve from the present time all the way back to the big bang. The locus of these points forms the outline of the lens shape, which when rotated around the T axis forms the two-dimensional surface representing the *local present.*

TABLE 2
GENERALIZED SLOPE OF THE LINE OF SIGHT
AT AN EARLIER GALACTIC TIME, T

Corner name	x coordinate	y coordinate	Slope
Top	x	T	$\frac{T-x}{T+x}$
Left	-T	x	
Right	T	x	$-\frac{T-x}{T+x}$
Bottom center	-x	-T	

The three-dimensional equivalent is a series of concentric spheres, each representing a marginally larger diameter sphere, up to the point halfway back to the time and place of the big bang. At this distance the diameter of the lenticular shape stops expanding and starts to get smaller toward the big bang. This poses an interesting challenge to visualize what amounts to a world that extends outward for a very long distance but then contracts. Of course, this is not what is actually seen. It should become more apparent that this halfway point is as far back in galactic time as a current observer can expect to see in the visible light range.

The shape of this lenticular curve is a very good approximation for most of the visible universe, but it also breaks down for distances through time that approach half the life of the present universe.

The equation relating x and T is shown below.

$$\left(x-\frac{1}{2}\right)^2+\left(T+\frac{1}{2}\right)^2=\frac{1}{2}. \qquad \text{Equation 51}$$

This is most easily plotted on x and T rectangular coordinates by separating the variables, yielding

$$T=\frac{1}{2}\pm\sqrt{\frac{1}{4}-x(1+x)}, \qquad \text{Equation 52}$$

where x is limited to values less than $1/\sqrt{2}$, and

$$x = -\frac{1}{2} + \sqrt{\frac{1}{4} + T(1+T)}, \qquad \text{EQUATION 53}$$

where T is less than 1.

The shape of the *local universe* as seen by an observer at the present time can be approximated in terms of the rectangular coordinates used in figure 26 as

$$x = r\sin\theta, \qquad \text{EQUATION 54}$$

and

$$T = r\cos\theta, \qquad \text{EQUATION 55}$$

where θ is the angle from the origin at the time and place of the big bang to the time and location of the light-emitting entity. The angle θ, in radians, also represents the velocity of the entity v/c relative to the position of the observer due to the expansion of the universe. This velocity is presumed to remain constant over the life of the universe.

The equation for the galactic surface at any time t, or T value, can be written as

$$r^2 = T^2 + x^2. \qquad \text{EQUATION 56}$$

However, once again, the distance to a galaxy at the local present time is not the x coordinate, but is rather measured along the arc of the galactic universe at the time the emitted light from the galaxy is observed by the present, earthbound observer. It is measured along the arc

$$s = r\theta \qquad \text{EQUATION 57}$$

and differs little from the value that would be obtained from a straight-line approximation.

For the larger picture, the divergence of the lenticular path and the assumed linear path produce markedly different results. The greatest difference occurs where the galaxy is being observed long in the galactic past, at a time when the universe was exactly $\sqrt{2}R$, where R is the present radius of the galactic universe measured in light-years. This situation is pictured in figure 27.

The velocity of the galaxy associated with the expansion of the universe is measured by the change in distance from the observer with time, counting the time interval as the age of the universe at the present moment. This time interval from the moment of the big bang to the observer's recent time is T, but the observer's curved line of sight places the galaxy at an earlier galactic time, t.

The true distance of the galaxy at the time of observation is, at the local present time,

$$s = r\theta = r\left(\frac{v}{c}\right). \qquad \text{EQUATION 58}$$

The error introduced by using the linear model reaches a maximum at the point where the emitting object is in the galactic past at a time when the universe was 0.707 times the present size, which is about 13.8 billion light-years. As the age of the universe is the radius divided by c, This puts the age of the universe at the earliest time we can observe it at about 9.8 billion years, and or about 4 billion years ago.

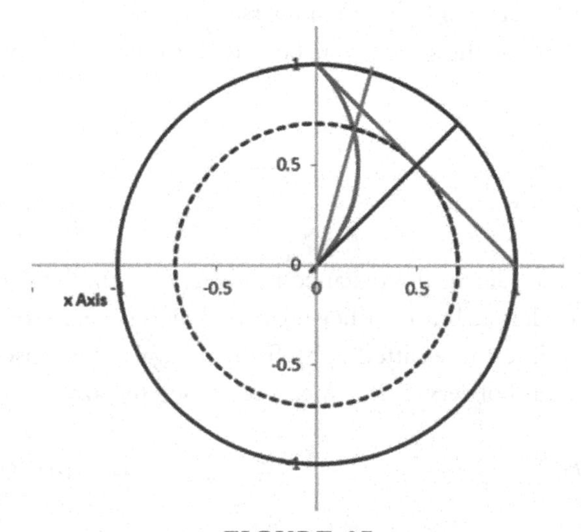

FIGURE 27
OBSERVING A GALAXY AT 4 BILLION LIGHT-YEARS IN THE GALACTIC PAST

The linear model says the distance of the object from the observer would be 4 billion light-years based on a flat universe and linear line of sight, or $r\theta = 9.75 * \pi/8 = 3.82$ light-years with the curvature of the universal "surface" neglected.

The lenticular model would place the galaxy at only 1.32 light-years. If the curvature of space were ignored, the galaxy would be at only 0.854 light-years, if the universe were considered approximately flat at this short a distance. At 4 billion years in the past, the curvature of space was considerably greater than it is now.

It seems apparent that the linear model, both relating to the curvature of the universe and to the curvature of the path of light being transmitted, introduces overwhelming errors in the translation of the observed local position and velocity of distant objects to the forecast positions and velocities they will probably have at the present galactic time. The errors are large enough that it seems reasonable to completely abandon the use of the galactic time reference system when dealing with events that occur at great distances and consequently at times in the remote galactic past.

Instead, the visual measurements of distance can be used to establish the galactic time associated with the object being observed, and the velocity can be determined by the degree of red shift, as has been done for many years. The present position by visual observation can be used to predict the position at the present time in reference to the galactic coordinate system. However, it must be kept in mind that this is a prediction of the position and not an actual measurement. The prediction is based on, from the galactic perspective, information that may be millions of years old.

Although the lenticular model of the path of light from the far distant past (in terms of the galactic system of coordinates) to the present is a significant improvement over the linear model used for the representation of light transmission from sources close to us—say, within a million or so light-years—it does not stand up to close scrutiny with respect to the basic requirement that the light path must be at forty-five degrees with respect to the surface representing the galactic universe, not only as it is now, but in all the configurations it must have had since its inception at the time of the big bang.

THE EXPONENTIAL SPIRAL MODEL

A strictly geometric approach to tracing the light path from an observer to the emission sources, no matter how far removed in space and time, leads to a result quite different from the lenticular model, particularly as regards the earliest times, near the time at which the big bang occurred.

One can trace the path back on a paper model by drawing a series of concentric circles representing previous galactic times in the history of the universe and placing a forty-five-degree triangle on the position of a present observer, with one edge along the apparently flat surface of the circle representing the observer's e axis, and one of the forty-five-degree sides pointing downward to the right (or the left) toward the next inner circle. It will not make a forty-five-degree angle with respect to a tangent to that circle at that point, but it will come close. The point of intersection can be marked as an approximate point on the path of light from sources at that time and place, or for earlier sources.

The triangle is then moved to the next point and the procedure repeated. The result of just such a procedure is shown in figure 28. Here each of the open circles represents a point along the pathway leading from the present observer all the way to the location of the big bang.

While this pathway is roughly approximated by the lenticular path described previously, it differs considerably in the region of the picture representing the early history of the universe. In particular, it seems to reverse the direction of light leaving the big bang and make the direction of its emission difficult to determine.

The shape of this path immediately suggests the possibility that this is a logarithmic spiral, which is a frequently recurring shape in nature.

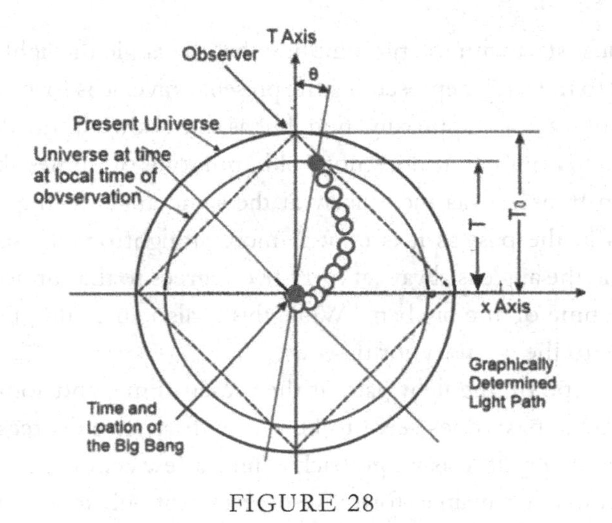

FIGURE 28
GEOMETRIC APPROACH TO THE LIGHT PATH

To make a long story a bit shorter, the equation of the logarithmic spiral in this particular case is

$$r = e^{-\left(\frac{4\theta}{\pi}\right)}, \qquad \text{EQUATION 59}$$

where

r = radius of the universe at time t
θ = angle from the time of the big bang to
any point along the light path.

The angle is measured counterclockwise from the origin at the time of the big bang.

The resulting curve can be plotted to illustrate the intricacy of the light path as the beginning of the universe is approached. Apparently, the spiral continues to wind around the starting point as the radius is decreased without limit toward a point, or toward whatever finite size the big bang is presumed to have had.

While this has a very similar configuration to the lenticular model described in the previous section, it is not contained within the upper-right quadrant of the circle representing the present universe, but seems instead to circle around the point representing the big bang.

One must start with the presumption that the angle the light makes with the tangent to the circle representing the present universe is forty-five degrees. It is apparently a good approximation, but as was shown in the development of the lenticular model, it does not hold up if one presumes that the path of radiation transfer was most likely at the same angle to the three spatial dimensions in the past as it is now. A more straightforward solution is to presume that the angle is always at forty-five degrees to the surface all the way back to the time of the big bang. While this is also an assumption, we have no evidence to the contrary for this one.

So the slope of the light path at the present time, and somewhat back into the galactic past, does seem to be exactly forty-five degrees. It appears to change relatively little as we go back in time a few centuries. However, the requirement that it remain at forty-five degrees, not only to the present circle representing the universe but also to all possible such circles representing past iterations of the universe, requires that we correct the angle of the line of sight in such a way that it is forty-five degrees at the present time but differs from this angle as we look farther back in galactic time.

The simplest such assumption is that the angle of light transmission through space is always at forty-five degrees, or $\pi/4$ radians. In the lenticular model, we assumed that this was also the angle at the time of the big bang, but it did not hold true for the intermediate configurations, particularly back toward the beginning of time.

But if one presumes that the light path is now at forty-five degrees with respect to the present universe at the location of the observer, a more consistent picture of the light path results. The angle decreases with respect to the opposition of the observer with each small increment of decrease in the radius of the universe representing an earlier galactic time.

And as the light path is followed back into the galactic past, the correction to the angle χ increases in inverse proportion to the radius of the universe as the universe is presumed to shrink back toward the point in space and time of the big bang, from its starting point of

$$\chi = -\frac{4}{\pi}. \qquad \text{EQUATION 60}$$

That is,

$$\frac{d\theta}{dr} = \frac{\chi}{r} \qquad \text{Equation 61}$$

and

$$\frac{d\theta}{dr} = \frac{4}{\pi r}. \qquad \text{Equation 62}$$

Integrating this as θ increases from 0 at the present time, going clockwise in on the graph in figure 28,

$$\int_0^\theta d\theta = \int_1^r \frac{r}{\pi r} dr \qquad \text{Equation 63}$$

and evaluating the integral over the limits indicated yields

$$\theta = \frac{4}{\pi} \ln\left(\frac{1}{r}\right) \qquad \text{Equation 64}$$

or

$$r = e^{-\frac{4\theta}{\pi}} \qquad \text{Equation 65}$$

This is the logarithmic spiral, which is approximated by the lenticular path of light for the last quarter of the life of the universe but departs considerably as one looks further back in time. The model suggests that the path of light emitted from the earliest hydrogen atoms curls around the point representing the big bang and leaves the location of emitted radiation entirely dependent on how big the initial point representing the big bang was. The logarithmic spiral would have to make an infinite number of turns to reach a zero radius.

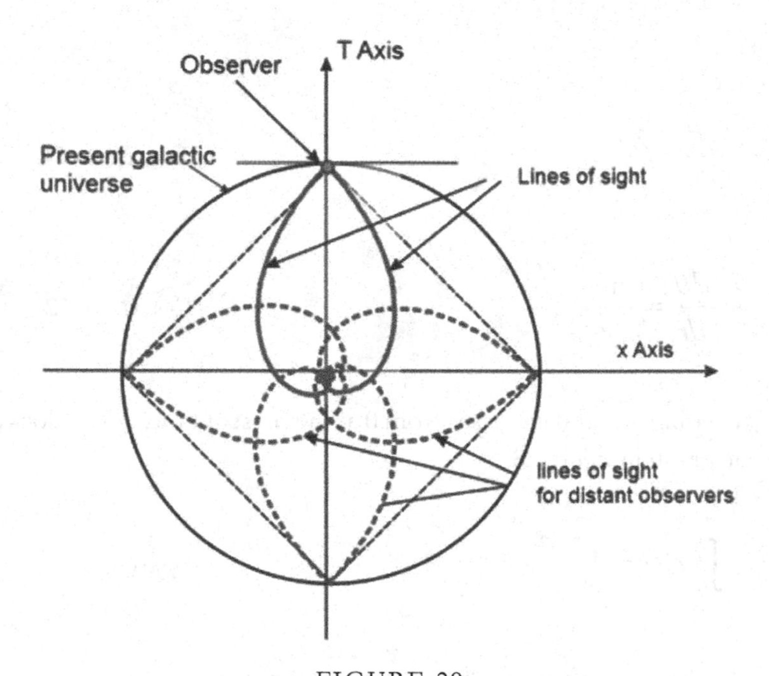

FIGURE 29
CALCULATED LINES OF SIGHT FOR A LOCAL OBSERVER

Figure 29 depicts the lines of sight for an observer located at a particular location in the present universe and shows the shape of his local universe as being somewhat heart-shaped, as opposed to lenticular. It also depicts the lines of sight that might be seen by observers located at the opposite "corners" of the universe. The one at the bottom represents the farthest possible neighbor, on the order of 35 billion light-years away.

Of course, this is a picture of a two-dimensional heart in the x = T plane and would be a two-dimensional heart-shaped surface of revolution if depicted as an x–y–T model. In the three-dimensional world, each of the circular cross sections would be a sphere centered on the observer, representing what he can see at the distance represented by the radius of the sphere. The farther out in space he looks, the further back whatever he sees is in galactic time. But, as in the case of the lenticular approximation, at about halfway back to the beginning of time, the universe would appear to be getting smaller and eventually disappearing altogether.

Table 3 is a tabulation of the x and T values calculated from equation 65, with time units as billions of light-years per year and distance units as billions of light-years. Figure 30 shows some of the data from this table, with the units given as fractions of the time and radius of the present universe.

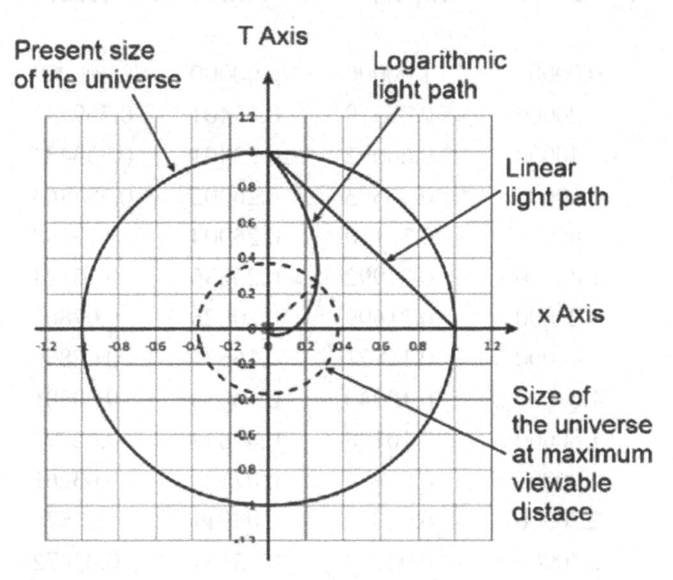

FIGURE 30
THE LINE OF SIGHT BACK TO THE BIG BANG

TABLE 3
CALCULATED COORDINATES OF LOGARITHMIC LIGHT PATH

θ Radians	r = exp4θ/π	x = rsinθ	T = rcosθ
0.00000	1.00000	0.00000	1.00000
0.20000	0.77519	0.15401	0.759737
0.40000	0.60092	0.23401	0.553483
0.60000	0.46583	0.26302	0.384463
0.80000	0.36110	0.25904	0.25158
1.00000	0.27992	0.23555	0.15124
1.20000	0.21699	0.20225	0.07863
1.40000	0.16821	0.16576	0.02859
1.60000	0.13040	0.13034	-0.00381
1.80000	0.10108	0.09844	-0.02297
2.00000	0.07836	0.07125	-0.03261
2.20000	0.06074	0.04911	-0.03575
2.40000	0.04709	0.03181	-0.03472
2.60000	0.03650	0.01882	-0.03128
2.80000	0.02829	0.00948	-0.02666
3.00000	0.02193	0.00310	-0.02171
3.20000	0.01700	-0.00099	-0.01697
3.40000	0.01318	-0.00337	-0.01274
3.60000	0.01022	-0.00452	-0.00916
3.80000	0.00792	-0.00485	-0.00626
4.00000	0.00614	-0.00465	-0.00401
4.20000	0.00476	-0.00415	-0.00233
4.40000	0.00369	-0.00351	-0.00113
4.60000	0.00286	-0.00284	-0.00032
4.80000	0.00222	-0.00221	0.00019
4.90000	0.00195	-0.00192	0.00036
5.00000	0.00172	-0.00165	0.00049

HOW FAR BACK?

The question "How far back can we see in the direction of the big bang?" relates to the conditions necessary for the transmission of radiant energy from one atom to another over distances in both space and time.

"How far can we see in space?" is almost equivalent to asking, "How far back can we see in galactic time?" but not quite. In the model that seems to work perfectly for distances up to thousands of light-years, distances in space are exactly equal to "distances" in galactic time. One might suppose that this holds true for objects that are also quite far away, but there are problems with this theory. The ability to see stars or galaxies is not limited only by the amount of emitted light being too small to activate the receptors in our eyes, but by the red shift reducing the frequency of the light out of the visible range. The further back in galactic time we see something, the smaller the universe was at that time. So we do not see or sense in any way the distant galaxies at their present positions in galactic space. About the maximum distance we can hope to see is the farthest away from our present position an object would have been in a much smaller universe.

THE RED SHIFT

The farther the stars or galaxies are away from the observer, the faster they are moving away from him on average. Red shift (the fact that one sees light from very distant stars is shifted in frequency toward the red end of the spectrum) is the first limitation. The red shift is proportional to the velocity of the stars or galaxies moving away from the earth. It is usually attributed to the Doppler effect, which is the apparent reduction in frequency of waves emitted by a moving object to have a lower frequency when the object is moving away from the observer and a higher frequency when moving toward the observer. This is true for sound waves, and appears to be the case for radar, based on electromagnetic signals. But if light does not consist of waves moving through the ether or through space, how can the frequency be changed by the motion of the source?

The answer is applicable to all observations of periodic operations, whether wavelike or not. If one observes a spinning, multicolored disk moving away from the observer but at a relatively short distance away, the rate of rotation of the disk will appear to be lower to the fixed observer than it would appear to an observer moving along with the disk. While this applies to the rotation of a wheel, it also applies to the orbiting of the electrons in energetic atoms, which are the emitters of visible light.

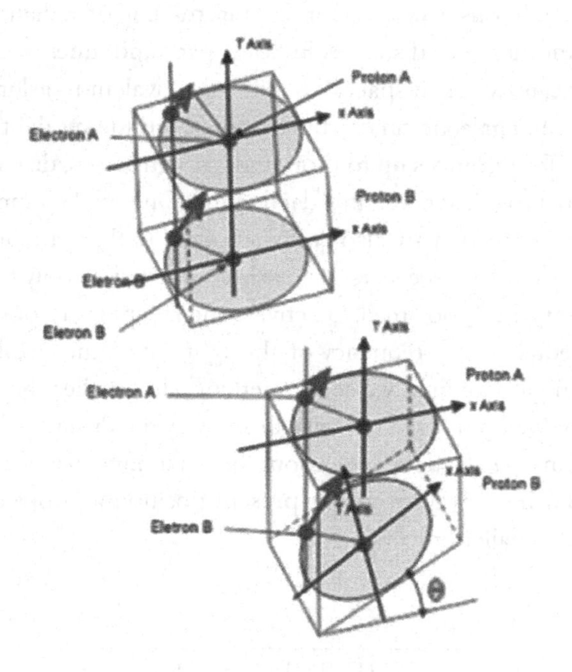

FIGURE 31
NONPARALLEL ORBITAL PLANES

In figure 31, the upper panel illustrates two hydrogen atoms with the proton and electron lying in parallel x–y planes. The lower atom has a larger orbital velocity than the upper one, and the two velocity vectors are pointed in the same direction. If these two planes actually overlap each other on the surface of the universal kernel, the faster one must either transfer its velocity to the slower one or the two electrons must change places so that the faster one now orbits in the upper of the two planes and the slower one in the lower plane.

In the lower illustration, the x–y plane of the lower orbit is at an angle, θ, with respect to the upper one. With the same higher velocity, only the component of velocity that is parallel to that of the upper orbital plane can be exchanged between the two orbits, so the energy transfer will be smaller in the lower illustration by an amount equal to

$$\frac{\Delta E_{lower}}{\Delta E_{upper}} = \frac{\mu(v\cos\theta)^2/2}{\mu v^2/2} = \cos^2\theta . \qquad \text{EQUATION 66}$$

where

ΔE = energy transferred
μ = electron mass
θ = angular misalignment.

So, if the planes are not parallel (that is, if the atoms exchanging energy are moving at different velocities), the frequency of the emitting atom appears to be lower and the radiation event that occurs involves less energy. This is, I believe, what we observe as the red shift of light arriving from distant galaxies on which Hubble based his theory of the expanding universe.

The red shift in the emission spectra of the light from nearby stars is generally attributed to the Doppler effect, which makes the apparent frequency of signals of any sort emitted by moving objects appear to be lower than they would appear to an observer moving along with the object. This is generally presumed to be the case for light, using the frequency of the emitted light as a wave frequency that moves through empty space.

However, it is the contention of the author that light does not actually cross the intervening space between the source and the receptor of the energy, but rather bypasses both space and time. It does not consist of waves at all, but is instead the transfer of direct energy between atoms. The frequency is that associated with the orbital velocity of the inner shell electrons in hydrogen and heavier atoms. The exchange of energy between an emitter and a receptor atom would be perfect if the two atoms were moving at the same velocity—essentially stationary relative to each other.

For observations of distant stars, this is not the case. This is because the direction of travel of the star being observed is significantly different from that of the receptor. Only a fraction of the angular velocity of the emitting electrons is exchanged with that of the receptor electrons.

Color	Frequency	Wavelength
violet	668–789 THz	380–450 nm
blue	606–668 THz	450–495 nm
green	526–606 THz	495–570 nm
yellow	508–526 THz	570–590 nm
orange	484–508 THz	590–620 nm
red	400–484 THz	620–750 nm

TABLE 4
RANGE OF HUMAN VISIBLE SPECTRUM

To put this in perspective, it is useful to consider that most of the light received from distant stars is emitted by hydrogen atoms at the range of energy levels the atoms can obtain before ionizing instead of entering into radiating energy transactions. The human visual range coincides with the band of frequencies emitted by very hot hydrogen, and the range of frequencies is roughly as shown in table 4.

The hydrogen spectrum covers this range pretty well, enabling humans to see all the colors within the human vision range in sunlight or reflected sunlight. However, if it is red shifted down below 400 THz (400,000,000,000 Hz), it is in the infrared range and invisible to the human eye. It can, of course, still be detected, down to near-zero frequency by infrared photocells, radar receivers, and radio telescopes.

It seems apparent that the energy transfer per transfer event is limited to dropping the frequency from roughly 800 THz to below 400 THz for visible light. This means that the sine of the angle θ between the emitting atom and the receptor is limited to less than 0.5, and the angle θ less than 30 degrees. As this angle equates to a velocity 0.524 times c, the *apparent speed of light,* visual observation of stars or galaxies is limited to those moving away from earth more slowly than this, using the galactic reference system. When measured by a real observer using the local time system, the observation would produce a velocity very close to c if there were some independent way of measuring the velocity of such distant stars.

VIEWING OBJECTS IN A SMALLER UNIVERSE

The logarithmic spiral light path suggests that we can never see or receive electromagnetic radiation of any kind from emission sources with a velocity higher than that which passes through the point of maximum x value on the curvilinear line of sight representing the local universe. This point has coordinates in space and time r = .53 times the present radius of the universe, and the galactic time of the emission is about 0.45 times the present age of the universe. The farthest away point actually observed is given by

$$s = r\theta = 0.26454,$$ EQUATION 67

or

$$s = 0.26454 * 17.8 = 4.71 \text{ billion light-years}$$
EQUATION 68

Where:

s = linear dimension in the x direction
r = radius of the past universe at maximum viewing distance
θ = angle from big bang to most distant point.

The maximum distance from the earth in any direction to the most distant star we can detect by radiation of any kind seems to be under 5 billion light-years. This is, of course, a measurement made with respect to the local time system. Were we to guess that the expansion of the universe is exactly constant with time and will remain so for the next 9 billion years, we would presume that the star would now be a distance of 1/.47 times as great, or 10 billion light-years away. This seems to place a great deal of faith in things staying the same.

So, 5 billion light-years seems to be the farthest away from us any galaxies can be detected if the difference between local time and galactic time is kept in mind.

By using detectors such as radio telescope arrays, which can detect radiation at much lower energy levels than the visual light range, we can detect emissions of radiant energy almost, but not quite all the way, back to the time of the big bang. The limiting factor is the apparent red shift in the radiation as the angle the motion of the emitting atoms in the x–T plane reaches ninety degrees. At which point none of the energy of the orbiting hydrogen or helium electrons would be transferred to those of an atom at the present time and location. The lowest frequency of radiation detected to date appears to be that known as background radiation, which comes from all directions and is probably the emission from hydrogen and helium atoms relatively close to, but not at, the location and time of the big bang.

While astronomers can only hope to see galaxies 5 billion light-years away in space, they can detect emissions originating almost all the way back to time zero, which seems to be about 17.8 billion years or so in the past by galactic standards.

THE IMPACT ON HUBBLE'S CONSTANT

Hubble's law, simply stated, is that the stars and galaxies tend to be moving away from the earth at velocities proportional to their distance away from earth, according to

$$Hs = v \qquad \text{EQUATION 69}$$

where

H = Hubble's constant
s = distance to the star of galaxy
v = velocity of the star or galaxy relative to earth.

Hubble's constant is easily demonstrated to be equal to the inverse of the age of the universe if the velocities are assumed to be unchanging with time. Likewise, the size of the universe is simply the velocity of expansion times the age, if the velocity of expansion is assumed to be c and is invariant with time.

The entire argument that light doesn't travel through the space between the source and the receptor atoms is based on Hubble's concept that our three-dimensional space is expanding, presumably in a fourth-dimensional direction. For distances that are relatively small compared to the radius of the entire universe, one need not be concerned about how the measurements are made. For most of the observations of nearby stars and galaxies, it is adequate to neglect the curvature of space and simply presume it is nearly flat. Similarly, the path of light through the transfer of radiant energy by radiation is assumed to take place between points lying in a straight line. But for great distances, where the velocity of expansion is significant relative to c, it is necessary to correct for the differences between the local observations and the galactic frame of reference usually used in scientific work. Also, it is necessary to take into account the curvature of space and also the curvature of the lines of sight, along which radiant energy transfers can take place.

The several correction factors are all negligible for nearby stars and galaxies, where "nearby" may be taken as anything closer than the tiny bit of the universe defined by an angle θ representing the velocity of a galaxy v_g/c less than 0.1 radians (about 0.1 * 180/3.14159 = 5.7 degrees), which encompasses that part of the universe within 1.38 billion light-years and velocities of expansion of 5,000 kilometers per second.

If the local measurements were presumed to follow a linear line of sight, the distances measured for a fixed time would be different by the ratio of the distance traveled in the same time period, as measured by both clocks. Thus, if a measurement of distance were made by the local observer as s, the corresponding distance in the galactic system would be

$$s' = v't'. \qquad \text{EQUATION 70}$$

When one looks at the stars, he is not seeing them at the present moment in *galactic time*, but rather at the present moment in *local time.* When Hubble's constant is calculated, ordinarily no attempt is made to correct the local time of the observations to the galactic system, so it is a *local time* which is measured. The geometry of the situation is shown in figure 32.

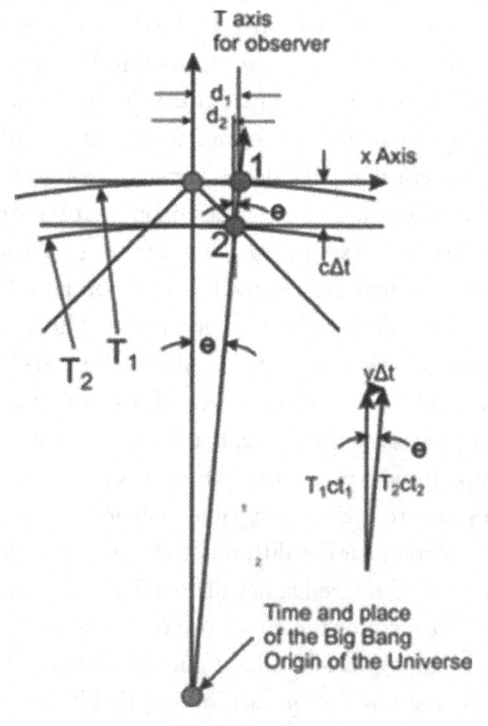

FIGURE 32
HUBBLE'S CONSTANT FOR NEARBY GALAXIES

The actual measurement of distance s at the time of the measurement defines the angle θ, and defined Hubble's constant as

$$H' = \frac{v'}{s'}, \qquad \text{Equation 71}$$

but neither the velocity nor the distance is directly measurable in respect to the galactic system.

Again, primes are used to designate values referenced to the galactic system of coordinates, and unprimed values represent measurements made in reference to the local time system.

This is clearly a measurement made in terms of the *local time*, where the relationship of the variables in the two systems can be established for either:

a) the situation where the reference times are taken as the local or the galactic time, and the time of the big bang, and the distance the galaxy in question has moved since the time of the big bang, and the velocity is proportional to this distance; or
b) the distance the galaxy has traveled since the big bang is considered to be the same, and the time differs between the two systems.

The former is of considerably more utility in the case where the velocity is that imparted by the big bang, as the beginning and ending time of the measurement is the same for both systems, and only the distance a particular galaxy has traveled during that time must be measured.

The measurement must, of necessity, be measured in respect to the local system, as the local observer can see the galaxy in question and the galactic observer cannot. So, the local observer obtains a sighting of the galaxy at a particular time and records his observation at the time indicated on his clock. This is, of course, the galactic time also. The time of the big bang can be supposed to be at time zero, again for both the local observer and the galactic observer.

The local observer can estimate the velocity of the galaxy with a fairly high degree of precision by inspection of the spectrum of interference bands on the light received. So, based on the red shift and the correlation with distance measurements of nearby stars, the model of the universe presented here was built and seems to provide an adequate basis for the observed local Hubble's constant. In the galactic model, the value of Hubble's constant should be corrected from the observed values using the presumption that the galaxy under consideration is located in an earlier iteration of the universe, along the line of sight from the observer, and traveling at the velocity indicated by the red shift.

In other words, the light is coming from a galaxy located at the intersection of the path of the galaxy at the angle θ from the T axis and the logarithmic spiral line of sight from the observer's position into the galactic past. This position is indicated in figure 32 as the actual position of the galaxy being observed. The values the observer can record during his observation are s, the local distance to the galaxy measured along the curved path in the earlier state of the galaxy, and t, the time of the observation.

It is apparent that the value of Hubble's constant, H', determined for the nearby galaxies, is slightly smaller if the logarithmic shape of the local universe is taken into account, although this difference is negligible for the closer galaxies. It should become apparent only for those quite far away. The following paragraphs are aimed at calculating the correction factor that should be applied for less remote galaxies, which is

$$s = r\theta ,$$ EQUATION 72

where

$$s = vt$$ EQUATION 73

and

$$r = ct ,$$ EQUATION 74

where t is the local time, which is identical to the galactic present time.

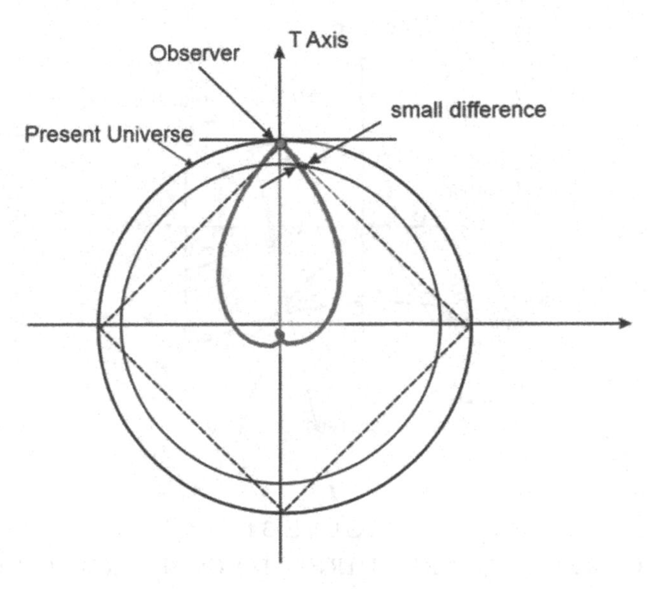

FIGURE 33
GEOMETRY OF THE ENTIRE UNIVERSE

Here it can be seen that the logarithmic-shaped projection of the present observable universe deviates from the right-angle cone shape at distances significant, as compared with the overall size of the universe. It is the slight difference in horizontal distance between the position of a distant galaxy as it appears to the local observer on the spiral and the position at which it was assumed to be on the forty-five-degree line.

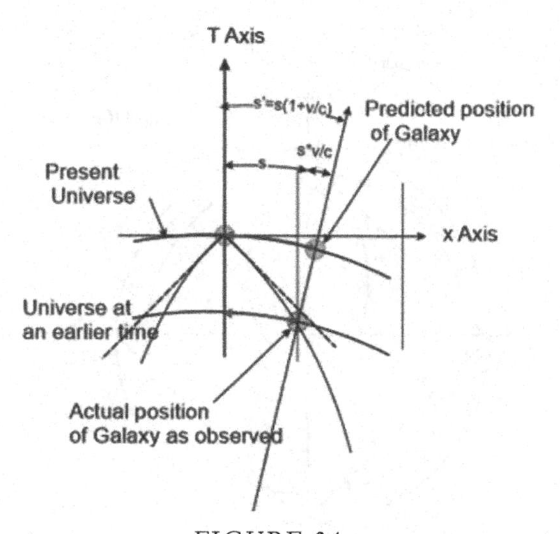

FIGURE 34
THE CORRECTION REQUIRED TO CONFORM HUBBLE'S CONSTANT TO THE GALACTIC COORDINATE SYSTEM

The linear model, which was used for the determination of Hubble's constant for relatively nearby galaxies, presumes that the path of light is essentially the straight-line elements of a cone, and that the galactic universe is for all practical purposes a flat plane located at a distance T from the point comprising the big bang. However, taking a larger view of the universe as it is at the present galactic time and has been at various past galactic times indicates that the path of light is curved. The galactic universe is better represented by a circle at any specific galactic time, as shown in figure 34.

So, it is apparent that the velocities measured in the two systems are not the same. The distance measure in the local time is the shorter distance, as shown in figure 34, so

$$\frac{v'}{v} = \frac{1}{1+\frac{v}{c}}, \qquad \text{EQUATION 75}$$

Just as was the case when the linear approximation, neglecting the curvature of space, was taken into account. However, it is not so simple. What is fairly apparent from figure 34 is that there are some proportionalities that may be helpful. If the present radius of the universe, R is taken as 1, and all the distances are proportioned to it, then the distance the galaxy has traveled in terms of local time is given by

$$s = r\theta \,. \qquad \text{EQUATION 76}$$

The distance relates to the galactic distance by

$$s' = R\theta = \theta \,. \qquad \text{EQUATION 77}$$

The present age of the universe is taken as

$$ct = T = R = 1 \qquad \text{EQUATION 78}$$

so the following ratios hold:

$$\frac{s'}{s} = \frac{v'}{v} = \frac{1}{r} = \frac{c}{t} \,.$$

In order to estimate the distance to the galaxy that is being observed to have a velocity v, based on the red shift of the light received, it is necessary to use the curved path of light derived in the previous section, which is at the point where the line representing the path of light in figure 34 is vertical. That is, at a point halfway back in time, when the radius of the universe was approximately half the present radius.

$$\frac{r}{R} = e^{-\frac{\theta}{4\pi}} \,, \qquad \text{EQUATION 79}$$

or

$$\theta = -\frac{\pi}{4} \ln \frac{r}{R} \,. \qquad \text{EQUATION 80}$$

The distance can be determined by the point where the radius θ intersects the circle representing the universe at an earlier time when the radius was r. At this time, the distance to the galaxy being observed is

$$\frac{s}{R} = \frac{r\theta}{R} = \frac{\pi r}{4R} \ln \frac{r}{R} = \theta e^{-\frac{\theta}{4\pi}} \,. \qquad \text{EQUATION 81}$$

As

$$\theta = \frac{v}{c}$$ EQUATION 82

and

$$\frac{s}{R} = \frac{v}{cR} e^{-\frac{v4}{c\pi}},$$ EQUATION 83

the distance can now be determined from the velocity indicated by the red shift and the known properties of the light path near the observer. So,

$$H = \frac{v}{s} = \frac{v}{\frac{v}{c} e^{-\frac{4\frac{v}{c}}{R\pi}}} = \frac{c}{R} e^{\frac{4\frac{v}{c}}{R\pi}} = \frac{1}{T} e^{\frac{4v}{\pi c}}.$$ EQUATION 84

Expanding the exponential as an infinite series,

$$H = \frac{1}{T}\left(1 + \frac{4v}{\pi c} + \frac{1}{2}\left(\frac{4v}{\pi c}\right)^2 + \frac{1}{6}\left(\frac{4v}{\pi c}\right)^3 + \ldots\right).$$

EQUATION 85

Because H is generally regarded as simply 1/T, this may be rewritten as

$$H = H' e^{e^{\frac{4v}{\pi c}}}$$ EQUATION 86

or approximated by

$$\frac{H'}{H} \approx \frac{1}{1 + \frac{4v}{\pi c}}.$$ EQUATION 87

The maximum angle that θ can assume is π/8. Because the radius of the universe at that galactic time was half that of the present universe, the correction to the conventional H' to a practical value would decrease from 1.0 for the nearest galaxies to 2/3 for the farthest ones that can be seen or communicated with. Beyond this distance, all dimensions are shorter if the size of the universe continues to decrease toward zero at the time of the big bang.

The correction factor is assumed to be based on the velocity of the galaxy taken from the red shift of light received from it and the calculated distance in three-dimensional space from a point where the stationary observer would be at that galactic time. The magnitude of this correction is plotted in figure 35 as a function of the angle θ in degrees. The solid line indicates the range of angles that can actually represent the path of light from a galaxy in the observer's local presence. The dotted portions are the extrapolation of the equation beyond the applicable range.

A more meaningful plot may be made by substituting the actual v/c ratio for the angle in degrees, as shown in figure 36. In figure 36, it is apparent that the highest observable velocity of recession is on the order of 0.4 c, because higher velocities would require the galaxy to be farther away than the radius of the universe at the galactic time the galaxy is being observed.

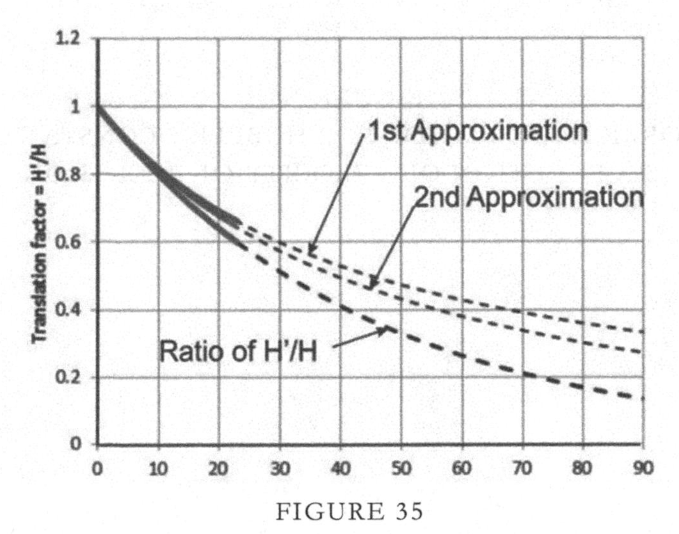

FIGURE 35

CORRECTION FACTOR FOR HUBBLE'S CONSTANT

That is, of course, based on the presumption that light has always been emitted and received in the galactic past according to the rules that appear to govern radiant energy transfer in the present time.

And, if radio telescopes, capable of detecting very low frequency radiation are counted as "seeing" distant galaxies, then it is reasonable to say that our limit is at the point where anything farther back in time is actually getting "closer" to our present position. This is at the position where the universe was half the present radius of 13.8 billion light-years or about 6.9 billion light-years.

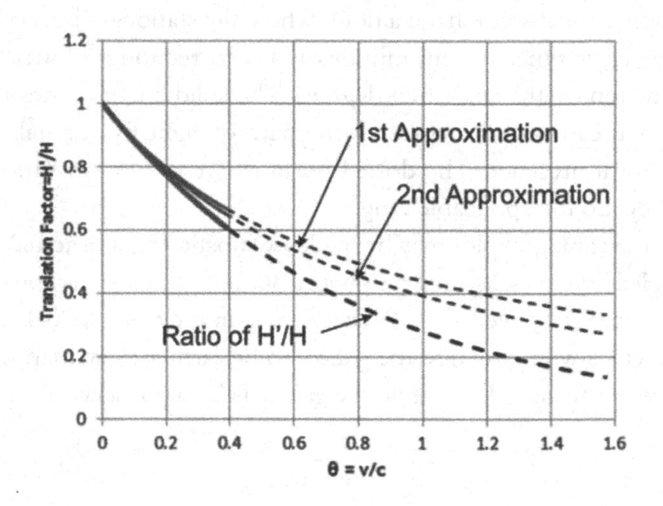

FIGURE 36
CORRECTION FACTOR FOR HUBBLE'S CONSTANT
AS A FUNCTION OF VELOCITY OF RECESSION

CONCLUSION

The *local universe*, which comprises all the objects we can see from any particular observation point in *the local present time*, consists of objects that are in the *galactic past.* We are limited in how far we can see into the galactic past by two things: the red shift makes it impossible to see stars or galaxies that are so far away that the light they produce is red shifted completely out of the visible spectrum., although more distant stars and galaxies could be detected by radio telescopes receiving radiation at frequencies far below the visible light range. Very sensitive visible light telescopes might be capable of detecting radiation from heavier atoms which were above the visible frequency range when emitted.

While it appears that nearby (speaking in terms of interstellar distances) objects are arrayed in concentric spherical shells around us represented by concentric circular sections of a cone in the two-dimensional analog of the universe, the shape of the *local analog universe* is instead a more complex figure bounded by a logarithmic spiral, which appears to be a cone near the time and position of the observer but turns inward and spirals toward the time and place of the big bang.

The conical appearance of the *local universe* does not extend very far (again, in terms of interstellar distances). This is because the lines of sight, which define the local present universe, are always at a forty-five-degree angle to the surface of the *galactic universe* at any time and place. As one looks backward toward the time and place of the big bang, these lines of sight have to be curved toward the surfaces of the smaller and smaller universes as one travels backward in *galactic time.*

The local universe increases in size as we go back in galactic time and reaches a maximum just beyond halfway back to the location of the big bang. Beyond this limiting distance, it would look like the galaxies farther away from us in time are actually closer to us in distance, with the big bang, paradoxically, looking as if it were very close by. However, we cannot see these galaxies visually, because the light emitted by hydrogen and helium in the stars comprising the galaxy would be red shifted far below the visual range.

It is possible to receive radiation from them but at frequencies below those in the visible light range, with the lowest of them consisting of radio-frequency radiation. These seem to be detectable from times almost as far back as the big bang. However, the individual galaxies emitting radiation of any sort cannot be seen at present at distances greater than about 5 billion light-years, although it would look like 10 billion light-years if the local time observations were confused with galactic time observations. The latter are simply predictions of what the universe will be like in another 8 or 9 billion years.

It is quite possible that the galactic background radiation, which appears to come from all directions, is in fact the light from the hydrogen and helium atoms close to the location of the big bang event, which are red shifted down to the lowest possible orbital frequency of hydrogen and helium above absolute zero.

CHAPTER 6

THE SOURCE OF BACKGROUND RADIATION

What is the true source of the cosmic microwave background radiation (CMBR)? This phenomenon was first discovered in 1964 by American radio astronomers Arno Penzias and Robert Wilson, which earned them the 1978 Nobel Prize in Physics. CMBR has been explained as the "leftover radiation" from the formation of the universe immediately after the big bang, when hydrogen was first condensing into ions, free radicals, and atoms.

I do not believe this to be the case, based on my picture of the way we perceive the universe by means of the transmission of radiant energy. In this chapter, I will explain why I think CMBR represents radiation from ordinary hydrogen and helium atoms near the location of the big bang that has been red shifted far beyond the visible light range and, in fact, to the lowest possible energy state above absolute zero.

The CMBR appears to come to earth from all directions in the universe at an almost—but not quite—constant intensity independent of direction. The frequency is most intense at 160.2 GHz, corresponding to a 1.9 mm wavelength, which would be emitted from a blackbody at a temperature of 2.725 K. The spectrum peaks in the microwave range and is only detectable when very large radio telescope dishes are used to collect the signals.

If one accepts that the limit of our vision (which is limited to the *local universe* at the present moment) allows us to see, as part of our *local present*, objects that are capable of emitting light that is in our *galactic past*, the farthest back we can see in time is to about half the present age of the universe to a time when the universe was about half the radius it has now. However, our vision is even more limited, as we cannot see the farthest extent of the earlier universe because the path of light, or any other radiation, bends toward the point where the big bang occurred. However, it is possible to detect radiation beyond this point, even though it is out of the range of visible light frequencies due to the red shift, which is in turn due to the velocity of stars and galaxies receding from each other. This radiation can be detected by infrared sensors at the higher end of the frequency scale and as radio waves of very low frequency toward the lower end.

These radio frequencies become weaker at the lower frequencies, and the background radiation described appears to be the lowest frequency observed to date. This radiation, if it pervades the universe rather than just the vicinity of the earth, must come from very far away, because the signal strength is very low. It is very likely to originate from atoms of hydrogen, which seem to be the predominant form of matter in the universe. It follows that the emission source is likely to be hydrogen comprising an emission source moving at very nearly ninety degrees to the motion of the solar system. The usual drawing shows the velocity of the various galaxies moving away from each other on an x–T diagram, where the angle from the point of the big bang to the location in time and space on the drawing is

$$\theta = \frac{v'}{c} . \qquad \text{EQUATION 88}$$

However, it is apparent that any body moving away from the observer will treat his own direction of motion on figure 37 as the direction in which time is moving and regard his own position as fixed. This should hold true for motion in any direction away from that of the observer. So, it is apparent that a point on the surface of an earlier version of the universe that is on the calculated light path toward the present observer would be emitting radiation at a ninety-degree angle to the angle at which the observer receives the radiation. Therefore, the frequency would be shifted all the way to zero. So, the background radiation cannot be originating from this point or anywhere beyond it. Therefore, it must be originating just short of this distance back in time and space.

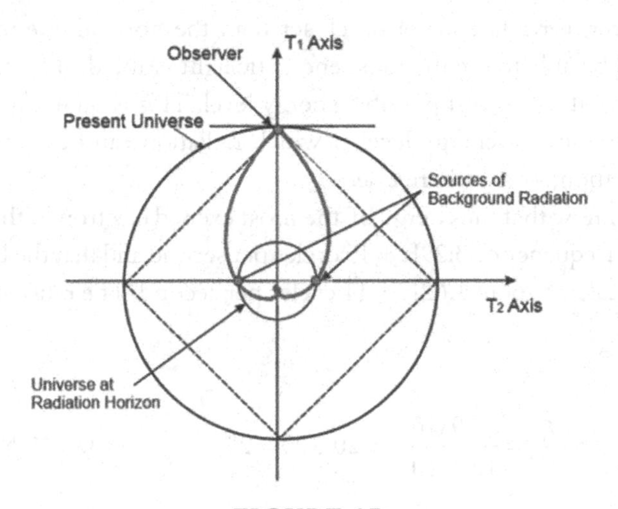

FIGURE 37
SIMPLIFIED PICTURE OF THE RADIATION HORIZON

This means that the two points shown in figure 37 represent the probable sources of the background radiation. They are not at the point of the big bang, nor are they precisely at the ninety-degree angle from the location of the present observer. The ninety-degree mark in either direction from the observer comprises the visibility horizon with respect to any radiation of any sort. This horizon is at about $(1-0.1415)*17.8=15.2$ billion years ago, when the universe was about 5.6 billion light-years in diameter.

It is proposed that the cosmic microwave background radiation is the radiation that takes place between the fastest moving hydrogen atom electrons located just this side of the visibility horizon quite a bit later than the time of the origin of the universe. If this is true, it provides a chance to further describe the mechanism of radiant energy transfer, because it gives way to assessing the slowest moving electrons permissible in the local time construct.

One may look at the emitting hydrogen atom and a receiving atom without regard for the space and time separation because it has been postulated that these are immaterial in the transfer of radiant energy. The rotational energy of the electrons cannot be transferred from one atom to another to any degree if the two atoms are moving at ninety degrees to each other, as the components of velocity of either would be zero with respect to the other atom.

However, this limit is so far away that it represents an enormous number of stars and galaxies, so there should be a lot of radiation emitted. We just can't see any of it.

However, for a line just a bit closer than the horizon line in figure 37, one should be able to see the most energetic light emitted, although it would appear to be at the lowest possible energy level. This is quite significant, for it may be the lowest energy level at which radiation can be received at our present location, or anywhere else.

So, we know that the energy of the most excited electron in the hydrogen atom is at a frequency of 3.29E + 15 cycles per second and that the background radiation peaks at about 1.62E + 11 cycles per second. The ratio of these two values is

$$\frac{v_0}{v_0'} = \frac{f_0}{f_0'} = \frac{3.29x10^{15}}{1.62x10^{11}} \approx 20,300 = 2^{14.3}. \qquad \text{EQUATION 89}$$

This suggests that there are a lot of possible velocities for the hydrogen atom—perhaps as many as 20,000+ discrete velocities.

In short, the background radiation seems to be simply the highest level of ordinary radiation from hydrogen red shifted down to the lowest level possible. The next step down would be no motion at all. Background radiation seems to come pretty uniformly from all directions, because at the distance the visible horizon is from us, there is an unimaginable number of stars in the relatively small universe, yet they surround the observer in his local universe.

CHAPTER 7

NUCLEAR ENERGY

My grandson, Joshua Jackson, is a smart, young college student (in 2012) and one of the few people with the patience to listen to my long story about the speed of light. We went fishing in Lake Michigan, and the fish were relatively uncooperative that day, so we had lots of time for conversation. After hearing me out, he asked me a couple of questions. They were good questions, and I was hard-pressed to answer at the time.

One of these was, "If you deny the conversion of mass to energy, what is it that *is* converted to energy when an atomic bomb explodes or hydrogen fusion takes place?"

I honestly hadn't thought about that, and not being able to answer would have spoiled the interesting conversation—had not some fish showed up and changed the subject.

I wasn't able to forget his questions and spent some time reviewing what I thought I remembered about nuclear engineering from when I was in college myself. Not all that much seems to have changed in the past sixty years. The basic problem in my mind was: if all electrons are identical to all other electrons, and protons identical to other protons, and neutrons to other neutrons, and all elements are made of these three building blocks, how can any mass disappear during a nuclear fusion or fission reaction?

HYDROGEN FUSION

Hydrogen fusion is much simpler than uranium fission, so it is best to start there in trying to figure out what gets converted to what during nuclear reactions.

I was particularly concerned that, in my simple view of nuclear physics, all atoms are made exclusively of electrons, protons, and neutrons. Only the latter two are part of the nucleus. I believed that all electrons are identical to one another and that the same thing was true of protons and neutrons. If so, how could deuterium (heavy hydrogen, containing a proton, a neutron, and an electron) and tritium (containing a proton, two neutrons, and an electron) fuse to form ordinary helium (two electrons, two protons, and two neutrons), with a neutron left over and a great deal of energy. The energy had to come from somewhere, and some mass must have disappeared.

A little review of the present literature is in order. I have included some references from Wikipedia, but they should still be on the internet if you care to look them up.

From Wikipedia:

> The electron is by far the least massive of these particles at 9.11 × 10−31 kg, with a negative electrical charge and a size that is too small to be measured using available techniques.[44] Protons have a positive charge and a mass 1,836 times that of the electron, at 1.6726 × 10−27 kg, although this can be reduced by changes to the energy binding the proton into an atom. Neutrons have no electrical charge and have a free mass of 1,839 times the mass of electrons,[45] or 1.6929 × 10−27 kg. Neutrons and protons have comparable dimensions—on the order of 2.5 × 10−15 m—although the 'surface' of these particles is not sharply defined.[46]
>
> Pasted from <http://en.wikipedia.org/wiki/Atom>

Aha! We have the first clue as to what changes in mass during a nuclear reaction. So far as modern physics is concerned, the neutron is not simply a proton and an electron bound together, which would weigh only the sum of the masses of the proton and the electron. The proton has a mass 1,836 times that of the electron, and the neutron ought to come out weighing 1,837 times the mass of the electron. But the proton mass can be reduced somewhat by changes to the energy binding the proton into an atom! And the neutron is 1,839 times as massive as the electron so it too is subject to an increase in mass due "binding energy."

This is very significant, because it is difficult to actually weigh any of the nuclear particles individually. However, the charge to mass ratio of the protons and electrons can be measured quite accurately in a mass spectrometer by creating a very strong magnetic field, essentially between the poles of a very big DC electromagnet. The path of a rapidly moving electron, proton, or ion is curved because the interaction of its electric charge with the magnetic field, so the radius of curvature gives a good measure of the ratio of the mass to the charge. If the charge on each electron is taken as −1 and each proton as +1, the masses of these simple particles can be established unambiguously.

The neutrons are a different, in that they have no measurable charge, and the mass cannot be ascertained by MS analysis. So, instead, the mass is calculated by adding an amount equal to the calculated "binding energy," which is the amount of energy released when the neutron decays spontaneously. Neutrons are not stable when not a component of the nucleus of an atom and decay into a proton, an electron, and an electron neutrino. This gives off lots of energy. The mass equivalent of this energy is assigned to the neutron, along with the mass of a proton and an electron. The "binding energy" suggests that it is not actually energy in the ordinary sense of the word, but rather a force of some sort which holds the nucleons together, like gravitational force, or electrostatic attraction, but much, much stronger.

However, when the mass of a nucleus containing one or more neutrons is measured in a mass spectrometer, it does not come out to be exactly the sum of the masses of the electrons, protons, and neutrons which compose it. This is ascribed to the binding energy which holds the nucleus together, and is calculated by subtracting the masses of the component nucleons and taking the leftover mass as the mass equivalent of the binding energy. The binding energy is not accounted for by electrostatic attraction and repulsion and gravity forces, but requires the addition of the strong force and the weak force, which only act over very short distances. Here we are talking about distances which are very short, on the order of 10^{-15} meter, or a few femtometers. For comparison, the radius of a helium atom is on the order of 31,000 fm.

The strong force, many times as strong as the electrostatic force, is called upon to account for the difference in mass of neutrons in different nuclei. And it is, somehow, a component of the binding energy.

So, the neutrons and protons are presumed to be the culprits that accounts for the variations in mass which takes place when atomic nuclei are altered by fusion or fission reactions. In order to explain how this can be possible, all sorts of new particles have been defined, the newest one always a little stranger than the previous ones. These are the quarks and antiquarks, which come in a wide variety of colors and flavors

Here is a sample, quoting straight from Wikipedia. I do not necessarily believe all this stuff.

> The nucleons are bound together by a short-ranged attractive potential called the residual strong force. At distances smaller than 2.5 fm, this force is much more powerful than the electrostatic force that causes positively charged protons to repel each other.[50] The nuclear force (or nucleon-nucleon interaction or residual strong force) is the force between two or more nucleons. It is responsible for binding of protons and neutrons into atomic nuclei.[6]

> … So by analogy, "color-neutral" nucleons may attract each other by a type of polarization which allows some basically gluon-mediated effects to be carried from one color-neutral nucleon to another … To a large extent, this force can be understood in terms of the exchange of virtual light mesons, such as the pions. Sometimes the nuclear force is called the residual strong force, in contrast to the strong interactions which are now understood to arise from quantum chromodynamics (QCD). This phrasing arose during the 1970s when QCD was being established. Before that time, the strong nuclear force referred to the inter-nucleon potential. After the verification of the quark model, strong interaction has come to mean QCD.

[6] Pasted from http://en.wikipedia.org/wiki/Atom.

> Since nucleons have no color charge, the nuclear force does not directly involve the force carriers of quantum chromodynamics, the gluons. However, just as electrically neutral atoms (each composed of cancelling charges) attract each other via the second-order effects of electrical [forces?] the virtual mesons which transmit the forces, and which themselves are held together by virtual gluons. It is this van der Waals–like nature which is responsible for the term "residual" in the term "residual strong force." The basic idea is that while the nucleons are "color-neutral," just as atoms are "charge-neutral," in both cases, polarization effects acting between near-by neutral particles allow a "residual" charge effect to cause net charge-mediated attraction between uncharged species, although it is necessarily of a much weaker and less direct nature than the basic forces which act internally within the particles.[1]

My couple of years of wondering and speculating about the nature of light, relativity, and atomic structure has suggested to me that there may be many commonly accepted physical terms that don't necessarily have real physical counterparts—terms like *photon*, *gluon*, etc.

I really don't believe in photons anymore. Gravitons and gluons have, in my opinion, gone down the drain with photons. I am not sure that "color-neutral" is very meaningful.

The conventional wisdom is that the strong force decreases the mass of the neutron in the nucleus. The strong force arises from quantumchromodynamics (which is held together by gluons.) The decrease in mass accounts for the energy emitted when the helium nucleus is formed from a heavy hydrogen atom and a tritium atom.

If one considers the fusion reaction to be in essence the conversion of ordinary heavy hydrogen (which has a neutron in the nucleus in addition to the proton of ordinary hydrogen), and tritium (which is has two neutrons in addition to the proton), probably in ionic form at very high temperatures, into ^{4}helium, then the helium nucleus has to be lighter than would be expected because of conversion of some of the proton and neutron mass in the ^{2}hydrogen and ^{3}hydrogen to lighter counterparts in the ^{4}helium.

From my point of view, the forces (all forces) are related to the warping of the time vectors at all the points in space occupied by matter, and the "strong force" would have to be likewise. The repulsive force between two protons is due to the fact that all protons twist space in the same direction, and when the spin fields around them approach each other, the spin vectors between them are pointed in opposite directions. This creates a hill in the x–y surface of the sphere representing the present universe and tips the time vectors for the two protons away from each other, just as the grass growing on the hillside is tipped away from the grass on the other side of the hill.

If the protons were forced together, say by the very high velocities created in the interior of a star or in a nuclear explosion, so that the spin vector fields (or the twist is space-time) around the two of them were overcome and they were moved to very nearly the same point in space, then the spin fields around them would become additive. They have to do this to hold more than one electron in orbit.

This is very like the situation where two parallel electrical conductors with the current flow in the same direction repel each other because of the magnetic fields (really the twisting of space around the moving electrons) rotating in the same direction around each of the wires but pointing in opposite directions in the space between them.

However, if they are forced together in spite of the repulsive force, the magnetic field now surrounds both wires and holds them together. The two fields become additive and hold the two wires tight together. Strongly together. There is no special "strong force" at work here.

Now, how would this appear to change the mass of the neutrons and protons? There would no longer be any space between them in the nucleus. Well, hardly any space between them. Certainly less than the femtometer diameter of the nucleus.

When two heavy hydrogen nuclei ($^{2}H^{+}$ and $^{3}H^{+}$) fuse to form a helium atom, the protons must be bound together after becoming enormously energetic in order to overcome the natural repulsion between them.

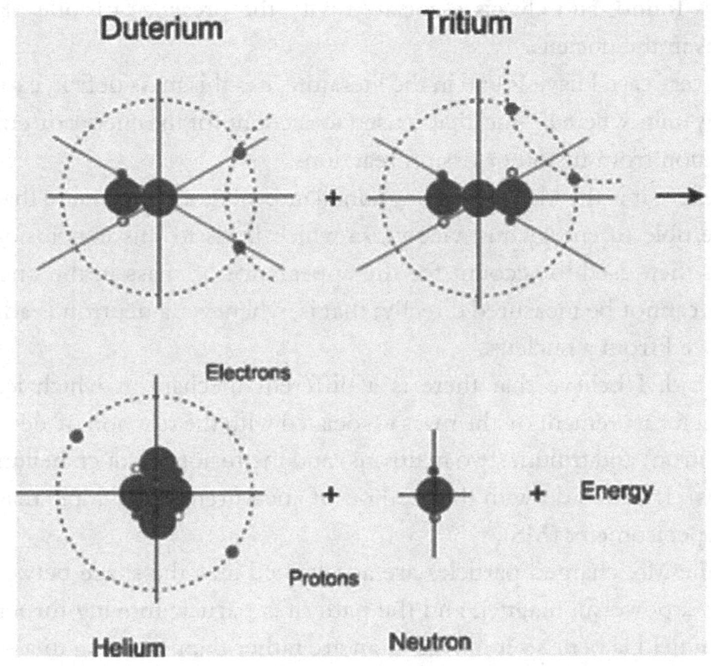

FIGURE 38
THE HYDROGEN FUSION REACTION

But how do the nuclei lose mass in the process other by presuming that they lose energy, and the energy equates with mass? As usual, I am quite willing to believe the measurements made by scores of careful scientists, but not so willing to believe the theories which they derive from their measurements.

Which takes us back to the measurement of the mass of the neutron. As one cannot measure the mass of the neutron directly in a mass spectrometer, it is necessary to measure it indirectly. If one measures the mass of deuterium ion (a single proton and a single neutron forming the nucleus of a molecule of heavy water), and then the mass of the proton alone, the remainder should give the mass of the neutron. This yields a mass for the neutron considerably greater than the mass of an electron plus that of a proton. Similar calculations for the mass of the neutron by measuring the masses of tritium and helium should produce similar results. But they do not give quite the same result for different cases. Always, there appears to be a greater mass of the neutron when it is in an atomic nucleus than the sum of the masses of the proton and electron which it decays into when removed from the nucleus. The mass deficit, as it is called, varies across the spectrum of atomic species, but it is always found, and always associated with the presence of one or more neutrons in the nucleus.

In every case I have found in the literature, it is this mass deficit, expressed in energy units where $E=mc^2$ that is used to account for the energy of emission of radiation from fusion or fission reactions.

I believe it is the idea, deeply ingrained into all modern physics, that mass is convertible to energy and vice versa which leads to this conclusion, and which is then used to account for the appearance of mass in the one place where it cannot be measured directly; that is, whenever a neutron is added to or removed from a nucleus..

Instead, I believe that there is a different mechanism which leads to incorrect measurement of the mass associated with the reaction of deuterium (one neutron) and tritium (two neutrons) and the fusion product, helium (two neutrons). It has to do with the method of measurement of ionic masses in a mass spectrometer (MS).

In the MS, charged particles are accelerated into the space between the poles of a powerful magnet, and the path of a particle moving through the magnetic field is bent so it moves in an arc rather than traveling in a straight line. The interaction of the electric charge on the particles with the magnetic field acts at right angles to the direction of the field—for example, straight up and down for the magnet poles facing each other with a horizontal gap between them, and also at right angles to the direction of motion of the charged particles.

This means that the charged particles will bend crosswise to the trajectory they would have if there were no charge on the particles or no magnetic field. So, the path will curve sideways. The charge on the particles causes the curvature, and the mass of the particles resists the sideways acceleration.

The location along the side of the mass spec unit where the particle exits depends on the ratio of charge to mass. The mass spectrometer measures the ratio of charge to mass. The lower the ratio, the less the particles will bend.

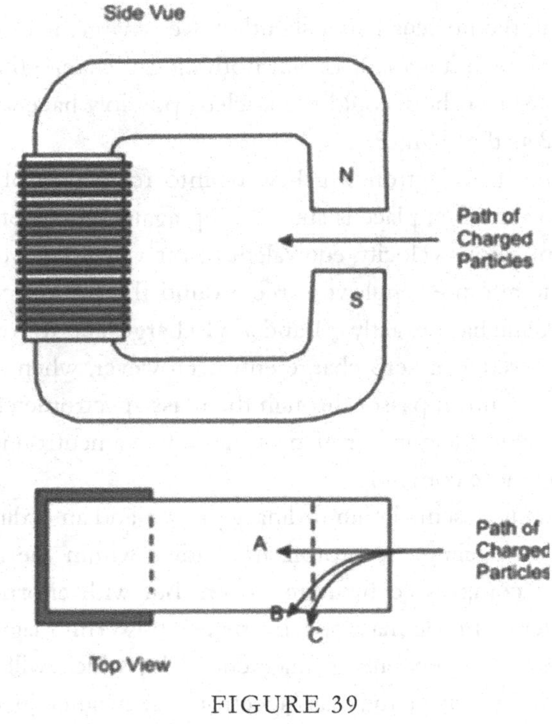

FIGURE 39
MASS SPECTROMETER

In figure 39, the path of an uncharged particle through the magnetic field is straight, as represented by particle A.

A particle with the normal charge (+1) of an ordinary hydrogen nucleus with a mass equal to one proton would trace a course like that of particle C. The deuterium ion would be expected to have substantially twice (actually (2*1836+1)/1836) the mass, but the same charge and traverse the path labeled B. However, it goes a little bit further, indicating a higher mass for the neutron than that of one proton plus one electron. The increment is taken as the equivalent of the energy excess in the nucleus due to the presence of the proton.

Were there no change in the constituents of the hydrogen and tritium nuclei when they are fused into a helium nucleus, one would expect the helium nucleus to follow a path consistent with a net charge of +2 and a mass equivalent to that of $^{2}H + ^{3}H$ less one neutron. Instead, it comes out lighter than expected, and the difference is regarded as the mass of the neutron plus the mass equivalent of the binding energy; the power of a hydrogen bomb explosion.

However, if the nucleus had a slightly lower charge, it would appear to be more massive than it actually is. But nothing can change the charge on a proton of electron, so how could the nucleus possibly have anything other than exactly +2 as the charge?

Suppose that the electron which went into formation of the neutron from a proton in the first place is snuggled up against the proton in a super tight orbit at enormous velocity, equivalent to the velocity it would have had to have to penetrate the repulsive force around the proton completely. It, and the proton, still have exactly −1 and a +1 charge, and for most purposes could be considered as a zero charge entity. However, when a positive ion not containing a neutron passes through the mass spectrometer, the positive charge is identical to the number of protons. When a neutron is present, the picture is a little more complex.

The neutron is, essentially, an ordinary proton and an ordinary electron, with the electron circling the proton at a radius within the radius of the nucleus, as in a compressed hydrogen atom, but with enormously higher velocity and energy. In the mass spectrometer's powerful magnetic field the orbiting electron also generates a magnetic field, which will line up with polarity opposite of that of the mass spectrometer magnet, just as hydrogen atoms do in a medical MRI (magnetic resonance imaging) machine. This reduces the strength of the mass spectrometer magnetic field locally, and produces the same effect as reducing the charge on the nucleus.

So, if the charge on the nucleus appears to be less than +2 for the helium nucleus, it would easily be misinterpreted as an increase in the mass of the helium nucleus over that of the deuterium and tritium which fused to create it. The missing mass would be interpreted as having turned into energy.

So, I believe the energy released during the fusion of ^{2}H and ^{3}H to form ^{4}He, plus a neutron and a great amount of energy, is a simple reaction during which the mass of the constituents is all accounted for, and the energy release is the kinetic energy of the electrons which collided with ordinary protons by virtue of having velocities approaching the *apparent speed of light* in reference to the galactic system of time measure, and many times the *apparent speed of light* in reference to the local system. The electrons keep this enormous kinetic energy by orbiting the proton in a tight orbit at incredibly high frequency.

I believe that the fusion reactions, which involve atoms with autonomic numbers of iron or higher, similarly show changes in the effective electric charge on the nuclei such that the reaction products of fusion appear to have a lower apparent mass than the parent atoms because of the incorrect assumption that the mass spectrometer reacts to the full charge on the electrons bound in the nucleus.

My short answer is that mass is not converted to energy at all. Rather, when a fusion or fission reaction takes place, the neutrons involved release some of the enormous energy of the electrons bound to them. It is this energy which makes the neutron unstable when it is not a part of an atomic nucleus, and which is released whenever the number of neutrons in a nucleus changes.

As with all my conclusions, this is simply a proposed alternative way of looking at the results of the measurements by hundreds or thousands of physicists but without the utter conviction they share, which is that Einstein's special theory of relativity, based on the presumption that light moves through space at about 300,000 km/second, and nothing can move faster than that. I don't believe that assumption is correct, so I am not limited to believing many of the deductions from it.

I could be wrong about this. I wouldn't consider it shameful to lose an argument with essentially all the physicists who have participated in the field in the past century. Most likely, every one of them is, or was, smarter than I am.

CHAPTER 8

A CLOSER LOOK AT THE SPEED OF LIGHT

My entire outlook on physics is based on the thesis that Michelson and Morley, and many others who attempted to measure the speed of light, instead measured something quite different. They measured, in my opinion, the speed at which the entire three-dimensional universe is expanding in a fourth-dimensional direction.

Light, in my opinion, represents the instantaneous transfer of energy from an excited atom to another, less excited one, which may be very far away from the source. The emission of energy and the reception are simultaneous events. The light doesn't actually traverse the empty space between the two points, but instead bypasses it, taking a shortcut through an extra-spatial dimension. In this respect, and in many others, light is unique.

The objective of this chapter is to review the history of the measurements of the speed of light performed over several centuries by researchers who did not consider the possibility that light was inherently different from both physical bodies and waves, which *do* traverse three-dimensional space.

There was, up until 1927, no clear indication that our three-dimensional space was expanding, and no evidence that there was a fourth spatial dimension into which the expansion was taking place. Physicists used various methods to measure the time elapsed between an event that could be seen and the perception of the event a known distance away. The distance divided by the difference in times of the two events was taken as the velocity. This works for everything else in the universe, so it seemed it should work for light also.

I do not believe it works for light, or radiation in general, but the experimenters had no knowledge of the motion of the universe through space, so there was no apparent alternative possibility.

My purpose in this chapter is to outline the early measurements of the *apparent speed of light* through 1887, when Michelson and Morley did their experiments aimed at determining speed of the luminiferous ether by measuring (or hoping to measure) the speed of light in different directions. The *apparent speed of light* was pretty well-known by that time, and the question was assumed to be the motion of medium of conduction of light through otherwise empty space.

After this famous experiment, Michelson continued for many years to refine his experiments to produce more precise measurements. He founded the physics department at the University of Chicago and did research there until his death in 1931.

In particular, I will describe the Michelson experiments, the results of which may have led directly to Einstein's special theory of relativity and contributed greatly to the establishment of quantum mechanics and much of modern physics.

EARLY MEASUREMENTS

Speculation about how fast light moves through space apparently goes back to the time of Aristotle, who quotes Empedocles as saying that the light from the sun did not get to earth instantaneously.

Galileo wondered about the speed of light and carried out some crude experiments, but he was only able to determine that it traveled at least ten times faster than sound in air.[7]

The first successful measurement is attributed to Ole Rømer, a Danish astronomer who measured the irregularities in the observations of Io, one of the moons of Jupiter. Io was eclipsed by Jupiter at regular but somewhat variable intervals. He reasoned that the irregularities were due to the differences in the distance between the earth and Jupiter. When Jupiter was far away from the earth, the eclipses seemed to occur later than when the planet was close by.

He deduced that the time differences from those expected divided by the difference in distances from the earth would be the speed at which light traveled. In 1696, he calculated a speed of 125,000 miles per second, which is about two-thirds of the currently accepted value of 186,000 miles per second for the *apparent speed of light.* The error was most likely due to the time difference being taken as 22 minutes, when it is really closer to 16 minutes. Still, this marks the beginning of the scientific measurements.

[7] http://www.speed-light.info/measurement.htm#Galileo.

FIGURE 40
OLE RØMER

Christian Huygens expanded on the observations of Rømer and went on to expound the wave theory of light in the *Treatise on Light*, 1678.[8]

Opticks, written by physicist Isaac Newton in 1704, recognized the earlier work on the speed of light and indicated that light moved at a velocity close to the currently accepted value. Newton wrote about the refraction, reflection, and absorption of light, and *Opticks* is considered one of the major milestones in the evolution of the physical sciences. In it, Newton proposed that light is transmitted as though it consisted of particles rather than waves.

By the beginning of the eighteenth century, it was pretty well understood that light appeared to move through space at a very high velocity compared to anything else we can easily observe. There was some question as to whether it was in the form of waves, as proposed by Huygens, or particles, as Newton believed.

[8] Michael Fowler, UVa Physics Department, *The Speed of Light: Early Ideas About Light Propagation.*

FIGURE 41
GODFREY KNELLER'S 1689
PORTRAIT OF ISAAC NEWTON, AGE 46[9]

It was also apparent that waves move through a medium, but there were other observations that seemed to require it to be particulate in nature and do not require a medium. But these fail to account for many of the properties light seemed to possess.

Thomas Young, a prolific English physicist, performed many experiments with both light and water waves that demonstrated that light had many of the same characteristics exhibited by waves in water, including the property of forming interference patterns when reflected from objects or when passed through narrow slits or very thin films, such as soap bubbles. He added a good deal of weight to the argument that light had to be wavelike in character and therefore needed a medium to conduct it from one point to another.

Thus it became fairly widely accepted that there was a medium pervading otherwise empty space, which conducted the light waves from the emission source to the point where they were detected visually, or with photosensitive equipment, such as a camera film. The medium was usually called luminiferous aether, or ether.

[9] George E. Smith, *The Cambridge Companion to Newton* (Cambridge Companions to Philosophy). Cambridge University Press; 1st edition (May 29, 2002).

MICHELSON'S EXPERIMENTS

Albert Michelson was a Polish-born American physicist who taught at several American colleges and did most of his experimentation as a member of the physics department of the various schools.

FIGURE 42
ALBERT MICHELSON[10]

He was appointed a professor of physics at Case Western Reserve. At Case, he continued to improve his techniques for the measurement of the speed of light. Like most of his predecessors, he was convinced that light was a wave form conducted through the luminiferous ether and that the properties of the mysterious ether would be sorted out by diligent research.

I will have to confess to remembering that the principle method used for the measurement of the speed of light in the Michelson-Morley experiments involved a multifaceted mirror that had to be rotated at precisely the right speed in order to reflect light back from the source to a receptor near the source.

[10] Photograph of Nobel Laureate Albert Abraham Michelson.
Copied from Wikipedia http://en.wikipedia.org/wiki/File:Albert_Abraham_Michelson2.jpg.

This was basically the approach used in Michelson's earliest experiments during his tenure as an instructor at the US Naval Academy. There he did his groundbreaking experiments on the speed of light, as a young man.

He used the method of Michel Foucault, which involved measuring the angle of deflection of a spinning mirror to time the transmission of light, presuming that the light passed through space like all other waves and bodies.

It is apparently the later experiments during which he used an octagonal rotating mirror to direct the beam of light over a precisely measured distance. And this is the one that I remembered.

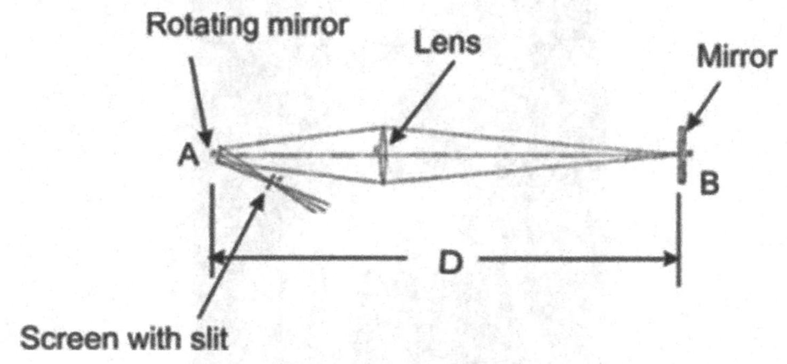

FIGURE 43
MICHELSON'S ROTATING MIRROR APPARATUS

While at Annapolis, he used a large room (measuring the speed of light in air, which is not quite the same as in a vacuum). Sunlight was used as the source of light, and it was caused to pass through a slit to form an image on a screen. When the mirror was turned at just the right angle, the sunlight passing through the slit would strike the mirror at A, be reflected from the flat mirror at B, back to the mirror at A, and onto the same spot on the screen as the slit. However, if the mirror was turned slightly, the reflected image would be moved away from the slit by an amount that indicated how much the mirror had been turned.[11]

When the rotation of the mirror R becomes sufficiently rapid, then the flashes of light that produce the second or stationary image become blended, so that the image appears to be continuous. But now it no longer coincides with the slit; rather, it is deflected in the direction of rotation and through

[11] Albert A. Michelson, *Experimental Determination of the Velocity of Light*, made at the US Naval Academy, Annapolis. Release Date: March 28, 2004 [EBook #11753].

twice the angular distance described by the mirror during the time required for light to travel twice the distance between the mirrors. This displacement is measured by the tangent of the arc it subtends.

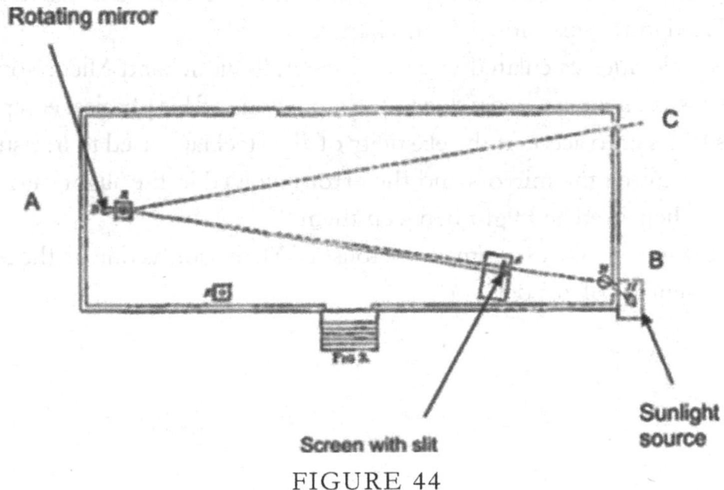

FIGURE 44
SITE PLAN FOR MICHELSON'S SPEED
OF LIGHT MEASUREMENT

To make this displacement as large as possible, the distance between the mirrors, the radius, and the speed of rotation should be made as great as possible.

In order to implement the experiment with the precision required for obtaining the best measurement of the *apparent speed of light* at the time, Michelson built a separate building and equipped it with a modified apparatus to make his determinations.

The speed of rotation of the mirror had to be just right to direct the beam of sunlight from outside the test room to the surface of the mirror and thence to the observation slit on the other side.

The building was 45 feet long and 14 feet wide, and raised so that the line along which the light traveled was about 11 feet above the ground. A heliostat at H reflected the sun's rays through the slit at S to the revolving mirror R, thence through a hole in the shutter, through the lens, and to the distant mirror.

The angular displacement of the second image at the screen with the slit is exactly twice the displacement of the mirror during the transit of the light across the distance D between the rotating mirror and the stationary mirror.

The measurement of the time associated with the rotation of the mirror through this angle required a great deal of care, as did the measurement of the distance between the rotating mirror and the fixed mirror.

His method of calculation and some of the experimental data are reproduced in the appendix to this chapter.[12]

The velocities calculated were very carefully done, and Michelson took great pains to eliminate errors due to the limitations of his physical equipment, such as taking into account the elasticity of the steel tape used to measure the distance between the mirrors and the error involved in the slight sagging of the tape when stretched tight between them.

The results of the experiment established Michelson as one of the leading optical scientists of his day.

---

[12] Albert A. Michelson, *Experimental Determination of the Velocity of Light*, made at the US Naval Academy, Annapolis. Release Date: March 28, 2004 [EBook #11753].

TABLE 5
CALCULATIONS OF THE VELOCITY OF LIGHT IN AIR[13]

1ST, 4TH, AND 5TH SETS

log	c' =	51607	51607	51607
"	T =	99832	99832	99832
"	d =	05131	05119	05123
		-------	-------	-------
		56570	56558	56562
"	r =	44958	44958	44958
		-------	-------	-------
"	tan φ =	11612	11600	11604
	φ =	2694".7	2694".1	2694".3
"	c =	49670	49670	49670
"	n =	41066	41066	41066
		-------	-------	-------
		90736	90736	90736
"	φ =	43052	43042	43046
		-------	-------	-------
"	V =	47684	47694	47690
	V =	299800	299880	299850

But what did he really measure?

There is no question that Michelson was a brilliant and careful scientist, and that he made very precise measurements. However, they were based on the assumption that light behaved like other kinds of waves and like physical bodies, which move through three-dimensional space in a predictable manner, occupying all the points in the space along their path sequentially as they progress. While there was no evidence that this was not the case at the time, there was also no evidence that it was.

Light cannot be observed as it moves from place to place. It is only defined when it actually reaches a receptor, such as the human eye or a photographic plate.

---

[13] Ibid.

Let us assume, for a moment, that light does not progress through space as other wave forms do and as physical bodies do, but instead is transferred from the emission source to the receptor as a pair of simultaneous events. Such instantaneous transfers take place only through a vacuum, of course. When light progresses through a physical medium, I do not believe it moves through the medium instantaneously, but rather from one atom to another instantaneously. When one transfer takes place, there is likely to be a time delay of very short duration before the conditions are right for another instantaneous transfer to take place to another receptor. Thus the speed of light within a physical medium is not infinite, and light does move through matter at a finite velocity, but not in a wavelike manner.

By measuring the distance the image of the slit was displaced when it was reflected from the rotating and the stationary mirror back to the slit that can be regarded as the source (actually, the sun was the initial source, but that doesn't really matter in this argument), Michelson did measure the elapsed time between two events. He assumed that the first was the movement of the sunlight through the slit in his screen and that the second was the appearance of the light after it had traveled from the screen to the rotating mirror, then made the round trip between the rotating mirror and the fixed mirror, and finally back to the screen. Because the timing was done by the rotating mirror, the speed of light was determined by the path length—twice the distance between the mirrors—and the time it took the rotating mirror to move enough to produce the flickering image on the screen. A schematic of the experiment stripped of all the inconsequential elements is shown in figure 45.

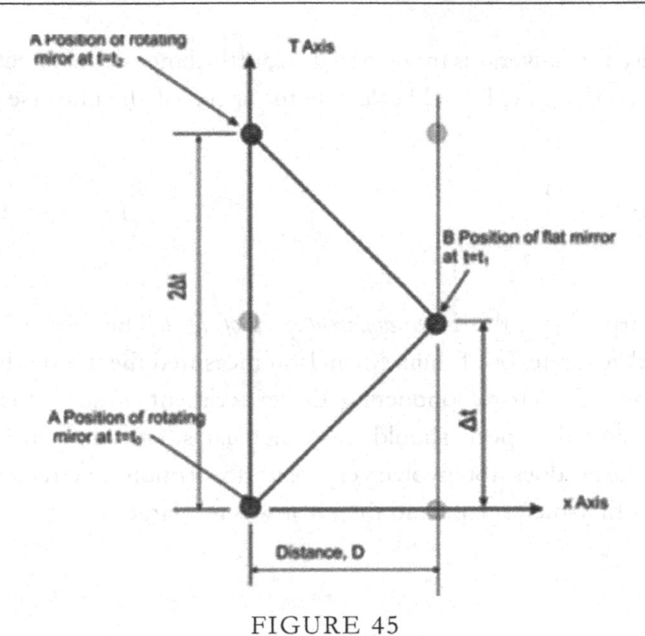

FIGURE 45
SCHEMATIC OF MICHELSON'S MEASUREMENT OF C

In figure 45, light moves instantaneously from the rotating mirror at A to the fixed mirror at B. However, the light does not travel along the x axis, which is moving upward at *the apparent speed* of light, c, but instead moves instantaneously to the location the fixed mirror will be in after Δt seconds have elapsed. It is reflected with essentially no loss of time and arrives back at the location of the rotating mirror, but again arrives at the location where the rotating mirror will be after a time period 2Δt.

The rotating mirror will have turned during this time period so that surface on which the light beam arrives is turned relative to the position at which it left.

While Michelson calculated the time velocity of light to be

$$c = \frac{2D}{2\Delta t}, \qquad \text{Equation 90}$$

I would say that the light arrived instantaneously at the rotating mirror's future location and that the observers did not catch up with that fact until they—and the rest of the universe—had reached that point in time.

Because the universe is moving in the fourth-dimensional direction at the *apparent speed of light*, c, I would calculate the speed of the universe as

$$c' = \frac{2D}{2\Delta t}. \qquad \text{EQUATION 91}$$

Not surprisingly, this is *the apparent speed of light.* The measurement was precise and accurate, but I think Michelson measured the wrong thing.

He was, of course, conducting the experiment in air, rather than in a vacuum, and the speed should be somewhat slower than in a vacuum. However, the air does not involve very many absorptions and reemissions of light over a fifty-meter path, and the error was not large.

THE NEED FOR ETHER

The objective of this chapter was to discuss the famous experiments done by Michelson and Morley where they found that, by not being able to measure any significant velocity for it, ether probably did not exist.

Huygens, Young, and others made a strong case for the nature of light being wavelike. This posed a serious problem, as waves of all other types require a medium of transmission. Sound waves move through air, water, or solids by setting up oscillatory motions of the medium. The speed of the wave propagation depends on the properties of the medium. Sound waves travel faster in the thin air at high altitudes and through hot air rather than cold air at the same altitude.

Light, on the other hand, seemed to move freely and with no attenuation whatever through the vacuum of interstellar space. The simplest assumption, at the time, was that the space is not empty but filled with a substance that has some esoteric properties, one of which is the ability to conduct light beams between the light source and receptor with little or no attenuation.

The substance was named (as is often the case when something is imperfectly understood) luminiferous ether, but there was no other information available about it. The name luminiferous ether, or simply ether, added to the apparent legitimacy of the substance, and the search began to measure its properties.

I must add here, parenthetically, that this suggests to me that there are many other things that have been given names and adopted into the scientific literature in similar fashion. Some candidates for this distinction (in my opinion) are photons and their relatives gravitons and gluons, for example. Force and potential energy are a couple of others.

Although no trace of luminiferous ether was identified, and it seemed to have no measureable properties that could account for the speed of light, only one of its properties seemed to be amenable to investigation. That is, if ether filled the spaces between all the astronomical bodies and conducted light throughout the universe, it should have some motion relative to the earth that could be measured by timing how long it took light to move a fixed distance in different directions. If the ether behaved like air conducting sound, then light would travel faster when moving in the same direction the ether was moving and more slowly when going the opposite direction.

THE AIRPLANE ANALOGY

An analogous situation exists when an airplane flies through an air mass moving relative to the ground. From the airplane pilot's perspective, the air is stationary and the plane flies through it at a velocity determined by the power input and the properties of the air. The true air speed is the same, no matter which way the airplane is headed. The ground speed, on the other hand, is determined by both the air speed (velocity of the airplane relative to the air mass) and the velocity of the air mass, or the wind, relative to the ground.

However, when the airplane makes a round trip to a destination in the direction the wind is moving and then returns to its starting point (presuming the wind hasn't shifted), the pilot finds it took a shorter time to get to his original destination than it took him to get home. His speed going was increased by the speed of the air mass, and his speed returning was decreased by the speed of the air mass.

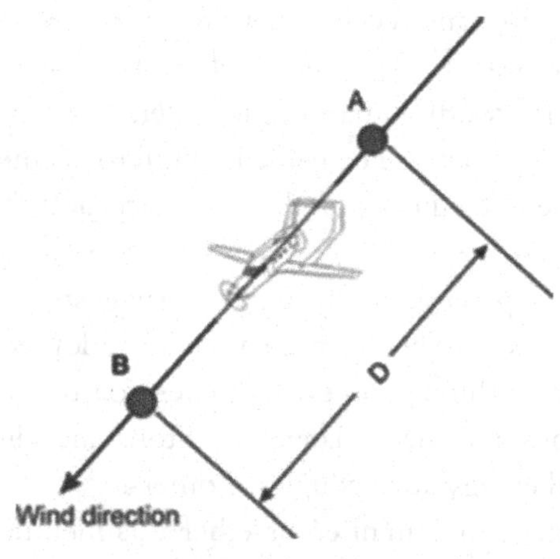

FIGURE 46
AIRPLANE ON A ROUND TRIP

If he knows the distance flown each way and the time en route each way, he can calculate not only his average speed, but that of the air mass. The wind speed, v, is simply the amount added to or subtracted from the true air speed of the airplane, V, as it makes the two legs of the trip each equal to the distance D.

The airplane's true air speed is known (measured by a Pitot tube and registers on the instrument panel), and the distance is known, so we can work out the speed of the air mass.

$$T_1 = \frac{D}{V+v}, \qquad \text{EQUATION 92}$$

where

T_1 = outbound trip time, hours
D = Distance between A and B, nautical miles
V = Aircraft true air speed, knots
v = Unknown wind speed, knots,

and

$$T_2 = \frac{D}{V-v}, \qquad \text{EQUATION 93}$$

where

T_2 = return trip time, hours.

The total elapsed flying time is

$$T_1 - T_2 = T = \frac{D}{V+v} - \frac{D}{V-v}, \qquad \text{EQUATION 94}$$

from which

$$T = \frac{D(V-v) - D(V+v)}{(V+v)(V-v)} = \frac{2DV}{V^2 - v^2}. \qquad \text{EQUATION 95}$$

This can be solved for v, the wind speed.

$$\frac{v}{V} = \sqrt{1 - \frac{2D}{VT}}. \qquad \text{EQUATION 96}$$

A stationary observer on the ground could tell what the average wind speed in the direction of flight was if he knew the true air speed of the airplane and the time for the round trip.

The picture is a bit more complex if the airplane does not happen to be flying directly with the wind or against it, but the mechanics of making the determination are similar.

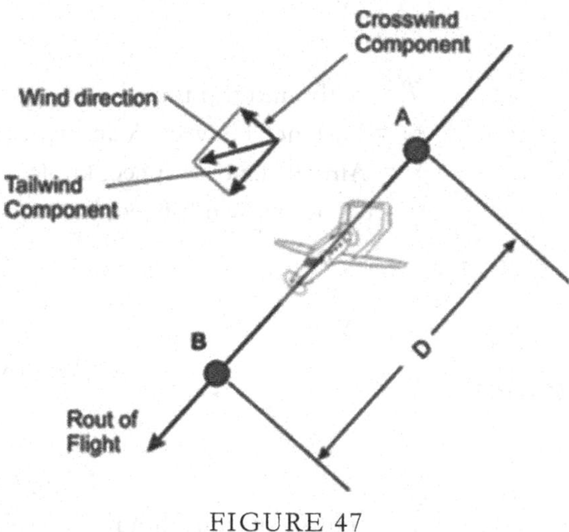

FIGURE 47
AIRPLANE TRIP WITH CROSSWIND

Assume that the airplane is flying with a quartering tailwind on the outbound trip and flies back home while the same wind direction and speed prevail, but it is now a quartering headwind. Two factors are different from the previous example.

First, the airplane does not benefit from the full force of the wind when flying with it but only from the component of the wind in the direction the airplane is moving over the ground. So, the velocity relative to the ground is not V on the outbound leg, but rather $V + v_T$. Secondly, the pilot must correct his heading and fly into the crosswind component of the wind, which means that, with reference to the air mass he is flying through, the pilot will have a longer trip because he will have to offset the crosswind component.

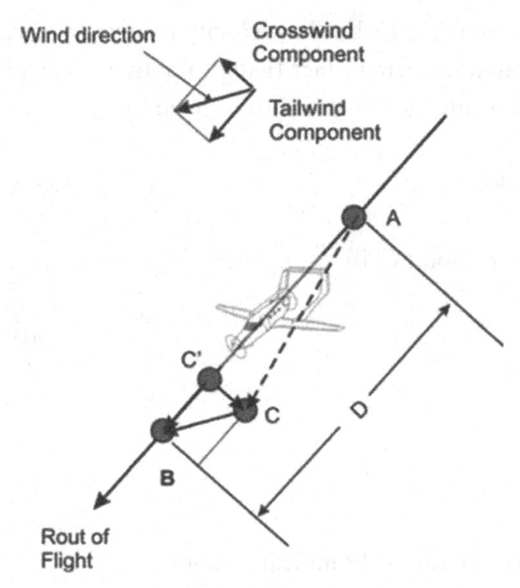

FIGURE 48
AIRPLANE ROUTE THROUGH AIR MASS

Repeating the above calculation taking into account the component of the wind, which is a headwind or tailwind, v_T, and the component of crosswind, v_C, which causes the airplane to fly a longer or shorter distance through the air mass, is a little tedious, but it is directly applicable to what Michelson and Morley were trying to do to identify the velocity of the ether relative to the earth.

The velocity of the airplane on the outbound trip with the wind at an angle θ relative to the outbound course is given by

$$V_1 = V + v_T, \qquad \text{EQUATION 97}$$

just as it was with no crosswind. However, the distance the airplane travels through the air mass changes. This is because the pilot must correct his course in the direction counter to the crosswind or he would not arrive at his destination. He would instead pass considerably to the right of it, having been blown off course by the crosswind.

He must fly farther, relative to the air mass, as though he were heading for point C in figure 48. Thus his velocity relative to the air mass, V, his true air speed, and the velocity of the wind, v, would add together as velocity vectors to carry him toward the destination point B.

The distance remains D, but his velocity relative to the ground must be calculated as though he were in fact flying to point C. The distance (through the air mass, not relative to the ground) is given by

$$AC = vT_1. \qquad \text{EQUATION 98}$$

The distance to point C' is

$$AC' = D - v_T T_1, \qquad \text{EQUATION 99}$$

and

$$C'C = v_C T_1. \qquad \text{EQUATION 100}$$

The geometry of figure 48 indicates that

$$\left(D - v_T T_1\right)^2 + v_c^2 T_1^2 = V^2 T_1^2 \qquad \text{EQUATION 101}$$

for the outbound trip, where the tailwind shortens the time en route but the crosswind lengthens the path. For the return trip, the equation is exactly the same, except that the tailwind is now a headwind and it lengthens the trip.

So

$$\left(D - v_T T_1\right)^2 + v_c^2 T_1^2 = V^2 T_1^2, \qquad \text{EQUATION 102}$$

and for the return trip,

$$\left(D + V_T T_2\right)^2 + V_c^2 T_2^2 = V^2 T_2^2. \qquad \text{EQUATION 103}$$

Because we have two unknowns in these two equations, we must know and use both the outbound time and the inbound time to solve for the downwind and crosswind components of the velocity.

For the outbound trip

$$\left(\frac{D}{VT_1} - \frac{v_T}{V}\right)^2 + \frac{v_c^2}{V^2} = 1, \qquad \text{EQUATION 104}$$

and

$$\frac{v_c}{V}=\sqrt{1-\left(\frac{D}{VT_1}-\frac{v_T}{V}\right)^2}\,. \qquad \text{EQUATION 105}$$

Likewise, for the inbound trip

$$\frac{v_c}{V}=\sqrt{1-\left(\frac{D}{VT_2}+\frac{v_T}{V}\right)^2}\,. \qquad \text{EQUATION 106}$$

From these two equations, the crosswind component can be eliminated by setting the right-hand sides of the two equations equal to each other, and it is apparent that the squared terms under the square root signs are also equal. Thus,

$$\left(\frac{D}{VT_2}+\frac{v_T}{V}\right)=\left(\frac{D}{VT_1}-\frac{v_T}{V}\right), \qquad \text{EQUATION 107}$$

and

$$v_T=\frac{D}{T_1}-\frac{D}{T_2}\,. \qquad \text{EQUATION 108}$$

Similarly, we can solve for the crosswind component, which adds to the time of the trip in both directions, by requiring the plane to fly farther through the air mass at its true air speed. The velocity, V, remember, is the speed through the air, not the speed over the ground. And the wind is assumed to continue at the same speed and direction during both legs of the trip.

We go back to equations 107 and 108, but instead of equating the two right-hand terms, we rearrange the equations, substitute $D/V_1 = T_1$, and then add them.

Rewriting,

$$\frac{D}{VT_1}-\frac{v_T}{V}=\sqrt{1-\frac{v_C^2}{V^2}} \qquad \text{EQUATION 109}$$

and

$$\frac{D}{VT_2} + \frac{v_T}{V} = \sqrt{1 - \frac{v_C^2}{V^2}}$$ EQUATION 110

are added to produce

$$\frac{D}{VT_1} + \frac{D}{VT_2} = 2\sqrt{1 - \frac{v_C^2}{V^2}}.$$ EQUATION 111

Solving for v_C,

$$1 - \frac{v_C^2}{V^2} = \frac{1}{4}\left(\frac{D}{VT_1} + \frac{D}{VT_2}\right)^2,$$ EQUATION 112

and

$$v_C = \sqrt{V^2 - \frac{1}{4}\left(\frac{D}{T_1} + \frac{D}{T_2}\right)^2}.$$ EQUATION 113

Were the timing only done at one end of the round trip, it would be necessary to time two round trips with different directions of flight in order to gather sufficient data for determination of both the wind speed and direction. Note that developing values for both the tailwind and crosswind components of the wind is equivalent to measuring its speed and direction, at least relative to the airplane's line of flight.

However, in order to make an accurate measurement of the wind speed with two round-trip measurements in different directions, the measurements would have to be quite accurate, and even slight variations in the wind speed would lead to significant errors.

But, if the experiment were repeated many times with a wide variety of flight directions (and the wind could be prevailed upon to remain essentially constant for the duration of the experiment), a pattern could be obtained that would eliminate much of the uncertainty.

For example, if we calculate the time required for the round trip at various angles, θ, of the wind to the direction of flight, the following equations can be used.

$$T_1 = \frac{D}{(V + v_T)} \frac{1}{\sqrt{1 - \frac{v_c^2}{V^2}}}, \qquad \text{EQUATION 114}$$

in which $(V + v_T)$ is the velocity corrected for the tailwind component, and

$$\frac{1}{\sqrt{1 - \frac{v_c^2}{V^2}}} \qquad \text{EQUATION 115}$$

is the effective distance corrected for the crosswind component.

The return trip time is

$$T_2 = \frac{D}{(V - v_T)} \frac{1}{\sqrt{1 - \frac{v_c^2}{V^2}}}, \qquad \text{EQUATION 116}$$

and the total time is

$$T_1 + T_2 = T = \frac{D((V + v) + (V - v_T))}{(V^2 - v_T^2)\sqrt{1 - \frac{v_c^2}{V^2}}}. \qquad \text{EQUATION 117}$$

This simplifies to

$$T = \frac{2D}{V}\left(\frac{1}{1 - \frac{v_T^2}{V^2}}\right)\left(\frac{1}{\sqrt{1 - \frac{v_c^2}{V^2}}}\right), \qquad \text{EQUATION 118}$$

where the first term is the time with no wind, the second is the correction for the tailwind component, and the third the correction for the crosswind component. When the total time is plotted as a function of the wind angle, the following graph results.

From figure 49 it is easy to see that the trip extension forms a sine wave pattern when plotted against the wind direction angle. To determine the wind speed and direction, it is only necessary to locate the angles of the peaks and valleys of the round trip time, which identify the direction of the wind and the maximum and minimum velocities relative to the known true air speed.

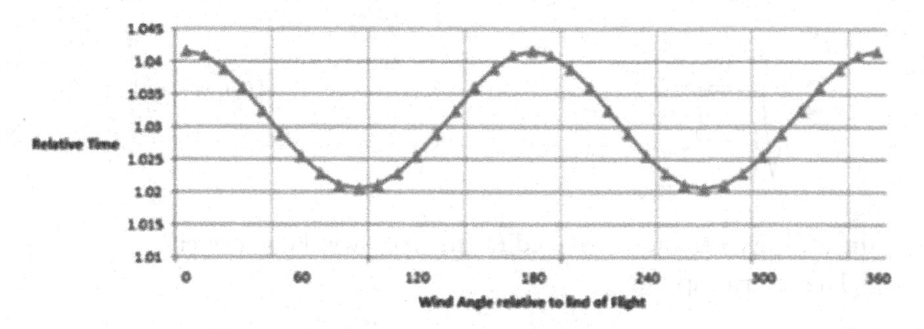

FIGURE 49
PLOT OF TRIP TIME VS WIND ANGLE

To further simplify matters, if the travel time information has been obtained for all the directions, as in the above example, it is apparent that the maximum time is experienced when the wind velocity is along the line of flight of the airplane (wind angle zero, or 180 degrees) and the minimum time is when the wind is a direct cross wind (wind angle 90 degrees, or 270 degrees).

The maximum and minimum times of the round trip under these conditions is given by

$$T_{Max} = \frac{2DV}{V^2 - v^2} = \frac{2D}{V}\left(\frac{1}{1 - \frac{v^2}{V^2}}\right), \qquad \text{Equation 119}$$

and the minimum time by

$$T_{\min} = \frac{2D}{V}\left(\frac{1}{\sqrt{1-\frac{v^2}{V^2}}}\right). \qquad \text{EQUATION 120}$$

The ratio of these two can be read from the chart and used to calculate v directly, from which

$$\frac{v^2}{V^2} = 1 - \left(\frac{T_{Min}}{T_{Max}}\right)^2. \qquad \text{EQUATION 121}$$

Although there does not seem to be much similarity between an airplane flying through a moving air mass and light waves being propagated through the all-pervasive luminiferous ether, the same calculations pertain to the determination of the wind speed and the speed of the ether relative to the earth as it orbits the sun. It is essentially equation 121 that Michelson and Morley used to calculate the velocity of the ether relative to that of the earth around the sun.

Also, the same limitations must apply. That is, the velocity of the wind (analogous to the velocity of the ether relative to the earth) must be constant in both direction and velocity during the experiments. We know the wind direction and velocity usually changes from day to day in the real world, but nothing, whatever, was known about the velocity of the ether.

TIMING A ROUND TRIP BY A LIGHT WAVE

If one presumes that light consists of waves propagated through the luminiferous ether at a fixed rate of speed, it should be possible to calculate the speed very much like the speed of the airplane was calculated in the foregoing example. One must, of course, presume that the luminiferous ether is moving in a relatively constant direction and velocity, and not wafting about with random motions, as the winds do above the earth.

If there were a component of the velocity that was affected by the velocity of the luminiferous ether relative to the experimenter's laboratory, experimenters should be able to measure the velocity by timing the round trip of a light wave and seeing how much it deviated from the fairly accurately known velocity of light. It is apparent from the above example that the procedure is analogous to timing the airplane's total round trip time rather than individual legs, so experiments would have to be made with more than one direction of the path of the light.

However, it was illustrated that the total time of flight would always be longer if there was a wind, regardless of whether it was a tailwind, headwind, or crosswind. One might reasonably assume that if measurements were made in a number of directions, those resulting in the shortest time would represent the experiments done with the light path moving in the direction of the ether in one direction and opposite the direction of the motion of the ether in the other. Then one could apply the formulae developed for the tailwind example and get a reasonable measure of the speed of the ether.

By the late 1800s, the velocity of light was relatively well established, with Michelson the foremost of the scientists involved with the measurement. It had been demonstrated to his satisfaction that light was transmitted as waves and was therefore conducted through a medium of some sort. He had speculated a good deal about the nature of the medium and the properties it would have to have in order to make the transmission of light according to wave theory possible. But there had been no direct evidence whatever of the existence of such a medium.

By this time, Michelson was a professor at Case Western University, and a prominent member of the scientific community. He undertook to determine the single property of the luminiferous ether that was most closely affected by his continuing study of the velocity of light: the velocity of the ether relative to the earth.

The reasonable presumption was that the ether would be moving through space at some speed and direction that, like the air masses in the paragraphs on crosswinds and tailwinds, was fairly steady, as opposed to wafting about at random. He pictured the earth as moving around the sun in an orbit that changed direction with respect to the motion of the ether, and further that the laboratory rotated with the earth and therefore was continuously rotating his apparatus with respect to the presumed constant flow of the ether.

Working with Edward Morley, he set up an experimental apparatus to measure the speed of light that could be rotated within the laboratory, in addition to the presumed rotation of the laboratory with respect to the ether by virtue of the earth's daily rotation and annual rotation about the sun.

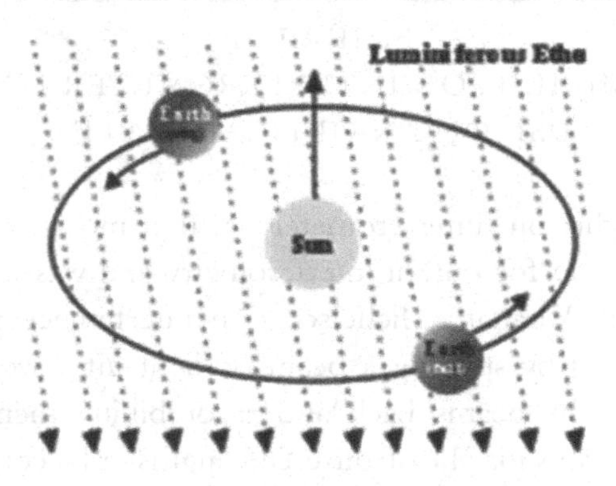

FIGURE 50
MOTION OF EARTH RELATIVE TO THE ETHER

Because they had no knowledge of the possible velocity of the ether relative to the earth, they chose to set up a very sensitive means for determining the speed of light and for detecting small changes in the speed.

Rather than using a rotating mirror or set of mirrors, as Michelson had done in prior experiments (and to which he returned in subsequent ones), he designed a unique interferometer aimed at using the diffraction pattern established by two beams of light passing through the interferometer after having traveled different distances from the light source.

The selection of an interferometer, the operation of which relied on the wave characteristics of light to produce interference patterns, further substantiates Michelson's firm belief that light was wavelike in character.

FIGURE 51
A MICHELSON INTERFEROMETER FOR
USE ON AN OPTICAL TABLE

> The Michelson interferometer is the most common configuration for optical interferometry and was invented by Albert Abraham Michelson. An interference pattern is produced by splitting a beam of light into two paths, bouncing the beams back and recombining them. The different paths may be of different lengths or be composed of different materials to create alternating interference fringes on a back detector. Michelson, along with Edward Morley, used this interferometer for the famous Michelson-Morley experiment (1887) in which this interferometer was used to show the constancy of the speed of light across multiple inertial frames, which removed the conceptual need for a Luminiferous Ether to provide a rest frame for light.[14]

Because they were not trying to measure the absolute speed of light, but rather the change in the speed when it was measured in the direction of the earth's orbit around the sun and at other directions at various angles to the orbit, Michelson and Morley did not need to rely on the rapidly rotating mirrors to give an absolute measure of the speed of light.

[14] From Wikipedia, the free encyclopedia.

To provide for rotation of the apparatus so as to measure the change in the speed of light at various orientations to the geometry of the earth's orbit, they used a much more compact arrangement than Michelson had used in any of his previous measurements of the speed of light.

The apparatus was, as was typical of Michelson, very carefully arranged to minimize any experimental errors he could foresee.

"The first named difficulties were entirely overcome by mounting the apparatus on a massive stone floating on mercury; and the second by increasing, by repeated reflection, the path of the light to about ten times its former value." This and much of the following material was taken directly from the *American Journal of Science* paper by Michelson and Morley.[15]

This cut the size down to a manageable plan area where it could be operated in any orientation relative to the surface of the earth.

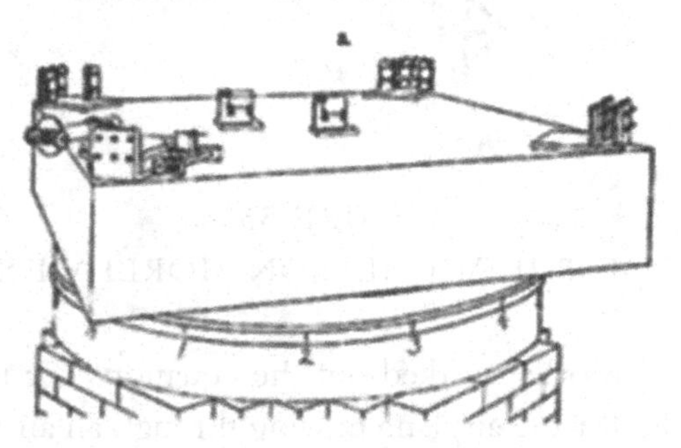

FIGURE 52
SUPPORT FOR THE INTERFEROMETER AND MIRRORS

A multiplicity of mirrors were set up to provide a path length long enough that they could make accurate measurements of the elapsed time between the initial beam of light striking the interferometer and the final beam after it had traversed the many paths between the mirrors. Although fairly complex in construction, the principle underlying the experiment was explained by a relatively simple diagram.

The elapsed time was measured by the displacement points at which the reflected light from the two mirrors could be observed using a telescope. The idea was that the motion of the earth through the ether (in the direction

[15] Albert A. Michelson and Edward Morley, "On the Relative Motion of the Earth and the Luminiferous Ether," *American Journal of Science,* 1887, 34 (203), 333–345.

s–c) would displace the light reflected from mirror, c, in the direction of the motion of the earth through the ether, whereas the light reflected from the mirror, b, would not be shifted. The difference in location of the two points of light should be a measure of the velocity of the earth through the ether.

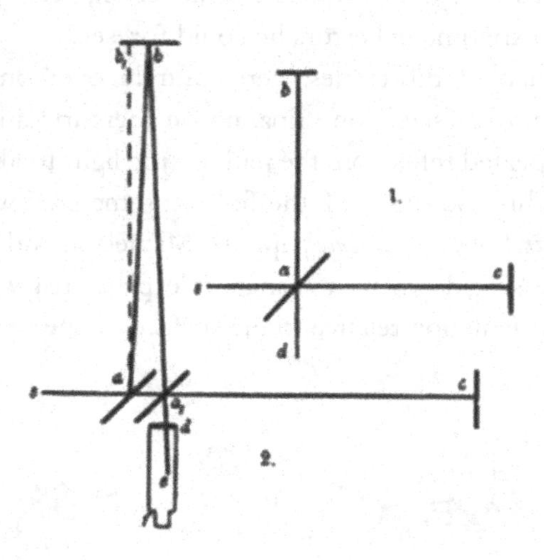

FIGURE 53
SCHEMATIC OF THE MICHELSON-MORLEY EXPERIMENT

Michelson and Morley worked out the equations for the speed of the ether much as I did for the airplane moving through an air mass at a known true air speed. The equations are repeated below as he explained them, using slightly different notation.

$$T = \frac{D}{V + v}, \qquad \text{EQUATION 122}$$

where

T = time, seconds
V= velocity of light [relative to the ether]
D = Distance
v = velocity of earth in its orbit.

The only thing different from my earlier examples is that I used wind velocity as v. Michelson used as the lower value the velocity of the earth's orbit around the sun, and he expected that the velocity measured would be the velocity of the ether relative to the earth, from which he could deduce the velocity of the ether relative to the sun.

In both cases, v is the slower of the two velocities. So although Michelson is dealing with three velocities—earth relative to the sun, ether relative to the earth, and light relative to the ether—he seems to have tacitly assumed that the earth/sun velocity and earth/ether velocity were going to come out the same.

This is not really a reasonable assumption, and the experiment would not have worked out well had there actually been ether permeating space and moving with a high velocity in any direction relative to the sun.

But the velocity of ether relative to the earth is not explicitly mentioned. It seems that Michelson presumed that the velocity of the ether would be constant with respect to the sun, and therefore v would be equivalent to the wind speed in my example.

$$T_1 = \frac{D}{V - v}$$ EQUATION 123

where

T_1 = Time for the return trip.

The total time for a round trip is

$$T + T_1 = \frac{D}{V + v} + \frac{D}{V - v},$$ EQUATION 124

or

$$T_T = \frac{D(V - v) + D(V + v)}{(V + v)(V - v)} = \frac{2DV}{V^2 - v^2},$$ EQUATION 125

and

$$TV = \text{Distance} = 2D\frac{V^2}{V^2 - v^2} = 2D\left(\frac{1}{1 - \frac{v^2}{V^2}}\right) \approx 2D\left(1 + \frac{v^2}{V^2}\right).$$

EQUATION 126

For the path at right angles to the rotation of the earth (the crosswind situation), to the same degree of accuracy as equation 126

$$T = \frac{D}{\sqrt{V^2 + v^2}}, \qquad \text{EQUATION 127}$$

and

$$T_1 = \frac{D}{\sqrt{V^2 + v^2}}, \qquad \text{EQUATION 128}$$

from which

$$T_T = 2D\frac{1}{\sqrt{V^2 + v^2}} = 2D\frac{V}{\sqrt{1 + \frac{v^2}{V^2}}} \qquad \text{EQUATION 129}$$

and

$$T_T V = 2D\frac{V^2}{\sqrt{1 + \frac{v^2}{V^2}}} \approx 2D\left(1 - \frac{v^2}{V^2}\right), \qquad \text{EQUATION 130}$$

By adding the approximations in equations 128 and 130,

$$\Delta T_T V = D\left(\frac{v^2}{V^2}\right). \qquad \text{EQUATION 131}$$

They figured that if the apparatus was turned ninety degrees, then the roles would be reversed and the displacement fringes observed would be given by

$$2\Delta T_T V = 2D\left(\frac{v^2}{V^2}\right). \qquad \text{EQUATION 132}$$

From this and the velocity of the earth's orbit around the sun, they calculated that the distance between the peaks and troughs of the presumed waves would be 2D * 10^{-8} meters.

As always, Michelson and Morley did a superb job as an experimenters, and their conclusions were impossible to refute. They were, in short:

> The results of the observations are expressed graphically in fig. 6. The upper is the curve for the observations at noon, and the lower that for the evening observations. The dotted curves represent one-eighth of the theoretical displacements. It seems fair to conclude from the figure that if there is any displacement

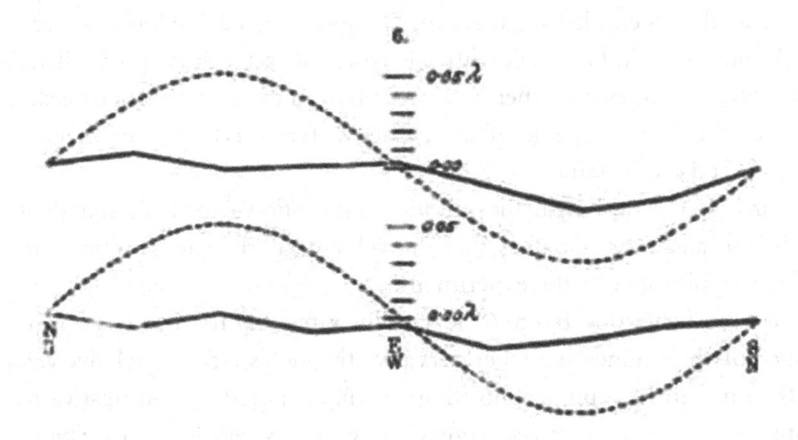

> due to the relative motion of the earth and the luminiferous ether, this cannot be much greater than 0.01 of the distance between the fringes.
>
> Considering the motion of the earth in its orbit only, this displacement should be
>
> $$2D\frac{v^2}{V^2} = 2Dx10^{-8}$$
>
> The distance D was about eleven meters, or 2x107 wave-lengths of yellow light; hence the displacement to be expected was 0•4 fringe. The actual displacement was certainly less

> than the twentieth part of this, and probably less than the fortieth part. But since the displacement is proportional to the square of the velocity, the relative velocity of the earth and the ether is probably less than one sixth the earth's orbital velocity, and certainly less than one-fourth.[16]

With this brief statement, Michelson made the case that if the ether was in fact the medium through which light was conducted as a wave form, it was apparently moving along with the earth, which of course makes no sense at all. The alternate explanation is that the measurement of the velocity of light does not depend in any way on the motion of the measuring apparatus, which forms the central theorem upon which Einstein's special theory of relativity rests. This is also equivalent to saying that the velocity of light does not depend on a conducting medium filling the vacuum of outer space.

While I can find no fault with the experimental technique of Michelson and Morley, I suggest that there is a trivial flaw in the analytical approach used and that there are a couple of altogether different conclusions that can be drawn based on the data.

First, let us deal with the implicit assumption (nowhere stated in the Michelson and Morley paper) that the velocity of the earth around the sun had any significance in the experiment.

While Michelson's figure 6 clearly illustrates that if there is a consistent motion of the luminescent ether pervasive through space, the relative velocity of the earth in its orbit around the sun will change direction relative to the motion of the ether as the seasons change, the experiments described were carried out over a few days time and did not wait for the earth's direction to change significantly relative to the remainder of the cosmos.

From the standpoint of measuring the motion of the ether, the speed and direction of the earth relative to the ether was completely unknown at the time the measurements were taken. Thus the origin for the coordinate system of the experiment was basically the center of the rotating table containing the light source and mirrors. The position and velocity of the sun during the experiments was of no significance whatever, save possibly as a reference velocity, although the speed of light seems to be a much more reasonable reference for the velocity of the ether.

---

[16] Albert A. Michelson and Edward Morley, "On the Relative Motion of the Earth and the Luminiferous Ether," *American Journal of Science*, 1887, 34 (203), 333–345.

The measurement, therefore, was a perfectly valid determination of the velocity of the ether, if one presumed that light was moving through the ether like an airplane moving through a moving air mass and the position of the earth relative to the sun had no more significance than it would have had on the timing of the airplane round trip times through the moving air mass.

A rather trivial comment involves the use of approximations by expansion as infinite series and then neglecting as trivial all the terms beyond the second one in making the conclusions. While this technique is generally quite acceptable and useful, it depends on an assumption of what will be significant and what will not. In this case, the tacit assumption was made that the velocity of the motion of the ether was very small compared to the velocity of light. This was demonstrated by the experiment, but the assumption was used in arriving at that conclusion. There was no firm basis for making this assumption prior to completing the program.

A more straightforward determination of the velocity of the ether, which does not require it to be trivial as compared with the velocity of light, was worked out in my airplane analogy.

$$\frac{v^2}{V^2} = 1 - \left(\frac{T_{Min}}{T_{Max}} \right)^2 .$$

EQUATION 133

This equation is exact and requires no assumptions about what the value of v will come out to be at the end of the experiment. Because it was found to be close to zero, it made no difference in the outcome.

My serious comment is that an altogether different conclusion can be drawn from what they measured with their apparatus. That is that they did not measure the difference in the velocity of light through the atmosphere in the direction of the earth's orbit and perpendicular to it, but rather the speed at which their apparatus was moving in the fourth-dimensional direction as the entire three-dimensional universe expands. This measurement velocity is independent of the motion of the earth or anything else in the three-dimensional universe.

The light waves, which they assumed were passing through the space between the source and the receptor in wavelike form—are instead transferred instantaneously from the emitter to the receptor without passing through the intervening space. Nothing I can see in the experimental technique would tell you which of these conclusions is correct. Either light moves through space at a speed that is independent of the direction of the light in space, or light does not move through space at all, but is transferred simultaneously from the source atom to the receptor without traversing the intervening space.

But of course you know which way I would vote on this question.

APPENDIX
MICHELSON'S 1887 EXPERIMENTAL RESULTS

The formulæ employed are:

(1) $$\tan\phi = \frac{d}{r}$$

(2) $$V = \frac{1592000'' x D x \eta}{\phi''}$$

φ =	angle of deflection.
d =	corrected displacement (linear).
r =	radius of measurement.
D =	twice the distance between the mirrors.
n =	number of revolutions per second.
α =	inclination of plane of rotation
d =	deflection as read from micrometer.
B =	number of beats per second between electric Vt_2 fork and standard Vt_3.
Cor =	correction for temperature of standard Vt^3.
V =	velocity of light.
T =	value of one turn of screw. (Table, page 126.)

These are taken directly from Michelson's paper on the results of the Naval Academy experiments.[17]

> Substituting for d, its value or d × T × sec α (log sec α = .00008), and for D its value 3972.46, and reducing to kilometers, the formulæ become—
>
> (3) $\tan\phi = c'\frac{dT}{r}$; log c' =.51607
>
> (4) $V = c\frac{n}{\phi}$; log c =.49670

D and r are expressed in feet and d' in millimeters.
Vt_3 fork makes 256.070 vibrations per second at 65° Fahr.

D =	3972.46 feet.
tan α =	tangent of angle of inclination of plane of rotation = 0.02 in all but the last twelve observations, in which it was 0.015.
log c' =	.51607 (.51603 in last twelve observations.).
log c =	.49670.

The electric fork makes ½(256.070 + B + cor.) vibrations per second, and n is a multiple, submultiple, or simple ratio of this.

[17] Albert A. Michelson, *Experimental Determination of the Velocity of Light*, made at the US Naval Academy, Annapolis. Release Date: March 28, 2004 [EBook #11753].

OBSERVATIONS

June 17. Sunset. Image good; best in column (4).

The columns are sets of readings of the micrometer for the deflected image of slit.

	112.81	112.80	112.83	112.74	112.79
	81	81	81	76	78
	79	78	78	74	74
	80	75	74	76	74
	79	77	74	76	77
	82	79	72	78	81
	82	73	76	78	77
	76	78	81	79	75
	83	79	74	83	82
	73	73	76	78	82
	-------	-------	-------	-------	-------
Mean =	112.801	112.773	112.769	112.772	112.779
Zero =	0.260	0.260	0.260	0.260	0.260
	-------	-------	-------	-------	-------
d =	112.451	112.513	112.509	112.512	112.519
Temp =	77°	77°	77°	77°	77°
B =	+ 1.500				
Corr =	− .144				

	+ 1.365				
	256.070				
	-------				
n =	257.426	257.43	257.43	257.43	257.43
r =	28.157	28.157	28.157	28.157	28.157

CHAPTER 9

THE QUESTION OF WAVE INTERFERENCE

The question of whether Michelson measured the speed of light or the rate of expansion of the universe has been dealt with tediously enough already. However, there is one facet of the Michelson-Morley experiments that raises a question that has been troublesome to me in many areas.

The question is, "If light is not propagated through space in the form of waves, why do so many experiments show light to exhibit interference patterns that look very much like those seen when water waves?" If it walks like a duck and quacks like a duck, it is very likely to be a duck.

I agree, a duck is quite likely to be a duck, but this is not necessarily so when it comes to identifying light as a wave form. It doesn't fit my prejudices. There must be something else that walks like a duck and sounds like a duck and leads us to err in this direction.

In particular, it was difficult to complain that Michelson and Morley used a Michelson interferometer (a tacit announcement that they believed light to be a wave form that exhibited interference patterns) when their work was so nicely done and has stood unquestioned for so long. But I will try just the same.

It is not hard to picture what Michelson saw when an interferometer, which depends on the supposed wave properties of light to produce bands of light and dark on a photographic plate, was used as his velocity measuring device. Or in this case, circles of light and dark seen through a telescope.

I will try to explain how interference patterns can be formed by radiant energy transfer without the existence of waves. Michelson's interferometer is a good place to start in understanding how such devices could work without the presence of waves.

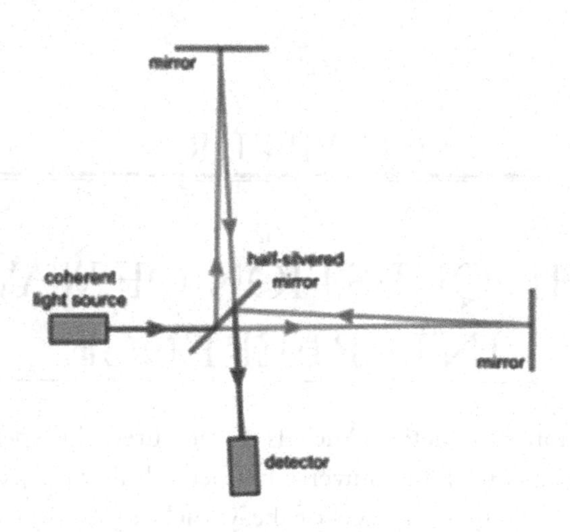

FIGURE 54
DIAGRAM OF THE MICHELSON INTERFEROMETER

The light source for the Michelson-Morley experiment was a sodium vapor lamp because he wanted to use as close as possible to a single wavelength or frequency (or to my way of thinking, single energy of emission of each energy transfer). This was presumably to avoid the differences in refraction of light as it was transmitted through the semireflective mirrors and telescope lenses.

Had lasers been in use at the time, he would have no doubt opted to use a laser for the light source, as they produce a monochromatic, coherent beam of light with all the emitting atoms having the same orientation within the crystal emitters. However, even with monochromatic light sources, the image produced at the target telescope or photographic plate is likely to consist of a target circular image in the center surrounded by circles or light and dark bands, usually presumed to be due to interference of the waves, which have slightly different path lengths from the source to the receptor and so arrive out of phase.

The rings are not, in my opinion, necessarily the result of the wavelike properties of light. I think they are instead the result of the interposition of devices that introduce refraction into the picture. Such is the case when a Michelson interferometer is used, but the argument applies equally well where ordinary lenses are used to focus the beam of light or when a telescope is used to observe the results.

Figure 55 shows a typical circular "interference pattern" from a Michelson interferometer. I do not believe interference of light waves is the explanation for such patterns; rather, it is the time difference between light that has been delayed by its passage through glass or some other optically clear medium and light that has not encountered any such material and makes the traverses the distance from the source to the receptor instantaneously, or nearly so when it is transmitted through air.

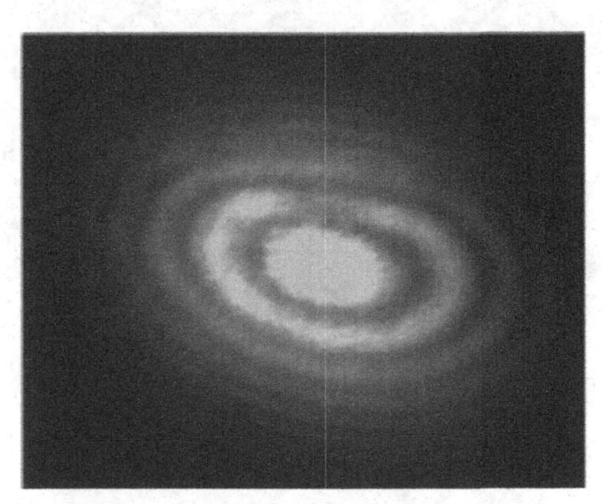

FIGURE 55
GREEN LASER INTERFERENCE PATTERN
USING A MICHELSON INTERFEROMETER

The explanation is a bit tedious but, I believe, straightforward. Figure 56 shows the essence of the experiment with the Michelson interferometer. A beam of light from a single source is split, and one half is reflected to a target screen (or telescopic viewer) and the other half is transmitted through the glass of the mirror (a flat lens) to a second mirror that is farther from the source, increasing the path length.

Figure 56 is superimposed on a grid representing the x–T plane through the *local universe* with a hydrogen atom having a proton at the origin at T (the *local time*) = ct, (*galactic time*) = 0. At this time, the electron orbiting the proton at position A transfers energy to a receptor at point B, in the interferometer, which receives it and with essentially no delay retransmits it to the screen location at C. Both points B and C represent positions of electrons orbiting protons that are in the future with respect to the electron at position A.

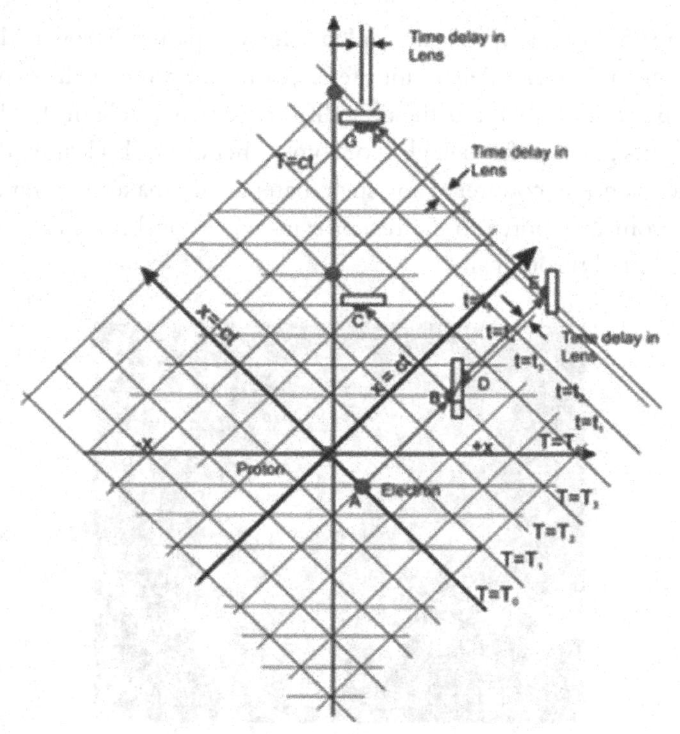

FIGURE 56
INTERFERENCE WITHOUT WAVES

At some time in the *galactic future*, but simultaneously so far as *local time* is concerned, the energy transmission is complete. An observer would be able to see the energy appear at point C, and he might assume, along with Michelson and Morley, that it was there because light waves had propagated from point A to B and then to point C, traveling through space via the ether at the *apparent speed of light.*

Of course, an observer would not be able to see the light emitted by a single atom and would have to have many, many such transactions taking place per second to register on his nervous system. But it is much simpler to talk about single radiant energy transactions than millions of them.

Now, assume that instead of one atom at the origin, there were two at essentially the same place, so that a second orbiting electron could enter into an energy transfer process from the same location, point A, and at the same time as the one already described. This orbiting electron at point A interacts with an atom on the surface of the interferometer lens at the same location, point B, but instead of being reflected in a near instantaneous transaction as in the previous case, this one interacts with an atom that retransmits the energy inward, so that it passes through the glass (a flat lens).

In the discussion of reflectivity and refractivity, it was pointed out that once energy was absorbed by a receptor atom, it would nearly instantaneously retransmit it if a second receptor was available. Thus reflection from a mirror to a final receptor is nearly instantaneous, whereas transmission through the glass of the lens requires many thousands of absorptions and retransmissions. Therefore, it takes a finite time for the energy being handed from atom to atom to reach the other side of the glass lens, where it ultimately reaches point D.

The energy impacting the glass lens is passed along through the glass and reaches the opposite side at point D only after the passage of some length of time, Δt. This is consistent with the observations that the velocity of light through matter is always slower than through a vacuum and is a function of the refractive index of the material, and to some extent, the frequency associated with the high-energy state of the electrons involved.

By the time the light reaches point D on the far side of the lens, all the objects shown in figure 56 will have advanced in the T direction by the distance $c\Delta t$.

At this time, the final transmission to the receptor screen will be simultaneous with the emission from the lens surface. However, the screen will not be in the same place in time as it was when the first energy transaction took place. It will have continued to move upward in the T direction. The point on the screen at which the refracted light is absorbed will not be in the center of the screen at point G, where the reflected energy transaction took place, but will rather be to the right of G, at point F, because of the time delay. Thus the second point of light will be displaced from the first in space because of its displacement in time.

It should be kept in mind that the only spatial dimension shown in this simplified drawing is the x direction representing the viewpoint from the origin to the right. If this is taken as zero compass degrees, it is apparent that the same argument would hold had any other direction been chosen arbitrarily. So one may assume that the off-center electron in the x direction might have just as well been off center in any other direction and that the reception of electrons at this same fixed distance from the center would occur.

This would account for the picture on the screen consisting of a very sharply defined dot in the center representing all the light from the electron at A that was reflected and surrounded by a clearly defined circle of zero width around the central point at a distance defined by the time delay, $c\Delta t$, that would be in turn set by the refractive index and the frequency of rotation of the excited atoms.

In reality, the emissions are not from a point source but from a small source comprising at least thousands of excited electrons in the filament of the sodium vapor lamp. This would account for the rather fuzzy circle in the center of the green laser light “interference pattern” in figure 55.

Similarly, if one imagines that each dot comprising the fuzzy circle has around it an invisible fine circle of light caused by the transmitted and refracted radiation from the thousands of atoms comprising the radiation source, one can see that rather than forming a single, distinct and well-defined circle around the central bright area, here would be instead a fuzzy ring comprising refracted counterparts of the many dots making up the central bright core.

Because the central dot is surrounded by void space inside the fuzzy ring and the central dot is not large enough to fill the ring, it is apparent that the ring will itself be surrounded by another dark space before the dots comprising the rings around the outward central core dots are encountered. Because there are fewer dots in the outer part of the central core, the next ring out will be fainter than the first ring.

It is as though I were describing the interference pattern shown in figure 55. Similar arguments can be made to explain the interference patterns seen in situations like the reflection of white light from thin surface films as a rainbow of different diffracted colors.

CHAPTER 10

MICHELSON AND MORLEY AND THE PIGEON EXPERIMENT

Is there a fatal flaw in my concept of the infinite speed of light? The theory of relativity? The structure of the atom? Everything?

A question came up that gave me some concern that my whole approach might be incorrect. As a matter of fact, it came up in a dream I had, from which I awoke with a feeling of foreboding. My problem went like this.

Suppose Michelson and Morley had, instead of attempting to measure the speed of light, set out to measure the speed of a carrier pigeon (a different, slower form of communication than a light ray) using basically the same technique they used for light. Instead of a mirror to reflect the light back toward them, they had a lab assistant receive the carrier pigeon at its destination and, in a negligible time, substitute a second pigeon trained to fly back home.

They would now measure the time interval between the departure of the carrier pigeon and the return of its counterpart. Dividing the distance the carrier pigeons traveled by the elapsed time, they would arrive at a speed of flight (about 80 km/hour).

Now if one were to postulate that carrier pigeons actually fly instantaneously from place to place and arrive back at their starting point in the three-dimensional world instantaneously, but that during the time interval the three-dimensional universe had moved into the future by the product of the time interval and the velocity of the universe in the fourth-dimensional direction, would not they conclude that the universe was moving in the fourth-dimensional direction at 80 km/hour (the *apparent speed of pigeons*), rather than the 300,000 km/second I have been using as the *apparent speed of light*?

In short, any time interval they measured between two events that appear to be separated in time by the speed of the moving object could be mistaken for the speed at which the universe is moving in the fourth-dimensional direction, could it not?

This would kill my whole argument that Michelson and Morley mistook their measurement for the speed of light when it was actually the speed of expansion of the universe. Obviously, my assumption would not apply to the carrier pigeon, so the question is, "Why does it apply to light but not to carrier pigeons?"

To clarify the situation, let's suppose we recreate the Michelson and Morley experiments using the pigeons instead of sunlight. Recall that their objective was to find out whether the speed of light would appear to be different when they were measuring the velocity in the direction of motion of the earth's orbit around the sun or in the opposite direction. In short, they made measurements when they were "in motion" and "at rest." So to be fair, we should measure the speed of the carrier pigeons when the experimenters were "moving" and "at rest." Let us suppose Michelson and Morley set their apparatus up on a railroad flatcar on tracks that run in the same direction as the pigeon's flight path.

Now let us suppose they do their initial experiment from their mobile laboratory with it sitting on the railroad siding and not moving at all (with respect to the earth). Their laboratory, the pigeon, and everything else will be, in my view, moving in the fourth-dimensional direction at the velocity that may or may not be determined by the experiment. The "stationary" experiment is depicted in figure 57.

The pigeon is released at the origin at time t = 0. As he flies toward his initial destination, some 40 km to the east, the earth and all the things stationary with respect to it are moving in the direction the universe is expanding into. The pigeon flies at 80 km/hr relative to the earth and to the stationary laboratory. It reaches its initial destination in half an hour and starts back (for simplicity, let's assume that this is a nonunion carrier pigeon who flies both ways).

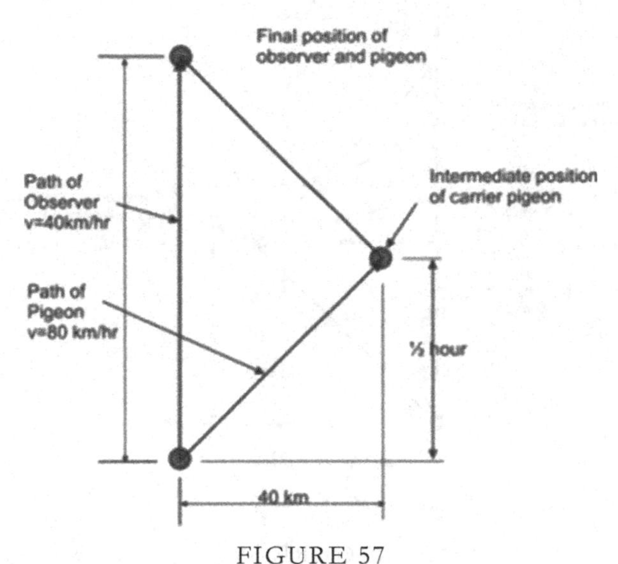

FIGURE 57
STATIONARY PIGEON EXPERIMENT

In a no-wind situation, it also takes half an hour for the pigeon to return, and Michelson and Morley calculate his speed to be 80 km/hr. They repeat this experiment with various directions to the destination and conclude that there is no wind (i.e., the luminiferous ether is not moving with respect to the earth).

They pause to wonder if the pigeon really moved 80 km/hr over the path length because they did not actually watch it fly away and return. They consider the possibility that the bird actually moved instantaneously from point A to point B and it was they, the experimenters, who moved from point A to point B in the hour via an unknown fourth dimension.

But being careful experimenters, they remembered that their task involved seeing if the bird appeared to fly at a different velocity if they and their laboratory were moving relative to the earth. So they arrange to repeat the experiment with the train moving at 40 km/hr, or half the bird's speed. The geometry of the second experiment is shown in figure 58.

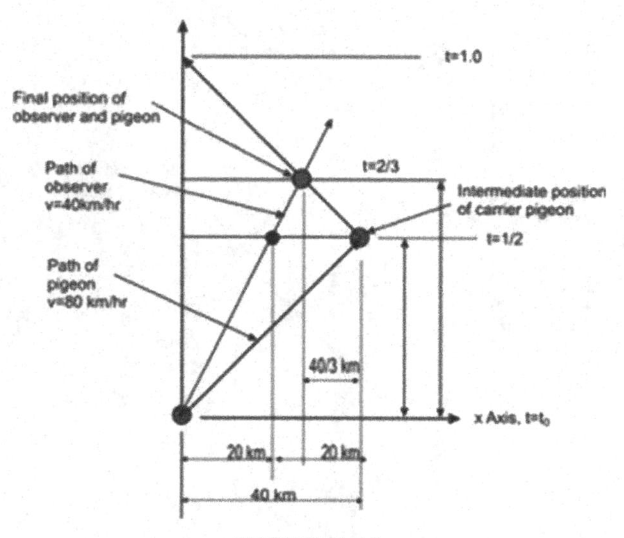

FIGURE 58
PIGEON SPEED FROM THE STANDPOINT
OF A MOVING OBSERVER

In the first picture, the bird's speed was taken as 80 km/hr, and the distance to the turnaround point was 40 km, therefore the elapsed time for the experiment is one hour. The bird returns from his 80 km round trip in one hour, giving him a calculated speed of 80 km/hr.

$$v_r = \frac{2D}{\Delta t} = \frac{80Km}{1hr} = 80Km / hr. \qquad \text{Equation 134}$$

Or, the universe was moving at 80 km/hr and the bird at infinite speed. One or the other.

In the second picture, the experimenter's apparatus is set up on the bed of the moving railroad flatcar and is moving in the direction of the bird's initial flight. The bird appears to be moving away from the laboratory at half the bird's speed of flight, or 40 km/hr.

$$v_r = 80 - 40km / hr. \qquad \text{Equation 135}$$

After the bird reaches his intermediate stop and turns around, it appears to be moving toward the laboratory much faster, at the sum of the lab speed plus the bird's speed relative to the earth.

$$v_r' = 80 + 40 = 120 Km/hr. \qquad \text{EQUATION 136}$$

To further complicate the problem, the pigeon's final destination is also moving east at 40 km/hr.

We can calculate the point at which the moving laboratory and the moving bird cross paths by writing the equation for the location of the bird as a function of time (we only have to do this for the return part of the trip), where the bird's location east of the starting point is given by

$$x_b = 80 - 80t, \qquad \text{EQUATION137}$$

where

$$x_b = \text{distance east, } km$$
$$t = \text{time, } hr.$$

The laboratory's location is given by

$$x_0 = 40t. \qquad \text{EQUATION 138}$$

When the bird and the observer cross paths, the two x values are equal, so

$$80 - 80t = 40t, \qquad \text{EQUATION 139}$$

and we can solve for t, the elapsed time:

$$t = \frac{80}{120} = \Delta t = \frac{2}{3} hr. \qquad \text{EQUATION 140}$$

The value of x at this time is

$$x = x_o = x_p = 80/3 \text{ K}m. \qquad \text{EQUATION 141}$$

The calculated distance the bird has gone relative to the moving laboratory is calculated from the following data points:

at t=0, $x_o = 0, x_b = 0$
at t=1/2, $x_o = 20, x_b = 40,$

$$\Delta D_1 = 20\ Km$$ EQUATION 142

at t=2/3, $x_{0=} 80/3, x_b = 80/3\ Km,$

$$\Delta D_2 = 40 - 80/3 = 40/3\ Km.$$ EQUATION 143

So the velocity of the carrier pigeon relative to the laboratory that released him is not 80 km/hr, as was measured with respect to the stationary laboratory, nor is it measured as simply the difference between the velocities of the bird and the laboratory. It is

$$v_r = (\Delta D_1 + \Delta D_2)/\Delta T = (20 + 40/3)/(2/3),$$

EQUATION 144

or

$$v_r = \left(100/3\right)/\left(2/3\right) = 50\ Km/hr.$$ EQUATION 145

The velocity of the bird is now measured as something more than the relative velocity of the bird and the train.

Both Michelson and Morley agree that the speed is definitely different when measured from a moving laboratory in contrast with the result obtained when they were checking for the velocity of light, which did not change when they were moving one way or the other. If they repeat this experiment with many railroad trains running in different directions, they again conclude that there is no wind involved in the experiment, so the wind velocity is announced to the world to be pretty close to zero. But it is also obvious to them that the bird did not move instantaneously from place to place, so they had mistaken the speed of the expansion of the universe into the fourth dimension for the speed of the bird.

Were this the case, the speed of expansion of the universe would depend on how fast their train was moving. Being realistic scientists, they conclude that they are not able to control the speed at which the universe is moving through the fourth dimension by moving the throttle of their locomotive.

They would conclude that the carrier pigeon really traverses the space between its starting point and its ultimate destination, as does just about everything else that moves from one place to another.

This leaves me free to go on claiming that light, or more generally, radiant energy transfer, seems to be the sole exception and jumps across empty space without actually going through it.

My theory withstood the pigeon test, but there will undoubtedly be many more situations that will arise where I may not be able to make a successful defense.

CHAPTER 11

THE IMPLICATION OF RADIATION INTO THE FUTURE

The possibility that light emitted and other forms of radiation consist of the simultaneous transfer of energy from an excited atom at one point in space and time to another distant point in space and time has an almost metaphysical implication. The obvious fact is that light is always transmitted from a "present time" and received in a "future time." If there is in fact an emitting atom and a receiving atom at each end of the transaction, the receiving atom must be in the "future" with respect to the emitting atom.

While it is easy enough to picture the mechanism proposed for this process for energy transfers that bring radiation from some point in our galactic past to the present or to other points in the past, the picture becomes hazy if you think about the transfer of energy into the future. Yet it can only be transferred into the future of the emission source.

If you presume that not only are our three familiar spatial dimensions wound around a tiny spherical kernel that brings many specific points in space and time into direct physical contact, but that the fourth dimension, through which the universe is expanding as time passes, is also wound around the kernel, the "past" takes on a different meaning than we usually assign to it.

When we look out at the night sky, conventional physics tells us that we are receiving light that was emitted from distant stars years ago, or centuries ago, or millions of years ago. In fact, some of the stars we see might have, in this view, already gone out of existence.

In my view, the present (which I have called the *local present* to distinguish it from the conventional view of time) consists of what you can see. That is, the stars you see comprise a part of your local present, not your past. Do they really exist right now, rather than a million years in the past? Paraphrasing President Bill Clinton, it depends on how you define "exist." Certainly there are things that are clearly in our past, whether local or galactic. The birthday cake eaten at yesterday's party is clearly in the past. You cannot see it now, nor will you ever be able to see it again.

The star is somewhat different because you can see it. I believe that the light emitted by the fusion of hydrogen into helium is being delivered to your eyes in the present time, and that, so far as can be determined by measurement, the emission and receipt of the energy are happening in the same instant. When we see a nova, to my way of thinking, it is happening right now, and we get the news immediately. The *galactic past* exists as long as you can see it. People at different locations may disagree about which items in the *galactic past* exist in their *local present*.

The metaphysical implications don't come up until you consider what happens on the starry night if you step outside and shine a powerful light into the night sky. To my way of thinking, the radiation from the light is not a one-sided affair, with the light simply going out into the void and traversing empty space, where it may or may not eventually find a receptor. To me, it is a process that requires both emitting atoms and absorbing atoms to coexist in the same *local present*.

This was, for a long time, a sticking point for me. I did not want to accept that the future was in fact already there, and we just couldn't see it until we got there. However, if for a moment you grant me that it is really there, you will have no problem imagining that at some time, like two days from now, we will be at that time and will be able to look back on the present as having become part of the past. Was our present there already, when we imagined it two days ago?

My simple answer has to be yes. The complete universe is there, waiting for us to grow into it. We cannot see it, because the transfer of radiant energy is a one-way street, with light always passing in the direction from the *galactic past* to the *galactic future*. Never the other direction.

The *galactic present*—the surface of the two-dimensional sphere in the analog universe used for illustration and the real three-dimensional universe—act like mirrors at our present location. When we try to look in the direction of the future (along our line of sight along the x, y, or z axis in our conical local present, when our line of sight reaches the T axis), what we see is the reflection of the galactic past along the other side of the T axis.

To get a little deeper into the metaphysics, let us consider the path of the light from a distant star that we can see at some particular moment. The "line of sight" stretches from the star to an atom within the optical receptors in our eye. This particular radiation event was completed when the energy left the star and was simultaneously registered in our eye.

However, there was undoubtedly a great deal of light that was given off by the distant star at nearly the same time that did not make the connection with our eye. Some lit up the landscape or was registered by countless other eyes looking up at the starry night. But presumably there was light emitted that failed to fall on the earth at all. Where did this light go?

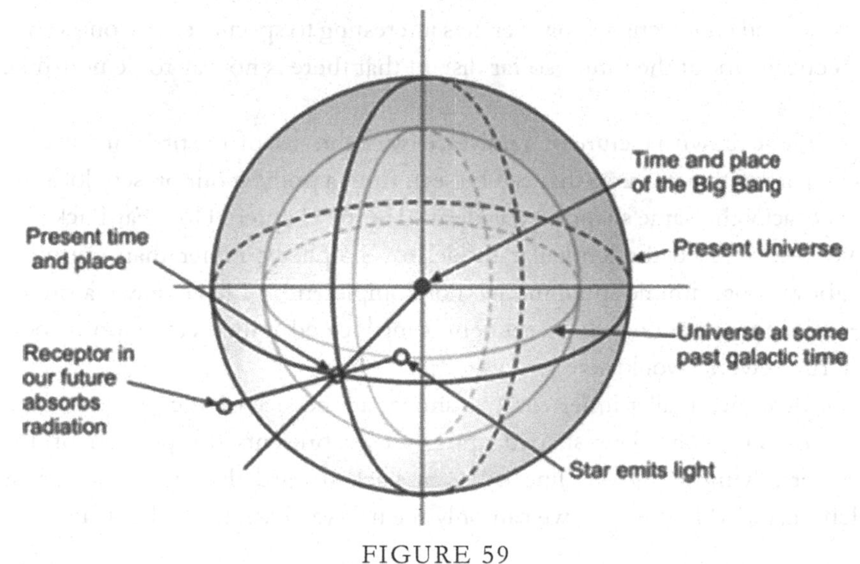

FIGURE 59
LIGHT EMITTED IN THE GALACTIC PAST
AND ABSORBED IN THE FUTURE

I believe it went past us in both space and time, and found a receptor in the future. A receptor that was there waiting and had the star in its *local present.* Let us look at the two lines of sight through both three-dimensional space and through the T dimension, as shown in figure 59. It is my contention that the light would not have been emitted by the star were the receptor not already in a position to receive it.

The suggestion is that the lines of sight that are wound around the universal kernel are continuous from the moment of the big bang to the present time, and they do not stop there but continue on into the future. What separates the past from the future (regardless of whether we are taking about the *galactic past* and future or the *local past* and future) is simply the position in four-dimensional space of the present three-dimensional *galactic universe.* The present moment in time lies at the apex of the local universe, which coincides with the *present galactic universe* at this point.

There is, therefore, a super universe that contains our present known universe, and all that it was, and all that it will be. While we are unable to see into the future, we can see into the *galactic past*, but only things that are relatively far away.

Which leads to speculation as to what this future contains. There is, of course, no way to predict the future beyond the painstaking methods of science and engineering. However, it is interesting to speculate—as long as one speculates about the future so far distant that there is no way to demonstrate error.

I have drawn a picture of a universe twice the size of the present universe. The part of this universe that can be seen from a point at our present location has exactly the same shape as was derived in the chapter "How Far Back Can We See?" I used the lenticular model for simplicity, rather than the more elaborate logarithmic spiral model. For completeness, I have drawn a similar envelope representing what a sentient being located at the exact opposite pole of the universe would see.

Here the smaller inner circle is shown as the size of the present *galactic universe*. The solid, lens-shaped upper area represents the portion of the universe lying along our line of sight back toward the big bang. It was demonstrated that at best we can only see halfway back to the big bang.

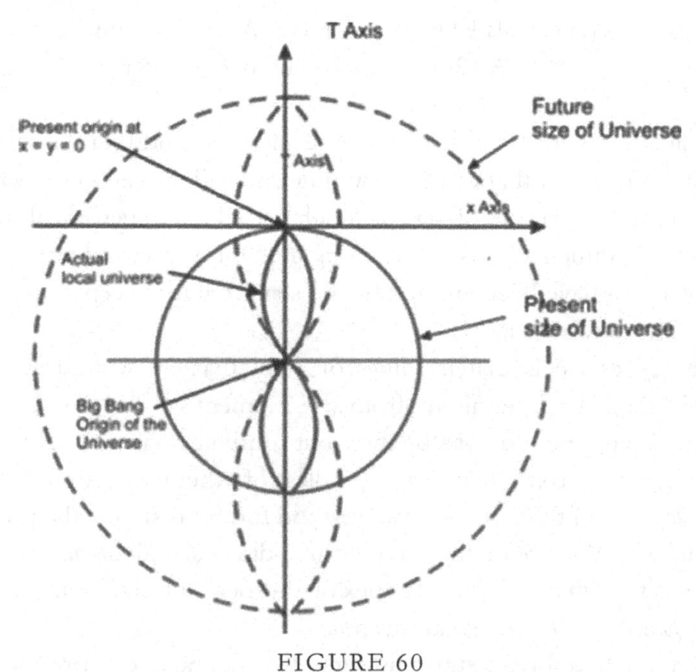

FIGURE 60
PROJECTION ANOTHER 13.5 BILLION YEARS

Now, one would expect that when the universe had expanded to twice its present size (there is no reason to suppose that the expansion will slow down or speed up because gravity has essentially no effect on expansion in the fourth-dimensional direction), the part of the universe that will be in the line of sight back toward the big bang will be represented by the dotted upper lens-shaped area—exactly like the present *local universe*, but larger. Now we have always presumed that the T axis is wound around the tiny universal kernel with an unimaginable number of layers that have no "thickness" in the fifth-dimensional direction.

Is there a possibility that the top lens-shaped *local universe* will bend around and connect with the bottom of the lens-shaped *local universe*, just as all the other possible lens-shaped local universes at the outer rim of the future galactic universe connect with their opposites on the other side? Would this not present the appearance of another big bang? Or would it be the original big bang?

CHAPTER 12

HOW DID NUCLEI FORM?

The proposed theory of light, gravity, and energy has not touched on the question of how nuclei work and how they came to be in the first place.

Unlike the velocity of light in a vacuum, this is not a problem that has bothered me a great deal. It fits more into the realm of interesting sidelines. To be more honest, my knowledge of physics is still at least fifty years out of date. While I am presuming to question the works of Newton, Michelson, Einstein, Planck, Bohr, and others, I don't even know the names of the scientists responsible for modern quantum mechanics and nuclear physics.

I suppose this ought to keep me from speculating about things that go on within the nucleus of the atom. But why not?

First, it is necessary to look at the formation of neutrons, which are ubiquitous but don't seem to have much purpose in life. They do not reap, neither do they sow. But they are there, and they have to find a place at the table, so to speak.

Unlike electrons and protons, they do not seem to have lives of their own, and for the most part they only exist within the nuclei of atoms. That is not to say they can't come out, but they are apparently very short-lived when they do. They have a half-life of only a few minutes before decomposing to give off an electron, a proton, and an electron neutrino. An electron neutrino? Yes, this is something theorized by Wolfgang Pauli in 1930 to account for some of energy that goes missing when the neutron decomposes.

The neutrinos are weird little devils. They are like electrons with no electrical charge, although they have a little bit of mass: 2.2eV vs 0.511MeV for the electron. It takes a heap of neutrinos to make an electron mass, and no amount of them will add up to the electron charge. If the physicists are to be believed, the air is full of these things, with something like 65 billion of them passing through each square centimeter of the earth's surface every second. They seldom interact with anything. Good thing!

Apparently, neutrons are not a simple, uncomplicated union of a proton and an electron, although they come close. In charge, they are neutral, as one would suppose them to be were they made by the joining somehow of a proton and an electron.

A reasonable explanation of why the electron and the proton have identical but opposite charges was explained by the association with the rotational energy imparted by the rotation of the universe wrapped around the universal kernel. Located on opposite sides of the kernel, the rotation is identical for the two particles but reversed in direction. The question would arise as to where on the kernel the neutron is located so that it does not share the rotation that influences the charged particles.

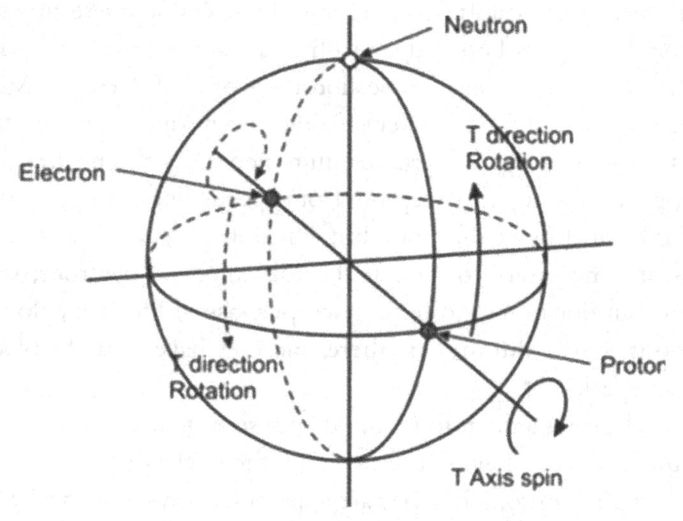

FIGURE 61
LOCATION OF NEUTRON ON UNIVERSAL KERNEL

And how, explained in a way simple enough for the mind of an aging, retired mechanical engineer, does the electron neutrino get involved?

There are several possibilities that would satisfy my limited knowledge of the behavior of neutrons in the nucleus of atoms. The nucleus is known to be relatively compact as compared with the volume of the entire atom, so there cannot be much displacement of the nuclear neutron from the location of the proton in an atom. However, it does not have the spin energy around the T axis associated with the electron and proton, which shows up as charge.

Possibly, the electron neutrino is simply a spin component around one of the three-dimensional x–y–z directions, rather than the T direction. This wouldn't have any charge associated with it, but it would involve some little bit of energy. Not mass, but energy, just as the photon (an imaginary particle in my mind) has energy, but no mass. The energy of a rapidly orbiting electron in one atom that is exchanged for the energy of a more slowly orbiting electron in a receptor atom does not involve any alteration in mass for the electrons, and does not need a photon to fly through the space between the source and receptor to deliver the energy.

One possibility is that the neutron is halfway between the proton and the electron in the T direction. That is, it exists slightly behind the proton in the T direction and at the essentially same position in three-dimensional space. Were this the case, the neutron would be formed by the fusion of a proton and electron, and an enormous spin energy would be retained in the neutron as the rotational energy of the proton and neutron, almost touching each other rotate as speeds approaching c by galactic standards, and an enormous multiple of c in terms of local time.

A possible position of the neutron in the nucleus of an atom of heavy hydrogen is shown in figure 62.

Another possible conclusion is that the neutrino is not really a particle at all, but rather a very high frequency radiation, representing the energy trapped in the neutron by the melding of the proton and electron. Very high in frequency because, rather than being located in the normal electron orbit, it is associated with the electron captured by the proton and bound into an orbit with a nearly zero radius. An electron forced into this small an orbit would have all the energy usually associated with a much larger, lower frequency orbit, but constrained in a very small orbit within an intensely strong positive field where it could be held tightly at enormous rotational frequency. This very high frequency could not be exchanged with an electron in the normal inner orbit of matter, and would, like X-rays, pass through relatively dense materials without interaction. Like any other form of radiation, it would normally interact only with a proton in a very, very heavy atom. This would explain why neutrinos pass through the earth like X-rays passing through wood or plastic, but reacting with lead.

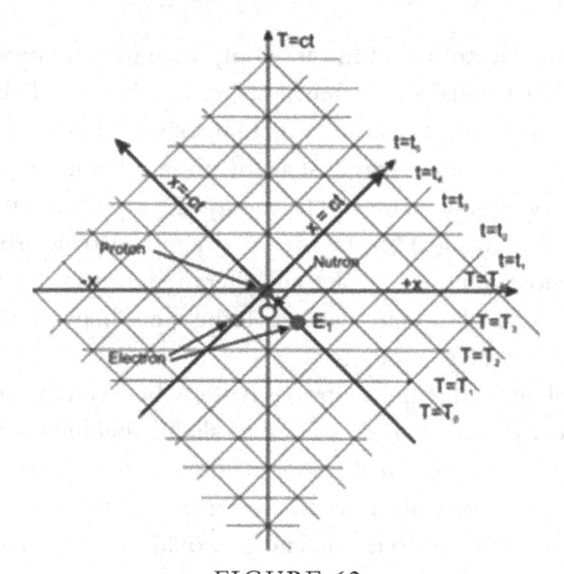

FIGURE 62
NEUTRON POSITION IN A HEAVY HYDROGEN ATOM

The proton is shown at the origin, with the *local present* time outline showing the x axis and T axis. The electron orbiting the nucleus orbits at a distance r_0 from the origin in the horizontal plane. The electron, so far as the proton is concerned, is at the same local time, while its counterpart on the same *galactic time* is in the proton's future.

The neutron is located at essentially the same x, y, z position in space, but is halfway between the electron and proton in the T direction. In this position, the mass of the neutron adds to that of the proton and helps prevent the electrons from escaping from orbit at higher velocities than would be the case were it not present.

The neutron shown on the surface of the universal kernel halfway between the proton and electron is also halfway between the proton and the orbit of the electrons in the T direction.

To pursue the matter a bit further, it is interesting to look at the geometry of the hydrogen molecule and the corresponding heavy hydrogen molecule with two neutrons per molecule. The picture of an ordinary hydrogen molecule with two protons and two electrons and no neutrons is shown below.

One proton, labeled B, is located at the local origin, $x = y = z = 0$. The two orbiting electrons, E_1 and E_2, are located at the opposite side of the universal kernel, and the second proton, labeled A, appears to coincide with the first one when viewed on the kernel but is two radii below it in the local time diagram.

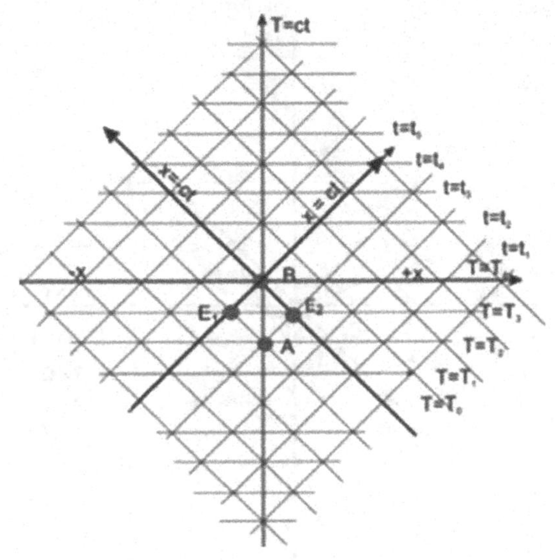

FIGURE 63
A HYDROGEN MOLECULE IN LOCAL TIME

Alternatively, proton A could be located at the same x and y coordinates as proton B, but at a different value of z, the dimension omitted from the diagram. While a little difficult to visualize, this would result in the same diagram were the section taken through the y = 0 plane and showed the x and z dimensions, save that the two protons would be shown side by side and the two electrons would appear as a single point with E_1 behind E_2.

Using the picture above, where do the two neutrons go to maintain the mass of the molecule and keep the charge balance?

The heavy hydrogen molecule picture above has the center of mass exactly where it should be, centered between the electrons, and has the proper charges located in the nucleus and the orbiting electrons.

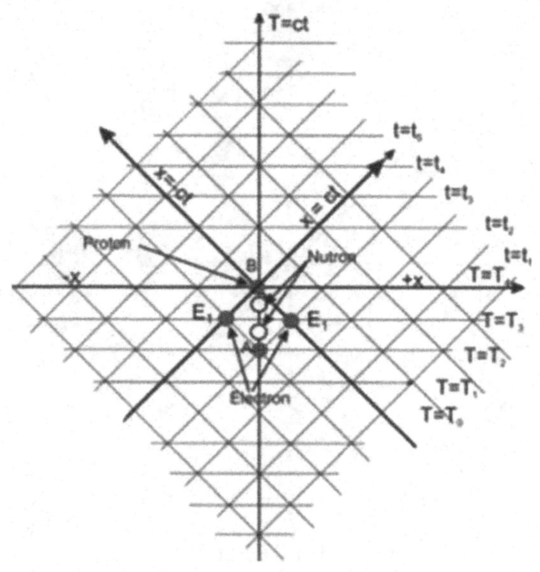

FIGURE 64
THE HEAVY HYDROGEN MOLECULE

For heavier atoms than hydrogen or helium, picture the inner orbital circle of the electrons as a sphere at a distance of r_0 from the center of mass of the atom which is a group of neutrons in the nucleus, again at half the distance between the protons and the inner orbit of the electrons.

So much for idle speculation.

CHAPTER 13

THE NEED FOR DARK MATTER

Much has been made over the possibility that 90 percent or more of the matter in the universe is not the stars, planets, galaxies, and other astronomical bodies that we can observe, but is instead dark matter. Something—and there is no agreement on what—that has an enormous amount of mass but does not give off any radiant energy we can use to detect it, permeates space, according to much of the current literature.

Speculation about the nature of dark matter has included everything from neutrinos, the tiny particles with almost no mass and no charge, to black holes, with unbelievably dense concentrations of matter that do not emit light but exert very strong gravitational forces.

The arguments for the existence of dark matter are not so complex and esoteric as are the proposed explanations of what it may be.

My picture of the way the universe is constructed does not require dark matter, but to understand the differences, it is reasonable to start with the conventional arguments for the existence of dark matter and then proceed to the alternative ways of satisfying the problems of the astrophysicists without the need for it.

Of course, if it doesn't exist, it is not really necessary to choose between the many alternatives forms it might be in if it really were there.

DID EINSTEIN NEED DARK MATTER?

The foremost argument for the existence of dark matter with perhaps ten times the mass of all the known stars, galaxies, and other visible matter in the universe is the inflation theory, which is based on the premise that gravity of the mass in the universe is somehow holding the universe together, and that a certain amount of mass per unit volume is required to keep stable. More than this critical amount will lead to a shrinking universe and eventual collapse into a black hole, while less than the critical amount will allow expansion at an accelerating rate without limit.

Albert Einstein, in his general theory of relativity, attributed the curvature of space to the presence of matter (or energy, as he regarded matter and energy to be interchangeable). For him, the curvature of space required a certain density of matter to be dispersed more or less uniformly throughout the limitless but finite three-dimensional universe. He believed, initially, that the universe was of stable size, as did most of his contemporaries.

However, his special theory of relativity attributed the curvature of space to the presence of mass, and he could calculate the mass per unit volume which would be necessary to account for his observations. The problem is compounded by the evidence that the universe is expanding. My own belief is that it is expanding at a uniform rate, which is unrelated to the gravitational interactions of the masses of the planets, stars, galaxies, and the like. The forces which we identify as gravitational, electrostatic, and electromagnetic are all due to relatively local differences in the way the universe is moving in the time-like direction. They relate, not to the properties of space, but rather to the direction of time, which is altered by massive bodies. But this is a minority of one opinion. The general approach to the argument that much of the universe must be filled with dark matter is summed up nicely in a web page which was published by the National Solar Universe. This web page is no longer on the site, but was reproduced by Wikipedia, from which the following excerpt was taken.

> The mass density of visible matter (i.e., galaxies) in the Universe is estimated at 3e − 28 kg/m^3 (3e − 31 times the mass density of water). The radius of the visible Universe is estimated at $1.78*10^{26}$ m (18 thousand million light-years) plus or minus 20 percent or so. This yields a total mass of the visible matter of about $6*10^{51}$ kg (1.3810^{52} lb), which is equivalent to the weight of $4*10^{78}$ hydrogen atoms. Since nine out of ten atoms and ions in the Universe are in the form of hydrogen, this is a reasonable estimate for the number of atoms in the Universe (based on the visible galaxies only). Maybe a correction factor of the order of 2 has to be applied to account for the warping of space on very large scales.

> However, there is considerable uncertainty about the mass density of all matter (visible and invisible) and energy (through Einstein's $E = mc^2$ equation). When one studies the movement of matter in and around galaxies, then it appears that up to about 10 times more mass is pulling at the matter (through its gravity) than is accounted for in the visible stars. This is the "missing-mass" problem. If this factor of ten holds throughout the Universe, then the total mass in the Universe would be about $6*10^{52}$ kg. If the missing mass were mostly in the form of hydrogen atoms (which is not at all clear) then the number of atoms would be about $4*10^{79}$.
>
> A currently popular theory of the formation of the Universe (the so-called Inflation Theory) predicts that the mass density of the Universe should be close to the so-called critical density that separates an open universe that always grows from a closed universe that ultimately collapses again. This critical mass density is currently equal to $6*10^{-27}$ kg/m^3. If the Universe is at the critical density, then the total mass of the Universe is closer to $1*10^{53}$ kg, and the number of atoms (assuming that most of the mass is in the form of hydrogen atoms) about $6*10^{79}$.
>
> It seems, then, that the number of atoms in the Universe is at least about $4*10^{78}$, but perhaps as many as $6*10^{79}$.

My contention is that the force of gravity has nothing whatever to do with the rate of expansion of the universe, in that the expansion is entirely into the fourth-dimensional direction while the effects of gravitational "forces" are contained within our three normal spatial dimensions. The universe is expanding at a constant rate, which just happens to be c, the *apparent speed of light.*

Gravity is the result of the changes in the direction of time which is warped locally by the presence of mass in three-dimensional space. Masses warp the time direction in a relatively local region around each mass, and I will argue a bit later, that the effect of this warping, and of gravitational effects in general do not reach very far from even the most massive bodies, when viewed on a galactic scale.

I have dismissed this idea on the grounds that the universe is expanding just about as fast as it possibly could, assuming that all the matter in the universe was given an initial velocity, c, at around the time of the big bang and that it hasn't changed much since then. The "force of gravity" works in the three spatial dimensions, and the universe is expanding in a fourth-dimensional direction perpendicular to the ordinary spatial dimensions. Gravity doesn't have any effect in this direction, so it cannot slow the expansion down.

Gravity probably had a lot more to do with the distribution of matter in space early on for reasons I will get to shortly, but it certainly is not what is holding the universe together now. If it were, we would be in trouble. It would require a lot of dark matter to do the job, and I don't think there is any. Or at least not much.

THE VELOCITY OF THE SPIRAL ARMS

A more cogent argument for the existence of dark matter is the observations by a number of astronomers that the spiral galaxies seem to be spinning around their centers, but the pattern of the spin doesn't follow the same rules that apply to planets orbiting a star. Instead, the mass of the galaxies would appear to be centered somewhere other than at the center of visible mass.

On the surface, it seems like it would be pretty hard to tell if a whole galaxy was rotating because they are so far away and so vast that they don't appear to be moving at all. Galaxies are part of the system of "fixed stars" because their relative positions, while they may be moving thousands of miles per second relative to earth, don't seem to be changing from day to day or month to month.

In order to describe the method used for determination that the galaxies are, or at least appear to be, spinning, I am going to lapse into the conventional terms used for description of the properties of light—frequency, wavelength, etc.—rather than try to substitute my preferences. This will avoid having to insert a lot of descriptive phrases, like, "which would be described as having a frequency of thus and so if light did in fact consist of waves …"

The astronomer's secret weapon is the spectrograph, which can split the light received from a single star in the outer rim of a galaxy into the various wavelengths and measure the exact frequency of each one. This enables them to determine the amount of change in frequency of specific emission bands from the hydrogen atom, from which they can determine the degree of red shift.

The red shift is a measure of how far away from us the light source is and how fast it is moving. This is much like a highway patrolman's radar. The radar receiver is capable of telling how far away an object is by calculating the time it takes a high-frequency radio wave to make the round trip from his unit to an object like an automobile, but it is also capable of telling how fast the automobile is moving by the change in frequency of the reflected signal.

Astronomers use the spectrograph for measuring the variations in velocity between the opposite extremities of spiral galaxies, and this leads to the conclusion that they are spinning around the center of mass, much as planets orbit around their sun.

The presumption is that if the stars on one side of the spiral galaxy are moving away from the earth relative to the center of the galaxy, and on the other side of the galaxy toward the earth relative to the center of the galaxy, this is indicative of rotation of the stars around the center of the galaxy. This is not necessarily the case. However, the conclusion is generally that the outlying stars are orbiting the center of mass, which should be at the center of the galaxy. But the velocities do not fit the pattern of planetary orbiting, in that the outlying stars appear to be moving just as fast as many of the closer-in stars.

This leads to the conclusion that there is a great deal more mass in the galaxy than is calculated by the relationship between the brightness of the stars making up the galaxy and the masses of the stars. This "missing mass," or dark mass, is either distributed throughout the galaxy or may be outside the main body of the galaxy. This would account for the peculiar orbital velocities.

However, there is another possibility that completely does away with the need for dark matter in the case of the spiral galaxies. Suppose that the motions of the outlying stars are not related to gravitational attraction at all, but rather to the random motions of the celestial bodies imparted at the time of the big bang origin of the universe.

This is entirely possible in that gravity is the weakest of the forces in nature, and the force diminishes with the square of the distance between the masses involved.

The expansion of the universe, on the other hand, brings about an acceleration of all the material bodies in the universe away from all other ones. Unlike gravity, this effect increases as the masses in question move farther away from each other. This acceleration is, in some ways, a form of antigravity in that it acts to separate masses. It will be demonstrated that it acts in a negligible way at short distances and becomes increasingly important at large distances.

By way of illustration, I have calculated the distance between two massive objects, m_1 and m_2, which are attracted toward each other by gravity and accelerate away from each other by the expansion of the universe. At some distance between the masses, these two "opposing forces" should just balance. At greater distances, the two bodies will move away from each other, and at lesser distances, they will "fall" toward each other under the influence of gravity. This distance is calculated by determining the acceleration due to the attractive force of gravity and the "expansive acceleration" due to the expansion of the universe and setting the two values equal.

This is done in the following paragraphs, and then the critical distance determined for our sun as one of the massive bodies.

First, the acceleration due to gravity is given by

$$F = \frac{m_1 m_2 G}{x^2},$$ EQUATION 163

where

F = force
m_1 = first mass
m_2 = second mass
G = Universal gravitation constant
x = distance between the two masses.

Also,

$$F = m_1 a_1 = -m_2 a_2 .$$ EQUATION 164

Taking m_1 for the more massive, central body presumed to be at the origin, and m_2 the lesser body, the acceleration of the second body produced by gravity at a distance x between the two bodies is

$$a_2 = -\frac{m_1 G}{x^2}.$$ EQUATION 165

In the above equation, the acceleration is shown as negative because it acts to reduce the distance between the two bodies, or reduce the value of x.

The acceleration of the second body away from the first can be calculated based on Hubble's constant.

$$v_2 = Hx,$$ EQUATION 166

where

v_2 = velocity of the second mass
H = Hubble's constant.

It was shown in my earlier book that Hubble's constant is numerically equal to the reciprocal of the age of the universe.

$$H = \frac{1}{t},$$ EQUATION 167

where

t = age of the universe,

which can be taken as a constant for purposes of this calculation. Also,

$$\frac{dx}{dt} = v_2,$$ EQUATION 168

so

$$\frac{dv_2}{dt} = Hv_2.$$ EQUATION 169

Substituting the value of v_2,

$$a_2 = H^2 x.$$ EQUATION 170

This acceleration is taken as positive because it tends to increase the distance between the two bodies and increase the value of x.

$$a_2 = \frac{m_1 G}{x^2}.$$ EQUATION 171

Setting the two accelerations numerically equal, as they should be at the point where the gravitational and expansion accelerations just cancel each other out,

$$\frac{m_1 G}{x^2} = H^2 x,$$ EQUATION 172

so

$$x^3 = \frac{m_1 G}{H^2},$$ EQUATION 173

and

$$x = \sqrt[3]{\frac{m_1 G}{H^2}}\,. \qquad \text{EQUATION 174}$$

$$H = \frac{1}{t} \qquad \text{EQUATION 175}$$

because

$$x = \sqrt[3]{m_1 G t^2}\,. \qquad \text{EQUATION 176}$$

This has been worked out for an example where the mass of the central object is taken as that of the sun. The minor mass can be any size so long as it is small relative to the mass of the sun.

From the above calculation, the distance at which gravity is just balanced by the acceleration of bodies away from each other due to the expansion of the universe is roughly 1,400 light-years. While this is a very large distance relative to everyday experiences, it is not very far in astronomical terms.

TABLE 6
CALCULATION OF GRAVITY/EXPANSION
BALANCE POINT X3 = MGT

Mass of sun is	1.99E+30	kg
G	6.67E-11	m3/kg-sec2
t	4.25E+18	Sec
x^3	2.40E+57	meters^3
x	1.33816E+19	meters
	1.338E+16	km
Balance Distance	1413.454332	light-years
light-year is 300,000* 60*60*24*365.25	9.46728E+15	meters

For example, the sun is toward the outer reaches of our spiral galaxy, the Milky Way. The Milky Way galaxy contains roughly 200 billion stars. Most of these stars are not visible from earth. Almost everything that we can see in the sky belongs to the Milky Way galaxy.

The sun is about 26,000 light-years from the center of the Milky Way galaxy, which is about 80,000 to 120,000 light-years across (and less than 7,000 light-years thick). We are located on one of its spiral arms, out toward the edge. It takes the sun (and our solar system) roughly 200–250 million years to orbit once around the Milky Way. In this orbit, we (and the rest of the solar system) are traveling at a velocity of about 155 miles/sec (250 km/sec).[18]

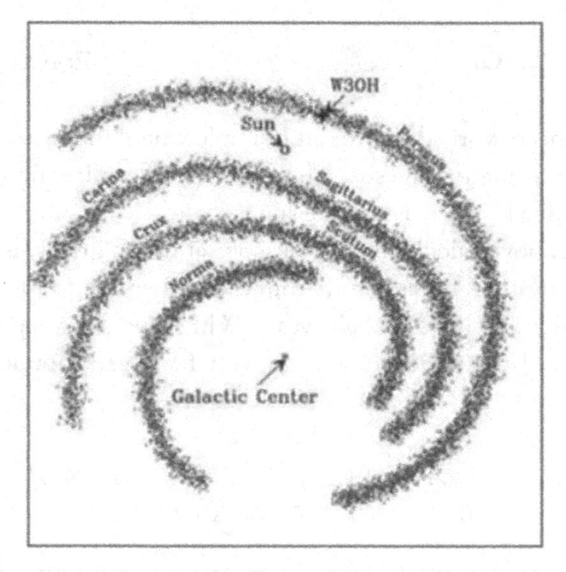

FIGURE 66
SKETCH OF THE MILKY WAY GALAXY

It is apparent that the gravitational attraction of the earth, while exerting what appears to be undiminished gravitational force on the planets in our solar system, is not likely to have any real effect on stars located near the center of our galaxy.

[18] Author unknown, Enchanted Learning Website, Our Solar System's Location in the Milky Way Galaxy, http://www.enchantedlearning.com/subjects/astronomy/solarsystem/where.shtml, 2010. [Note: this site is aimed at readers in third and fourth grades.]

Pluto's distance from the sun at aphelion is only about 7.275×10^9 km, or on the order of 1/10,000 of a light-year.

It is clear that the effect of gravity (presuming you believe the foregoing calculations) works at planetary distances, but is not so likely to be a substantial factor in the motion of stars within the spiral galaxies.

Of course, the presence of many stars of much greater mass than the sun at any point near the center of the galaxy might be capable of exerting sufficient force to bring about rotation of the stars in planetary fashion around the center of mass, but it does not seem likely that this is the case and does not explain the anomaly in the pattern of rotation.

Dark matter, unless it comes in exceedingly large lumps, is not likely to be influencing the trajectories of the stars in the spiral arms of galaxies. Of course, black holes, which have all the requisite characteristics of dark mass, could conceivably meet the requirements, but they would have to be distributed in space in a way that is unlike the distribution of matter which emits light.

Dark matter is not required to account for the curvature of space and would have no influence on the curvature of space (other than producing the local gravitational effect). It certainly does not have any influence on the rate of expansion of the universe, which is in the direction of the fourth spatial dimension, while gravity only acts in the ordinary three-dimensional space.

On balance, I do not believe dark matter exists, other than in the occasional black hole or possibly in relatively small quantities of dust or other cold matter that is too small in size to be detectable by reflected light.

I do not believe we are failing to account for 90 percent of the universe. Perhaps a little, but not most of it.

[illegible] distance [illegible] about [illegible] km [illegible] of light [illegible]

[illegible] or galaxy [illegible] believe [illegible] within the [illegible] galaxies.

[illegible] of the [illegible] mass [illegible] than the [illegible] point [illegible] center of the galaxy [illegible] distance [illegible] planets [illegible] does not seem likely that this [illegible] and [illegible] explain the [illegible]

[illegible] not likely [illegible] black holes [illegible] characteristics of [illegible] would have to be [illegible] of matter which [illegible]

[illegible] of space [illegible]

[illegible] other [illegible] galaxies [illegible]

CHAPTER 14

TRANSFORMATION OF COORDINATES

In general, the equation giving the relationship between the three-dimensional spatial coordinates in our everyday world and the fourth, time-like direction, T, has been characterized by the presumption that the three-dimensional universe we inhabit is expanding in the fourth-dimensional direction.

$$r = ct. \qquad \text{EQUATION 177}$$

For the ordinary three-dimensional world,

$$r = \sqrt{x^2 + y^2 + z^2}, \qquad \text{EQUATION 178}$$

which represents an expanding sphere with the center at the big bang.

When a fourth dimension is added,

$$r = \sqrt{x^2 + y^2 + z^2 + T^2}, \qquad \text{EQUATION 179}$$

it still has its center at the big bang.

This is the equation I used in the previous book to describe the expanding universe:

$$x^2 + y^2 + z^2 + T^2 = ct^2. \qquad \text{EQUATION 180}$$

Now the question is simply one of readdressing the coordinates so the origin is on the surface rather than at the center of the four-dimensional universe. This means that the values should all be referenced to a point on the surface, where at any time, t,

$$(x - x_0)^2 + (y - y_0)^2 + (z - z_0)^2 + (T - T_0)^2 = c^2(t - t_0)^2.$$

EQUATION 181

If the origin is taken as x = y = T = t =0 as the center of the four-dimensional sphere, you get the equation I used. If, on the other hand, you take the origin to be at some point on the surface and still take T = ct, it looks like the equation 181 is only valid for values of

$$x^2 + y^2 + z^2 << T^2.$$

EQUATION 182

This approximation works just fine if the spatial dimensions under consideration are small compared to the size of the entire universe. That is, millions of light-years would be considered a small distance as compared with the 27 or so billion light-years diameter of the entire universe.

However, it is worthwhile to look at the mechanics of the transformation of coordinates from the center of the four-dimensional universe to the location of the three-dimensional universe at the present time. We are interested in looking at the overall history of the universe, back to and including the big bang, and also to the opposite side of the universe, diametrically opposite us on the other side of the big bang.

The transformation from the absolute coordinate system, with the origin at the location in space and time of the big bang, to a local coordinate system with the origin at an arbitrary point in time (such as right now) and location on the surface of the two-dimensional spherical analog of the real 3-D universe (for example, at our present location) is somewhat complicated mathematically.

Figure 67 shows the geometry of this transformation.

In the illustrative picture, an arbitrary point on the surface of the sphere is assumed to have coordinates x_1, y_1, z_1, T_1, with respect to the origin at the center of the sphere. If the origin is moved to the point on the surface of the sphere, where the x', y', and T' coordinate axes meet, the same point will now have coordinates x_1', y_1', z_1', and T' referenced to the new coordinate system.

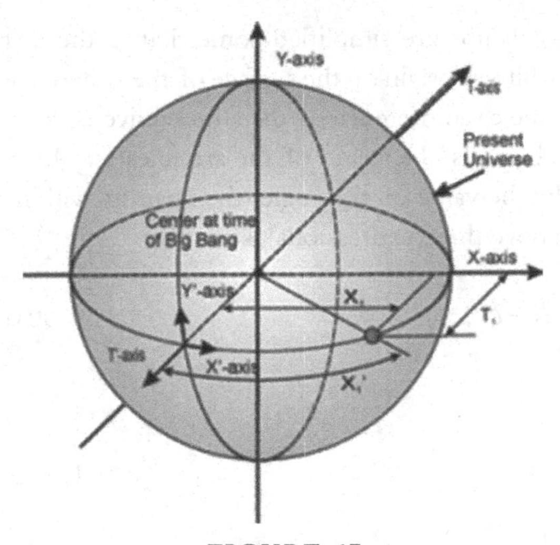

FIGURE 67
TRANSFORMATION OF COORDINATES

The translation from one set of coordinates to the other is complicated by the fact that the second set is measured along the surface of a sphere.

The following equations hold:

$$T_1' = T_1 - ct \,, \qquad \text{EQUATION 183}$$

where the values with primes indicate the correct measure along the spherical surface, as opposed to the linear measurement in an orthogonal (noncurved) space.

$$x_1' = 2\pi ct_1 ArcSin\left(\frac{x_1}{2\pi ct_1}\right), \qquad \text{EQUATION 184}$$

$$y_1' = 2\pi ct_1 ArcSin\left(\frac{y_1}{2\pi ct_1}\right), \qquad \text{EQUATION 185}$$

and

$$z_1' = 2\pi ct_1 ArcSin\left(\frac{z_1}{2\pi ct_1}\right). \qquad \text{EQUATION 186}$$

These relationships are simplified somewhat if the distances involved away from the arbitrary origin on the surface of the sphere are relatively small compared with the circumference of the entire universe. For distances up to a few million light-years, the values of the arc sines may be considered to be approximated by the value of the angle (the quantity within the parenthesis in each of the above three expressions), so

$$T_1' = T_1 - ct, \qquad \text{EQUATION 187}$$

and

$$x_1' = x_1, \qquad \text{EQUATION 188}$$

$$y_1' = y_1, \qquad \text{EQUATION 189}$$

$$z_1' = z_1. \qquad \text{EQUATION 190}$$

In short, for most purposes, the coordinates in the two systems may be used interchangeably, except that the T coordinate must be taken as zero at the reference time chosen for the coordinate time system, so long as the distances involved are relatively short by astronomical standards.

How about the fifth dimension?

A logical extension of the system of coordinates would be one in which the tiny universal kernel, also presumed to be spherical, is added.

The characteristics of the kernel are:

1) It is presumed to have a circumference of $2r_0$, where r_0 is the radius of the inner orbit of the hydrogen atom's electrons.
2) All three spatial dimensions plus the time-like T dimension are presumed to be wound around it. The equations that need to be factored in are

$$2\pi r = 2r_0 \qquad \text{EQUATION 191}$$

and

$$R^2 = x^2 + y^2 + z^2 + T^2 = c^2t^2, \qquad \text{EQUATION 192}$$

where

R = the radius of the present universe.

If the coordinates are wound around the five-dimensional kernel, an x–y–z–T origin can be identified on the surface of the sphere, and each coordinate axis is presumed to go around it many, many times. We can show the x and T axes wrapping around it as I have done for the three-dimensional analog, but the other two axes have to wrap around it just as well.

Using r_0 as the unit of distance, two points overlap if the value of r, the distance from the origin, for the two points differs by an integer times $2r_0$. We can presume that the value of R, the radius of the universe, can be represented by $R - R_0$, where R_0 is the value at a particular instant $t = t_0$. This represents a circle of growing radius around the origin, which is expanding at the velocity $dr/dt = ct$.

CHAPTER 15

THE FINE STRUCTURE CONSTANT

One of the values that appears frequently in calculations of physical constants is the fine-structure constant. This is usually referred to using the Greek letter α and calculated as

$$\alpha = \frac{Ze^2}{hc} \cong \frac{1}{137}, \qquad \text{EQUATION 193}$$

where

Z = Coulomb's law constant
e = Charge on a single electron, Coulombs
h = Planck's constant
c = the apparent speed of light.

This rather striking number is interesting in several ways. First of all, it is unitless, so it should apply no matter what set of units are used to calculate it. Secondly, it seems to be very close to being the reciprocal of the integer 137, a prime number. While it does not appear to be exactly equal to 1/137, it is very close.

Much has been made recently of the ability of quantum mechanical experiments to determine the value of the fine-structure constant to very high degrees of accuracy, and the argument has been made that the physical properties of matter throughout the universe have been shown to be constant by determinations of the fine-structure constant for distant stars.

All the problems I have with modern physics and the standard model used by physicists are wrapped up in this equation. Let me describe a few of these problems and then see if I can provide some simpler interpretation of the fine-structure constant.

Both of the terms in the denominator are somewhat objectionable to me. The first of these is Planck's constant, which, as I have pointed out, is defined as the ratio of the energy transferred in a single radiation event, which Planck defined as the emission of a photon. However, his definition relates the energy to the "frequency" of the light emitted in a linear fashion. As I pointed out in the previous book—and somewhat belabored in this one—the actual quantity of energy transmitted during a radiation event is proportional to the square of the orbital frequency of the electrons in the emitting atom, not to the first power of the frequency. I have proposed that instead of

$$E = hf \,, \qquad \text{Equation 194}$$

the proper expression should be

$$E = Hf^2 , \qquad \text{Equation 195}$$

where

E = energy transmitted during the radiation event
H = modified Planck's constant
f = frequency of either the orbital rotation of the emitting atom or apparent frequency of the energy exchanged.

In addition, the value c is given as the speed of light in a vacuum, whereas I believe it to be the velocity at which the three-dimensional universe is expanding in the fourth-dimensional direction, although the numeric value is correct.

These objections do not suggest that the fine-structure constant is without meaning, but rather that it, like so many of the fundamental parameters in physics, might have some interpretation other than the ones usually accorded it.

ELIMINATING H

The first thing I would like to do is to try to eliminate Planck's constant from equation 194. This is not difficult.

In the definition of Planck's constant, I have used the energy associated with an electron in orbit around a hydrogen nucleus that is a potential source of radiant energy at the frequency of rotation of the electron around its orbit, which also determines the amount of energy that will be transferred in a radiation event,

$$h = \frac{E}{f} = \frac{\frac{\mu v_0{}^2}{2}}{\frac{v_0}{2\pi r_0}} = \pi \mu v_0 r_0 .$$ EQUATION 196

I consider the effective mass of the electron, the orbital velocity of the electron, and the radius of the inner orbit of the electron much more fundamental than is Planck's constant.

So the fine-structure constant, using this value for Planck's constant, is

$$\alpha = \frac{Ze^2}{hc} = \frac{Ze^2}{2\pi \mu v_0 r_0 c}.$$ EQUATION 197

Inserting the synchronous values for v_0 and r_0 determined by Bohr's calculations, where

$$r_0 = \frac{Ze^2}{\mu v_0^2}$$ EQUATION 198

and the electrostatic force holding the electron in orbit is just balanced by the "centrifugal force" tending to make it fly out of orbit. This sets the maximum energy that the electron can have when orbiting the hydrogen nucleus and thus the maximum energy level in a transfer of visible light from the sun.

This very fundamental relationship must hold when dealing with hydrogen. So

$$\alpha = \frac{Ze^2}{\mu v_0 r_0 c} = \frac{Ze^2}{\mu v_0 c \frac{Ze^1}{\mu v_0^2}} = \left(\frac{v_0}{c}\right).$$ EQUATION 199

The fine-structure constant (at least when used in conjunction with the calculated properties of the first electron orbit of the hydrogen atom, the most common element in the universe), is just equal to the synchronous velocity of the electron measured in terms of the most fundamental velocity in the universe: the rate of expansion into the fourth dimension.

In the foregoing discussion, I used the definition of Planck's constant to simplify the expression for the fine-structure constant. I would have felt more comfortable had the modified Planck's constant, H, been used, where

$$E = Hf^2 . \qquad \text{EQUATION 200}$$

Of course, the derivation would have come out exactly the same, because the fine-structure constant would have been defined as

$$\alpha = \frac{Ze^2}{Hfc} = \frac{v_0}{c} . \qquad \text{EQUATION 201}$$

MORE ON BOHR'S MODEL

In developing his model of the hydrogen atom, Bohr assumed that the electrons are wavelike in nature and used the relationship

$$\mu rv = nh, \qquad \text{EQUATION 202}$$

where

h = Planck's constant
n = the "quantum number" of the electron orbit.

He described this by defining the angular momentum of the electron to be an integral number of Planck units, but also implicit in the assumption that the electron has wavelike properties and that the maximum wavelength, corresponding with the minimum frequency of rotation, is exactly equal to the circumference of the orbit. This is the wavelength corresponding with n = 1, which is the only value n can have for the innermost orbit of the hydrogen atom because any higher number would involve a velocity greater than the synchronous velocity, and the electron would fly out of the orbit. In essence, Bohr pictured the electron as moving somehow in a wavelike way as it traveled around the orbit.

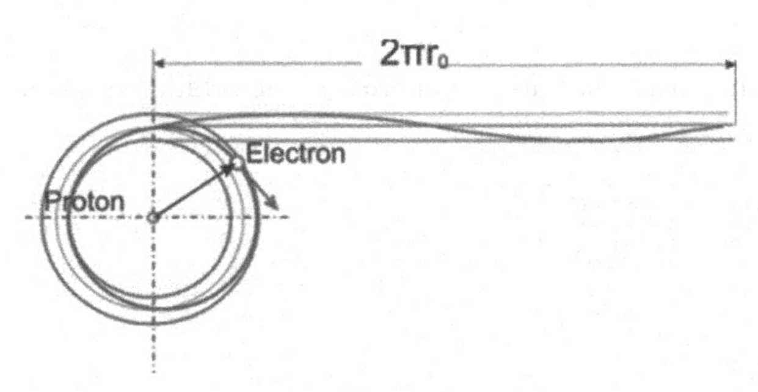

FIGURE 68
BOHR'S MODEL OF THE HYDROGEN ATOM

He did not go into detail as to what the waves consisted of, just that they were characteristic properties of the electron.

Had Bohr instead presumed that the energy levels of the electron were proportional to the velocity squared, which is consistent with the mechanics of the situation, and used the more fundamental relationship

$$H = \frac{\frac{\mu v_0^2}{2}}{\frac{v_0^2}{(2\pi r_0)^2}} = \frac{\mu (2\pi r_0)^2}{2}, \qquad \text{EQUATION 203}$$

from which

$$2\pi r_0 = \sqrt{\frac{2H}{\mu}}, \qquad \text{EQUATION 204}$$

and then presumed that the frequencies have to be integer fractions of the time increments along which atoms exchanging energy must lie (c/N), he could have written

$$E = Hf^2 = \frac{\mu}{2}\left(\frac{c}{N}\right)^2. \qquad \text{EQUATION 205}$$

One can equate this with the energy of the orbiting electron

$$\frac{\mu v_0^2}{2} = \frac{\mu}{2}\left(\frac{c}{N}\right)^2 \qquad \text{EQUATION 206}$$

to obtain

$$v_0 = \frac{c}{N} \qquad \text{EQUATION 207}$$

or

$$\frac{v_0}{c} = \frac{1}{N}. \qquad \text{EQUATION 208}$$

The value of N was established in the previous section as approximately 137, the reciprocal of the fine-structure constant.

This procedure gives exactly the same values for v_0 and r_0 as does Bohr's derivation. The major difference is that Bohr postulated that there could be only one velocity of the electron in the orbit—the synchronous velocity. This was the lowest energy level, as all the other energy levels for the electron had to be higher due to the "potential energy" due to the greater distance from the proton.

In my picture of the hydrogen atom, the velocity of the orbiting electron can assume any integral fraction of the value of v_0, so that

$$\frac{v}{c} = \frac{\alpha}{n}, \qquad \text{EQUATION 209}$$

where n is the quantum number, satisfied by all integer values between 1 and approximately 20,000. The latter corresponds with the value associated with the frequency of the background radiation received from outer space in all directions. It is perhaps reasonable to say that "infinity" is also a legitimate value for the quantum number, representing the state of the atomic orbit at absolute zero temperature, where presumably all motion ceases.

CHAPTER 16

THE MYTH OF THE AGING TWIN

It is widely accepted by physicists and the general public that if one moves fast enough, time slows down. I just read another sci-fi story based on this "fact." By working as a crewman on a "near light-speed" space craft, the leading character's father aged so slowly he eventually became younger than his son. Or, rather, his son aged enough to become older than the father.

This created a double paradox. Not only could the astronaut not have fathered his son if his son had already been born, but the whole premise is based on what I have called the "aging twin" paradox. It is this aging-twin problem I would like to deal with here and hopefully lay to rest the notion that if you are moving fast relative to something or other, your clock runs slower and your body ages more slowly.

I made up the story of twin brothers named Romulus and Remus at some time in the distant future by their whimsical parents. The twins grew up in the early days of interstellar travel, when the fastest starships were only able to accelerate to velocities on the order of 0.94 times light speed (the *apparent speed of light*). Both joined NASA's exploration program but were assigned to different crews with different destinations.

On their twenty-first birthday, both boys left on voyages that happened to be in exactly opposite directions. Before long, they were moving away from each other at 0.984 times the speed of light—or maybe at a lower velocity, but let's use the simple arithmetic for now. It doesn't make much difference in the long run.

The NASA officials on earth, familiar with Einstein's special theory of relativity but having not previously sent anyone on such a long journey, would know for a fact that both of them would be experiencing the time contraction factor commensurate with the speed, or 0.03. In the sixty earthly years that pass during their voyage, each would experience only 1.8 years of time passage—neglecting the bit of time it took to accelerate the spaceship to cruising speed and the week they spent at their destination before heading home.

When they returned, two generations of NASA people would have been replaced, but the new regime expected to get back two seasoned but still young crewmen ready to go on their next voyage.

But what would Remus and Romulus expect? They certainly did not expect to see the same guys at NASA who had sent them out only a couple of years ago, but who had now aged miraculously and were either well past retirement age or had passed on.

After all, so far as the twins were concerned, they had spent most of the trip with no sensation of motion whatever as they coasted through space. The earth, or the solar system, would have seemed to them to be receding at 0.94 times the speed of light, one would presume. So while they experienced a sixty-year trip, their bosses sitting back in the office were, from the twins' point of view, moving at high velocity in the opposite direction and enjoying their own version of the time contraction. They each expected to see a young earth-based staff, ready to pension them off, and put them out to pasture.

What would Romulus expect to see during his scheduled reunion with Remus? While Earth had been rushing away from him for half his adult life and toward him for the second half, Remus had been moving twice as fast in both directions. Romulus would expect his twin to have aged even less than the 1.8 years he was presumed to have aged by his earthbound staff.

But of course, the only difference between the two twins was that one was going one direction and the other the opposite direction. Certainly, Remus would have no reason to believe that either Earth's coordinate system had anything to do with his life expectancy, nor did Romulus.

Obviously, all three parties were expecting the other two to have experienced a time contraction that they, themselves, did not experience. Who was right and who was wrong?

All three were right about the time they experienced themselves. Each was wrong about the passage of time experienced by the others.

The problem is that the time contraction is, in a sense, illusionary. It is based on observations of what goes on in systems moving with respect to our own. These are based on the use of visual observations (the use of light) to see what is going on in the moving system. It is very much like using the sound of a siren on an approaching ambulance to determine the frequency of the sound it is actually emitting. From the reference system of the ambulance driver, the siren sounds the same whether it is moving relative to some other system or not. The contraction of time for systems moving with respect to our own is entirely illusionary, an artifact of our measuring system.

Similarly, some of the other characteristic changes in objects that are moving relative to our own reference are also illusionary, artifacts of our measuring system that we try to explain away mathematically. These include the increase in the mass of moving objects and the shortening of length. Imagine that we are trying to reproduce the mechanical design of the siren on the ambulance by listening to the sound of the siren as it is approaching us at high speed. Surely we would build a smaller, faster rotating device than were we listening to one driving away from us at high speed.

Romulus and Remus took part in the mythical founding of Rome, and perhaps they can be of help in the correction of the myth of the aging twin syndrome.

For the more stubborn-minded, I will try to picture what actually happens when bodies move away from each other and then return to proximity with velocities that are significant relative to the speed of light.

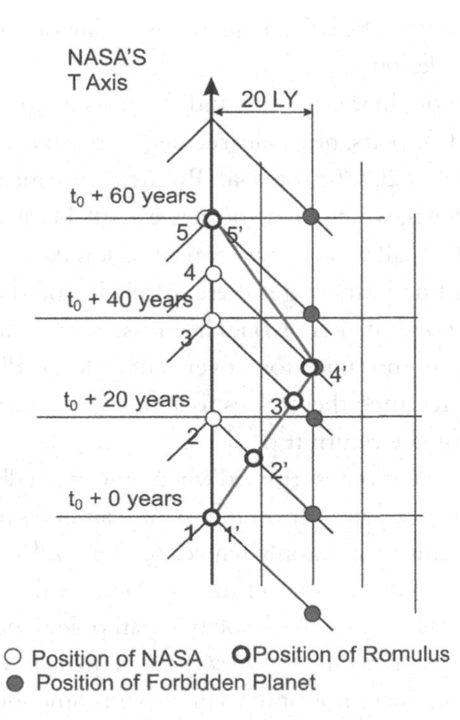

FIGURE 69

VIEW OF ROMULUS'S FLIGHT IN NASA LOCAL TIME

I have used more modest velocities 0.67c relative the *apparent speed of light* in order to make the picture a little clearer., and plotted Romulus's course in figure 69.

I have presumed, as before, that he starts at time t_1 at NASA's location on earth and accelerates very quickly to 0.67c. He then coasts along at this velocity until he is essentially at his destination, the Forbidden Planet, t_4. He slows down to a walk in a very short time and makes one circuit around the destination planet, but he is, of course, forbidden to land.

Still using NASA's coordinate system, he speeds back up to 0.67c and heads back home, arriving right on schedule sixty years after he set out.

What the people at NASA observed was a little strange. They knew his ship would grow more massive and shrink in size as it reached its cruising speed, and that the onboard clock would slow down. However, their clock would continue to keep accurate time, and they could plot the position of Romulus's ship by nearly continuous observations.

However, it would appear to the NASA controllers that Romulus was laying down on the job, because after the first twenty years had passed, he would apparently not yet be halfway there, averaging only 0.5c rather than the 0.67c his ship was designed for.

Their opinion of their astronaut and the mission grew more pessimistic when, after forty-five years, he finally seemed to reach the target. His average velocity was down to 20/50c, or 0.4c. By their best measurements, he was actually slowing down, which made no sense at all, because he was supposed to be coasting in free fall with no fuel consumption during almost all the fifty years. It took him fifty years to get there; surely it would take him fifty years to get home, and none of them would live to see his return.

But because communication over such long distances was very problematic, they resigned themselves to a very late return and cut down on the observations of the return trip.

Naturally, they were very surprised when, unexpectedly, Romulus radioed in for landing clearance precisely on the sixtieth anniversary of his departure, having made the return trip in only ten years, or at an Einstein-defying 2.0c.

I spent a good deal of time on this problem in the first book, where I pointed out that determining the velocity of an object moving at a relatively high velocity compared to the *apparent speed* of light is very tricky, because the position of the object not only changes with time, but the time interval you are using also changes with distance. The observations of the position of the spaceship were always made with respect to the *local time* at the NASA headquarters, and based on what they could see or hear via radio.

Had they been able to make observations using *galactic time*, they would have found the behavior of the spaceship quite on spec.

But the question is still, "How old is Romulus when he gets back home?"

The NASA people, who weren't expecting to see him at all, thought he would have aged much less than they. Romulus, who had been away from the initial time until the final time, would have looked at things from his own point of view, as shown in figure 70. This is, in almost all details, a mirror image of figure 69.

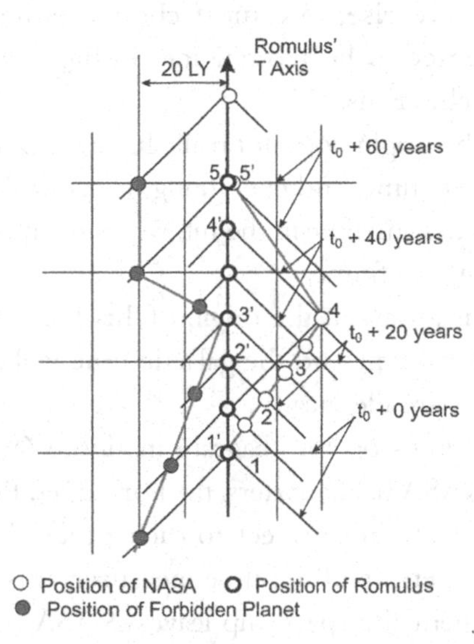

FIGURE 70

THE TRIP FROM ROMULUS'S POINT OF VIEW

Here we are using Romulus's T axis, which, because it is always pointed in the direction Romulus sees himself moving through the fourth-dimensional space, always points straight up.

At the beginning of his trip, he is at NASA headquarters, and his clock agrees with NASA's. He can look out his window and see the Forbidden Planet's star twenty light-years in the distance. Of course, it is in his local present, or twenty years ago according to galactic time. But he can only make observations in his local time and is not even sure the Forbidden Planet will still be there thirty years in his local future.

When his ship leaves, he sees the earth moving away to his right and the Forbidden Planet moving toward him on his left.

While NASA regards Romulus's spaceship to be the only body moving (assuming that the Forbidden Planet is essentially stationary with respect to the earth), Romulus has two milestones to watch.

But let us first look at Romulus's clock. His spaceship, using his own coordinate system, is fixed in space, and anything changing in distance from his ship has a velocity and presumably a different time scale. However, one thing is certain: whereas there are two ways of looking at time with respect to any coordinate system, at the origin of that system, the local time and the galactic time are the same. This is true only for the origin. Everywhere else, one must choose either the galactic time coordinates, represented by horizontal lines in figure 68, or the local time, represented by the chevrons.

An observer at the origin does not really have much choice, as he can see things in his *local present* time, and everything in his *galactic present* time is not going to be visible until sometime in the future. So he must make his estimates of distance in his *local time* frame.

But because he is always at the origin of his local coordinate system at any given time, the local time and the galactic time will register the same on his clock because they are identical.

There are three times on the diagram in figure 69 where the all three objects of interest (NASA headquarters, the Forbidden Planet, and Romulus's spaceship) are all at rest with respect to each other. At those three times, the distance measurements and the time measurements will all be identical. They are at the moment the spaceship leaves NASA before it immediately accelerates to 0.67c (i.e., 67 percent of the velocity at which the universe is expanding in the T direction); as Romulus stops at the Forbidden Planet to have a look-see; and when he returns safely to NASA.

At these three times, because there is no velocity of any one of the subjects relative to the other, the distance measurements should be identical. So, at point 3, we should be able to agree that the time on Romulus's clock reads thirty years elapsed, the distance to the Forbidden Planet is essentially zero, and the distance to earth is twenty light-years. It has taken Romulus thirty years to move twenty light-years, so he accepts that he has been moving relative to the earth and the Forbidden Planet at 0.67c, as advertised in the spaceship operating manual.

He sets his course for earth, and arrives, to his way of thinking, at exactly sixty years from his embarkation date. He is eighty-one years old and rather short on human companionship.

The NASA people, in that time, have experienced nothing out of the ordinary, save for their peculiar measurements of Romulus's velocity change as he reversed course and came toward earth instead of going away from it. They too have aged sixty years during the voyage, even though they moved a much shorter distance through three-dimensional space (and four-dimensional space also, for that matter) than did Romulus.

This is because Romulus's coordinate system showed his journey through four-dimensional space as a straight line in the T direction, whereas NASA saw it as the hypotenuse of a triangle. Their calculation showed that he went a total distance of twenty light-years in three-dimensional space plus the sixty light-years in the T direction, while he only counted the sixty years in the T direction. Thus, Romulus's time, t', is used in his calculation

$$c\Delta t' = T \,, \qquad \text{EQUATION 210}$$

whereas that same T value for NASA was

$$T = \sqrt{x^2 + c^2 t^2} \,, \qquad \text{EQUATION 211}$$

because

$$x = vt \,, \qquad \text{EQUATION 212}$$

$$c^2 \Delta t'^2 = \Delta t c^2 - v_t^{\,2} \Delta t^2 \,, \qquad \text{EQUATION 213}$$

which leads directly to

$$\frac{t'}{t} = \sqrt{1 - \frac{v^2}{c^2}} \,. \qquad \text{EQUATION 214}$$

This is simply Einstein's correction for the fact that you misread the clocks on the moving spaceships when you observe them from the stationary NASA headquarters. But you have to keep in mind that Romulus also misreads the clock on the NASA control panel, and he thinks their time is slowing down rather than his.

Finally, there is the troublesome fact that the spaceship appeared to make a remarkable journey back from the Forbidden Planet and seemed to actually move at twice the *apparent speed of light.* Common knowledge tells you that nothing can do that.

Well, this is true and it is not true, depending on how you look at it.

Remember that from a galactic standpoint, nothing can exceed the *apparent speed of light* because that is the velocity given to all matter at the time of the big bang or shortly thereafter. Nothing can go faster simply because there is nothing already moving faster that could run into it and speed it up. However, this is making measurements with respect to the galactic system of geometry wherein all the points are at the same *galactic time,* like in the current three-dimensional hypersphere. Unfortunately, this is completely invisible to us, save for the pinpoint location where we are right now. All the rest of the *galactic present* is in our *local future.*

All we can see or experience is in our *local present.* The difference between the horizontal lines in figures 67 and 68 and the inverted v's represent our *local present* as we move along our own local T axis as time passes. We can only make measurements in the *local present.* We don't really have any way of showing that the *galactic present* is actually out there, although I am willing to take it on faith that it is.

The point is that when measured with respect to our *local present* coordinate system, c is the rate of expansion of the universe, not the speed of light. The speed of light is infinite. The velocity of objects measured within the *local present* coordinate system is not limited to the speed of light. The upper limit is infinite. The energy associated with the movement of bodies measured in this system can also be any finite value at all. It is not limited to mc^2.

Romulus returned from his voyage (the earlier one) an old, old man who had hoped to see his brother a mere stripling and was disappointed. He had hoped to see the crew at NASA that had wished him bon voyage, but they had all retired or died after having written both Romulus and Remus off for lost because of the long time it appeared to take them to get to their destination.

Romulus, for his part, felt that he had given it his best shot, stayed right on schedule, and all he found out for sure was that things are not always as they appear to be.

Relativity got that all wrong because it was based on the assumption that the speed of light was limited to 300,000 km/sec. in the *local time* sense, which is the only one in which we can make observations.

CHAPTER 17

THE ONLY CHAPTER WITHOUT EQUATIONS

Many months have passed since the publication of the previous book, *A New Light on the Expanding Universe*, and I have had some feedback, some additional thoughts, and some additional time to think about the problems addressed. The result was this book.

I will try to share with you the insights that came during these months and give you a progress report of sorts on my attempt to convince all the physicists in the world that they have got some of the basics wrong.

FEEDBACK

I have had a lot of interesting comments on the material in the first book, although precious few of them were from actual card-carrying physicists. There has been a lot more interest than I expected from people whom I would have thought to have little interest in physics beyond that required to drive a car, sail a boat, or play games with balls.

I have tried to name the people who read enough of the book or listened to my monologue on the subject enough to formulate good questions that I could not answer without some prolonged thought. Several of these questions resulted in individual chapters in this book; namely, the ones on dark matter, background microwave radiation, and nuclear fusion. I have tried to answer these questions, and I hope the chapters provide suitable answers.

For the most part, I have not gotten much in the way of comment from any real physicists. I can't say this reaction was unexpected, as I am in a way attacking some of their most entrenched beliefs.

The sole exception so far is Professor Russell Betts, Dean of Arts and Sciences at Illinois Institute of Technology. Dr. Betts was gracious enough to review my book and spent some time with me discussing it. He was sympathetic and polite, and recognized that it took some effort on my part to get the book together.

However, his principle message for me was that there really was no question that light is in fact an electromagnetic wave that moves through the vacuum of outer space at 300,000 km/sec or thereabouts and that the speed is set by the properties of space, which include the dielectric constant and paramagnetic constant. In short, but very kindly put, I am dead wrong in my presumption that this is not the case.

He did point out that, in order to be a valid theory, my proposals should have some consequences that could be tested by experiment to prove me right or wrong. This is a perfectly valid point, and one I have had trouble with. All of my theoretical calculations seem to produce essentially the same results as the widely accepted theories. In a way this seems necessary, as the current standard model is based on experimental data and agrees with it. To the extent I am able to calculate things, so does my model.

But Dr. Betts offered me a gleam of hope that I might be able to demonstrate the usefulness of my approach. He said that astronomers have been puzzling over an observed deviation from Hubble's law that states that galaxies are receding from our own at velocities that are roughly proportional to their distance from our own galaxy. This did not come into question until the Hubble telescope made observations of very, very distant galaxies. Based on the red shift, these galaxies seem to be moving away from us less rapidly than predicted.

Aha! This was something that I predicted. I do not believe that Hubble's law is inaccurate, but we are observing the motion of the galaxies in our *local time*, rather than in *galactic time*, and Hubble's law applies to the position of the galaxies in *galactic time*, which requires a correction factor.

I had already written chapter 5, "How Far Back Can We Look?," describing the shape of the *local universe* (the universe we can see from here and now), which suggests that there is no way to see all the way back to the big bang because all radiation from that *galactic time* would have been red shifted down to zero frequency. It also suggests that when we make observations on really far away planets, we aren't looking at where they are now, from a galactic standpoint, but where they were a long time ago. So, Hubble's law will appear to be in error by a correction factor. I calculated this correction factor, and included it in chapter 5.

I am not sure this correction factor is what the astronomers need to sort out the problem Dr. Betts described, and I have not checked. However, it is a prediction that might have some value.

Unfortunately, my prediction is that there should be a small correction applied to a very inaccurately measured parameter (Hubble's constant has to be the least accurately known of any physical constant), so I am not sure this will be meaningful.

But maybe this is better than nothing.

SUMMARY OF FINDINGS

The second and third chapters of this book are simply embellishments of the basic theme I presented in the first book.

Chapter 2 is an attempt to explain how the basic laws of optics are compatible with and perhaps explained by the notion that light moves instantaneously from atom to atom—not passing through the void between the atoms but bypassing the space altogether. However, when light passes through matter, it is a different story altogether. It still jumps instantaneously from atom to atom, but it has to go stepwise through glass, air, water, or other transparent materials. This is not an instantaneous process because the conditions for transmission from atom to atom are not always present. The delays while the emitter and absorber atoms come into suitable positions for the transfer accounts for the finite velocity of light through media other than a vacuum.

This finite velocity is slower than the infinite velocity through a vacuum, and it varies with the frequency of the light being transmitted (i.e., the orbital velocity of the electrons in the emitting atom).

All the optical properties associated with light can be accounted for by the mechanism proposed. Refraction, reflection, and absorption make a lot more sense to me than when simply presented as "the way light works."

Because the frequency of the radiation is so important in all the optical properties of radiation, it was necessary for me to backtrack a bit and mitigate some of my harsh criticism of Planck. I did this in chapter 3. I still think he used a bad basis for Planck's constant, but so much of optics deals with the frequency (orbital frequency of the electrons in the emitting atom) rather than the energy transmitted that it is necessary that I extend an olive branch toward the specter of Max Planck.

Chapter 4 also includes a little backtracking.

In the first book, I drew some pictures of a universal kernel in a five-dimensional space, with two of the four spatial dimensions depicted on the surface. In this picture, I placed both the protons and electrons in a rudimentary atom at the same point. I subsequently made the point that the electrostatic and electromagnetic properties of electrons and protons had to be based on their having a spin around the fourth-dimensional axis, with the electrons and protons spinning opposite directions.

This is pretty hard to picture if they are located at the same place on the spherical kernel. Were this rotating about the fourth-dimensional axis, both the electron and proton would spin the same direction. My bad!

In order for them to spin opposite directions, it makes more sense for them to be located on opposite sides of the five-dimensional sphere. This relocation doesn't cause any other problems I have been able to see and looks like a matter of housekeeping.

In chapter 5 I took a look at the presumption that one can observe only things in the local present, as opposed to the galactic present. All we see, including far off galaxies, lies in our local present. We can't see anything at all in the galactic present, although we may be able to see it sometime in the future.

Our local present defines the local universe. It is everything we can see right now. Because the nature of light is that it can be transferred from atom to atom along lines that are at forty-five degrees to the surface of the galactic universe at any given galactic time, our local universe has a sort of lemon drop shape with points at both ends.

I spent a lot of time developing the equations that define this in the two-dimensional analog universe for which we can draw pictures and extending it to the three-dimensional universe for which we cannot.

From this model, it is apparent that we can only see back about halfway to the time and place of the big bang. Anything beyond this "horizon" is red shifted to the point where the radiation has no energy at all.

This led rather quickly to the discussion of the source of background radiation in chapter 6. The farthest we can "see" can't actually be "seen" at all. The light coming from about 6.8 billion light-years away is red shifted to the point that light in the visible spectrum, largely emitted by incandescent hydrogen in the stars, is red shifted all the way down to zero.

However, just this side of the horizon are stars whose hydrogen atoms are radiating outward toward us, but with a red shift that almost erases them. In fact, the energy level is so low it comes to us not as visible light, but as microwave frequency energy at 16.7 mHz, or at about the frequency we would expect to get from a blackbody at 2.7 degrees Kelvin. In short, it is the background radiation generally assumed to be leftover from the big bang.

It was my grandson, Josh Jackson, who asked me what background radiation was. That got me started on chapters 5 and 6, which I hope provide a satisfactory (although far from proven) answer.

Chapter 7 was also triggered by one of Josh's questions. Namely, "If I don't really think mass can be converted to energy, despite the accuracy of E

$= mc^2$ as a statement of the inherent energy in all mass, where does the energy come from that is released by uranium fission in a power plant or hydrogen fusion in an H-bomb?" I had to think about that a bit.

Again, I have an answer, but not one that provides anything quantitatively different from the standard model used by physicists.

Chapter 8 was written for my own satisfaction more than anything else. I have maintained that Michelson, and later Michelson and Morley, did their experiments on the measurement of the velocity of light and the velocity (or lack thereof) of the luminiferous ether believed to conduct light correctly, but they failed to consider the possibility that light was actually transferred instantaneously. So, they measured the rate of expansion of the universe in a fourth-dimensional direction and thought they were measuring the velocity of light swimming through the vacuum like a fish swims through water.

I went back and looked carefully at how they did their experiments and came away with great respect for their ability as researchers. However, I am more convinced than ever of the notion that if you conduct an experiment with some expectation of what the result will be, you are more likely to get that result.

Michelson, and essentially all the other experimenters who measured the speed of light before and after them, worked on the assumption that light moves through a vacuum like a physical body, occupying successive positions that start out close to the source and move in a continuous fashion closer and closer to the receptor. Michelson, in particular, was convinced that light consisted of waves, much like sound waves, that are conducted through empty space as sound is conducted through air or water.

Despite all sorts of evidence that light is different from any other physical phenomenon, Michelson and Morley did not consider the possibility that it could somehow bypass the space and get where it was going instantaneously. Of course what they measured was the speed of light through a vacuum. That is what they were expecting.

I still think they were mistaken.

Chapter 9 deals with the question of interference patterns.

The thing that caused me the most trouble with Michelson's and Morley's experiments was that, in the measurement of the velocity of the luminiferous ether (although not in Michelson's earlier and later experiments on the speed of light), they used an interferometer.

The formation of interference patterns when beams of polarized light are mixed is one of the strongest arguments for light being basically an electromagnetic wave. Waves cause interference patterns. There is no question of this, as can be illustrated with water waves. How then could Michelson and Morley use interference patterns to measure the speed of light if it is not an electromagnetic wave—if in fact it has no existence at all outside the originating and the receiving atoms?

Basically, interference patterns can be formed by waves cancelling each other out in places and reinforcing each other in other places. However, similar patterns can be formed by the statistical distribution of electrons hitting a target when allowed to pass through two or more separate openings or when light transmissions are allowed to follow alternative paths.

The pictures come out the same. I made some reference to this in the previous book when discussing how Schrödinger's wave equation doesn't appear to describe waves at all, but rather probabilities.

Chapter 10 is a follow-on to the discussion of Michelson's and Morley's experiments involving the measurement of the speed of light. My thesis is that he mistook the speed of the universe moving in the fourth-dimensional time-like direction for the speed of light.

It occurred to me to question whether experiments aimed at measuring other velocities might also mistakenly measure the speed of the universe in the fourth-dimensional direction. This wouldn't help my case at all if it were true. But I wasn't able to think up a simple way of demonstrating that it isn't true in a general sense. So I chose instead to make up a silly story about Michelson and Morley setting out to measure the speed of a carrier pigeon making a round trip between two laboratories.

The silly story has a point though. You have to be careful to keep track of whether or not your laboratory is moving if you want to measure the speed of something outside it. The outcome was that they were able to measure the speed of the pigeon at about 50 mph when there was no wind, but the speed relative to the laboratory was different for each different speed of the laboratory. There was no doubt they were measuring the velocity of a thing actually moving through space and not the velocity of the universe.

Chapter 11 is a bit whimsical, but it calls attention to one of the things that has bothered me the most about my proposed mechanism of light transmission and the kind of universe that would permit this to be true. The problem is that if you shine a light out into the night sky, my theory says that the energy does not leave the filament in the lightbulb until it has a receptor lined up to receive it.

The receptor for any emission from any atom must be in the future. Light doesn't shine from the present into the past; it only goes the other way. So there must be atoms out there in the future ready to receive the energy simultaneous with it coming out of the flashlight. The future has to be there before we have gotten there to experience it.

This is a little spooky. I can't find any way around it though.

While I was in a speculative mood, I wrote chapter 12, which is pure conjecture about how atomic nuclei formed. There is every suggestion that electrons and protons were formed in about equal numbers at or near the time of the big bang and that they all started out pointed in random directions, each with the velocity c. They banged around together until they had found their way out of the tiny space they were in, all headed in different directions, and their positions at any time define the three-dimensional universe as we know it. There isn't any place in this picture for neutrons, which seem (in spite of the proton being made of two up quarks and a down quark, and a neutron being made of one up quark and two down quarks) to be pretty much like a proton and an electron combined. Possibly with an electron neutrino thrown in for seasoning.

In my picture, the mass of the proton and electron are pretty close to that of a neutron, and the charge is pretty close to the sum of the charges. The problem is, where did the spin that accounts for the electrostatic and electromagnetic properties of the proton and electron go if they combined to make a neutron? More speculation, and no hard science here.

Chapter 13 deals with dark matter. The popular conception is that only a small fraction of the mass necessary to hold the universe together via gravitational forces can be accounted for by the mass of all the stars estimated to exist in the solar system. A more specific and compelling argument for the existence of more dark matter than there is visible matter lies in the observations that the arms of the spiral galaxies seem to be moving faster than could be accounted for by the orbital velocity around the center of gravity of the galaxies, based on the estimates of the mass of the visible stars.

I don't need any dark matter to hold the universe together, because gravity, which is what we observe in three-dimensional space, has no effect whatever on the motion in the fourth-dimensional direction.

The spiral galaxy arms requires a little more thought. I calculated that the expansion of the universe is, in a sense, an antigravity force in that it tends to accelerate masses away from each other, and its effect increasing distance rather than with decreasing distance.

Thus there is a maximum distance at which we can expect normal gravitational forces to be stronger than the trend for the stars and galaxies to accelerate away from each other. I calculate this distance to be about 1,400 light-years, which suggests that gravity has nothing to do with the behavior of the stars in the outer arms of the spiral galaxies, as they are much farther away from the center than the 1,400 light-years.

Gravity just doesn't enter into the problem very much. The cosmologists need some other explanation for the motion than missing mass. Could it be that the arms on the far side of galaxies are moving faster simply because they are farther away from us?

In chapter 14, I got back to basics. In the first book, I spent some time discussing the coordinate system that I used to describe my picture of the expanding universe. The simplest system was one taking the x, y, z, and T coordinates at the place and time of the big bang. It is easy to write the equations for a four-dimensional hypersphere expanding continuously with time. However, it is darned hard to work with a coordinate system that has its origin somewhere else than on this earth and at a time very, very long ago. I did some transformation of coordinates and used one somewhat like the geographic coordinates used on earth, except that I used x and y instead of latitude and longitude, and T, the distance in the direction the universe is expanding, instead of altitude above sea level.

The actual mathematics of the transformation of coordinates I brushed off as "somewhat complicated." However, I had rather painstakingly worked them out and shown that they could be greatly simplified if the distances were kept small (say within a few million light-years) relative to the overall size of the universe, but would have to be taken into account for consideration of large scale observations.

On second thought, I decided it would probably be better to include them and suggest that anyone not terribly concerned with the geometry of enormous distances skip over the derivation. So there it is in chapter 14.

Chapter 15 deals with the fine-structure constant, which is one of the values that recurs when one is making calculations involving light, atomic physics, the composition of the stars, and lots of other widely scattered subjects.

This chapter makes the point that the fine-structure constant involves two concepts that I see differently from current-day physicists. The first involves Planck's constant, which I feel attributes properties to radiant energy (photons) that are not correct, so Planck's constant ought to be eliminated from the definition of the fine-structure constant in favor of something more concrete and fundamental. Secondly, it utilizes the *apparent velocity of light*, c, which I have no problem with as a velocity. I just think it is the velocity of all matter in the universe, not the velocity of light.

So, manipulating my own version of Planck's constant and combining it with the derived velocity of the electrons in the hydrogen atom at the synchronous value (the highest velocity they can have without escaping from the atom), I got a very simple definition of the fine-structure constant. It is exactly equal to the v_0/c, the synchronous velocity of the hydrogen atom electron divided by the speed of the expansion of the universe.

Chapter 16 is an attempt to poke fun at the relativists who take Einstein seriously when he said that objects moving relatively fast as compared with the speed of light experience time as passing more slowly than us people standing still and that their dimensions grow shorter as they accelerate and their masses become larger, approaching infinite as their speed approaches 300,000 km/hr.

I fully agree with Professor Einstein that people who are moving with respect to ourselves experience time differently that we do, but I must call attention to the fact that there is no good reference system from which to measure the velocity. We are all moving very fast relative to some distant galaxies, but I am sure that our rate of aging does not depend on which galaxy we choose as our reference system. Nor does our lunch pail grow heavier if we choose to base our measurements on the center of the sun instead of the surface of the earth.

My tale of Romulus and Remus, the twin astronomers dispatched to opposite ends of the galaxy in near light-speed ships, was written to illustrate my point.

WHERE DO I GO FROM HERE?

While I have so far not been discouraged from my attempts to convince the physicists of the world that much of the basis of their present standard model of the universe is based on a mistaken measurement, I have mainly succeeded in convincing myself that I really understand very little of the physics that I am attacking. There are several lifetimes worth of subjects that I really need to try to learn about.

In particular, a solution to the problem of how one could set up any sort of experiment that would provide evidence for or against my picture of how things work would really be useful. I will continue to think in this direction and would welcome any suggestions from readers.

I will be trying to get my first book distributed a little more widely and possibly even going to the extreme of putting some effort into publicizing it while at the same time trying to learn more about the subject I am pretending to know about.

Comments and criticisms are very helpful.

ACKNOWLEDGMENTS

For the most part, I can't blame anyone else for anything that appears in this book, save for the physicists and other researchers I have quoted.

However, I would like to acknowledge with thanks the help of my daughter, Pat Jackson, who invested a good deal of her time and energy in proofreading the manuscript.

Thanks a bunch, Pat.

ABOUT THE AUTHOR

Les Hardison is an eighty-five-year-old retired engineer. He graduated from Illinois Institute of Technology in 1950 with a degree in mechanical engineering. During his working years, he was a petroleum process design engineer for UOP, Inc., and later technical director of UOP Air Correction Division.

During the last twenty-five years of his working career, he was president of ARI Technologies, Inc., a small air pollution control company that developed, among other things, the LO-CAT Hydrogen Sulfide Oxidation Process.

He has recently been awarded a US patent for the development of a system for viewing ordinary TV programs in 3-D without special glasses or alterations to the television set or program production.

He has never had any special training in physics or cosmology and recognizes that if he knew more about them, he would probably not have written either the first book, *A New Light on the Expanding Universe*, or this one.

Printed in the United States
By Bookmasters